Idle Hands

John Ruttley

Also by John Ruttley

Fiction

The Devil Finds Work…

Non-Fiction

Mowbray the people's Park

Prisoners In The North

IDLE HANDS

ISBN No 978-0-9543366-3-9

© 2007 John Ruttley

The right of John Ruttley to be identified as the author of this work has been asserted by him in accordance with the Copyright, Designs and Patents Act 1988.

All right reserved. No part of this publication may be reproduced, stored in a retrieval system or transmitted, in any form or by any means without the prior written permission of the publisher, nor be otherwise circulated in any form of binding or cover other than that in which it is published and without a similar condition being imposed on the subsequent purchaser.

All names, characters and events in this publication are fictitious and any resemblance to real events or persons, living or dead, is purely coincidental.

Published by Holroyd Publications.

Printed by
Stonebrook Print & Design Services
Buddle Street
Wallsend
Tyne & Wear
NE28 6EH
Tel: 0191 2633302

Foreword

Idle Hands is John Ruttley's second novel and there's always a certain amount of uncertainty as to whether a new writer can produce a second novel as good as the first. Well reader, he can, and he does it in trumps. Without giving away any of the plot, I can tell you that this is every bit as good as his first novel, The Devil Finds Work, and doesn't disappoint, or let you down in any way. Reading Idle Hands is like finding a buried treasure chest just waiting to be dug up and the treasure coming to the surface is the writing of John Ruttley. An intriguing plot, studded with great dialogue and peopled with strong, realistic characters you can believe and relate to, are woven together and waiting to unfold for you as you read. These ingredients are the stuff of great tales; they're all here and make an excellent read. It made me laugh and it made me sad. I know these characters, we all do. I cheered on the good guys and booed the bad guys. This is a cracking tale with all the ingredients of a good thriller, written by a true thriller writer, who tells a story that races along in a ding dong way. John Ruttley has a huge talent with a great writing style that is very easy to read. But beware, this book is a joy to pick up and read, but very, very hard to put down again until you've reached the very last word. Read it, enjoy it and then ask when the film is coming out.

Mike Elliott
September 2007.

Man should live according to his own nature. He should concentrate on self knowledge and then live according to the truth about himself. What would you say about a tiger who was a vegetarian?

Carl Gustav Jung (1875-1961)

This book is dedicated to my uncle, James Blakelock Ruttley

Prologue

Max had discovered all the details of the couriers' route without any real difficulty. Now he and two of his men waited for the couriers to arrive. Max had carefully selected the two men to help him. He required them to be trustworthy, able to carry out his orders without question, but they were also to be expendable, as he wanted absolutely no witnesses to his double cross. A pity to lose good men, but Max had learned through hard experience that if you leave any loose ends untied, they tended to come back and create problems for you.

They waited in the darkened warehouse as the van arrived and watched quietly as the two couriers opened the shuttered door and drove the van in. They waited until the door was closed again before showing themselves. The couriers were slow to react, a poor choice, Max thought, considering the value of the cargo they were entrusted with, but then they didn't know its value, any more than his men did, he conceded charitably.

Max and his men worked all night to cellophane wrap and pack the cash in Dutch tulip bulb boxes, which were conveniently at hand. These were loaded onto a lorry that Max had arranged to take the consignment to England, calculating that the money would never be traced there. The existing consignment of German video recorders was unloaded from the back of the lorry to make way for the tulip boxes.

Max planned to invest the cash in various business ventures he was involved in throughout Europe. It would enable him to expand his lawful operations and make a complete break with crime and be totally legitimate at last. The British lorry driver would be completely unaware of his valuable cargo, being simply an employee of the haulage company Max used. The owner of a warehouse in Birmingham was the only person in the UK who knew that the cargo was worth exceedingly more than its face value, and even he didn't know what it was, or just how valuable it was. Max had known him for years and knew he was totally loyal.

The two men sweated with exertion as they moved the last of the boxes.

Max watched with interest. "That the lot?" he asked.

"Yes. They're all on," answered the bigger of the two men.

"Good. All we need now is to make sure the paperwork is in order. Will you please fetch it from the office?"

Both men jumped from the back of the vehicle and the bigger man started to walk towards the office at the other end of the warehouse. Max walked a few steps behind him before producing a pistol from under his jacket and shooting the man between the shoulder blades. The man stumbled and fell. Max turned and shot the other man, who was about five yards away, in the face, making a small hole below his right eye. The man staggered three paces backwards, a surprised expression on his face, before his legs crumpled and he collapsed onto the floor.

Max shook his head. It was a pity to have to lose two good men, but it had to be done. He pulled the bodies behind the lorry by their legs, careful not to get any blood on his clothes. The bodies of the couriers already lay there. He pulled a large tarpaulin over them all then made his way to the office, picked up a telephone and dialled a number.

The call was answered almost immediately. "Yes, it's me. I need to have some rubbish disposed of as quickly as possible. Four bundles at the usual rates."

1

Summer 1988

Situated on the exposed top of the steep hill, the allotment huddled amongst the other fifty or so like it, as if seeking comfort amongst its neighbours.

The two men appeared to be relaxed and comfortable in the allotment's shed, which, despite smelling strongly of paraffin, creosote and tobacco smoke, was a comfortable home from home. The wooden structure was as warm and weatherproof as they could possibly make it. The roof was coated with a type of bitumen that would repel cascading seawater from the cargo hatch covers of merchant ships in the most severe of storms. This was actually what it had been designated for, before being 'appropriated' from the yard by Joe, the younger, leaner, and more hirsute of the two men. The structure was fitted out with two old, worn, but comfortable, well-upholstered armchairs, an old sofa, stuffing peeking out from a few splits in its fabric, a kettle and a table holding various mugs and assorted tea-making utensils. The table also supported a battery-powered transistor radio, an ashtray, some crumpled copies of that morning's newspapers, a large cabbage and some soil-stained carrots. There were also various wall cupboards in the shed, and these contained stores of food and alcohol. The men were partners in running the allotment, sharing the work, expenses and the acclaim when their vegetables took first prizes at the local workingmen's club's annual Leek and Flower Shows, which they invariably did. They were also workmates, both being employed as nightshift labourers at a local shipyard.

Joe was seated on one of the armchairs, his legs stretched out before him. His friend, George, overweight and sweating, untidy even in his dress clothes, sat opposite him, lounging on the old settee. George had been working with Joe at the allotment for nine years, taking over after the death of Harry, Joe's previous partner. He'd also taken the dead man's job as a crane driver at the yard. To any casual observer the friends seemed to be at ease, but they weren't happy. They were in pensive mood, discussing the options open to them if the yard closed and they became redundant.

"Well, I think it's a dead certainty. Yule's will close and we'll all be out of a job," Joe said, folding the copy of the News of the World he held and dropping it on the table where the others lay, adding to the untidy pile.

"You really think so?" asked George, lifting a pint glass full of brown ale from the floor and putting it to his lips.

"Nothing surer, mate. It stands to reason doesn't it? Yule's is one of the last shipyards on the river now, the order books are almost empty and all these rumours can't be wrong. There's no smoke without fire, is there?"

George took the glass from his lips, its contents now considerably reduced. "Well, I still don't know if it's right. I wouldn't worry too much. It always seems to be the same old story. There's no work, this is the last ship on the order list, the yard's going to close and then suddenly, just before the ship is launched, the company announce that they've got another order. Amazing."

He shook his head in disgust. "I think they do it like that deliberately to stop the unions asking for more money." He wiped the froth from his lips with the back of his hand. "There have been rumours about closure going around for ages and nothing has happened up to now. But this time's different. You mark my works. The place will close down in the next few months."

The men quietly reflected on this possibility for a few moments.

"You worked out how much redundancy money you'd get if it did close down?" George asked, pulling an old battered pipe and a small round tobacco tin from one of the pockets of his jacket.

"Yes, I have, and it's not a lot, I can tell you."

"Same here. But the chances are it'll be even less that you expect."

"What makes you say that?"

"Well, I've got it on good authority," George said, pushing his flat cap to the back of his bald head, "from that pen-pusher in the office, him that drinks in the club on a weekend, that they'll probably pay us the bare minimum they can legally get away with. Which I'll bet is a lot less than you're reckoning on. So we'll be out of a job, virtually skint and with no chance of getting another job in any other yard."

"There's not many bloody yards left now, not around here there isn't. Anyway this pen pusher's probably got it all wrong. They're hardly going to tell him everything are they? Don't worry, we'll walk away with a fortune and get fixed up somewhere with a job, man. The yards aren't the be-all and end-all, there's always plenty of work on construction sites, factories and places."

"You really think so?" George asked without conviction. "I've never fancied the buildings, too much bloody fresh air. I suppose my mate at the brewery could get me a start there. That'd be a turn up, eh? Me, working in a brewery." He started to fill his pipe with black, evil-smelling chips of tobacco. These he cut with difficulty with a pocketknife from a hard, black block that looked like a piece of coal. "What do you fancy doing, then?"

"Me? I don't know. I'll sign on and see what's available, I suppose," Joe answered.

There was a lengthy period of silence while the men considered their options and George completed the complicated process of filling the pipe to his satisfaction.

"I suppose we could use the redundancy money to set up some sort of business and work for ourselves," Joe suggested tentatively.

"Doing what?"

"I don't know," Joe said slowly, biting his lower lip in concentration. "We'd have to look around and figure what would be the best option, the best business to get into. The one with the greatest chance of success, I suppose. We could buy a franchise, maybe?"

His companion shook his head dismissively. "We haven't got any experience of setting up and running a business, mate. We're not that type. We'd go down the drain in a few months and that'd be what little money we do get, gone," George said as he tentatively lit the tobacco in the pipe's bowl and drew smoke into his mouth.

"The money will soon go anyway. It'll just get frittered away on odds and sods," Joe said.

"Odds and sods?" George blew thick, foul-smelling smoke up towards the wooden ceiling, where it billowed outwards in a mushroom-like cloud to fill the whole shed.

"Yes, you know? We'll pay off the debt we've got, buy some new carpets and furniture and spend a few quid on one or two luxuries. Maybe have a holiday; a few quid to the wife and kids and that'll be about it. All gone."

"You're right about it not going far. I don't think it'll take long to spend the pittance we'll get. And I wouldn't worry too much about a holiday. Anyway, we shouldn't have to wait long to find out. The launch is in a couple of weeks so they'll have to tell us what's happening then, if not before. Either they've got another order on the books, or they'll close the yard down. So we'll know one way or the other," George said, opening another bottle of brown ale, pouring it carefully into his glass and drinking half of it straight off.

"At least we'll get off bloody night shift if the yard closes," Joe put in.

"Maybe, maybe not. Your new job might be worse."

"Well, if it is, then I'll chuck it and get another one. Or I'll go on the dole permanently, like a few others I know."

"Steady on now, Joe. You'll be aspiring to get on the social club committee next."

"I'd really be joining the ranks of the aristocracy then, eh?" Joe talked faster now as his enthusiasm grew, his friend's comments about the likely poor redundancy payments pushed to the back of his mind. "Mind you, a holiday is definitely on the cards. Trev wants us to book a Mediterranean cruise. He's all for it. Probably thinks he'll meet a glamorous heiress with loads of money. You know what he's like with women."

"A different girl every night, lucky bastard. I wish I looked like George Best."

Joe shook his head. "I really thought he would settle down with that young lass, the musician, Fiona. He thought the world of her but they split up, shame."

"I heard she was two-timing him."

"Aye? A pity, she seemed like a nice lass, but that's how it goes, I suppose. Trev always used to have a bad opinion of women, you know. Probably because his mother done off and left his father with the kids when he was only a toddler. He really fell for that Fiona and his attitude changed altogether, but now he's right back to square one."

"Well, he's back to his old ways again now and no mistake," George said, puffing contentedly on the pipe, which was now, after repeated poking and prodding, apparently drawing to his complete satisfaction.

"Anyway, Trev's still young and single. He doesn't have a wife and family to support and he will be able to afford to go on a cruise. That sort of holiday will put a big hole in your money, supposing you do get enough to spend on a holiday. But like Trev said, it's a once in a lifetime opportunity and we shouldn't miss it. If we don't spend some of the money on something like a cruise, it'll go in dribs and drabs and we won't feel any benefit from it at all."

"What's Brenda got to say about it, I bet that she's not keen on a cruise?"

"She is actually. I thought that I'd never be able to talk her into it, but she said yes straight away. She didn't even take time to think about it. I think she's got the same idea as Trev, take the opportunity while it's there, because we're not likely to get a second chance."

"What about Mickey, he tempted by a cruise?"

"No. We asked him, but there's no way he'll spend that sort of money on a holiday, not Mickey. Anyway, the way Tracy is, she couldn't travel anywhere. Bag of nerves she is. Always fretting about something or other. What about you, you fancy going on a cruise?"

"Me, on a cruise? No, I've told you I'm not expecting to get that much redundancy to be able to go on a cruise, or any other holiday for that matter. It's a pity though, that might have changed our lass's mind and tempted her back. But she'll not be tempted back by the pittance I'm expecting to get, so there's not much chance that she'll come back at all now. Getting on for seven months it is, since she left," he explained needlessly to Joe, who was well aware of his friend's marital difficulties, and had been for the last seven months and more.

Another period of silence descended on the pair and each sat with his thoughts.

"I saw Alan this morning." Joe was the first to break the silence, deliberately changing the subject. "He was cleaning out his pigeon cree. Him and that Nobby, him that thinks he's Elvis."

"He's working at the yard as well now, isn't he? That him I've seen knocking about in the shed with the leather jacket and long sideboards?"

"That'll be him. He's been there a couple of months now. He and Alan are partners with the pigeons. He's been looking after them while Alan's was inside. Apparently he goes in for those talent contests. He impersonates Elvis and is quite good from all accounts. He's in that big Elvis impersonators' competition that Supreme Leisure's running at the moment."

"Alan's out again, eh? How is the robbin' bastard?"

"Alright. He's been out about three weeks now. They've given him a start back at the yard, but how long for is debatable."

"His little spell inside might cost him a fair bit this time," George said.

"How's that?"

"Well, being sent to prison, even for a few months, means he's broken his service, doesn't it? So if the yard is closed he'll not be entitled to any redundancy payment at all now. Not a penny."

"I never thought of that," Joe said. "That's a pity isn't it? He's been there a lot of years."

"Well, he shouldn't be such a bleedin' rogue, and then he wouldn't have got locked up, would he? It's his own fault, no one else's."

"Still, all the same," Joe said, "it's a bit rough on the bloke, isn't it? He said he wanted to go straight after his last spell inside and seemed to be doing okay."

"You're too soft, Joe. You believe what anybody tells you. Just because Alan hasn't been locked up for a while doesn't mean he's been going straight. I seem to remember him being up to court a few times over the years and only getting probation. From what I've heard, Alan's been burgling for years. And it depends on how you look at it, doesn't it? If yours was one of those houses that he burgled, you might just consider him being gaoled to be his just deserts. And Trev still swears it was Alan who stole his wage packet that time."

"Being locked up might have taught him a lesson, I suppose."

"Not him. He'll never learn, not that one. Hardly surprising really. His father was a real crooked bastard and Elsie, his mother, is still the queen of the shoplifters. I hear that she's inside now as well."

"I suppose you're right, he'll never change. He's already talking about pulling some job. Apparently somebody he met inside told him about a lorry load of something that'll be easy as pie to nick."

"What, he's got something lined up already? You've got to hand it to the lad, haven't you? He's very enterprising. He doesn't let the grass grow under his feet."

"You know what Alan's like, full of shit most of the time."

George drank the remainder of his beer and picked up and opened another bottle of brown ale.

Joe watched his friend pour the dark frothy liquid carefully into his glass, lift it to his lips and drink long and deeply. The distaste he felt was obviously showing on his face.

George removed the glass from his mouth. "What?" he snapped, interpreting Joe's expression correctly. "Don't say you're going to start nagging me now? I've just got rid of her, gob on a stick, and now you're starting."

"I'm not going to nag you, mate." Joe said quietly, taking in his friend's unkempt appearance, his creased and marked clothes and greasy shirt collar. "It's up to you if you want to drink all day. But do you really think that will bring her back? You're drinking far too much for your own good. And, you're not looking after yourself properly. You're sleeping here at the allotment more and more, and you're not eating well. You'll kill yourself if you carry on like this."

"Don't you worry about me. I've never felt better. And if I want to sleep up here now and again, where's the harm in that? I can keep an eye on the prize vegetables. We don't want anybody sabotaging those now, do we? Not this close to the annual Leek Show," George smiled, calming down and making a joke of it, knowing he had over-reacted to his friend's genuine concern. Since Violet had left him, walking out after that stupid argument, his life seemed to have lost its colour, its meaning. He missed Violet like he'd miss his right hand. Nothing was the same when she'd left. He always seem to have a feeling of dread, a feeling that something terrible was about to happen. He was constantly irritable and bad tempered. Food had lost its taste and he had no appetite. Sleep evaded him and when he did manage to drop off he'd wake from some nightmare in the small hours, covered in sweat, with a dreadful feeling in the pit of his stomach. As the months went by, he'd gradually learned to live with the pain, which had settled into the dreary ache of depression, but was still taking anti-depressants and felt ill and empty inside most of the time. Even so, the only way he could he manage a short relief in dreamless unconsciousness, was by drinking huge amounts of alcohol, despite his doctor's warnings about mixing the medication and drink.

"All the same, you shouldn't be drinking as much as you are. There's nothing wrong with liking a drink, mate, but lately you've been right over the top."

George nodded his head but said nothing.

"Look it's only natural that you're a bit depressed, but it's not the end of the world. You don't need to rely on her, you know? You can manage without any woman. Anyway, there are plenty of other fish in the sea. Why don't you look in the ads in the local papers?"

"For what? Another woman? Join a lonely bleeding hearts club for the over forties? No thanks. It's got to be her or nothing. I can't help it; it's just the way I feel."

"You might find yourself a woman with loads of money. Just fancy that, George."

"Yes and pigs might fly."

"How's that history project coming on? You still working at it?" Joe asked, deliberately steering the topic of conversation away from women.

"Oh yes. We're about half finished now," George answered enthusiastically. The local history book was being compiled by members of the local history society of which George was an active member. Becoming involved in contributing material towards the project had really helped him keep his mind occupied since his wife had left and kept him sane. "We've covered the time up to halfway through the Industrial Revolution already, but now's where it gets really interesting. The others are completing that, but they want me to start writing my own recollections down. You know, what it was like when I was a lad."

"That sounds interesting. What sort of stuff you putting in, then?"

"Well, there's a lot to choose from, too much really. Some things the youngsters haven't experienced, like the housing conditions, outside toilets and tin baths in front of the fire, things like that. I've put a fair bit down as I remember it and will have to sort it out later. Edit it and take the unsuitable bits out."

"Sounds good. Let's know as soon as it's published and I'll buy a copy."

"Sure." George looked at his watch. "Is that the time?" he said, changing the subject. "Bloody hell, Joe. Come on then, if you're coming. We've only got two hours drinking time on a Sunday lunch session, and we don't want to waste any of it sitting here in the bleedin' shed, gabbin' like a couple of old wives." He drank off the remaining beer in his glass, grabbed his coat and made for the door. Joe was right behind him.

2

She smiled at him as she pulled on the pump. At least he thought that she was smiling at him. The barmaid was cross-eyed. In fact her estranged eyes were not even on nodding terms with each other and he was never one hundred percent certain who she was looking at. She was one of four barmaids coping with the opening rush into the pub at noon. Men crowded around the bar, three deep, impatient to be served. Trays of pint glasses were placed at strategic points on the counter, already half-filled to save precious time and waiting to be topped up.

"There you are, pet, a nice pint of Scotch Beer," she said as she placed the pint glass in front of him on the bar counter.

Sure now that she was addressing him, Trev handed over the money and picked up the pint glass. He had wedged himself into a corner between the bar counter and a wall and so was managing to avoid most of the jostling, as men pushed to the bar to be served. As he raised the glass to his lips he heard George's voice, "Come on then, get them in."

"You must have been waiting out there for me to come in first," Trev joked, pulling money from his pocket and signalling to the barmaid.

"You've guessed," George said joining him at the bar. "Joe's on his way down as well, so you might as well get him one in. He's just popped home with a cabbage and some carrots for the Sunday dinner."

"You think we'll hear anything this week, then?"

"I don't know. There's supposed to be a statement issued sometime soon. If the yard is going to close they'll have to announce something to the press and we'll find out soon enough." He looked anxiously toward the barmaid. "Do you think that she's getting those pints, or what?" George said with irritation, "I'm fair parched here."

"I think so, but you're never bloody sure with her, are you?" Trev renewed his efforts to attract the barmaid's attention, waving a five-pound note in his hand.

The barmaid came across after serving a group of shipwrights. "I'm not blind you know. Another pint of Scotch is it?"

Trev nodded. "Make it two, please."

By the time Joe arrived there was more space at the bar, as men bought their first drinks and found seats. The rush had abated and the crowd thinned. The three friends drank a number of pints and although George had a quite a head start on the others, he wasn't noticeably any worse for drink than they were. The main topic of conversation in the pub was, of course, the possible imminent redundancies at Yule's. Most of the pub's clientele were shipyard workers of one kind or another, shipwrights, platers, welders or labourers.

Because of the exciting possibility of impending redundancies and the atmosphere of expectation, Joe allowed himself to drink more than he usually would. It wasn't that he disliked alcohol, or had any religious or moral grounds for not normally consuming a lot, it was just that he had a duodenal ulcer and if he drank more than a couple of pints, it gave him problems.

George sat down to play dominoes, persuading Joe to join him.

They were playing partners. Partners was played very seriously in this pub. Some said that hand signals had been used in some high-stake games, which was considered to be the worst form of cheating. Everyone was on the lookout for such infringements of the rules. George and Joe won the first two games straight off and so naturally their opposition's concentration was very intense on the third and deciding game.

Joe kept glancing at his watch every few minutes and one of the opposing team, on the look out for possible signals, challenged him.

"Hey, that's the fourth time that you've looked at your watch in the last few minutes. Just what's your game, eh? You're bloody signalling to your mate here, aren't you? He's signalling to his mate here, Dave," he repeated to his playing partner, as if the man, who was sitting opposite him at a distance of about four feet, couldn't hear what he had just said. "I'll bet the bleeder's got double five," he accused. "He must have. He can't have double six because you've got it …" Realising his faux pas, he hurriedly tried to cover it up. "It gets to be something when you can't trust the mates that you work with, doesn't it?" he protested to Dave.

"Now look here," George said, placing his dominoes face down on the board, "don't you go accusing me and Joe of cheating. We're as honest as the day is long, we are. Well, Joe is anyway," he amended.

"Then what's he looking at his watch all the time for, then?"

"Probably the same reason that you look at your watch. To see what bloody time it is," George answered.

"That's right," Joe put in. "I promised Brenda that I'd only have a couple of pints and I'd be back for one o'clock, because she'll have my dinner ready for me on the table."

"Oh aye?" Joe's accuser said disbelievingly. "You promised, Brenda, did you? Well, then, if you promised your Brenda that you'd be in at one, then why are you still here when it's …" he looked up and over Joe's head at the large clock on the grubby wall of the pub, "… nearly a quarter to two, then, hey?"

"Well, I got into conversation, didn't I?" Joe defended himself. "And I can have a game of dominoes, can't I?"

"And, anyway," George contributed, "Joe's the boss in his house. He's not hen- pecked." He looked across the board at Joe. "You're not hen-pecked are you, mate? He wears the trousers and is the man of the house, so if he wants to have a few more pints, then that's his prerogative, isn't it? And his wife will just have to put his dinner in the oven and keep it warm until he comes home. That right, mate?"

Joe nodded, but not too convincingly. "That's right."

Just then, further discussion was abandoned as the players became aware that all conversation had gradually ceased and the room had fallen completely silent. All eyes went to a slight figure standing in the pub doorway. A woman had just entered the bar. Now the bar was strictly men only, the only females ever allowed inside its sacred space were barmaids, who were tolerated only because they served the drinks. This code had always been rigorously adhered to, and never challenged for the hundred and sixty years the public house had been open, even by the most strident 'women's libbers', not that there were many of those in this part of the country.

Accounts of what happened next vary and are sometimes contradictory, as they tend to be with such astonishing events. The men closest to the domino board were generally thought to be the best positioned to give the most reliable of accounts. Except possibly for the boss-eyed barmaid, who happened to be on the customer side of the counter collecting empty glasses, and was one of the only two totally sober persons in the room. Her account was the one that tended to be believed, once whoever she was speaking to realised that they were being addressed, but her account was never conclusively confirmed one way or the other by the only other totally sober eye witness.

The silent spectators stopped whatever they were doing and stared fascinated, as the woman at the door, holding something out before her, began to move purposefully through the crowd of men, which parted before her like the Red Sea parted before Moses and the Israelites. She walked slowly towards the domino table.

The domino players looked up, somewhat taken aback.

"Brenda," Joe said, starting to rise, surprised by his wife's sudden appearance in the bar. "What are you …?"

His words faded away to nothing and he sank back down in his seat, as she strode resolutely the few remaining steps through the crowd of astonished men and towered over the seated domino players.

Brenda was a strikingly attractive woman and at the moment also a very angry one. She had a voluptuous figure with prominent breasts and looked a veritable Amazon as she stood there holding a plate of steaming hot Sunday roast dinner in her hands, complete with Yorkshire puddings. A tea towel protected her hands from the heat of the searing meal. She plonked it squarely in the middle of the domino board, splashing a little onion gravy across the board in the process. The four players gaped in amazement at this unprecedented event.

"There you are. I told you that your dinner would be ready by one o'clock, and that if you weren't back I'd come down here with it, didn't I? Thought I wouldn't dare, didn't you? Well you were wrong. If I say I'll do something, then I will. If you won't come home, then you can eat it there, on your darling domino board." Having dumped the steaming dinner plate, Brenda pulled a knife and fork from her apron pocket and threw them on the board. Then she turned on her heel without another word and, folding the tea towel, walked out of the bar.

The men watched her exit silently, and none spoke until the door had closed behind her. Then everyone started to talk excitedly.

Joe stood up, nearly upsetting the board, dominoes, Sunday dinner and all. He grabbed the table to steady it, and himself. "Brenda, wait a minute, Brenda," he spluttered as he hurried to follow her out of the bar. He stopped at the door, hesitated for a second and then returned to the board, put the knife and fork in his pocket and picked up the steaming dinner plate, using his coat to protect his fingers, as Brenda had left with the tea towel. Joe removed the plate and himself, as quickly as he possibly could from the bar, the men's laughter loud in his ears.

"She not left the salt, then?" someone shouted after him causing more hilarity.

The game of partners summarily abandoned, George got up from the board and joined Trev at the bar counter. George laughed and shook his head in admiration. "She's some woman that Brenda, isn't she? Joe doesn't know how lucky he is." He paused and puffed hard on his pipe, trying to keep the embers in the bowl alight. Finally satisfied with his efforts, he smiled. "Women are supposed to be the weaker sex, but that's a load of rubbish. If they want something and are determined to get it, then you might as well give in straight away and agree, because you just can't win with them, can you?" he said philosophically, his words slightly slurred, the amount of alcohol he'd drunk seemingly finally taking effect.

"I can't and that's for sure," Trev muttered. "Not where it counts, anyway."

George pretended he hadn't heard Trev's comments. "But still, they're lovely, man, especially barmaids." He looked behind the bar and added, "Well, most barmaids anyway. We'd be lost without them. Before I got married I always made a point of knocking around with barmaids, you know," he continued in reminiscent mood. "Come to think of it, they were the only women that I ever met. I had it all worked out before I met our lass. I worked permanent dayshift then, and was out on the drink every night with the girlfriend while she was at work, and it didn't cost me a lot. I'd always stand at the end of the bar so as to be able to speak to the lass, but was always careful not to get in the way of anybody wanting to be served. Every now and again, when she got the chance like, she'd slip me a pint for nowt. Then later on I'd slip her one, eh?"

Trev and the other men standing near him laughed loudly.

"No, seriously though," George went on, "barmaids are the best. They know what it's all about, and they're not stuck-up buggers like some women that I've known."

Trev readily agreed. "There's only one drawback though, if you fall out with the barmaid, then you have to change your local and find somewhere else to drink," Trev said.

They laughed again.

"That's why I used to drink in the town centre, plenty of pubs in a small radius."

3

George walked with a slight stagger through the shipyard gates, his legs rubber-like. Any casual watcher could see by the exaggerated way each step was placed carefully on the ground and by the swaying of the body, that he was drunk. He was drunk as a result of two diametrically opposite emotions. One was his general state of depression and despondency and the other, elation resulting from a horse win that afternoon. He'd received a tip for that particular horse, from a friend's relative who supposedly worked in a trainer's stable. George had placed a lot of money on the animal, most of it borrowed from one doubtful source or another, and he was overjoyed when it came in at twelve to one. He had spent all that Monday afternoon in the pub playing dominoes and had drunk a total of nine pints of best beer, plus a number of celebratory whiskies and he still had money left over. He knew that he had to go into work that night and he had no intention of staying off. If he did he would be letting his squad down and besides, he knew that this was very probably be one of the last chances to work for quite a while. He knew that the rumours were more than likely true and that the yard would probably close soon. He was going to work tonight, no danger. The chances were that it would be a quiet shift anyway, and even if he was busy, he could handle that, even with a drink inside of him. He'd done it before, countless times.

Normally drink didn't affect George adversely. He never got aggressive and generally just went to sleep if he'd drunk a lot. But tonight there was something on George's mind, and he was determined to do something about it. He'd been waiting for an opportunity to tell the welders' foreman exactly what he thought of him and if the yard was closing he'd have to be quick. He'd decided that tonight was the night that he'd get it off his chest.

The inebriated man made his somewhat unsteady way through the yard to the high- roofed shed and along to the small office where the foreman spent most of the shift. He gave a sharp rap on the wooden door with his knuckles, and pushed it open without waiting for an invitation to enter. He could see the white-clad figure in the corner of the room standing behind the desk.

The small group of labourers standing beside the small gas fire some yards away, watched as George harangued the white-clad figure inside the office. Although they couldn't make out what George was saying, they could tell by his body language and from the tone of his raised voice that he was angry. He came out, slamming the door shut and walking away a number of times, but then, deciding that he had something else to add, returning to the door, opening it again and resuming his tirade. George finally considered himself spent, and to have communicated his displeasure fully. He walked away from the office door, and made his way unsteadily towards the labourers. "That's told him and no mistake. Bloody foremen," George said as he passed them on the way to his crane.

The men looked puzzled as they could see the welders' foreman quite clearly across the other side of the shed where he'd been talking to a group of welders for the last ten minutes.

"What's he on about?" Joe said as they watched George start his unsteady climb up the sixty-foot ladder to the crane.

George's climbing technique was heart stopping for the spectators. He first swung far over to the left as he removed both his right hand and foot from the rungs, then pulled himself back to the centre and placed his free hand and foot on the next rung up. Once he'd attained the next rung, he let go of the ladder with his left hand and took his left foot off the rung below and swayed alarmingly way across the to right, his free arm and leg swinging out into space. He repeated this time after time and made his way slowly upwards. This display was worrying enough when he was only a couple of feet from the ground, but at forty or fifty feet in the air, as he made his progress skywards, it was terrifying.

"He's pissed," Trev said, shaking his head. "He'll kill himself if he falls off that ladder."

The men watched in silence as George made his slow and perilous way the sixty-feet to the top, then clambered across the rails and into the cab of the crane. Once inside the cab he sat down and promptly fell asleep.

"I'd better go and see who he's been talking to in the office," Joe said. "God knows who he was having a go at, but it certainly wasn't the welders' foreman." He ran along to the office and opening the door looked in, and then ran back.

"Well, who's he been upsetting this time?" Trev asked.

"Nobody. There isn't anybody in there at all. Just a pair of old white overalls hanging up on a peg behind the desk. Silly old sod," Joe said smiling. "He's been sounding off to a pair of overalls."

The routine of the shipyard gradually commenced, and the inside of the shed became a hive of activity. Joe set to work with the fore-end squad and almost immediately a lift by the crane was required. It took some time and some determined hammering on the supporting metal stanchion to wake George up, but once aware that the services of his crane were required, he moved it into position above the men and lowered the hook. A metal strop had already been attached to the plate that was to be moved. The plater placed the strop over the hook and indicated to George to raise the hook. As the strop took the stain, the thin plate bent alarmingly and then lifted slowly off the ground.

It swayed slightly as it hung suspended from the crane.

"That bloody thing doesn't look safe to me," Joe said with alarm.

"It'll be alright. Just keep to one side of it," the plater replied. He peered upwards and indicated to George which direction he wanted to move the plate, and then he and Joe set off up the shed, following the smoothly moving crane, with the plate hanging precariously between them. Joe made sure that he kept well away from the plate by the simple expedient of holding it at his arm's length. He desperately tried to keep the thing from swaying around. They'd got about halfway to where the plater wanted it, when at the side nearest the plater, the small, lightweight shoe-clip holding the plate came loose. This type of attachment relied purely on the weight of the plate to hold it in place. The weight of the thin, light plate had somehow shifted and the plate dropped free, its sharp edge dipping quickly and dangerously towards the plater's right leg. The metal shoe, now loose, went whizzing dangerously around the crane strop like a helicopter rotor blade.

Joe was aware of it flying through the air towards his head. He ducked. Everything seemed to slow right down. He watched as the falling plate slanted downwards in slow motion and threatened to take off the plater's leg as he desperately tried to get out of its way. The plate hit the metal frames already welded onto the shell laid on the floor of the shed, and bounced upwards sending a shower of sparks across the retreating man's legs. Again and again the plate fell, sending out a fresh shower of sparks, and then it bounced upwards again, every time getting nearer and nearer to the plater's legs as he tried to run backwards away from the danger. The edge of the plate left a trail of fresh scars across the top of the metal frame it had come into contact with, until finally the angle of the falling plate became too acute, and the thing slid flat onto the frames. It remained there wobbling and vibrating as its energy depleted, being absorbed into the metal frames below it.

Joe, shocked by the sudden violence, was now aware that everything suddenly came back to normal speed. He ducked again as the flying shoe whizzed past his head and spun repeatedly around the crane strop, increasing in speed, until it finally stopped, completely wrapped tightly around it. The plater, pale-faced, lit a cigarette, and offered one to Joe. His hand shook as he lit them both.

"I told you it didn't look safe to me," Joe said, with an attempt at wry humour.

"No, it bleedin' well wasn't, was it?" the plater replied seriously. "It could have had my leg off. I could have been killed there." He spat onto the now still plate. "I'm going to make sure that piece of shite is welded up to this fucking thing good and proper tonight if it's the last thing I do."

Joe's colleagues came across and the details of the accident were recounted again and again. It had been a close thing, and the plater was very lucky that he hadn't lost at least one of his legs.

"Serve the greedy bastard right if it had hit him," a labourer said nastily. "He should have got a lug welded on the plate and lifted it properly, instead of trying to save a few minutes. If he'd have used the proper gear it wouldn't have happened."

"Aye. I don't mind one of them getting hurt if they want to cut corners, but it could have been you that lost a leg, Joe, not him," another chipped in.

John Gore, the night shift foreman arrived on the scene. "All right, lads. Get yourselves back to work now. Nobody's been killed, have they? We're not closing the yard, are we?"

"Not tonight, anyway," one of the labourers muttered as he walked away.

The men drifted back to where they should be working. Gore beckoned to Joe. "You alright?"

"Yes, fine, except my stomach's kicked off again," Joe said, holding his hand to his midriff.

"You got some tablets or something?" the foreman asked.

Joe nodded.

"Well, if I were you, I'd go and make a cup of hot, sweet tea and take some time to drink it. Don't start work again until after the next break, and then only if you feel well enough. Okay?"

"Fair enough, but I'll be okay."

Joe did exactly as the foreman had suggested and watched while the others worked around him.

"Bloody hell, Joe, I hear that was a close thing," said a voice behind him.

Joe turned to see Trev.

"You alright?"

"Yes, I'm okay. These bloody platers only think of their bonuses, man. Everything is rush, rush, rush. They never seem to do things properly and take basic safety precautions."

"Yes, they're always in a hurry. Instead of using a proper clamp or welding a lifting lug on to the thing, the plater just shoves the shoes on to it, but the plate is too thin isn't it? Not heavy enough. And one of the shoes comes off and very nearly takes the plater's leg off as well. Really lucky, he was."

"You're right about them cutting corners," agreed Trev. "I've been working out on the slipway and they're berthing a double bottom tonight. You know what the plater asked me to do? Crawl underneath with a marking line. There's this huge double bottom that must weigh a hundred tons, hanging by the crane about three feet off the ground and I'm wondering what he's playing at. I watched him chalk the string and then he gives me one end and says, 'just nip under there and hold the line against the plate while I mark it'. Nip under? I ask you. And what happens if one of those lugs come flying off the thing, and the whole great bastard lot falls on top of me?"

"What did he say?"

"Nothing. He just gave me a dirty look."

"Did you go underneath with the marking line then?"

"Did I shit! I refused point blank. I've not risking a flat head, not for the money they're paying me here. No way. No, he had to get under himself. Mind, I've never seen anybody move so fast in all my life. He crawled under, got the line in the proper place. We twanged it, he made sure that the plate was marked all the way across and then he was out. Like a ferret coming out of a drainpipe he was."

"It get berthed alright?"

"No, it bloody didn't. One of the lifting lugs came off when they started to lift it into position, didn't it? It went spinning around in the air like a bleedin' fairground ride. The whole unit dropped about two-feet at one end. You should have seen us run. We got out of the way as fast as we could. I thought the other lugs were going to come off as well, what with the uneven strain on them. We had to get the crane to move the thing back and lower it down to the ground again. It'll have to be checked out to make sure that it hasn't buckled or anything," Trev smiled. "The plater nearly had a heart attack when it happened. He had to go and have a sit down and a smoke. White as a sheet he was. All he could say was, 'that lug could have come off while I was underneath it'. 'Yes,' I said to him, 'and it could have come off while I was underneath the thing, if I'd have been daft enough to do what you asked.' He's still not right. Still sitting out there looking like a ghost."

"Do you think you should get him up to the ambulance room or get him first aid or something?" Joe asked.

"No. He doesn't want anything like that. He'll be alright after a while. Anyway, it'll make him think on next time he wants anything like that doing. He should have chocked the thing up on blocks before trying to mark it," he paused, shaking his head disgustedly.

"Well, we won't have to bother about things like that soon. The word is that there's going to be an announcement made this week. According to the platers' shop steward, it could even be as soon as tomorrow morning."

"It's funny, isn't it? We keep talking about the yard closing, but somehow when it actually is going to close, it doesn't seem to be real," Trev said.

"I know. It's a funny situation we're in, mate. This job's not ideal by any means and the money's not very good, but we've been doing it for so long that it's in our blood."

"Yes, you're right. We're going to be like fish out of water if we do have to look for new jobs. It'll take us some time to settle down and get used to doing anything else."

"You got anything in mind?"

"No, not a thing. But I'm definitely going to have a good holiday first, before I even think about looking for another job."

The launch of the last ship took place later that week. The union called a meeting for the yard's tradesmen the following Wednesday at a local workingmen's club and informed its members that a redundancy situation was almost certainly imminent. Although they were still in crisis talks with the yard's management, it looked almost certain that the yard would close within weeks, as there were no new orders on the books and none on the horizon.

The next day Yule's Shipbuilders Limited sent a letter to each individual employee at their home address announcing that the yard was to close the following week. In a statement which was later given to the press, the board of directors declared that they had reluctantly decided to take this drastic measure owing to the lack of production orders, intense competition from foreign builders, especially the Japanese, with whom competition was very difficult because of the differential in labour costs, and the uncertain financial climate in the country as a whole and the shipbuilding industry in particular. The management had reached agreement with the various trades unions concerned after prolonged negotiations and a fair package of redundancies was being calculated.

4

Max Westlik had dined particularly well that evening. He now sat comfortably in the big padded leather armchair in his study, surrounded by shelves of leather-bound books, and savoured the taste and aroma of the newly lit, large, expensive Cuban cigar. He blew smoke in a thin blue steam towards the glowing end of the Havana, turning the cigar to spread the burning leaf evenly. Satisfied with the cigar, he dropped the spent matchstick into a chunky crystal ashtray, then picked up a large brandy schooner and drank deeply and appreciatively. The expensive spirit joined the equally exclusive and well chosen food and wine in his stomach and added to his sense of wellbeing. Contented with himself and his surroundings, he turned his thoughts to the project he was considering. He always found he concentrated better after a nice meal.

   Max had become financially very well-off because of his criminal activity. He had lots of money and could afford to live well, but he never forgot his younger, hungry days in Berlin. Max swallowed the remainder of his brandy, poured himself another generous measure, puffed contentedly on his cigar and smiled. He never did things without considering all aspects thoroughly beforehand. He was a very intelligent and careful man and had given due consideration to his decision. There were still a number of problems to resolve, but when he was very young he'd learned something that he had never forgotten, that you never, ever, let an opportunity pass you by. If fortune was kind enough to place anything of value in your reach, then it was the height of bad manners, and an insult to fortune, to refuse to take it. Max realised that this large amount of money, in cash, was more than he could resist and he was determined to steal it.

5

The last shift was a somewhat surreal experience for the men. The only work left to do was to tidy up the yard. The foreman organised the labourers into groups and sent them off to various parts of the yard, more to keep them occupied than to get them to do anything productive. Trev and Joe were in a group of six that was sent to the slipway to clear away the blocks and timber remaining after the recent launch.

The men busied themselves at a pace that seemed appropriate and they prepared to pass the next couple of hours until break time.

"It seems strange in here tonight, doesn't it?" Joe said to Trev.

"It does and that's because this is the very last time that we'll be working down here, mate." He stood up straight and looked around. "And it's the quietness. This is the first time I've not been able to hear some sort of noise. There's no hammering from the platers, no welding or burning, no shouting and swearing. It's eerie."

The shift passed surprisingly swiftly. Dawn broke and lightened the sky. It was a bright, clear, summer's morning. The sun brought with it some warmth and it promised to be a pleasant day, the birds were already singing, bees and butterflies about early and fish jumping in the river.

Trev took deep breaths and smiled. "This does your heart good, doesn't it? This is the only part I really like about night shift. It's a special time of day."

"Well, make the most of it, mate, because it'll probably be the last one that you see, at this yard anyway. But don't worry too much; you'll probably still see plenty more walking back from some girl's place after taking her home."

Alan wandered along the silent shadows of the slipways, vigorously throwing welding rods at the large river rats that infested the debris littering the water's edge. He loved hunting the rodents and he loved the quietness of dawn, especially this last strange sunrise, eerily quiet, none of the noise, the racket of ship construction which generally emanated from the yard. Alan also liked the feeling of superiority, being wide awake when most of the city was asleep in their beds. It gave him a feeling of power, of supremacy. Lifting his eyes from the scurrying rats, he watched the early birds, mainly gulls, flying down the river and soaring overhead, looking for their breakfasts and screeching their welcome to the new day.

The foreman walked around about six o'clock and told them to get their gear together and get off home. "Don't bother clocking out, lads, just go home. That's it, the yard's finished."

Normally an early finish, or a flyer as they called it, would have cheered the lads up, but today it didn't. Most of them were somehow reluctant to leave the yard. It had been their place of employment for so many years and the scene of so many memories, both good and bad. They slowly retrieved their coats and haversacks, took a last look around and made their way, subdued, to the main gates where they exited for the last time.

"It's kind of sad, isn't it?" Joe said as they trudged up the bank.

"You're in a right maudlin mood, aren't you?" Trev answered. "Try to be positive, man. It could be a lot worse, you know? You could be coming back in to work again tonight. Just think of all that lovely redundancy money you're going to get and the lovely ten-day Mediterranean cruise that we're going to book in a couple of weeks. That should cheer you up, mate."

"Hey, I haven't said for definite that we're going on that cruise. But even if we do go, we've still got to come back afterwards, haven't we? We'll still have to find new jobs in a bleedin' factory or foundry or somewhere." He shook his head. "It's hard to explain, I thought that once we knew what was happening, I'd feel better, but I feel depressed. It's just a strange feeling, that's all," he said, placing his hand on his stomach.

"Sure to be strange, mate. How long have we worked here? Since we left school. That's getting on for sixteen years or so. It's sure to feel a bit strange, mate. Sure to, you'd not be human if you didn't."

"It's more than that. It's hard to explain, to put into words, but it's like we've been rejected. Tossed out with all the other rubbish. Not wanted. It doesn't do much for your feelings of confidence and self-worth, does it?"

"I know what you mean, mate. Your confidence just disappears and you feel useless. But we shouldn't feel like that at all, man. Think positive."

"Alright I'll think positive." He remained silent for a while before speaking again, "I've had a think and I'm positive that I'm depressed."

Trev laughed. "You shouldn't think about it like that, mate. Look on it as an opportunity. I've got a book about positive thinking and this guy reckons that all things change. Everything is always changing. The world is always changing, the seasons, everything."

"And traffic lights," Joe muttered.

"What?" Missing the joke entirely.

"Nothing. So how does all that change affect us, then?"

"Well, we should accept change because it's a natural thing. More than that, we should welcome it because change is opportunity. We all like the nice sort of changes, don't we? But we don't like any sort of change that we can't control, and we think that we're going to be worse off. So we try to resist it. But when we think positively, and start to believe that things might just turn out pleasantly for us, instead of crap, then sometimes it does just that."

"All that positive thinking stuff is just a pile of shit, man."

"It is, if you think it is. Believe me, there's some good stuff there if you believe in it. I'll dig that book out and you can have a read. It'll do you the world of good, might even help you to stop worrying."

"Don't bother, mate. All that stuff is a load of crap."

Trev smiled at his friend's totally negative response. "Anyway, where are we going to have this last celebratory drink with all the lads, eh?"

"I suppose we'll just go around the town and have a few bevvies," Joe said uninterestedly.

"That all? What about a proper sit-down meal in a restaurant or something? If we have something a bit posh like that, it'll give us a bit of practice, won't it?"

"Practice? Practice for what?"

"For the cruise. Come on, man, wake up."

"Talking about that, I'm not sure that I'd like all that dressing up for dinner and that."

"That's all part of the enjoyment, man. We'll get a few photographs of us done up like dog's bollocks, stick them in a frame and put them on top of the telly. Then every time Brenda's got Corry or some other crap on TV, and she won't let you watch the match on the other channel, you can look at the photos and remember our lovely, luxurious, Mediterranean cruise holiday," Trev said enthusiastically.

"I just hope that George keeps off the drink long enough to look after the leeks properly. I don't know, but I've got a funny feeling about those leeks this year."

"What do you mean a funny feeling? Is this another one of your funny feelings, or the same one you had before? You're full of funny bloody feelings, you are."

"I don't know, it's hard to explain."

"You're having a right old, 'hard to explain' night tonight, as well, mate, aren't you? You're full of hard to explains and funny feelings. Are you going though the change or what?" Without waiting for an answer, Trev went on. "You know what you need?"

"No. What?"

"You need a bloody good drink, mate. That'll sort out your stomach and all these, hard to explain feelings. I think most of them are probably just wind anyway," Trev laughed.

"Bugger off. If you had my stomach, you'd know about it alright. It's no laughing matter, I can tell you. The pain I've had recently is terrible."

"I'm only joking, mate. Don't get shirty. It's all the worry about the yard closure that's kicked off your stomach this time. You're much too sensitive, mate. The least bit of stress and it plays up. It's always the same. You can bet money on it kicking off when you get tense."

"You're right there. And, these bloody tablets the doc's given me are almost useless," Joe complained, popping another pill into his mouth.

"It's not the tablets' fault, mate. I've told you before; you're supposed to take them regularly, every day. Not just when you get a pain in your gut. It's too late then. It's like drinking a pint of milk after you've just drunk ten pints of best ale. You've got to drink it before the ale and build up a lining on your stomach to protect it."

Joe nodded, but remained silent.

"Anyway," Trev said, changing the subject slightly, "you bought your seasickness tablets yet?"

"Seasickness tablets? Why would I need seasickness tablets?"

"Well, we are going to sail around the Med, aren't we? Or have you just been having me on all these weeks?"

"We might be. We'll have the money to buy the tickets soon, and we've applied for our passports and everything," Joe answered defensively.

"Well, then. You'll need some seasickness tablets, won't you?"

"But why? Those liners are huge, aren't they? And the Med's as calm as a millpond all the time, isn't it?"

"Who told you that, then?"

"Who told me that? You bloody told me that. You said it was like a duck pond. You said that it was always so calm that you could sail a toy yacht in it."

"I said that?"

"Yes. You bloody said that." Joe was getting a bit irate now and Trev decided to back-pedal a bit.

"Oh yes. You're right, mate. I was forgetting, I did say that, now you come to mention it."

"So, why would I need to buy seasickness pills, then?" Joe persisted.

"Just as a precaution, mate. In case it got a bit rough, just on the off-chance, like."

"Rough, in the Med? That's not very likely is it?"

"Well, you never know nowadays. At one time you could guarantee the weather, but now, who knows? Even in the summer, it can be a bit iffy."

Joe looked at his friend. "You are having me on, aren't you?"

"Yes, that's right, mate. I'm having you on," Trev said, but he made a mental note to remind Brenda to buy some seasickness tablets for Joe anyway, and make sure that she packed them. If they ever did actually manage to get on this famous cruise, he'd probably need them.

The labourers were called to a meeting in the yard canteen the following afternoon. They were addressed by a union representative and informed of the level of their redundancy packages. The men were shocked as their individual details were handed to each of them.

Joe looked at the paper in his hand with disbelief. "This can't be bloody right," he exclaimed.

"I wish it wasn't, but I think it is," Trev said sadly, holding an identical piece of paper.

"But this isn't even a quarter of what I was expecting," Joe said despondently.

"Same here, mate, nowhere near what I'd reckoned on," Trev said quietly. "That's fucked up the positive mental attitude theory."

Joe looked at him quizzically.

"You know, it's in that book I lent you. The theory is that you always get what you expect to get, but I expected to get a lot more than this."

"There must be some mistake, surely. We were told that the redundancy packages would be much better."

"You heard the union man, the company's virtually bust and are paying the minimum amount of redundancy required by law, twelve weeks' pay, which is the maximum anybody will get, tradesmen and labourers alike."

Joe shook his head. "There isn't enough here to pay off half my bloody debt. How are we supposed to pay the mortgage and what are we supposed to live on until I get a start somewhere else?"

"We're all in the same boat, mate," Trev said despondently. "But get back to the positive mental attitude and look on the bright side, eh?"

"The bright side, what bloody bright side is that then?"

"Well, at least now you needn't worry about being seasick on that cruise."

The following Monday morning Joe went to the unemployment office and signed on. He completed a mound of paperwork and was interviewed by a small, thin man, who asked a lot of questions and filled in more forms with the answers Joe supplied. Eventually he informed Joe officiously that he wasn't entitled to any unemployment benefit because of the redundancy money he'd recently received from his previous employer. Joe already knew this, but let the man enjoy himself by informing him of the fact and looking suitably pleased with himself as he did so.

"Yes, I know that, mate. I know that I'm not entitled to any dole. I want a job, not dole money. Is there anything in at the moment that might be suitable for me?"

"Don't you call me mate. I'm not your mate, I'm a government official. And you want a job, a job?" the man repeated as if it was the last thing he'd have expected anyone to ask for.

"Yes, a job," Joe said loudly. "This is a bleedin' unemployment office, isn't it?"

"Yes it is and there's no need to take that attitude. I'll have to ask you to keep your voice down, or else I'll be within my rights to refuse to deal with you."

"I'll bet you know all about your rights," Joe said.

"Yes, I certainly do. I happen to be the shop steward for the union here and we civil servants stick together, we back each other up, we do."

"Look, you can't tell me anything about unions. I've had my fill of them. All they're good for is taking your subs and getting your place of work shut down. You want to keep well away from unions, mate."

"That's rubbish. And, I'll remind you again not to call me mate. I'm not a mate of yours and doubt if I ever will be. Just sign that." He pushed a piece of paper across the desk to Joe.

"What's this, then?"

"It's a list of regulations regarding your signing on. What you can and can't do. Sign the top sheet and keep the bottom copy for yourself."

Joe ran his eye down the list, which looked innocuous enough, and signed.

"Right then," the clerk said. "I'll go and have a look at today's vacancies and see if there is anything that might be suitable for you." His tone suggested that there being something suitable for Joe was highly unlikely, if not impossible. He returned some time later carrying another piece of paper. He sat down before reading it. "There's a number of factory machinists required here," he said questioningly while looking at Joe. "They want another four. You want to try for one of those positions?"

Joe shrugged. "Might as well, where is it?"

"Trenchers Components. That's up on the Westwood industrial estate. They're interviewing Friday morning."

Joe nodded. "Alright, I'll give it a go. Anything else on there?" he asked, indicating the list still held in the clerk's hand.

"Another machinist's position … ah no. That's semi-skilled, no good for you," he said dismissively. "A general labourer wanted, no, that's just been filled. No, that's it. That's all there is, I'm afraid."

He didn't look afraid, Joe thought. In fact he looked quite pleased with himself.

George had an interview the same morning and his was a lot easier.

"I see that you have relatives working here, Mr Atkins," the personnel manager said, while reading the employment application form in front of him on his desk.

"Yes, that's right," George lied confidently. Fred, his friend who was also a member of the local history group, and who had spoken for him, wasn't exactly a relation; in fact they weren't related at all, except through drink, as George like to put it.

"Well then, I've no doubt that Fred has given you all the relevant facts regarding employment here with us?"

"He's told me a lot about the brewery, yes," George answered.

"It'd be pointless me going over all that stuff again then, wouldn't it? Are there any specific questions that you would like to ask me?"

"Er, no, I don't think so," George said, desperately trying to think of a question so as to appear keen and interested in the job, but he couldn't think of any at all.

"No? Okay then, we'll leave it at that," he paused and looked at a clipboard that was hanging from a hook on the wall. "Can you start, let's say a week Monday? Would that be alright for you?"

George nodded. "That'd be great. Thanks."

"Okay then, we'll see you then. Just turn up at half-seven at the main gate and ask for Mr Walker, the foreman."

Trev, thinking positively, had attended a number of interviews in the weeks before the closure, and started work as an insurance agent immediately the yard closed.

6

When the lads did at last receive their long-awaited, but unexpectedly paltry, redundancy cheques, they decided to celebrate anyway, if celebrate was the right word, by having a night out. It was more a case of drowning their sorrows than a celebration. They met early in the evening at one of the pubs in the city centre and put money into a kitty for their drinks. Almost all the yard labourers turned up and Joe was elected to hold the money, as everyone trusted him. Joe was the one they all turned to when they wanted advice, or even just his opinion about something. He was always genuine, trustworthy, sympathetic and reliable. Alan and Nobby were invited along anyway for the drink, even though they didn't have any redundancy package due to them. The lads agreed that under the circumstances, they should be exempt from contributing to the kitty and so were given a free night. All of the lads had made an effort and were dressed for a night on the town.

Most of the labourers had arrived and were already drinking when Alan and his diminutive younger friend, Nobby, walked into the bar. Alan wore his characteristically suspicious scowl as he swaggered into the pub, his eyes darting everywhere as he weighed up the customers, as if looking for any threat he might need to deal with, or any weakness he could use to his advantage. He instinctively knew that attack was the best form of defence and would attack without hesitation if he thought he would win. Alan always appeared to have a chip on his shoulder and to be aggressively wary. He considered the average man to be a mug, working to make someone else rich. His attitude to women was similar and he thought any man who tied himself to a woman was a mug.

Nobby seemed to be in a world of his own. He had really outdone himself tonight and was resplendent in a new pair of black leather trousers, an open black leather bomber jacket with 'Elvis The King' spelled out in studs on the back, and his boots were black, chisel-toed, with inch-and-a-half Cuban heels. In contrast to the rest of his outfit, he wore a powder blue, open necked, frilly fronted shirt, with an upright, severely starched collar, and a two-inch wide leather belt with a large ornate silver buckle was prominently visible at his waist.

Nobby's appearance brought quite a few admiring looks and a lot more stares of disbelief. With his prominent long, broad sideburns and dyed, jet-black hair, greased and shining, swept back to a ragged DA at the back and a dangling quiff pulled forward over his eyes, he looked like a short, demented, Elvis look-a-like.

"That Nobby's done up like a dog's bleedin' dinner. It wouldn't look so bad but he's only about four foot eleven. He looks like a bleedin' pantomime star. I'll bet good money that some clever bastard has a go at him tonight, dressed like that," Trev remarked to Joe. "Who invited the plonker anyway?"

"It'll have been Alan, won't it? The pair of them are as thick as thieves," Joe answered quietly.

"They're thieves all right, but I suppose we can afford to buy them a few pints. Look on the bright side, here we are complaining about how little redundancy we got and those buggers didn't get a penny. There's always someone worse off than you, and that's a fact," Joe said philosophically.

The large group toured the bars. Small splinter groups split from the main core now and again, but rejoined their friends as they moved from bar to bar. There was no trouble and everyone was enjoying themselves, except George, who had gradually lapsed into one of his silent drinking modes. The others tried unsuccessfully to jolly him along and get him to become involved in their jocular conversation. Even Joe's repeated efforts to get him to talk about the history project were to no avail.

The evening wore on and the alcohol began to take its toll. At around nine o'clock, Trev would have won his 'good money bet' if someone had taken the wager. Nobby had just entered a bar a few paces in front of the others, as he didn't have to buy a round he didn't at all mind leading the way, when a large and obviously drunk man grabbed him around his shoulders. "Look everybody, it's little Elvis!" he shouted to the room at large. "Little Elvis is in the building. Come on, little Elvis, give us a song. How about Jailhouse Rock eh? I like that one, it's my favourite."

The big man wore a light grey Teddy Boy suit, with a knee-length drape coat and drainpipe trousers. His suit was complemented by black velvet collar, cuffs and pocket flaps, and set off with a black shirt. The shirt was resplendently decorative, with glittering sequins down the front and topped with a loosely tied, cowboy-type, steer's head, string necktie. Suede, crepe-soled, beetle crushers completed his outfit. Anyone else dressed so outlandishly would almost certainly have attracted some critical comments, but this was Sid the Shiv Shearer.

"Oh fuck," Trev said to Joe. "It's Sid the Shiv."

"Who's he when he's at home, then?"

"He's supposed to be one of the hardest bastards in the city. From all accounts he's a right bastard all right, and his brother is in that Elvis look-alike competition Nobby's entered. His brother's semi-professional, stage name's Ricky Fontain, or something."

"Why do they call him Sid the Shiv and what's with all the teddy boy gear?"

"'Cos he carries a knife and the bastard uses it. And he and his mates think dressing like Teds make them look hard."

Now, Nobby considered himself to be a lot more than just an Elvis look-alike, he really thought that he was the spitting image of his idol in his younger, leaner years, and if he'd only been a bit taller he would have been Elvis's double. He knew he could sing any of Elvis's songs at least as good as, if not a great deal better than, the King himself.

Nobby had entered, and won, a number of Elvis competitions in the past and had now reached the semi-finals of a current contest run by the Supreme Leisure Ballroom Organisation. So, he was not at all put out by the big man's request, even though he knew he was being sent up. In fact he was rather pleased and was just about to let belt with his rendition of Jailhouse Rock, his lip curled, right hip stuck out, leg bent and foot up on the tips of his toes, right arm held high above his head, just as Elvis used to stand, when Alan appeared beside him.

"Fuck off, Sid, you bastard," Alan snarled at the big man. "Don't you take the piss out of my mate."

Nobby tried to calm Alan down. "It's alright, I know the song right through and I can sing it great."

Alan had weighed the situation up quickly and his intervention wasn't as foolhardy as it appeared. He'd noted that Sid was the worse for drink and had probably been on the drink all day. He was accompanied by only two of his hard bastard Teds. Of the other four with him, Alan knew, and got on well with, the two that worked at the yard and he'd been in prison with one of the others. He reasoned, correctly as it turned out, that including Sid, there were only four to account for if it came to a fight. And there were ten behind him, on his side, most of whom could handle themselves. No contest.

By now all the lads were inside the bar and lined up opposite the big man and his friends.

"I knew this would happen," Trev said to Joe, as he pushed past him and stood alongside Alan and Nobby. Trev stared at the big man and knew from the way he stared right back that there was going to be trouble. "Look, mate," Trev began, but that was as far as he got. The big man attempted to punch him on the jaw, but Trev saw it coming, moved out of the way and was hit on the side of the head instead. The blow knocked him sideways to the floor.

As Trev fell, Alan attacked the big man, hitting him on the head with an empty bottle he snatched from a nearby table. The bottle smashed over the man's head and blood immediately streaked through his hair and ran down his face. He grabbed at Alan as the others closed in around them. Alan and his large opponent struggled, swayed in the crowd and then fell over, upsetting a table and sending glasses crashing to the floor. Alan landed on top, making sure both of his knees hit the Ted in the stomach, and then struggled to his feet and kicked out at his prone adversary. There was a general melee and confusion for about thirty seconds and then, as so often is the case, the various parties involved in the conflict disengaged themselves and reformed into their original groupings as the bouncers piled in to restore order.

Sid the Shiv was winded, very bloody and very, very angry. "I'll sort you out later, Spencer," he snarled, bent almost double and holding his stomach in pain, his knee length coat was covered in blood from his split head. "Just you fucking wait, you twat."

The lads helped the groggy Trev, who was the only real casualty on their side, outside, where the fresh air revived him fully. He seemed to be alright apart from a slight headache and they moved onto the next pub and resumed their pub crawl.

The rest of the evening was uneventful, the lads continued to drink until the pubs shut and then the younger and more energetic ones went on to a night club.

At closing time in the early hours of Saturday morning, Trev left a nightclub with two girls, and walked them home across the bridge. One of the girls left them at the tower block where she lived. Trev and the other girl continued arm in arm to the house she lived in with her parents. The house was in the middle of a large Victorian terrace near the sea front. It had a small porch, and so offered the couple protection from the elements and from prying eyes as they said their goodnights. While engaged in an opening kiss and cuddle, Trev managed surreptitiously to open her coat and get his hand around her back, where he made subtle, but determined efforts to get it inside her skimpy top. Once inside he nonchalantly tried to move his hand around to the front. This he gradually managed to do, and as his progress was rapid, he soon felt confident enough to take hold of her hand and rub it against his groin. It was then that she started to protest. What sort of a girl did he think she was? She must really have known what sort of a girl he thought that she was, because she went on to tell him she wasn't that sort of a girl. He must be a pervert or something to try and do something like that to her, a good, decently brought up girl. She didn't show any serious sign of going inside however, or of removing his hand. So Trev, holding a positive mental attitude and believing he'd get what he thought he'd get, kept at it, and eventually, as a lot snogging couples tend to do, they came to an unspoken, but nevertheless mutually understood arrangement.

She gradually stopped protesting as he kissed her hard on the lips, indeed she appeared to like it, and now more or less kept her hand where Trev kept placing it on his trousers. He was excited and encouraged by her passive resistance, nearness, and not too forceful protestations, and so he went a stage further and unzipping his fly, took out his erect member and placed it in her warm hand. She didn't give any indication of being disgusted, or even a little put out. All she said was, "It's hard isn't it?" as she proceeded to move her hand up and down gripping his swollen erection tightly in her hand. She continued with this motion until things reached their natural conclusion, then she quickly bent down, grasped the doormat, bearing the legend WELCOME, which had been the recipient of his ejaculation, and presumably so as not to offend the sensitivities of anyone using the mat the following day, flipped it over on the floor so that the unaffected side now showed upwards.

Perhaps she didn't like the idea of anyone wiping his or her feet on that? thought Trev, as he zipped up his fly, still surprised by her sudden but fluid movement. Walking home alone later, after she'd said a firm goodnight, pushed him out into the street and closed the door behind him, Trev realised that she must have performed the self-same manoeuvre many times in the past to be so proficient at it. Well, he certainly had a 'well-cum' all right. He shook his head and smiled.

7

The lads had arranged to meet up again in the pub on Monday evening. Alan, Nobby, George and Joe were there on time. George bought the drinks and carried them on a tray across to where the others were sitting. One bottle of brown ale, three pints of lager and a pint of still orange for Joe, whose stomach was still recovering from the previous Saturday evening's alcohol consumption. He placed the tray of drinks carefully on the tabletop without spilling a drop from any of the glasses.

"Trev's late, but I've got him one in," George said, picking up one of the pints and downing about half of the contents in a couple of swallows. He placed the half empty glass on the table in front of him and wiped his mouth with the back of his hand. "He said he'd be here at half-seven," he complained.

"Your ulcer playing you up again, Joe?" asked Nobby.

Joe nodded. "A bit."

"My uncle Norris had an ulcer," Nobby offered thoughtfully. "It killed him in the end."

"Thanks for that, Nobby," Joe said disgustedly. "It's just what I needed to hear."

"Well, it was his ulcer and the beer that killed him really," Nobby qualified. "He was in bed with a bad stomach when his mate called and said they were giving free pint tickets out at the club."

The others waited expectantly, but Nobby didn't elaborate further. He picked up his glass and took a long drink.

"Well?" Alan asked.

"Well what?" Nobby asked, putting his pint down on the table and looking innocently at the others, who were all looking at him expectantly. "Oh, you mean my uncle Norris? Well, he was in such a hurry to get up the club for his free pint tickets that he tripped over his braces when he was trying to put his trousers on, fell over and broke his neck."

"I wonder what's happened to Trev," Joe said, making no comment about Nobby's uncle Norris's misfortune.

"He'll be along, don't worry," Alan said, picking up his drink.

"You think he'll still speak to us now that he's working again?" George said with a smile.

"Trev had the right idea taking that insurance agent's job. He's doing all right from all accounts. On Saturday night he was telling me some right tales about his customers," Alan said. At that exact moment the door opened and Trev walked in. "Speak of the devil."

"We've been hearing all about your new job. Alright is it?" George asked the smartly dressed newcomer, while indicating his drink already waiting on the table.

"Great. Funny hours, mind. I've just this minute finished. Been out all day with a salesman, but it's an awful lot better than working down the yards. I go to work everyday with a suit on, keep my hands clean, and at least I know that I'm going to get a full week in, no lockouts or strikes there, mate."

"I'll bet you do all right with all them bored young housewives as well, eh?" Alan asked with a leer.

"That'd be telling wouldn't it?" Trev said, taking his first taste of the lager.

"What about the bookwork, Trev? I hear that it's a right pain in the arse?" George asked.

"Yes, that it is. I must admit that I don't like doing the administration. It's the worst part of the job, but they reckon that you should do a bit every day, so that it doesn't get out of hand. Always keep on top of it. But I'll tell you what the worst thing about the job is, dogs."

"Dogs?"

"Yes dogs. They're all the same. They come up to you and sniff your crotch, you know, when you go into different houses to collect the money. As soon as one comes near to you and touches you, it leaves its scent on your trousers and when you go into the next house their dog has to come over and have a sniff as well. It really pisses me off, I can tell you. Great smelly hairy things nudging their noses in my balls, while I'm trying to count the money and mark the customer's books."

"Puts me in mind of the time we went to that grab-a-granny dance that Thursday night over in South Shields," Alan said.

"What, marking the books?" Trev asked, puzzled.

"No, you daft sod, the great hairy things nudging their noses in your balls." They all laughed.

"One of the lads who's been doing the job for donkey's years gave me a tip. 'Get some Anti-mate and spray it on the bottom of your trousers. That'll keep the dogs off you'. So I decide to try it. I had nothing to lose, did I? So off I go down to that pet shop in the market. The queue was right around the corner. I waited well over ten minutes to get served, and when I finally get to the front, who's serving but that big blonde lass who used to work behind the bar in the club, her with the huge tits, remember?"

Apparently the huge tits were very memorable because no further description by Trev was required, they all remembered. "Well she's serving behind the counter, and she says to me, 'can I help you?' All innocent and sweet like. Now being a gentleman I didn't tell her how she could help, but asked if they sold Anti-mate. She goes looking all over the shop for it but can't find it, can she? So she comes back with something she says is just as good and asks me if that would do. I have a look, but they're tablets and I say there're no good, because I need a spray. So she asks me exactly what I need it for. And I say because I'm an insurance agent, trying to impress her, like, and when I go into different houses all these dogs come up to me and smell my trousers. So what does she go and do? She only shouts through to the back of the shop, doesn't she? She shouts as loud as she can, 'there's a man out here asking for something to stop dogs smelling his crotch'. Well, there's still a quite sizable queue behind me. Very popular that pet shop is. When the people in the queue hear her shouting that about my crotch, they all push forward to get a closer look at me, don't they? The manager comes out from the back, and I have to go through the whole story again, I'm sure he only did it to embarrass me in front of all those people. Anyway, people in the queue kept making remarks about my trousers, and I very nearly cracked one guy who thought it was funny." He stopped to take a long drink from his pint.

"So what happened then?" George asked with a smile.

"Well the manager hums and haws for a while, and then he finally recommends this spray in an aerosol tin. Just spray a tiny amount on your trouser turn-ups, he says and dogs won't come anywhere near you. So I bought the spray, didn't I? Well next day was Friday, my busiest collecting day, so I sprays this stuff on the bottom of my trousers, just a quick little squirt like the manager said, but then I thought I'd better give it a bit more 'cos it didn't seem to be much, and then off I drive in my car. Well, I drive about half a mile and the fumes from this spray have got my eyes watering. I couldn't see a thing. I had to pull the car over and open all the windows. When that didn't help, I had to get out and walk up and down to clear my head, which was absolutely ringing by now. That Anti-mate stuff is absolute dynamite. It didn't half have a nasty effect on me."

"That's because you've probably got a bit of dog in you somewhere," George said.

"He's certainly been out with a few," Joe put in.

"Yes, you could well be right there," Trev said good-naturedly and continued his tale. "So after about ten or fifteen minutes, when my head's cleared a bit, I get back into the car and drive to the debit.

The fumes seemed to have dispersed somewhat, but I still had to keep the windows wide open. I get to the first house that I collect on, old Mrs Jones. She pays me forty pence a fortnight, and when I take the money, mark her book and give it to her back, she puts the next fortnight's forty pence in the book and puts it away in the sideboard again. So I say to her why don't I take that money now, and I'll come back again in a month's time instead of a fortnight? 'Oh no, you can't do that,' she says. 'You come here every fortnight, not monthly.'" He shook his head in despair. "Sometimes it's like pissing against the wind. Anyway she's got this daft bleedin dog that just loves my crotch." He paused long enough to take another long drink from his glass. "You lads ready for another?" He saw their hesitation. "It's alright; I'm okay for a couple of rounds. I know how it is being out of work, remember?" He got up and started for the bar. "Come on lads, drink up. I've told you that I'm good for a few drinks. You still on the orange juice, Joe?"

He returned with the drinks and despite his encouragement, the others continued to drink slowly and nurse their pints, not wanting to scrounge off their friend.

"It's okay then, the job, apart from the dogs?" Alan asked.

"Champion, man. Best move that I ever made. It was bit iffy at first, what with having to learn about the collecting, the administration and the policies like, but I soon picked that up." He took another drink, well pleased with himself. "You do meet some right funny people, though," he shook his head in amusement. "There was the axe killer, did I tell you about her?"

"I'm sure that we would have remembered if you had, Trev," George said, smiling.

"Well," Trev said, settling down to give an account. "I call at this house to collect the premiums, and the wife says will I go next door because the woman there has just moved in and wants some insurance. Now, we've always got to find new business, so this is music to my ears, and I'm off round there double quick time. This young lass opens the door and says yes, she would like some life and house insurance, so I sit down and fill in all the forms, ask all the proper questions and everything. Nice lass she was, a bit dim maybe, but then we all can't be rocket scientists, can we? Anyway, she signs all the forms and I tell her exactly how much it will cost every week, so I ask her if she can pay the first week's premium today. 'Oh, I don't want to start it off just yet', she says. 'Didn't my neighbour tell you?' 'No,' I say. 'Why don't you want to start it off now?' 'I told her to tell you so that you'd know what it was all about,' she says. 'Well, she didn't tell me, so what is it all about then?' I ask her. 'I can't start it until I've been to court', she says. 'When is that?' I ask, assuming that she's up for shoplifting, or fiddling her gas meter or child benefit book or something. 'Not until the back end of the month,' she says. So I ask her why she's up at court, what had she been up to, like? 'For murder,' she says, calm as anything. Bleeding murder, I ask you. She told me the whole story. She'd been knocked about regularly by her boyfriend, and was getting a bit sick of it, you know, as you would, I suppose, once the novelty had worn off. Anyway, he comes home drunk one night and starts on her again, so she ups and hits him in the head with an axe. Killed him stone dead she did. I come out of the house thinking perhaps it was just an excuse because she couldn't afford the insurance or maybe she didn't like the look of me.

"Anyway, she said that she'd contact me after the court case, if she's still out and about, that is and not locked up in prison, and off I go. I didn't think much of it, in fact I'd nearly forgotten all about it. Then there she was the following week, her photo right on the front page of the local newspaper. And big headlines right across the top of the page – 'Axe Killer Acquitted'. It goes on to give an account of the trial; the details were exactly the same as she'd told me. Well, you could have knocked me down with a feather." Trev took another long drink, as his friends digested the recently imparted information.

"So what happened when you went back, did you get the money then?" Nobby, who had listened to the account enthralled, asked.

"Are you daft or what man? I didn't go back. There's no way that I was going to collect on an axe murderer was there? If I had upset her once, I'd have been a dead man. I'd have shit myself every time I knocked on her door. Can you imagine her having a fire claim disallowed or something? No fears, man. I certainly didn't go back there."

"But surely it was a one off?" Joe said.

"What?" Trev queried.

"You'd be quite safe. She'd only ever kill the once. And that was because she was being abused by her husband," Joe maintained.

"You think so?" Trev asked doubtfully.

"Yes. Look, put yourself in her position for a second. You get knocked about regularly and are sick of it, so you retaliate. That doesn't make you a lunatic axe killer, does it?"

Trev thought about it. "No, probably not, but I'm still not going back and chancing it, mate. No way."

The men laughed, and Trev bought another round of drinks despite their protestations. "Just drink it," he said as he sat down again.

"It'll be a bit of a problem always looking for sales then, Trev?" George asked.

"I suppose that it could be, but you've got to keep a positive mental attitude. And I suppose it's just like the bookwork, if you keep on top of it, it's not so hard. It's all about having the right attitude. That's what you need, keep that and the business rolls in, just like you expect it to. Anyway, usually people ask me for business, or give me referrals to their friends and relations." He took another drink. "And the money's good. If you work hard then the rewards are there. No overtime bans, no lockouts, no short time, I can work as long as I like, and I'm more or less my own boss, no foreman sitting on my shoulder all day. Best move that I ever made," he said again. "Just to think, I worked all those years in the yards when I could have been doing something as cushy as this."

"I wish that I was a few years younger and I knew what I know now. I'd have been out of the yards like a shot," George said wistfully.

"What? You leave the yards? Never would have happened," Trev said. "It was only the redundancy situation that forced you out. You would have never have left otherwise."

"No. Not now, but when I was younger. If I were your age, for instance, I'd have been off like a shot. I don't know why we stuck it for so long. It never got any better did it? There were always strikes and walk-outs."

"Well there never was a lot of work outside the yards for us to pick from was there? It's not as if everywhere was shouting out for unskilled workers," Alan said defensively.

8

Hans was tired, desperately tired. The long, high-speed autobahn drive had left his eyes sore and his muscles aching from the long periods of concentration. Thank God he was almost there, only another couple of kilometres to go now. He'd be glad to deliver the packages to the warehouse and then be free to have a long sleep in a comfortable bed. He didn't know what was in the packages; he wasn't interested, but presumed they contained drugs of some description.

He saw the flashing lights of the police traffic patrol car behind him and veered over to let it pass, not realising at first that it was him they were signalling to stop. The traffic car pulled alongside him and the policemen indicated for him to pull over, pointing to the side of the road. A glance at his controls told him why, he was well above the speed limit for this stretch of road, which was in a built-up area. Hans considered his options. He should really outrun the police car. There was plenty of fuel in the tank as he'd filled up when he'd left the autobahn. He knew the vehicle he was driving had a supercharged engine, all his employer's cars did, and could outrun anything the police had. But he was tired and weary from the long drive, he had cramp in his calf muscle, and he'd had almost no sleep the previous night.

Too late now anyway, Hans realised as the traffic car edged in front of him and forced him to stop at the side of the road.

Hans knew his papers and the car's, although forged, were sufficient to pass a cursory police computer check. Max was always very insistent about the thoroughness of small details like that. It was one of the things Hans admired about his employer, who was a very intelligent man, much like himself, Hans liked to think.

One policeman got out of the traffic car and walked back towards him. The other stayed in the car and spoke into his radio, checking his index plate, no doubt, thought Hans.

Hans produced his documents as the policeman approached the car. He wound down the window. "Good evening, officer. Is everything all right?" he asked politely.

"Do you know what speed you were doing?" the officer asked bluntly.

"Er, not exactly, officer. Was I going too fast?"

"Yes, you were," the policeman said as he took the proffered documents from Hans.

"I've just left the autobahn, officer. You know how it is when you've been travelling at speed for a while?" Hans said.

The traffic officer didn't reply, but continued to examine Hans's documents.

The other patrolman, still in the car, shouted something through the open window to his colleague. Hans didn't catch what he'd said, but the officer at his car reacted immediately.

"Step out of the car please, sir," he said and stepped back to allow Hans to open the door and get out.

Hans could hear a police siren approaching. He checked that his automatic pistol was to hand in the door storage compartment, before he opened the car door and placed one foot on the ground. "Is there anything wrong, officer?" he asked, his mind racing. A speeding ticket was one thing, a trifle, but this looked as if it was becoming serious. The siren was getting nearer.

"Step out of the car please, sir, and hand me your keys."

There was no way Hans was going to allow these policeman to search the car. Max's packages were in the trunk and if they saw those …. "Look, officer, if there's anything wrong, I'm sure we can put it right," he said persuasively, pulling a wad of large denomination banknotes from his pocket.

The policeman wasn't impressed. "Get out of the car now," he demanded. "You're in enough trouble without adding attempted bribery to the charge sheet."

"But what is wrong, officer?" Hans asked, stepping out of the car but leaving the door open and still not relinquishing the keys.

"Your index plate was not issued to this car. It does not tally with this make and age of vehicle and was on a car involved in a serious crime recently. Now, will you give me the car keys?"

Hans smiled. "Of course, officer, of course," he said, proffering the keys in his outstretched hand. As the policeman moved forward to take the keys, Hans bent and took the automatic pistol from the car and fired once at the man at point blank range. He couldn't miss and shot the policeman in the face with the nine millimetre bullet, making a small neat hole in his forehead. The patrolman fell as if poleaxed. Hans ran to the police car and shot the other officer as he got out of the vehicle and attempted to draw his weapon. Hans shot him again in the chest and he slid down the side of the car to the ground.

Hans ran back to his car and pushed the gear lever into reverse. As the car backed away from the patrol car, door still swinging open, another police car, siren wailing and lights flashing, rammed into him from behind. Hans jumped from the car and emptied the automatic's magazine, shooting indiscriminately at the police car without taking aim, He made for the hedge alongside the road and crashed through it. He ran some way along the hedge and then took off over a ploughed field. There was no pursuit, so he thought that either he'd shot the occupants of the second car or, more likely, they were attending to their injured colleagues. Either way, he made good his escape.

Max wasn't going to be happy about his property being lost. There'd be hell to pay and somebody was for the high jump. Hans intended to make sure it wasn't him. He was already rehearsing what he'd tell Max. That it was a police vehicle stop check because they'd noticed the false plates. He'd keep quiet about the speeding. Luckily Max was a reasonable and logical man and he would understand why it couldn't be Hans's fault.

9

Trev was out collecting. It was a very busy day for him. He'd started early and planned to work for seven hours solid and collect a lot of money, a large percentage of his total weekly collections. He'd been going for about a couple of hours when he arrived at a row of houses, one of which was his next call.

    Trev opened the garden gate and made his way up the path to the back door, ducking and dodging under the two short washing lines as he went. The lines were both full, full of very skimpy and exotic underwear. The underwear was an assortment of colours and designs, but none of it would cover very much at all, he mused as his head brushed against a pair of red, black-frilly-edged, crotchless panties hanging next to a matching bra. He knocked on the back door and, as was the custom in that area, turned the handle and walked straight in, announcing his presence by shouting. As he waited in the kitchen, there was an answering call from upstairs. "I'll be down in a minute," the female voice told him.

    Trev waited. He looked around the small room and out of the

window at the lingerie again. "I think I've been here before," he told himself and smiled. His mind wandered and his imagination was playing havoc, when he heard movement upstairs.

"Could you please come and help me?" Trev immediately stepped forward in his best saving a damsel in distress mode as soon as he heard the plaintive cry, determined to assist in any possible way that he could. He bounded up the stairs three at a time and reached the top only slightly out of breath. The object of his intended rescue was in a bedroom to the left. She was obviously very much in distress; Trev could see that from the way she was half-lying on the bed dressed in a sheer, black, low cut, see-through negligee. The crotchless knickers she wore were the exact twin of the ones on the line outside except they were black with red frilly edges.

Trev walked towards her. "You all right?" he enquired, rather inanely.

"It's my back," she answered in a soft quavering voice. "I think I must have twisted it."

"Well, don't you move," Trev told her quietly. "I'll try and help you up."

"I think I'd be better off if you laid me down properly," she simpered.

"Oh, alright then," Trev said, grasping her by the shoulders and easing her backwards.

"Oh, your hands are freezing," she complained, wriggling herself into a more comfortable position on the bed, and reaching up her arms towards him.

"Give me a minute then," Trev said, breathing on his hands and then rubbing them together to warm them. He grasped her again, this time around her waist and pulled her further up the bed. The bed was soft and she sank back into it, holding his shoulders as she did so. Then her arms went right around his neck and pulled his head down to hers.

"I'm really glad you came in like that, otherwise I might have been here all day, what with my husband being away until the weekend," she breathed into his ear. Her breath was warm and sweet, as was her perfumed body. The nearness of her semi-naked body was affecting Trev physically and he knew he'd have to do something about it.

"He's away until the weekend, is he, Mrs Gillan?"

She nodded. "And I'm not expecting anyone else to call. In fact there's no one else that could call, not today, and please call me Ginger."

"It is a good job that I came round then, isn't it, Ginger? Otherwise you'd have been lying here groaning all day, wouldn't you?" he said, pulling her hair back from her face with his fingertips.

"I hope I still might be groaning all day," she replied with a sexy smile and lifted her face to Trev's to be kissed. Trev kissed her, a long lingering kiss. He felt the desire rising within him and tearing himself away from her clinging lips, moved downwards, parted her panties with his left hand and kissed her mound of Venus. She gasped and the little button of her clitoris immediately became prominent. Trev concentrated his attention on this, while sliding his right hand under her pert little bottom. She wriggled and forced her bottom further down onto his fingers as he pleasured her with the tip of his tongue. She gasped and panted, arching her back as she sought release. Trev slowed his tongue and went slower the more excited she became, until she finally arched her back and climaxed with a shudder.

Trev kissed her again and unable to wait any longer, pulled off his clothes, threw them aside and slid between her legs. He kissed her and slipped his enlarged penis inside her. She was well lubricated and ready for him. He made love to her slowly, withdrawing almost completely and then thrusting as far as he could inside her. He was too excited to last for long and he came with a violent convulsion, as Ginger clung to him and climaxed for the second time.

They were both exhausted and lay quietly for a few minutes. But Ginger was soon restless and became engrossed in licking his chest and nipples. She traced her tongue down his body to his still half erect member and took him in her mouth. He was soon more than ready again and they had wild sex on the bed, the floor and the stairs in a variety of positions. They moved onto the floor after a leg at the bottom of the bed collapsed, sending them sprawling to one side as they made love in the doggy position. She gave a surprised scream of pleasure at the unexpected movement, but try as they might, they couldn't repeat the sensation, although they did manage to also break the headboard from the top of the bed. Her back seemed to have made something of a miraculous recovery and she proved to be supple and very imaginative. When Trev remarked on this, she put her hand to her mouth and said, "Oh my God, it's a miracle. You must have healing hands, or something," she said with a dirty laugh. "You're a real miracle worker with that magic wand of yours."

They made love enthusiastically and repeatedly and Trev was utterly worn out when he finally left. He'd made many previous half-hearted attempts to leave, but was always persuaded by her to stay for just a little longer. Finally, he just had to go, as he absolutely couldn't make it just a little longer, any longer.

It was only as he left the house, light-headed, weak-legged, and exhausted, to resume his work that he realised that he hadn't taken her insurance money, and after due deliberation, he decided that there was no way he was going back for it, not today, anyway. Trev was over five hours late for the rest of his collections that day. He missed huge chunks of his customers out, and raced round the remainder trying to catch up.

When he finally did get finished and drove home in the darkness, he was almost two hundred pounds down in his collection money, worn out and ready for bed. He turned in as soon as he got home, without bothering with anything to eat or drink and slept for a good ten hours solid.

"Sit down please," the personnel officer was stiffly formal and gave a strong impression that he wished he were somewhere else. He read slowly through Joe's application form, his face indicating that he wasn't impressed. "So, you've had no previous machine work experience?"

"Er, no. But being a plater's helper is a sort of semi-skilled job. You've got to know what you're doing."

"Right," the interviewer answered doubtfully. "Well; it's not so much the experience that's required here, more being able to fit in and work together productively as part of a team," he rattled the phrase off pat as if he'd memorized it from some management manual, which indeed he had.

"Er, yes. I'm all right working with other people. Done it for long enough at the yard," Joe answered.

"If you're successful, you'll be working on a machine, which will have been preset for you by a skilled, time-served tradesman. All that you'll have to do is to turn out large quantities of components. These components have to be within certain specifications and you'll be trained on how to measure these so that they stay within the allowed tolerances." He was warming to his theme now. "If you find any of these tolerances are out, or beginning to go out of the allowed limits, then you contact one of the tradesmen who will adjust the set-up and put it right, you understand?"

Joe nodded. He was listening intently.

"Good. Now a lot of these components that we manufacture, although small, are very special and very expensive. They have very tight tolerances and if these tolerances are breached then they are no good and have to be scrapped. So you must keep an eye on them and check them regularly." He paused to add emphasis to his words. "In the rare event of any of them being scrapped, then it would cost the company a lot of money." He stopped speaking and looked at Joe expectantly.

Joe thought that he was expected to say something in response. "Well, you could always take the money out of my bonus," he said jocularly. It was exactly the wrong thing to say.

"You don't seem to be taking this very seriously. These things are very expensive to produce. The materials used to make them are very expensive to buy. The machinery used to manufacture the things is expensive to buy and to maintain and it costs the company a lot of money to employ machinists, designers, draughtsmen, managers, foremen, labourers, and canteen staff to feed all of these and you say that we can stop the money out of your bonus?"

Joe was dumbstruck. "It was a joke," he mumbled.

"A joke? A joke? The only joke around here is you. You come in here begging for a job and then talk stupid like that." He picked up Joe's application form and threw it into a metal waste bin on the floor near to his desk. He picked up the next form from the stack on the corner of his desk. "Right then. I think I've got everything that I need. Thank you for coming in," he said curtly without looking up, already reading through the first page of the next application form.

"Er," Joe said apologetically.

The personnel officer looked up as if astonished that Joe was still there. "Yes?"

"Er, have I got the job, then?" Joe asked quietly.

"We'll be in touch," he said curtly and went back to studying the form. As the door closed behind Joe, the personnel officer muttered, "but don't hold your breath."

Joe didn't get the job of course and never quite understood why. He could never understand why he didn't get the next three jobs he had interviews for either.

10

George arrived at the brewery and clocked in at seven-fifteen, a quarter of an hour early. He wanted to make a good impression on his first day. He made his way to the locker room where he had been told to leave his coat and haversack. As he made his way through the brewery he saw a man standing near a stack of beer kegs with a bottle in his hand. As George approached him the man backed behind the empty beer kegs and put the bottle of brown ale to his lips. He drank greedily until the bottle was empty and then placed it amongst other empties in a nearby crate. He wiped his lips with the back of his hand and belched loudly, a long, satisfied belch. "Morning," he said cheerfully to George. "First today, you can't beat the first one can you? Nothing like it. Lovely."

George reported to the foreman and was taken to where the kegs were filled. He was told that he'd be working there for his first few weeks, and then moved around each department to get experience in each, until they decided where he was to be placed permanently.

The other men who worked in that department showed him the

ropes and what to watch out for. One of the first things they showed him was how to steal beer and where to hide it.

"Don't worry; they expect you to take it to make up your wages," one of his new workmates told him. "They'll cut back on anything to save money – wages, health and safety, anything, but they turn a blind eye to you nicking the beer, as long as you're not blatant about taking it. It must cost them next to nothing to make."

George thought that he was going to be very happy working at the brewery and that this just might be the best job that he'd ever had in his whole life.

The three-man kegging team worked very well together in a well-practised operation developed by themselves over many years. The empty kegs where filled on a large, complicated-looking machine. Once the keg was topped up with beer and released from the filling machine, one of the three-man team rolled the newly filled kegs across the floor to the stacker.

Stacking the full kegs was supposed to be a two-man job, and they were supposed to use a hydraulic lift, but the machine had been broken for months, wasn't repairable and had apparently proved too expensive to replace. But one man was able to lift the kegs alone and stack them on top of one another. George was shown how to do it by his workmates. He was told that the first thing to do was to forget all about what was supposed to be the correct way of lifting by bending the knees and so on. The secret was to straddle the keg with legs wide apart and stiff, bend and grasp the handle space on the keg with both hands. Then, keeping the arms, legs and back stiff, straighten up, bringing the keg up between the legs to waist height and then drop it down on top of the others. Using this method it was surprising easy for one man to lift and stack the heavy kegs two high, quickly and with minimum effort.

This method of working also meant that two of the team could easily do the work of three, and subsequently, by switching positions regularly, every half-hour, each of the three men could have half an hour off after every hour worked. George decided very early that this was a very civilised way to work.

His workmates were a varied bunch. Most drank far too much,

but could generally hold it well and never appeared to be the worse for drink, even though they drank all day. A few didn't touch any alcohol at all, at least not while at work.

George had been at the brewery for a couple of days and had settled in nicely, working on the kegs. It was heavy work, but not particularly taxing physically because of the rota system. One morning he had a visitor. The man walked casually across the wet floor and looked around proprietorially. He nodded to George and cast a knowing eye across the stack of empty eight-gallon kegs.

"Keeping busy then?"

"Never stopped," George affirmed.

"New aren't you?"

George nodded. "Been here a couple of days."

"Thought so." The man looked around as if everything he saw confirmed his suspicions. "I'm the loading bay foreman," he indicated vaguely with his head towards the other side of the kegging section.

"Oh," George said.

"Aye. It's a responsible job, you know. Took me twelve years to work my way up to foreman. Not a bad job really, but responsible, you know?"

George nodded his understanding.

"Biggest problem I've got is those crates."

George followed the foreman's gaze and looked upward to the conveyer belt, which carried crates of brown ale from the bottling plant across the kegging area to the loading bay.

"Oh yes?" George said, noncommittally.

"Aye. You'll never believe this, but some of those crates have bottles missing when they reach the loading bay and guess whose responsibility it is to make sure that they're all topped up again with full ones?"

"Yours?" George guessed.

"That's right. Mine. So I've got to keep checking all those crates before they're loaded and if there are any bottles missing, then I've got to walk all the way over to the bottling hall, get the required number of bottles and put them into the crates to replace the missing ones."

"Never?" George said in mock disbelief.

"It's a fact," the foreman affirmed with emphasis. He took out a packet of cigarettes and placed one in his mouth, then offered the packet to George. He then lit both cigarettes with a disposable gas lighter, casually ignoring the strict no smoking regulations.

"That'll be a nuisance, then?" George said, blowing smoke upwards towards the conveyer belt.

"You can say that again. It's a great bloody nuisance and that's a fact," the foreman said, also blowing smoke upwards. "In fact, it would save me a great deal of time and trouble if whoever was taking those odd bottles, would just take the whole bloody crate, then I wouldn't have to keep topping them up, would I?"

"That's right, you wouldn't." George said, agreeing with the man's faultless logic and made a mental note to take a crate at a time, rather than the odd bottle. He couldn't make all that extra work for the foreman, could he?

The foreman looked around at the stack of kegs again. "Draught is alright, but it's flat as a fart straight from the keg without any gas, isn't it?" Without waiting for a reply, he nodded to George and ambled off back towards the loading bay.

After a couple of weeks in the kegging department George was moved. He and another workmate were allocated a morning's work loading empty wooden beer crates onto a lorry. The men were then transported on the lorry to a storage depot where the empty cases were to be stored. Upon arrival they discovered their entry into the store barred by a large lorry discharging wooden barrels. As they couldn't get in to unload the empties, the men decided to go to a pub for lunch. They had pints with their pies and got involved playing dominoes with some of the local customers. The games stretched way past their allocated meal break and when they returned to the lorry they found the foreman waiting for them. He wasn't very happy at all and they were ordered to report to the brewery manager the next morning.

The men duly presented themselves at the manager's office the following morning at the required time and after a brief hearing, at which they were allowed to put their excuses, they were found guilty of deserting their posts and punished with a day's suspension without pay. This unpaid day off could be taken any time they chose, as long as they gave notice to the foreman at least a week beforehand, as explained in the company rulebook. The guilty men accepted their day's suspension and took it when it suited them after giving the required notice.

George actually read the rulebook after he was sentenced to the suspension. He was surprised by the comprehensive amount of detail contained in the slim volume. The rules regarding suspension and just about everything else you could think of were contained in a small, pocket-sized, book that every employee was presented with upon being appointed. The rules were many and varied and included what was, and was not acceptable in the workplace regarding smoking, gambling, swearing and spitting. All of the above were definitely not permitted. There was a full two pages of rules on statutory Health and Safety regulations, almost none of which were paid even lip service to. George was surprised to read that a minimum of two workers must be present at any time when employees were operating machinery, or working at any significant height above floor level. The rules were relaxed somewhat in regard to drinking. Allowed drinking was restricted to the allocated 'stagger' ration. Stagger was the nickname given to the two bottles of beer allocated free to each man daily by the brewery. This weak and disgusting tasting brew was rumoured strongly to be the mixture of all the returned bottles that were past their sell-by date. No one knew for sure because no one with any choice drank the foul stuff, preferring instead to steal good, strong, delicious beer from various points around the brewery.

The rulebook also explained in detail about the bond. A bond of ten pounds was required to be deposited with the company by the employee soon after his or her appointment. The money was designed to ensure that, in the event of being dismissed for any type of misbehaviour, the employee would subsequently lose the bond and the company would be reimbursed the cost, or part thereof, of any damage or misappropriation caused by the above-mentioned dismissed ex-employee. The bond could be paid weekly, deducted from wages at the rate of fifty pence per week. Interest was accrued on the ten pounds while held by the company and paid together with the capital sum upon leaving. The rulebook explained all this. The whole exercise was entirely pointless as the legal standing of the rule was questionable to say the least, and anyway, the company had never once failed to return a bond plus interest to even those sacked for misconduct of any description, or even for theft.

The brewery's drays and horses had been a familiar sight around the city for years. The huge horses were very well looked after, more so than the human employees in a lot of ways, and always looked resplendent. They were certainly never overworked and were given plenty of rest on the brewery owner's country estate. As well as the dray horses, the brewery's owners, prominent members of the county set, also kept a number of thoroughbred horses for hunting, carriage driving, both ceremonial and sporting and point to point events.

George and the others watched as the horse was led around the road surrounding the stables. They couldn't help but compare the shambling, listless animal before them now to the lively, spirited creature that had impressed them all the previous week. That was the trouble apparently. The colt had been a bit too lively and spirited for the stable manager's liking, so they'd castrated him, or de-bollocked him, as George put it succinctly. The horse was having trouble recovering from the castration and had fallen into a deep and listless lethargy.

George shook his head. "That just about sums up what life does to us doesn't it?"

"How's that?" asked his friend, Fred.

"Well. I mean look at that young horse last week. He was prancing and pawing, kicking and carrying on. He was a magnificent animal, full of himself, proud, confident, and daring; he'd have a go at anything, especially any mare that came into view.

But look at the poor bugger now. Shambling, head down, beaten, and just about ready to lie down and die from the looks of him."

"So how does society do that to us, then?"

"How? Just take a look at yourself, mate. Or look at me. Look at all of us. We were all once just like that colt was last week. We were young, confident, and full of ourselves. We all had big plans about what we were going to achieve. What we were going to do with our lives. And what happened? Life happened, that's what. We got married and got wives. And we got bills. Furniture bills, bills for carpets, cookers, beds. Electricity and gas bills. We got kids and we got more bills. We sure did get bills then. We got school uniform bills, birthday and Christmas present bills. And how do we pay these bills? We get jobs that pay us just about enough to be able to survive on after we've paid tax and national insurance. We're simply surviving from one payday to the next. We don't get paid enough to save any money, or if we do manage to save a little, then the money's got to be used for emergencies. Emergencies like the gas bill, or the TV licence, or something else that we've got to pay to live. We're on a big merry-go-round, mate, and we'll never get off." He paused and shook his head. "I look at myself now and think what the fuck has happened? Where did all those years go, all those big plans and ambitions? I'm like that horse there. Castrated. They, that is, our so-called civilised society, have taken my bollocks off as sure as if I'd been castrated. They don't do it violently, but they do it gradually and just as surely as if they'd used a great big knife. They cut them off and then take them away."

"Steady on, George, don't take things so seriously. It's not as bad as all that, man."

"Isn't it?" George replied doubtfully, still watching the horse stumbling around the stable yard.

Fred passed George a bottle. "There you are. Get that down your neck and you'll feel better."

George opened and drank from the bottle.

Fred tried to cheer his mate up. "How are you getting on with your recollections for that history project? You got some good examples of the good old days to put in it?"

"Haven't really spent a lot of time on it lately, what with one thing and another, but I'm always on the lookout for material. Why, you got something I could use?"

"Well yes. You remember when we used to go to those Saturday morning matinees? We'd get a cartoon and two half-hour short films, a Pathe newsreel and a full-length feature film, all for what was it? One and six?"

George nodded. "Yes, we used to go every week. It was a good show for one and six, or was it just sixpence? Anyway it cost something like that. What was that song we all used to sing before the films started?"

"Something about the ABC, wasn't it?"

"That's right. The cinema chain was called the ABC, wasn't it?"

"Aye. We all had those luminous badges with ABC on them. If you stood in the cupboard under the stairs, they used to glow. Easily pleased we were then. Not like the kids today. You couldn't fob any of them off with a luminous badge and tell them to go and play under the stairs, could you?"

"Not bleedin' likely," George was enjoying the memories flooding in now. "We used to buy a bag of whelks, eat them inside the pictures with a pin, which could be a right job in the dark, I was always sticking the bleedin' pin in me fingers."

They both laughed.

"And then during a boring bit of the film, you know, the love bits, when the hero kissed his girl, we'd throw the empty shells down the front."

He shook his head and smiled. "You ever notice that when they were being chased by the baddies, it was always the girl slowed them down 'cos she twisted her ankle or something?"

Fred nodded his agreement. "That's right, they always did, didn't they?"

"Anyway, after we'd thrown the shells down the front, the kids down there started to complain about being hit on the head, they'd put on all the lights on and stop the film. Then we'd all bang and stamp on the floor with our feet. Right noisy little bastards we were."

"Aye," Fred put in. "There used to be a serial on every week, Rocket Man and the other one, what was he called? Jungle Jim, that's him. And, every week when the half-hour show came to an end there would be the hero, Jungle Jim, thrown into a pit and hungry lions were running towards him and attacking him. He was sure to be killed, torn to pieces, but we'd have to wait until next week to see what happened to him. We could hardly wait until the next Saturday morning came around and we were off to the pictures again to see Jungle Jim get eaten alive by those lions. But next week, when the serial came on, there was Jim, hanging onto a tree branch over the lion pit. Now, we were sure that we'd seen him actually thrown into the pit last week by the baddies, and the lions actually mauling him, but no, there he was, plain as day, hanging from a branch over the pit. We couldn't understand it. We must have been mistaken. And then that week a similar thing would happen, Jim would be inches from death when the film ended, but again the following week, there he was, with an escape route that we'd overlooked the week before. We kids were starting to doubt our own eyes and our sanity," he shook his head.

"And what about Tarzan? There was always a Tarzan film on about once a month. All those elephants charging about, hundreds of them in darkest Africa, and they were all bloody Indian elephants, with the small ears, weren't they? And a lot of those natives were a bit suspect as well. They just used to tell us anything, they did, and we'd bloody well believe it. No wonder that I don't trust anybody at all nowadays. We were conned something rotten, we were," George said, laughing.

"It's bloody amazing just how much things change over a few years, isn't it?" George said. "I know I sound like an old bugger, but even chocolate biscuits are different."

"Biscuits?"

"Yes. Like Wagon Wheels. Remember them when you were a kid? They were that big, you had to cut it in half to get it on a plate. Now you can get a whole one in your mouth without any trouble, they're so small."

Fred nodded his agreement. "That's right, now you mention it."

"And what about policemen on point duty. You never see police doing that nowadays, not unless the traffic lights have failed or something."

"Aye, you're right," Fred agreed. He thought for a moment. "When I was a kid there was a man who used to stand right in the middle of the road and pretend he was directing the traffic. He used to cause havoc on a Saturday afternoon, especially if there was a match on. Buses used to go around the bugger. They reckon he was suffering from shell shock from the war, but I think he was just pissed, you only ever saw him do that after the pubs closed."

The men fell quiet, still watching the horse. George picked up the bottle, drank the remaining alcohol and looked at his friend. "You've been good to me, mate."

"Aye, right."

"No, seriously, you have. You got me the job here, showed me the ropes when I started and kept me right."

"Anybody would do the same, George."

"No. No they wouldn't. Not everybody. No Fred, you're a good 'un and no mistake."

"You're pissed, that's what you are, you drunken old git. Look, I've got to get back and see if that bleedin' silo's full up with grain yet. My mate's had to go to hospital so I've got to do it all myself today, bleedin crime that's what it is."

"That why you're not drinkin', eh?"

"Aye, it's criminal, isn't it? Here it is, half past one and I haven't had me first yet."

"The rule book says it's illegal for you to be working in there on your own, did you know that?"

"That right?"

"Aye. It's in the rule book in black and white. You should refuse to work unless they get you another mate."

"Oh, aye. If I told them that, I'd be out of the door before the end of the week, man."

"They couldn't sack you for that."

"No, but they could sack me for pinching beer or having a half-hour off every hour, couldn't they? They'd find something to sack me for if they wanted to, mate."

George knew Fred was right. "Why don't I come up with you and give you a hand then?"

"Great, if you'll not be missed here."

"I'm on a late lunch break, so I'm okay until two or thereabouts. Come on, I'll go up with you."

The two men made their way across the brewery complex to where the silos containing the grain were located. A large tanker, parked in the lane was pumping the grain into the top of a silo through a flexible pipe. There was no sign of its driver. A cloud of fine dust floated above the silo, gradually settling on top of the tanker and the ground around it.

"Here we are," Fred said when they reached the base of the giant containers. "I'll nip up and have a look, see how far we're on." He climbed the steel ladder fixed to the side of the metal silo and was soon at the small platform on the top. He peered down into the rapidly filling container. The fine cloud of dust coming from the top indicated that there was still movement of grain inside. "Filling nicely, but it'll be a while yet," Fred shouted down to George. He then picked up a large paddle and began to shove grain from the centre of the pile to the sides, evening the level.

"Can I help?" George shouted up. "Shall I come up there, or what?"

"No, it's alright. You can bang on the sides of the silo if you like, shake the stuff inside down a bit."

George looked around for something to hit the sides of the silo with, and saw a shovel leaning against the side. Picking it up, he started banging on the sides at various points and heights. He worked his way all the way round the large container until he was back where he'd started. Putting the shovel back where he'd originally found it, he wiped the thin film of sweat from his brow and looked up. Fred wasn't in sight, so he shouted up. "How's it going up there, mate?"

There was no reply, but George thought that he could hear a muffled sound. He shouted again, expecting to see his friend's head peering over the top of the platform. There was still no reply.

Becoming concerned, George started to climb the steel ladders. Still nothing. He increased his pace and reached the top. As he raised his head above the platform he was half expecting Fred to throw something at him. He was certain that it was some sort of trick. Fred's footprints were visible in the dust on top of the silo, but no Fred. "Where the bloody hell has he gone?" George mumbled to himself as he scrambled onto the platform and looked around.

Puzzled, George walked to the edge of the platform and peered down. Nothing. He walked slowly around the circular structure, looking down all the way around it. Nothing. He looked into the silo, which was now almost full of grain. Still nothing. He scratched his head. "Where the bloody hell has he gone?" he said to himself. He turned and peered into the silo again and was just about to shout again, when he thought he saw something move just under the surface of the grain. Quickly and with a terrible feeling of dread, he grabbed a paddle and pushed it into the grain where he'd seen the object.

The end of the paddle encountered something more solid than the grain. George pushed it further towards the object and it broke the surface. It was Fred and he was unconscious. He'd obviously swallowed quite a great quantity of the grain and his body was already starting to bloat. The body turned over again and sank beneath the rippling wave of grain. The surface undulated, like liquid. George, shocked, lost his grip on the paddle and it sank like a stone, sucked down into the seething mass.

George was panic stricken. He resisted his first instinct, which was to jump in and try to save his friend, realising that the thing wasn't like water or any other liquid he could float in and he'd quickly drown. There was nothing that he could use to reach Fred; the only object he could possibly have used was the paddle that had now sunk to the bottom of the tank. Fred was nowhere in sight and George's imagination flashed images of his body turning slowly at the bottom of the silo, his mouth opening and closing, grain pouring down his throat and swelling his body even further. Suddenly he knew what to do. He pushed the pipe, which was still spewing grain, away from the opening in the top of the silo and shoved it over the edge, where the grain spilled onto the floor. He then slid down the ladders, his feet and hands on the outside of the supports and ran for help.

At the door he saw a man and he shouted to him to help. He ran with George to the silo. Fred was still out of sight under the grain, but with no more grain being pumped in, the surface had stopped rippling and become calm.

"Is there some sort of outlet pipe where we can empty this thing?" George asked desperately.

"Aye. There's a wheel valve on the other side there, but you can't open that, not without the foreman's permission, it'll ruin the grain."

"Fuck the foreman's permission and the grain, where is the thing?"

The man pointed it out to the distraught George.

George found the valve, a large wheel that operated a sliding door in the bottom of the silo. He strained and pulled at the wheel before it would move, but once started it spun wildly around and the door began to open. The grain so recently pumped in now started to spill out again. It spilled out onto the floor, piling up around the opening and had to be constantly shovelled away to allow more gain to escape. Both George and his companion used shovels to do this and soon there was grain spread right across the floor of the silo room. They were engaged in this when more help arrived in the form of another four men and the foreman.

"What the bloody hell are you doing?" the foreman screamed at them. "Do you know how much that stuff costs? You can't do that. Stop it at once!"

"Fuck off," George told him without ceremony. "My mate's in there somewhere and I'm going to get him out. I don't care what the fucking stuff costs."

"There's somebody in there? Oh my God. You men grab some of those shovels over there and start to move some of this stuff. You come with me," the foreman ordered and started up the steps to the platform, followed by one of the other men.

The silo eventually emptied and they recovered Fred's body. He was dead, of course. Had been for a while. His body was bloated and swollen and was hard to recognise as belonging to the affable, genial man George had known.

The brewery manager arrived with the police and George gave statements explaining what had happened. There was an immediate unofficial investigation and an enquiry that came to the conclusion that it was a pure accident and that there was no individual person to blame. The official enquiry and inquest later came to the same conclusion. But George blamed himself, reasoning that if he hadn't had a lot to drink he might have found Fred sooner, or been able to rescue him somehow. His friend's death really deeply affected him. Coupled with the distress caused by his wife's leaving and his redundancy, it caused a profoundly depressive reaction and he was soon on a steep downward spiral.

11

Trev's collecting percentages were down and his new business figures were not meeting target. He'd had a number of extra training sessions organised by his supervisor, none of which seemed to help. Finally he was called to the manager's office.

"What's the problem, Trev?" the manager asked. "You were doing alright initially, but now everything appears to have gone to hell, especially your new business. What's happened to your production figures?"

"I'm doing my best," Trev protested.

"Well, son, the answer to that is that your best is just not good enough," the manager answered.

"Not good enough? I'm working all bloody hours that I can. It's not my fault that there's no new business about."

"Look, it doesn't matter how many hours you put in, what matters are the results you achieve. The first rule is always to make sure you get your collections in. If you don't, then your arrears go up and the auditors will always be on your back. They'll think you're fiddling. So you've got to spend more time and effort doing your collecting, even if the sun's cracking the pavements or it's raining cats and dogs. The second rule is to always write new business. There's always new business out there to be written if you go the right way about it. Don't try and tell me that it's not there. Of course it's there. It's always there; you're just not looking in the right places for it." He looked at Trev over the top of the specs perched on the end of his nose. "Have you tried cold canvassing?"

"Er, no, I haven't," Trev, admitted reluctantly.

"Well then, there's a place for you to start. Pick out a street on your debit where you don't have a lot of calls and nip around after tea, when you'll catch them all in, and give them a knock. Introduce yourself, tell them you have lots of calls in the area and you'd like some more because you're saving up to get married, want to buy a house, or something. Give them any old sob story and I'm sure that a personable, good looking lad like you will be able to get a lot of new business."

"But cold canvassing has always seemed like the hard way of doing things to me," Trev said.

"It is, but then there isn't an easy way. At least, if there is then I certainly haven't found it yet and I've been doing this for nearly thirty years." He paused and looked at Trev again. "Look, Trev. You've got the makings of a good agent. You're honest, reliable and could be a good salesman with a bit more experience. You can make a lot of money at this game, believe me, but, and it's a big but, you've got to work at it. It won't just fall into your lap." He paused again. "Having said that, sometimes it is ridiculously easy. People ask you for business, or you are given prospects from existing clients. They'll tell you that their daughter, sister, or brother has just got married or moved, or had a baby and wants some insurance. It can be easy at times like that. Now when that happens, anyone can go along and sell a new policy. What differentiates a good agent from a bad one is that a good one will get business even when that doesn't happen. When there are no referrals, he'll go out and find the business somewhere else, he doesn't just accept it. He'll go off debit, or sell a policy to his friend or his own mother come to that.

But cold canvassing is a good place to start. It's a very effective way of producing new business. It's been proved time after time. Knock on so many doors and you will get a sale. The number of doors varies, but on average, over a period of time, you will succeed. All you have to do is to keep at it. When you get knocked back and get refusal after refusal, just console yourself with the thought that you are now that much nearer a sale. You've got to keep a positive mental attitude."

Trev listened intently to every word, but remained silent, his eyes taking in the large, inspirational, printed texts in frames hanging on the office walls, You're only beaten when you think you are. Another, Don't give up, the next call might be a sale, and so on. The manager finished speaking and Trev nodded his agreement. "Okay, I'll try that." As he left the manager's office, one text on the wall near the door caught his eye; You are what you think about, the words of wisdom stated. Trev smiled to himself and nodded, I must be a right tit, he thought.

That evening Trev set off knocking on doors, full of affirmations and positive thoughts. A young woman obviously preparing to go out opened the first door Trev knocked on. She was dressed, or more accurately, half-dressed for a night on the town and smelled of some exhilarating perfume that made Trev's nostrils flare and his groin twitch.

"Sorry, are you on your way out?" Trev asked apologetically.

"Yes," she smiled. "As a matter of fact I am," she replied, her voice surprisingly husky.

"Oh, alright then, I won't bother you," Trev said.

"It's all right. I've got a bit of time. Come in for a few minutes."

Trev followed her into the living room, and admired the way her rounded buttocks swayed as she walked. She pointed to a chair and sat herself down in an identical one on the opposite side of the room.

"Now then?" she smiled at Trev.

"Er, yes. I'm an insurance agent for Capital Growth and this area is my patch. I've got lots of customers, sorry, clients around here, so I thought I'd give this street a knock and try to get some more ..." he finished lamely.

She nodded. "I've seen you going past. Tuesday mornings you're around here aren't you?"

"Yes, that's right," Trev confirmed eagerly. "Every fortnight."

"You're new, aren't you? You've only been coming around for a few weeks or so, that right?"

Trev nodded. "You're very observant."

"You're not doing so bad yourself," she said smiling.

"What?" Trev said, confused.

"I said that you're pretty observant yourself. The way you keep looking up my skirt like that."

Trev blushed a deep red right down to his neck. "Oh, I'm sorry," he started to apologise.

"Don't be daft. I'm only joking. In fact I'd be really put out if you didn't try to cop a peek, after all the trouble I've gone to getting bloody ready."

"Oh," Trev said, unsure of what to say next.

"You go to Ginger's don't you, in Patterdale Street?"

"Yes, I do."

"Her man works away a lot?"

"Does he?"

"Yes. And he's a terrible jealous one he is. Nearly killed a bloke who was looking at Ginger in the Club one Saturday night a few months ago."

"Oh, right," Trev said and swallowed hard.

"So how much are your policies then?"

"Well, it depends on how you want to pay," Trev said, cheering up considerably. "You'll get a much better deal if you pay direct debit through your back account, than by paying cash at the door."

"Oh, I don't want to pay through the bank. I want the sort that you have to come around regularly and collect. That's the sort I'd like. What time do you normally get here on a Tuesday, about half nine, isn't it?"

Trev nodded, pulling the proposal forms from his pocket.

"Right then. Sign me up for one of those at a pound a week. And mind, when you call next Tuesday, just walk straight in, don't hang around on the doorstep like a debt collector, okay?" She winked at him. "And if I'm still in bed, then we'll just have to see what comes up."

Trev nodded and smiled. "That sounds alright to me." He completed the proposal form and took all her personal details and a pound for the first week's premium. He patted his pockets as if searching for something. "I don't think that I've got a receipt book on me. I can get one from the car …"

"No, that's alright. You can give it to me when you come on Tuesday, you can bring a book as well," she smiled. "When you come next time I'll give you the names and addresses of a couple of my friends. They were thinking about taking some insurance as well." She saw him to the door. "Sorry I don't have any time tonight, but I've got to be in town by half past. Never mind it'll keep until Tuesday. See you then."

Trev left the house elated. He'd not only managed to get his first unassisted policy sale, but he'd also got a new customer and an attractive and game one at that. He got to the garden gate before he realised that there was a very good chance that he was going to be late and well down on his collections again next Tuesday.

12

Max had discovered the couriers' identities and details of their route without any real difficulty, and with a clever ruse, changed their original delivery destination and diverted them to his warehouse. Now he and two of his men waited for the couriers to arrive. Max had carefully selected the two men to help him. He required them to be trustworthy, able to carry out his orders without question, but they were also to be expendable, as he wanted absolutely no witnesses to his double cross. A pity to lose good men, but Max had learned through hard experience that if you leave any loose ends untied, they tended to come back and create problems for you.

They waited in the darkened warehouse as the van arrived and watched quietly as the two couriers opened the shuttered door and drove the van in. They waited until the door was closed again before showing themselves. The couriers were slow to react, a poor choice, Max thought, considering the value of the cargo they were entrusted with, but then they didn't know its value, any more than his men did, he conceded charitably.

Max and his men worked all night to cellophane wrap and pack the cash in Dutch tulip bulb boxes, which were conveniently at hand. These were loaded onto a lorry that Max had arranged to take the consignment to England, calculating that the money would never be traced there. The existing consignment of German video recorders was unloaded from the back of the lorry to make way for the tulip boxes.

Max planned to invest the cash in various business ventures he was involved in throughout Europe. It would enable him to expand his lawful operations and make a complete break with crime and be totally legitimate at last. The British lorry driver would be completely unaware of his valuable cargo, being simply an employee of the haulage company Max used. The owner of a warehouse in Birmingham was the only person in the UK who knew that the cargo was worth exceedingly more than its face value, and even he didn't know what it was or how just how valuable it was. Max had known him for years and knew he was totally loyal.

The two men sweated with exertion as they moved the last of the boxes.

Max watched with interest. "That the lot?" he asked.

"Yes. They're all on," answered the bigger of the two men.

"Good. All we need now is to make sure the paperwork is in order. Will you please fetch it from the office?"

Both men jumped from the back of the vehicle and the bigger man started to walk towards the office at the other end of the warehouse. Max walked a few steps behind him before producing a pistol from under his jacket and shooting the man between the shoulder blades. The man stumbled and fell. Max turned and shot the other man who was about five yards away, in the face, making a small hole below his right eye. The man staggered three paces backwards, a surprised expression on his face, before his legs crumpled and he collapsed onto the floor.

Max shook his head regretfully. It was a pity to have to lose two good men, but it had to be done. He pulled the bodies behind the lorry by their legs, careful not to get any blood on his clothes. The bodies of the couriers already lay there. He pulled a large tarpaulin over them all then made his way to the office, picked up a telephone and dialled a number. The call was answered almost immediately. "Yes, it's me. I need to have some rubbish disposed of as quickly as possible. Four bundles at the usual rates."

13

Joe did finally get a job. His interviewer at the factory seemed unconcerned about his lack of previous experience, ability to do the job, or his attitude. He was only interested in when Joe could start, which was the following Monday.

Joe wanted to create a good impression on his first day on the new job and so was on time. In fact he was a few minutes early and had to wait outside for a while before someone turned up to open the front door. Joe thought that the man walking towards him was somehow familiar and as the man got nearer Joe realised why. It was because he was familiar. Much too bloody familiar. It was someone that Joe had worked with some years ago. The man had started work at the yard and worked in Joe's squad. Joe tried hard, but couldn't remember the man's name. But he could remember that he was absolutely useless as a labourer and a lazy bastard into the bargain. Joe hadn't liked the man from the first shift and had tried to keep as far away from him as possible. They'd had a number of arguments and run-ins as he tended to disappear and leave Joe to do all the work. They hadn't got on very well at all. The man had worked at the yard for about three or four months before being sacked and Joe and the rest of the squad had been glad to see the back of him. He nodded to the man as he approached Joe and was acknowledged in return.

"You the new man?" he asked.

"That's right," Joe answered. "First day today."

The man nodded.

Joe still couldn't remember his name. "I know your face; did you use to work at Yule's?"

"That I did," the man said. "Worst bloody few months of my life. Right load of wankers worked there," he said shortly, and produced a set of keys from his pocket and proceeded to open the front door. Joe followed him inside and waited while he turned off the alarm system with another key.

"I can see that you're a key man around here," Joe attempted a joke.

"You could say that," the man replied, obviously taking his comment seriously. "I'm the foreman."

Joe was given a day's training and allowed to stand alongside another experienced operative and watch how he worked for a further day. Joe quizzed the other men about the work and the conditions in the factory and was told in no uncertain terms that they thought he'd made a big mistake in coming to work here. "The bonus system is crap. You can't make any money. The machines are all crapped out. The foreman is a bastard and the management is even worse," one told him.

"If it's that bad, how come you're still working here, then?" Joe asked the man.

"Because I can't get another job anywhere else," he was told. "These bastards won't give me a proper reference and I actually owe the company money because I'm so far behind with my production."

"How can you owe them money?"

"Fucked if I know. But that's what they keep telling me. They've got a bonus system here that you'd need a degree in advanced mathematics to work out." He shook his head. "If I were you I'd get out now, before they start accusing you of owing them money."

Joe shook his head and smiled. He couldn't accept that he could actually end up owing the company money. "It can't be that bad, surely?"

"I'm not kidding you, mate. What I've just told you is the truth. You get out while you can, before you start on the production, they can't say that you owe them any money then."

Joe made a point of asking the other machinists about the bonus system during their break. Most wouldn't confirm what the other man had said and just made vague references to the way the system worked, although none of them could explain the details of exactly how it did work.

The machinery was quite old. "Bloody ancient," was how Joe described it when he first saw it. There were a number of lathes, both capstan and centre and these took up the bulk of the factory floor space, almost all of them old Ward or Whitworth machines that had seen better days. In addition there were a couple of old milling and drilling machines as well as a number of grinders, both fixed and hand-held. The factory produced engine components. Most of these were brought in from a nearby foundry as casts and machined to various specifications to suit the various engines. The finished components were then transported to various assembly points around the country and to the docks for export abroad.

The castings were made and bought quite cheaply and the company did everything it possibly could to keep the processing as cost effective as they could. The unskilled men were paid well under the nation average hourly wage and even the time-served turners were on poor money.

Joe quizzed the foreman the next time he appeared and was told that the others were all lazy bastards and that the reason that they couldn't make a lot of money on the machines was because they wouldn't work.

Joe started on his own machine the following morning and after a quick introduction by the foreman, was left on his own to knock out a few thousand components. Joe set to work full of vigour, convinced that he would easily make enough to have a sizable bonus in his pay packet come the weekend. He operated the machine exactly the way he'd been instructed, so as to get the maximum performance out of it and soon had a sweat on his brow from his exertions. He worked out exactly how many of the components he had to produce every hour to hit his targets and intended to do a certain amount more than that, so as to get ahead of target and have a bit of a cushion in case of emergencies.

He worked relentlessly and without stopping right until the mid-morning break, when he sat down and poured himself a cup of tea from his flask. He ate a chocolate biscuit while counting the number of components he'd produced in the first two hours. He counted them twice and then again. "That can't be right, surely?" he muttered and counted them all again. But the numbers were right. He had only three quarters of the amount he needed to achieve his bonus and something more than that behind his own personal target he'd devised to give himself a cushion.

Joe decided that he must have been doing something wrong. He re-ran every part of the operation on the machine in his mind, trying to identify what was amiss, what was slowing him down, but he couldn't identify what it was.

He started again after the break had ended, with renewed vigour. He tried to increase his speed and the efficiency of his movements, but was slowed down by the machine itself, which he couldn't hurry while it was completing its operations. He soon realised that he was doing everything he could to produce more components but the machine would only work at its own set pace and no faster. He was force to accept, reluctantly, that he couldn't produce the components any faster than he was now, because the machine wouldn't allow him to. He complained to the foreman about the situation and was told in no uncertain terms that if he wanted to make any bonus, then the only way to do it was to get his head down and his arse up and turn out some components.

There was a union representative in the factory but he was unwilling to take up Joe's case. None of the other employees wanted to make a fuss because they were convinced that would inevitably lead to their dismissal on some pretext soon or later. The exact same thing that had happened to other, previous employees who had dared to kick up a fuss.

Joe wasn't happy at all. He couldn't make any money working there, but couldn't leave because then he'd get no benefits for six weeks. He asked to see the manager. The foreman hummed and hawed but eventually Joe was allowed five minutes of the manager's very valuable time.

The foreman escorted Joe upstairs. As he entered the office he knew straight away by the expression on the manager's face that he was on a hiding to nothing.

"I understand that you asked to see me?" the manager said bluntly without an attempt at any sort of cordial greeting.

"That's right, I have," Joe said and sat down opposite the man without waiting to be asked. The foreman remained standing and positioned himself behind Joe.

"When I started here, when I spoke to you at the interview, you told me that the machines I'd be working on were state of the art, modern machines and that I would be easily able to produce enough components to hit my targets and to make a lot of bonus."

"Yes, that's right," the manager said cautiously. "What about it?"

"What about it?" repeated Joe. "What about it? There's no way that I can make enough of those bloody components to get anywhere near my targets and make any bonuses at all, that's what about it."

"Look, if you can't make any money it's got nothing to do with me. Nothing at all. You've only been here two minutes. It's hardly my fault if you're not good enough at your job to make anything, is it? You can hardy blame me for that, can you?"

"It's got nothing to do with me not being able to do the job," Joe protested. "It's because the machine that I'm working on is a clapped-out old wreck. The bloody thing is older than I am, a lot older."

"Well how come that the others can make money? They don't come in here complaining to me about it. They just get on with it and knock the things out, hit their targets and collect big fat wage packets."

"Most of the others are in exactly the same position as I am. Fair enough one or two can hit their targets, but they're the brown-nosed bastards, the ones working on the newer machines. There are a few others who have lower targets and can just about do enough to make a little money, enough to keep them here, just, but the vast majority on the shop floor are not able to make anything at all." He stopped speaking and took a deep breath. He realised that he was beginning to get excited and that his speech was getting faster and faster. He made a determined effort to slow himself down and remain calm. "Look, you're not stupid and I'd appreciate it if you wouldn't treat me as if I am. There's not a hope in hell of me making any money on that machine, none at all and you know it." He paused again, allowing himself time to collect his thoughts. "I can't make any money, I spend more on bus fares and bait than I can earn here in a week. I can't leave voluntarily because if I put my notice in they'll stop my dole. So, would you do me a favour and sack me?"

"Sack you?"

"Yes sack me. If you sack me then I'll qualify for benefits straight away and not have to live on nothing for six weeks."

The manager sat right back in his chair, made a steeple out of his fingers and peered over the top of his hands at Joe. "But why would I want to do that?"

"I've just told you. I want to leave but I can't leave voluntarily," Joe said. "You don't want me here when I don't want to be, do you?"

"I understand all that. But why would I want to sack you when that would leave me a machinist short. The factory's production would go down." He sat forward suddenly. "You realise that we've spent a lot of money recruiting and training you, don't you? Why, we've even given you safety glasses and special shoes with steel toe caps to protect your feet."

"You take money for the safety equipment off our pay every week. You haven't given us anything. Nothing except a crap bonus system." Joe was beginning to get angry now. He was also aware of a familiar pain starting in his stomach.

"We subsidise the cost of the safety equipment. Get your facts right, you're wrong about the equipment the same as you're wrong about the bonus system. Instead of sitting here complaining, why don't you get out there and start producing some components? You want money, well get out there and make some." He paused and leaned back in his leather chair. "Look, the company has ordered some new machines and they will be delivered soon. When they arrive, it's possible you might be able to change machines. And there's a pay rise pending, so you could well be better off anyway. So why don't you get yourself back on your machine and get to work."

Joe didn't believe a word the manager had said. The pain in his stomach was getting uncomfortable, so he stood and left the office without another word. The foreman remained behind in the office with the manager.

Not long after he'd complained to the manager Joe was informed that the long-awaited and long overdue pay rise was about to be implemented. The tradesmen were to receive an extra three pence an hour, the semi-skilled men two pence, and the unskilled one penny. This was good news to everyone, although they had all been expecting a much larger increase than that. They begrudgingly accepted the offer after being advised by the union representative to do just that as it was the best offer that the company was going to make.

Joe asked the representative why there was a disparity between the skilled, semi-skilled and unskilled when there was already a huge division of their wage rate to start with.

"It's to maintain the differential, isn't it? I was involved in the negotiations and the company wanted to give a flat rate increase of three pence an hour across the board, for everybody, skilled, unskilled, the lot. But the tradesmen's rep wouldn't have it. He rejected that offer, insisted there be a differential between the grades, and instead proposed the one that has been implemented. The management couldn't believe it, man. They were over the moon. We actually insisted on an increase that was less than they had already offered us."

Joe shook his head. "But that's absolutely ridiculous. Who the bloody hell are these tossers who are negotiating on our behalf?"

"Tradesmen are all the same, mate. They all seem to have an agenda that is different from ours. All we are after is a fair and decent living wage, but they're all into politics and the broader picture and all that stuff." He shrugged his shoulders. "Beats me. But that's what we've accepted and it's too late to shout about it now."

Joe did his best, which never got him within smelling distance of any bonus. He tried looking for other work, any work paying as much or more than he was getting now, but unskilled jobs were few and far between and he didn't have much of a chance against all the youngsters out there who were also looking for work, as they cost less to employ. He scanned the ads in the local and national press and even called into the unemployment exchange at every opportunity on spec, to see if anything new had come in.

In the meantime he put his thinking power into devising ways to increase his production. He even went so far as to remove the head of the machine and pack the bearings with grease before replacing it. He then experimented with much higher speeds and with different tools to see if the job could be done any faster and so enable him to reach his targets. No luck. The only result was that he managed to cause the machine to overheat. Smoke was coming from the machine head together with the smell of burning grease. It was the smell that caught the attention of the foreman who strode across and immediately turned off Joe's machine. The foreman guessed what had happened and reprimanded Joe. Joe made the mistake of arguing with the man and was duly hauled before the manager for yet another reprimand and a formal warning about his conduct. He was told in no uncertain terms that if he stepped out of line one more time, he'd be out on his ear. The foreman, standing behind the manager's chair, smirked openly at Joe's discomfort and Joe knew that he'd have to be very careful and watch his every step in future, dismissal for misconduct also meant he'd be disqualified from any benefits for six weeks.

Joe removed his cap and scratched his head with a finger. "They can't be serious," he muttered to himself. "Look at the state of these bloody things; they're straight out of the ark, fucking antediluvian." He walked around the low loader. "In fact some of these look like they are even older than that," he added. Joe walked to the driver's cab, where the driver had just switched off the engine and was climbing out of his cab.

"You're at the wrong place with these, mate," Joe said officiously.

"Oh aye?" the driver was surprised.

"Yes. You got a delivery note?"

The driver produced the delivery note.

Joe looked at the note and nodded, as if it confirmed his suspicions. "I thought so. They've only put the wrong address on again, haven't they?" he tut-tutted. "You just can't get the staff nowadays, can you?" he said authoritatively.

"Er no," the driver answered, unsure who he was talking to.

Joe took a pen from his overall pocket and scribbled another address on the note. "There you are, that's where they need to go," he said and handed back the delivery note to the driver. "Carry on up that road then you take the first left. Once you're on the dual carriageway, just follow the signs. You'll be there in about twenty minutes."

"Thanks a lot," the grateful driver said and climbed back into his cab and drove away with a wave to Joe.

"The manager wants to see you." It was a command, not a request.

Joe followed the foreman to the manager's office and stood before the symbol of authority, his large desk.

"You think you're funny, do you?"

Joe feigned surprise. "Me?"

"Yes you, you bolshie bastard."

"I don't know what you mean, Mr Turnbull."

"You don't know what I mean?" screamed the manager.

"No."

Turnbull stood up angrily; in the process he pushed his chair back violently against the wall, where it deepened the groove in the plaster, the result of countless previous collisions. He paced the small office. He walked backwards and forwards half a dozen times before regaining a semblance of his composure.

Turnbull stopped in front of Joe and picked up a piece of paper from his desk and shoved it under Joe's nose. "Is that your writing?" he demanded.

Joe moved his head back slightly so as to allow his eyes to focus. "It's hard to tell from that, Mr Turnbull, but I suppose that it could be."

"Could be. Bloody could be. It bloody well is and you know it is. That's your writing. You were seen redirecting the bloody lorry with the machines on it. The driver described you to a T, right down to your bloody bolshie attitude."

"Oh. Is this to do with the new lathes?"

"Yes. It's got everything to do with the new lathes. We're all sitting here like idiots waiting for them to arrive and you send the driver to the bloody Beamish Industrial Museum."

"That's right, Mr Turnbull."

"Oh, so you admit it now, do you?"

"Well, I did send them to Beamish, alright. I thought that they'd made a mistake. I thought that they were so old that they must have been sent here in error. There was no way they could be the brand new machines that you told us to expect. I mean, there's no way that we could increase production and reach our new, increased targets, working on those old rattlers, Mr Turnbull, was there?"

Turnbull was incandescent with rage. Joe and the foreman watched enthralled as the manager's face changed colour. It went a bright red, then changed to puce, then finally a deep purple.

"Are you alright, Mr Turnbull?" the foreman asked with concern.

Turnbull's mouth was opening and closing but he was making no sound.

The foreman pulled the chair away from the groove in the wall and pushed it behind Turnbull's knees. This had the effect of pushing the manager's legs forward and he sat down heavily in the chair.

"I'll get your pills, Mr Turnbull," the foreman said, opening a drawer in the desk. He found a small bottle and spilled two pills onto the desk. "I'll get some water," he said, picking up a cup.

The foreman indicated to Joe that he should follow him out of the office. Once in the corridor, the foreman turned to Joe. "If I was you, I'd get your stuff together and get out. I think that you can consider yourself out of a job."

"He didn't say that," Joe protested.

"He will. He'll sack you as soon as he pulls himself together and finds his voice again."

Joe went home on the bus with his P45 and the money due in wages in his pocket and a familiar ache starting in his stomach.

14

"Sit down," said Max sharply, his back to Hans.

Hans swallowed hard and sat in the chair facing the large desk, one of Max's bodyguards towering right behind him.

"Look, Herr Westlik—"

"Shut up. I will tell you when to speak," Max said, still looking out of the window, his hands clasped behind his back.

Hans sat quietly, trying to banish the dreadful thoughts from his mind. Although a cold-blooded killer, Hans considered himself to be an educated man. He was self-educated, well read and was an intelligent, reasonable and logical type of man, with an IQ well above most of his work colleagues. He was afraid of Max, but prided himself on being a very good judge of character and was convinced that if he explained what had happened, Max would have no option but to accept his reasonable explanation. After all Max was also an intelligent man and had to think and behave logically. After what seemed an age, Max turned and sat down in the padded leather chair behind the desk opposite Hans. He looked belligerently into Hans's eyes for a full minute, further unnerving his employee. Finally, he spoke. "What happened?"

Hans had mentally rehearsed his answer countless times and couldn't get the words out fast enough, he licked his lips. "It wasn't my fault, Herr Westlik. The police pulled me over for a routine check and found the stuff. I couldn't do anything about it at all," he gushed.

Max stared at him for what seemed to Hans to be a full minute. "Why did they stop your car?"

"They said the plates didn't match the make and age of the vehicle," Hans said, his mouth was getting drier and he could feel beads of sweat forming on his brow.

Max nodded, as if Hans had just confirmed what he'd already known. "What happened then?"

"They asked to see my documents, started to search the car and …" he hesitated, "and would have found the stuff in the trunk."

"What happened then?"

"Well, I wasn't going to be taken, so I tried to reason with them, you know, offered them money. No good. So I pulled my gun, one went for his pistol and I had to shoot them both."

"Dead?"

"I think so."

"And then?"

"Then I got back in the car and tried to drive off, but another police car arrived and blocked me in and others were coming up behind …"

"And?"

"And so I ran off. I was lucky to get away."

"And you left the stuff?"

"I couldn't do anything else, Herr Westlik."

"Do you know how much that drug consignment was worth?"

"No, Herr Westlik."

Max was silent for a few minutes and appeared to be deep in thought. Hans was distinctly uncomfortable. He knew of his employer's reputation for ruthlessness, in fact had witnessed it on a number of occasions and certainly didn't want to experience it, but reassured himself again with the fact that those people had deliberately crossed or betrayed Max. He hadn't crossed Max, just been unfortunate enough to lose a quantity of his drugs.

When Max spoke again, the sound alarmed Hans so much he jerked upright in the chair. "Who arranged the car?"

"I don't know. It was already loaded and waiting for me when I arrived at the warehouse." A sense of relief began to flood slowly through Hans's body. He knew he'd been right. Max was logical and reasonable and he was off the hook.

Max nodded to the bodyguard, who was still standing so close behind Hans that he could feel the man's breath on the back of his neck. "Find out who arranged the plates." The man left the room.

"Okay, the plates weren't your fault," Max said to Hans. "More care should have been taken. I will deal with whoever put the mismatched plates on the car." He stared at Hans and Hans felt a quiver of fear through his entire body, he knew he wasn't quite off the hook yet.

"But you, you shouldn't have stopped. You should have driven away and outrun them." He shook his head in disgust. "I thought you were better than that, Hans." He sat forward in his chair and leaned over the desk, shortening the distance between them. "This is the first mistake, the first I am aware of anyway, that you have made in the what, three, four years that you have worked for me?"

"Yes," Hans answered nervously.

Max nodded again. "Because of that, I will overlook this one error on your part." He stared at Hans, his eyes hard. "Any further errors I will not be able to overlook. You understand?"

15

"When's the bastard going to stop?" Nobby whined.

"How the fuck do I know? I thought he'd have pulled over long before now," Alan answered. They'd followed the lorry from the ferry terminal, banking that the driver would stop sooner or later. "What's wrong with you, anyway? You've been moaning like an old woman all day."

"Nowt."

"Oh yes there is. Come on, let's have it."

Nobby hesitated. He knew Alan would keep on at him until he found out. "Well, it's just everybody is going on at me for entering this Elvis look-alike competition. They all take the piss 'cos I'm not as tall as Elvis was."

"You're not even half as tall as Elvis was," Alan said.

"See, even you are doing it," Nobby complained.

"It was a joke, for fuck's sake. Look, you are a good impersonator. You've got his mannerisms off to a T, can sing all his songs and look just like him on stage as long as there's nothing next to you for comparison, to show you're a bit on the small side. Anyway, all good things come in little packages, mate."

"That's as may be, but I'm thinking about giving it up. I've had enough of all the snide remarks about little Elvis. I'm sick to death of it all."

"Why don't you try impersonating someone else?"

Nobby looked at Alan before answering, trying to figure out if he was joking. But Alan was poker-faced as he drove, eyes fixed firmly on the road.

"Someone else? Like who?"

"Well, how about Sleepy?

"Sleepy?"

"Yes, Sleepy. One of the seven dwarfs?" Alan laughed.

"Fuck off; I should have known you were taking the piss."

An hour later and the shadowing pair were beginning to think the lorry wasn't going to stop at all. Then, finally it turned into a small service station car park and came to a halt.

Nobby was forced to park the van next to the lorry in the café car park, as it was the only space left vacant. The pair crouched down in their seats and studiously avoided eye contact with the lorry driver, who climbed out of his cab and walked past their van to the café entrance.

"Bollocks, he's just clocked us," Alan said. "I told you we should have nicked another van and not used yours."

"He hardly glanced at the van and didn't see our faces, so don't worry."

"It's too bloody late to worry now anyway. Wait here a minute while I sort my gear out," Alan said, rummaging with trembling fingers in a canvas tool bag on the floor. Despite his bravado, Alan was nervous. Nervous of being caught and most of all terrified of going back to prison. "Right, that's it, I've got everything."

"You sure you'll be able to get in that thing alright and start it?"

"Sure I will. You just watch me, mate," he declared confidently.

Alan left the van and took the couple of steps to the front of the lorry. Nobby watched anxiously as his friend nimbly jumped up to the cab door and fiddled with the lock for about thirty seconds and then was inside, fiddling with the ignition mechanism under the steering column.

Nobby tapped the steering wheel with his hands impatiently, while keeping watch on the café entrance through the rear view mirror. Another agonizingly slow thirty seconds passed before Nobby heard the lorry engine splutter into life, then promptly die again. As the engine stopped, Nobby was dismayed to see the driver come out of the café again and begin to walk towards them. Nobby sounded the horn as a warning to Alan, but nothing happened. Alan was still busy in the cab. Panicking, Nobby opened the van door and ran around the front of the van to the cab, shouting a warning to Alan. He reached the cab door just as the lorry's engine fired into life once more, much more strongly than previously. Alan slammed the cab door shut, not even aware that Nobby was outside and with a hiss of released hydraulic brakes, the lorry shot forward somewhat shakily. The vehicle turned out into the road and picked up speed. Nobby ran the short distance back to the van, jumped in and followed the lorry out of the car park.

Some time later the lorry was parked up on a dark, narrow, country road, and Alan and Nobby explored the stolen treasure at their leisure. They forced the lock on the back doors and climbed aboard. The lorry was packed with plastic boxes and Nobby pulled one from the top of the pile and opened it expectantly. "What the fuck's this?" he said in disbelief.

Alan had also opened a box and looked at the contents with amazement. "They're bulbs," he said quietly. "Dutch tulip bulbs." They looked at the other boxes. All were the same size and colour.

"Bollocks," Nobby said loudly. "You said the lorry was full of video players. You said we'd make a fortune selling the things. What the fuck are we going to do with tulips?"

"It was supposed to be full of video players," Alan said defensively. "There must have been a change at the last minute."

Nobby was puzzled. He held one of the bulbs in his hand and was peering at it closely. "Here, you an expert in flowers, or what? How do you know that these are Dutch tulip bulbs, then?"

"Because I'm psychic, aren't I?"

Nobby looked more puzzled than ever. "What?"

"I know that the boxes have Dutch tulip bulbs in them because all the boxes are stencilled 'Dutch Tulip Bulbs' in big black lettering on the sides, you nugget," Alan said pointing the stencilling on the boxes out to his companion.

"Let's just leave the bastard things here and cut our losses," Nobby said, not amused at all.

"Wait a minute, wait a minute. Just give me a bit of time to think, will you." Alan rubbed his chin ruminatively.

The pair sat silently for a while, Alan seemingly deep in thought while Nobby glared angrily at the boxes of bulbs.

"Look, we might be able to make something out of this yet, with a bit of luck."

"Oh aye? How?"

"Well, I know some keen gardeners who just might be interested in buying some of these tulips."

"Who, George and Joe up at the allotment? They're not likely to buy all these, are they?"

"No, but they might buy some and their friends might buy some, and their friends, etc, etc, etc. I'll have a quiet word with George tomorrow."

"It's going to take a lot of friends to get rid of all these."

"Well, what other options do we have, then? It's either that or we just walk away and leave the things here and there's not much money in that, is there? Come on, let's get the lorry out of here and somewhere safe, we might as well give it a go." He pushed the reluctant Nobby to get him to move.

16

George arrived early at the allotment the following morning and was busying himself with some routine gardening work. The annual Leek and Flower Show wasn't that far off and runaway wife, redundancy, Fred's death, depression or not, George was determined to put up as good a show as he always did. He'd been awake since half past three that morning and looked tired and completely washed out. He'd stopped taking the anti-depressants because they were reacting with the alcohol and making him feel ill and he'd realised that either the drink or the tablets had to go. No contest.

Alan turned up some twenty minutes later, the squeaky gate announcing his arrival.

"Come on in, mate," George welcomed him with brash cheerfulness. "Go in the shed, I'll be along in a minute. Just stick the kettle on while I check on the marrow."

Alan filled the kettle with water, stuck it on the Calor gas and then sat down and made himself comfortable. After a few minutes George arrived and took a seat as Alan poured the tea into two chipped mugs.

"You'll make someone a great little wife, Alan," George joked.

"That right? Well it certainly won't be you, you ugly, old, fat, baldy git," Alan replied pleasantly, slightly taken aback by George's washed-out appearance. "How's the new job going? I heard you've started at the brewery, plenty of free beer, eh? You've landed on your feet there, alright." He paused, that wasn't all he'd heard. "Terrible about Fred, eh?"

"Terrible is the word alright, he was a good mate. Anyway, the job's not that good. They want their pound of flesh the same as every other firm. It's no holiday working in a brewery, I can tell you."

"You don't know when you're well off," Alan teased, sipping his tea.

"Well off? I don't think so. Even if there's a bit of free beer around, the wages are crap. They expect you to pinch the beer to supplement the measly wages they pay you. Now then, what are you after? You after a start and want me to put a word in for you? Because I can't. I'm on the sick at the minute and the way I feel I'll be off for quite a while."

"I'm sorry to hear that you're not a hundred percent, George, but no I don't want a job at the brewery, not on your life, mate. I wouldn't want to work there for anything." Alan didn't ask George what was so wrong with him that he'd gone sick, reckoning that he'd tell him if he wanted him to know.

"Go on then, when you're ready. What's brought you up here?" George asked.

"Okay, I'll explain." Alan paused as if gathering his thoughts and then began. "We're all more or less up the creek without a paddle, job-wise, would you agree?"

George nodded.

"Right. What if I could show you a way to make some money, easily, safely and quickly?"

"But not legally?"

Alan smiled and nodded. "Not strictly double legally, no."

"I might be interested," George said slowly. "I might be, if it's quick, safe, nobody gets hurt and there's absolutely no risk of us being caught whatsoever, and it'll make us rich beyond our wildest dreams."

"Look, George," Alan said earnestly, "I've been inside, remember? In fact it's not that long since I got out. And I've got no intention of going back again, ever. I'm a rogue, a thief and a villain, but I'm not stupid. You believe me, this is safe as houses."

"Alright. You're the expert, the master criminal. I'll take your word for it. So how does it work, then?"

"Well, without going into too much unnecessary detail, a large quantity of very valuable merchandise has come into my possession. It'll be easy for us to sell these valuable items without any fuss or upset and … well, basically that's it. We've got the stuff, you can sell some of it and we'll all live happily every after."

George looked at Alan silently.

"Well, what do you think?" Alan asked impatiently after twenty seconds of silence.

"Think about what?" George said. "You've told me next to nothing, man. Not a thing, just a very brief and garbled outline. You can't expect me to make a decision with only that to go on. And who is the 'we' you mentioned? Who else is involved in this?"

"Just Nobby and me."

"Nobby?"

"That's right. Just me and him."

George shook his head. "Nobby? You mean Elvis? Why is he involved?"

"Nobby's alright. I needed somebody to help me get the stuff and help to shift it. It's because of his help that I've managed to get hold of this valuable merchandise."

"And just what is this valuable merchandise?" George asked impatiently.

"Dutch tulip bulbs." Alan paused and waited for a response.

George laughed out loud. "Tulip bulbs? I was expecting gold bullion at least, the way you were talking. Valuable merchandise you said and it turns out to be tulip bulbs," he shook his head and laughed again. "Whatever made you steal Dutch tulip bulbs, for God's sake?"

"I was acting on information received from a very reliable source, which subsequently proved to be incorrect. We were expecting a lorry load of video recorders, not bleedin' bulbs." He sighed. "Look, are you interested or not? There's lots of other people would jump at the chance of buying these, you know, but I thought I'd give you the first refusal seeing as you're a mate."

"How many have you got then?"

"About two hundred."

"Two hundred bulbs?"

"Boxes."

"Boxes? How many are in a box?"

"Couple of dozen."

"You've got, what," George did some quick mental arithmetic, "four thousand eight hundred Dutch tulip bulbs?"

"Something like that. How many do you want?"

"Well, I don't really go in for growing flowers. Joe and I go more for vegetables, but I suppose we could try some for next spring. If they're half decent when they've grown they'll always sell."

"Great. So how many shall I put you down for then?"

"How much are they?"

"Couple of quid a box."

"Okay then, say four boxes."

"I'll get them now; I've got some in the van. You want to give me a hand? What about your mates in the other allotments, they'll want some, won't they?"

The men walked to the van and Alan opened the rear doors. Leaning inside, Alan pulled some boxes towards him.

"They're posh boxes, plastic. The only other bulbs I've seen were in cheap wooden orange box things," George said.

Alan broke open the seal and pulled the top off one of the boxes and George put his hand inside to examine the bulbs. He rummaged around amongst the tissue paper and pulled out a cellophane-wrapped bundle about six by four inches and about ten or twelve inches long. Both men stared at the bundle.

"What the bloody hell have we got here?" George said pulling at the cellophane wrapping. He stripped away the tight wrapping with difficulty and stood staring wide-eyed at a large bundle of twenty-pound notes.

Alan grabbed the bundle from George, looked around to make sure there was nobody watching, and flicked though the notes, dong some mental arithmetic. "There's got to be twenty grand here," he estimated.

"Well, let's see if there's any more," George said and shoved both hands into the open box. A moment later he pulled them out holding an identical bundle. When stripped of its coverings the bundle revealed a similar amount of twenties.

They quickly opened another box and found two similar bundles.

"Four bundles of twenty grand, that's eighty grand," Alan said quietly.

George gave a low whistle. "It looks like you've struck lucky after all, mate," he said.

"What about the other boxes? Let's have a look at them, you never know, do you?"

The rest of the boxes gave up more money, but not every box contained cash, some were disappointingly filled with a couple of dozen Dutch tulip bulbs. The two men didn't bother to remove the cellophane wrapping from the new finds, but merely placed the bundles together and counted them up. There were forty bundles.

"Is my arithmetic right, George?" Alan asked doubtfully.

"Depends what total you've got, mate."

"Let's assume, just for figures, that there's twenty thousand pounds in each bundle of notes, right?"

"Right."

"And we've got forty bundles."

"Right."

"So that's twenty times forty."

"Right."

"Which makes eight hundred thousand pounds."

"Right." The men grabbed each other's shoulders and danced a crazy, ecstatic jig around the van.

"Wait," Alan shouted. "Wait a cotton pickin' minute. We only put about fifty boxes in the van, we've got another hundred and fifty in the lorry up at the clubhouse."

"What clubhouse?" George asked.

"Mickey's clubhouse, the boys' boxing club, where he coaches. The lorry's right out of sight up there. We asked him if we could park the lorry behind the clubhouse for a while, until we got sorted out. He's the only one using the dump at the weekend, so it's safe enough for a while."

"I'm surprised that Mickey even considered getting mixed up with anything dishonest. That's not like him."

"Oh, he doesn't know the stuff's nicked. I just told him I was delivering stuff for a mate and could only get so much in the van at a time."

"Well he better not find out the truth or you'll be eating hospital food, mate. He'll not like you getting him involved with this lot."

"Don't you worry about Mickey. I'll think of something to keep him quiet."

"Come on then, let's get up to the club and see if there's any more cash in the other boxes."

The men closed the van's rear doors.

"Er, wait a minute. I think it might be better to move the lorry out of the way of the club before we start opening the boxes. I wouldn't want Mickey getting wind of this amount of cash," Alan said.

"Mickey's honest enough; he'll not steal any of the money."

"That's the problem. He's too honest. If he finds out what's in the boxes he'll never sleep again until he's done something to ease his conscience. He's a right bleedin' heart, he is. Anyway, he'd have a fit because I told him porkies about the things in the first place. No, we'll leave them up there for the time being and find somewhere to stow these buggers first. What the hell are we going to do with all this?" Alan said, scratching his head.

It'll take some spending and that's for sure," George said. "Look, we'll have to hide it somewhere and quick. All these boxes are a dead giveaway."

"But where? It's got to be somewhere safe and where nobody can see it."

George had a brainwave. "Why not hide them in your pigeon loft?"

Alan considered the suggestion. "In the cree? There's not that much room in there for all these boxes." Then Alan had a brainwave of his own. "Why don't we put some in your allotment? There's a lot more room there. You've got a tool store there as well as your shed and the greenhouse. Come on, the allotment would be ideal. It's quiet up here. Nobody goes in there except you, and there's plenty of space there to hide the stuff."

"Aren't you forgetting something?" George asked quietly.

"What? What am I forgetting?"

"Joe. He's my partner up here, remember? He'd have a fit if he knew all this money was up there. You know what a worrier he is. He'd probably bust his ulcer if he saw this little lot."

"He won't find out if we hide the stuff when he's not here. And it's not like it'll be staying here forever, is it? It'll only be temporary, until we find a permanent hiding place for the loot. Anyway, even if Joe does find out, he'll not shop us, will he? And we can always cut him in to keep his ulcer quiet. Will Joe be here today?"

"No, not today. He's got a hospital appointment, got to see a specialist about his stomach. Then he's meeting Brenda in town. He shouldn't be back up here until tomorrow."

"That's it then. We'll do it now."

George agreed reluctantly. Mainly because he couldn't think of anywhere else suitable to hide the cash.

17

They reversed the white Escort van as near to the allotment fence as they could. There were a few allotment holders pottering about their gardens, but they were too far away to be able to see what the pair was up to. The conspirators spent an extremely busy morning transferring the boxes from the van to the allotment. The boxes filled the tool store and the greenhouse completely and they stored more in the shed, but there were still a lot more to hide.

"What are we going to do with the others up at the boys' club? We'll not get many more in the shed and the greenhouse is completely chocker," George said.

Alan looked around thoughtfully. "We can't leave them here and that's for sure." His face brightened as his eye fell on the leek trench. "If we take the cash out of the boxes, but leave it wrapped in cellophane, we can bury it in the leek trench."

"Are you daft, man?" George said, obviously shocked at the very thought of tampering with the leeks. "They're prize vegetables, they are, not just any old leeks. Joe will bust a gut if they're damaged."

"Come on, mate, get your priorities right. What's more important, hiding this cash or those bloody leeks?"

"Well okay, but we'll have to be careful to take the leeks out and put them in again when we've finished. Anyway, I can't see us getting them all in here," George complained.

"They'll have to go in and that's all about it," Alan said, shortly. "There's nowhere else that we can hide the stuff. It's got to go in here."

"But look, we've emptied the van and that's what, about a quarter of the boxes? And the allotment's nearly full; we've got boxes all over the place. We'll have to think of something else."

"We'll just have to empty some of the boxes. If we do that the cash will take up much less room and we can ditch the boxes and the bulbs."

They worked steadily for another hour or so, moving piles of banknotes and bulbs around, and managed to identify more possible hiding places for quite a lot more. The empty boxes and surplus tulip bulbs were thrown behind the shed.

The pair were so engrossed in their task that they got a shock as the screeching gate announced a visitor. It was Nobby. He stood in the doorway and looked around, taking in the pile of empty boxes and the bulbs lying around. "You two have been busy, haven't you? You've moved an awful lot of tulip bulbs," he said, clearly impressed. "But you'll have to get rid of the boxes. They're a dead giveaway if anyone sees them lying there."

"Well, you're standing there doing nothing, so why don't you move them?" Alan answered, without stopping his unpacking.

"What's wrong with him?" Nobby asked George.

George shrugged his shoulders. "He'll be alright once we get this lot sorted." He looked at Alan. "You want to tell Nobby here about the money?"

"Money?" asked Nobby keenly. "What money? You sold some of these bulbs already, then?"

Alan sat Nobby down and explained quietly about the money they'd found.

Nobby was very sceptical at first and said that he thought he was having his leg pulled, although that wasn't exactly the term he actually used. However, eventually they were able to convince him, more by showing him some of the actual banknotes, than by their explanations.

The ecstatic Nobby left the others to the unpacking and turned his attention to the empty boxes, which he rightly considered to be a priority. He tried to break them up and push the pieces into a large black plastic bag. After a few minutes he stopped and went back to the shed door. "This is no good. The bloody things are like elastic and won't split." He rubbed his chin ruminatively. "We'll just have to burn them, that's all."

George came to the door. "Bloody hell, they do take up some room, don't they? But if we burn them it'll cause really thick black smoke that'll be visible for miles, so we'll have to do it at night. We'll burn them with the garden rubbish, that'll be best."

George and Alan emptied about half of the boxes of their contents and piled the bundled cash they hadn't yet found a hiding place for along the walls of the shed. Nobby stacked up all the empty boxes and piled them as best he could behind the shed and covered them with black bags containing garden waste. They sat down to rest after their work and George put the kettle on for some tea.

It was obvious that the boxes were the biggest problem and the three men talked over their options.

"There's far too many to burn. The fifty here are bad enough but there's another hundred and fifty still in the lorry yet."

George snapped his fingers. "I've got it. We'll put some next door," he said. "That garden's been empty for a couple of months now; the council hasn't re-let it since old Ralph passed away. The empty ones we'll dump with the lorry."

"Ralph's dead?" Alan asked. "I didn't know that."

"Yes. He was working at that scrap yard near the river. He got hit on the head with a magnet, one of those big electronic things hanging from a crane what they use to lift scrap metal with. Killed him outright."

"Hit on the head with a magnet? Was he on iron tablets, then?" Nobby asked innocently. The other two looked at each other, but ignored the remark and made no comment.

Nobby and George helped Alan to throw some of the boxes over the adjoining fence and then, using a ladder, they all climbed over and hid them in the adjoining garden.

Most of the boxes safely concealed, they returned to the shed and put the kettle on again. While they waited for the kettle to boil, the three men sat and gazed at the huge amount of money in the shed.

"Somehow, seeing it like this, laid out in front of us, seems strange," George said.

"That's because it is bleedin' strange, mate. Not many people have seen that much money all together in one place, believe me," Alan answered.

"Too true," George said. "What's troubling me is where are we going to hide the other stuff that's up at the boys' club? The chances are there's a lot more cash up there."

"There might not be any more," Nobby said.

"You could be right, but the chances are that there is, mate," George maintained.

"George's probably right. It's not very likely that we just happened to grab the only boxes with cash in, is it? There's almost certainly more in the lorry and we'll have to find a place for it all. I've been thinking about it," Alan said. "We'll get a fair bit more in here, in the shed, under the work bench there and stowed under the seats, and we can get about the same again in old Ralph's greenhouse next door, but I think we're still going to have a fair bit left over."

"So?" Nobby asked. "If you've been thinking about it, what's the solution?"

"We'll have to dig out the whole leek trench and put some in there."

"What?" George said. "Look here, I've told you there's absolutely no way that I'm digging up that leek trench. My prize leeks are in there and they're coming on fine, there's no way that they're going to be disturbed, not this close to the annual leek show. No way," he added for emphasis.

"It's all very well for you to chunter on about your bleedin' prize leeks, but what about this money? If anybody sees it lying around then we're for it. Would you rather protect your leeks or end up in prison or even worse if whoever the money belongs to catches you with it?" Nobby argued. "What are you bothered about the leeks for anyway? You've got enough money there to buy the bloody leek club, lock, stock and barrel, and you're worrying about a few prize leeks, you can't even eat the bloody things anyway."

"'Course you can eat them. They're lovely fried with a bit of bacon, or baked in a leek an' potato pie," George answered.

"Well I wouldn't eat them. Not after seeing what you put on the bloody things. Yuk," Nobby said with a grimace.

"Home grown veg is a lot tastier than the shite you buy in the supermarkets. It's fresh, got no chemicals in it and you know how it's been grown," George insisted.

"Will you two shut up about the bloody leeks!" yelled Alan. "We can probably tuck them down the side of the trench without damaging the bleedin' leeks anyway."

"That's a good idea. I'll do it though. I'll put them down the side, I don't want you two touching the thing," George said, glad of a chance to gain a reprieve for his precious leeks.

They got to work again when they'd finished their tea. Nobby and Alan carried the money out and George began to carefully dig out the borders of his leek trench and bury the wads along the edge. They worked quickly and quietly until the trench would take no more.

"That's it," George said. "We can't get any more in here, not if we want to keep them out of sight."

"But there's still quite a few left," Alan said.

"There is, isn't there?" George answered. "But don't worry, I've been thinking and I've got a solution."

"What's that then?" Nobby asked.

"Easy. We put the rest in your pigeon cree over there," he pointed towards the brightly painted wooden structure in the site adjacent to the allotment.

"Now wait a minute," Alan protested. "You can't put any in there. You'll disturb the birds. Some of them, the good ones, are very sensitive to disruption, especially that close to their nesting boxes."

"It's the only place left. We've filled the tool store, shed, greenhouse and even my bloody leek trench, so it's got to be the cree. Anyway, it's the ideal hiding place, isn't it? Who in their right mind would go looking for something in there? It's full of bird shit and stinks to high heaven."

After more prolonged argument, Alan was finally forced to agree to use the cree to store the remaining cash. They hid the banknotes, covered with rags, under the nesting boxes. And the rags were already collecting a layer of bird droppings by the time they'd finished. The ammoniacal smell was eye watering and would certainly be a strong disincentive to anyone being too nosey and looking for anything in the cree. The birds viewed the human activity with disinterest and their only silent criticism was to defecate on the men's heads occasionally.

The money all safely stowed away, except of course for a small amount held by each of them for spending money, they felt safer. They'd also agreed to hide a small amount of cash in the shed, ready at hand, for emergencies.

"Right, as soon as we get the chance, we'll bring the rest down, get rid of the boxes and the bulbs and that'll be that. All trace gone," Alan said. "Everything linking us to the lorry will have been sorted."

"We'll have to dump the lorry," Nobby reminded them.

"And the empty boxes, and there'll still be all the cash here," George said, hesitantly. "What happens if somebody finds that?"

"We'll have to take turns to sleep up here until we've moved it somewhere safer," Nobby said.

"I sometimes sleep up here anyway. That's no great hardship," George said.

"There's no way anybody can prove that it was from the lorry hijack, even if they found the money, can they?" Alan said confidently.

"No, but it'll still be bloody hard to explain away, won't it? I'm sure that we could be still be done for something or other," George maintained.

"They'd have to prove it. Believe me, there's no way we can be touched. As soon as those boxes are gone, we're in the clear. Anyway, officially there were only tulip bulbs in those boxes, that's all. It says so on the paperwork."

George didn't seem convinced.

"Don't worry, mate," Alan said.

"I'm not worried, not at all, but Joe will be when he finds out what we've hidden in the allotment."

"Yes, that's right, he will won't he? I'd forgotten about Joe. But then Joe is always worried about something. In fact he's always worried about everything. I think he'd be really worried if he caught himself not being worried about anything," Alan said.

"George's got a point though, about all the money. We'd have a hard time explaining where it came from," Nobby put in.

"Maybe, but they'd have a hard time trying to prove it came from an illegal source. You're innocent until proven guilty, remember that." Alan paused. "Anyway, what else can we do with it? We can't stick it in a bank. You try that and they want to know where it came from and everything. It's the same with any type of building society account or investment. It's getting harder and harder to stick money anywhere without everybody and their uncle wanting to know where you got it from in the first place."

"What we could do is to stick the maximum into Government savings and stuff, premium bonds and the like," George said.

"Look, mate. If we bought premium bonds you know what would happen, don't you?"

"What?"

"We'd bloody win a fortune that's what. Sod's law, isn't it. If you've got no money, you'll never win anything. But now that we're literally sitting on a fortune, we'd be sure to win lots more."

They both laughed.

"The only thing that's certain is it's not legal. And somebody somewhere must know it's been stolen. They must do. Whoever owns the bulbs and the cash will have just a small inking that they're gone, won't they?" George said.

"The owners are probably a bunch of greedy criminals who are bringing the proceeds of their illegal activities here. I know that the videos that were supposed to be in that lorry were iffy, the cash has got to be from the same source. Once the money's here they probably planned to process the money through various legitimate business interests, so that it's laundered clean. And then they can whiz the cash straight back out of the business and do what they want with it. They've probably done it countless times in the past and gotten away with it every time. This time they haven't gotten away with it. They won't be very happy, but they'll simply accept the loss as a business expense, write it off, and devise another way to beat the system," Alan deduced.

"That's some write-off business expense," Nobby said.

There was a moment's silence before George spoke again. "So the money was being transported from Holland?"

Alan shook his head. "It came in on a lorry from Germany via Amsterdam, according to the paperwork it was dispatched from Berlin. Don't ask me why there're bringing in English currency from Germany, because I haven't figured that out yet. I was expecting the lorry to be carrying electrical goods. But   think about it. We've really fallen lucky here. Just you think of the options. What else are we going to do? The yards were bad, and dangerous, but at least we knew what we were doing and what to expect. You've tried other employment, which is even worse than working in the yards. The only jobs out there for us now are the shite no one else will do. Now you won't need to work again, ever, you can forget job interviews, dirty shipyards and smelly breweries. You're in clover for the rest of your life now, mate, we all are."

18

The theft of the money was a huge shock to Max. He spent a long time thinking over the situation and was almost a hundred percent certain that the theft was a fluke. He couldn't believe that the thieves had known what was in the lorry. He sent for Hans, who he knew was eager for a chance to redeem himself after his recent failure.

Hans felt a lot more comfortable sitting in front of Max's desk than the last time he'd been in this room, but still had a nagging sense of unease deep inside him.

"I have a job for you, Hans," Max said. "A very important job. Some property, very valuable property, belonging to me has been stolen in England and I want you to go across and retrieve it."

Hans nodded. "I will get it back, Herr Westlik."

"Yes, you will, Hans. I want you to have some help. You will take Ernst with you."

Hans's heart sank. Ernst was Max's nephew and a total waste of time as far as Hans was concerned. The lad had no intelligence, was bad tempered and hot-headed, vainer than a teenage girl and only interested in building up his muscles at the gym. To facilitate his bodybuilding, it was said he was taking large amounts of illegal steroids and was also becoming increasingly dependant on other drugs of one sort or another.

"I could handle it easily by myself, Herr–"

"I want Ernst to go with you," Max cut him short.

Hand nodded. "Of course, Herr Westlik."

19

Nobby opened the gates and closed them again quickly after Alan had driven the lorry out from behind the boys' club. Nobby climbed into the cab and Alan drove away as fast as he could in the dark. He was nervous and had trouble finding the gears and crashed through them as he picked up speed. His heart was in his mouth when he slowed at a roundabout. He prayed that he wouldn't have to stop in case he stalled the lorry. The way was clear and he negotiated the roundabout all right and was soon making good time on the dual carriageway. He expected to hear the sound of sirens behind him and see the flashing blue lights of police cars at any second, but nothing happened. He hadn't been this concerned when he thought the lorry was carrying a load of video recorders, but somehow knowing the cash was in the back made a big difference. He kept within the speed limit and was only a couple of minutes behind schedule when he turned off the dual carriageway. He drove up the hill to the allotment, bumped the vehicle up over the curb and onto the grass verge and parked as close as possible to the garden fence

Alan stopped the lorry and turned off the engine and the lights. He jumped down and ran to the back doors of the vehicle.

George was already there waiting for them. "Where've you been? I've been stood here bloody ages."

"Don't exaggerate. Come on, don't stand there moaning like an old woman, give us a hand to unload the stuff," Alan ordered as he swung open the back doors. The lorry was about three-quarter full of boxes. They both scrambled inside and rummaged around, moving the boxes to the rear of the lorry.

"How do we know which are the right ones?" Nobby asked.

"We don't know. We'll just have to open them all."

"Open them all? Bloody hell, that's a job and a half and no mistake," George complained. "We haven't got time to open them all."

"Well, try just shaking them, then. We might be able to tell if they've got money in them instead of bulbs by the weight or the way the contents move."

The three men picked up boxes from various parts of the lorry and shook them around. After they'd moved a few, it did become apparent that some felt different from others. Alan opened one such box and sure enough it contained banknotes. "Cracked it," Alan said triumphantly. "The heavier ones have got the bulbs in them; the lighter ones hold the cash."

"But most of those I've picked up are light," Nobby said. "All those can't be full of money, surely?"

"Well, just for now, put all the light ones over there on that side of the lorry and the heavy ones on this side, then, when they're all sorted, we'll open them up and see just what we've got."

It took the three of them a good twenty minutes to separate the boxes and then Alan used his penknife to slit open all the seals on the top of the lighter ones. All of them contained money. Every one.

"It looks as if we've got more than we were expecting," Nobby said in wonder.

"It does that," Alan agreed, staring at the boxes in amazement. "I think I'd better open the other, heavier ones, just to make sure that there's no bloody cash in those as well."

"Yes, there could be fivers in those, maybe?" Nobby joked.

Nobby started to examine the notes in one of the boxes while Alan opened the others. All the heavier ones where filled with bulbs, as expected.

Nobby turned to Alan. "So just how much is in each box, then, mate?"

Alan looked at him strangely. "Have a guess."

"Fuck off, Alan, I'm not in the mood for games. How much?"

"I make it two bundles of twenty grand in each. That's forty thousand pounds in twenty-pound notes, same as the others."

"Good. And how many boxes have we got?" Nobby started to count.

"One hundred and five," Alan interrupted him.

"Good," Nobby said again, automatically. "Then that makes a grand total of … let's see now, one hundred and five boxes, times forty thousand pounds per box …"

"It's four million, two hundred thousand, fucking pounds," Alan said staring at his pocket calculator with wide, disbelieving eyes.

"How much?" Nobby demanded.

"Four million and two hundred thousand fucking pounds," Alan repeated.

"It can't be that much, you daft git. We've already got eight hundred thousand stashed here at the allotment. It'll be four hundred thousand two hundred, that's what it'll be. Give me the calculator here." He did the sums on the calculator. "That can't be bleedin' right. There must be more in that box than in all the others, let's count another one."

Nobby counted another one and another and another. Alan and George counted a number of boxes selected at random. They all contained the same amount. Their total haul was four million two hundred thousand pounds in used twenty-pound notes, plus the eight hundred thousand already hidden away.

"Fuck me gently," Nobby said with feeling. "That's five million pounds altogether."

"Do you think we'll get all these in Ralph's allotment?" Alan asked doubtfully, in mild shock, totally ignoring the huge monetary value of their haul and concentrating only on the logistics of their storage problem.

"We'll have to, either that or we'll have to eat the stuff," George said. He shook his head. "This much cash is going to be a big problem, you mark my words."

The men worked industriously by torchlight and did manage to conceal a lot of the boxes in the garden next to George and Joe's allotment. They managed it by filling all the outhouses and then simply burying as many as they possibly could under the rich dark soil. The remainder they hid in and around the pigeon cree and George's allotment. The boxes soon became mixed up, so that boxes containing cash were buried along with others containing bulbs. The lads didn't worry too much about it; they could always sort them out later, or so they thought.

When all the boxes had been hidden, they loaded the empty ones onto the back of the lorry along with the loose bulbs. Then Alan drove the lorry away to a predestined, remote spot where he thought it shouldn't be discovered for some time.

20

The two tough-looking Germans arrived on a flight from Amsterdam at 8 a.m. the following morning. They cleared Customs without incident and took a taxi to the city centre, where they booked into a hotel overlooking the river. The older of the two, Hans, made a telephone call from their room to Max in Berlin to inform him they'd arrived.

Max gave Hans further instructions over the phone. "I've had time to study the details of the theft and there are only three employees who could have given the information to the thieves. Two, this side, have been interrogated and discounted, so the most likely suspect is the driver employed by the haulage company. We are still looking into his background. It is extremely unlikely that he knew what he was carrying but you need to check him out. You pay this driver a visit and find out if he has any knowledge of the theft. And, Hans, don't be particularly gentle with him. Use your initiative and investigate any information you might turn up, but report to me daily. I want my possessions back quickly, but quietly. I don't want the police involved any more than they are at the moment and I definitely don't want any publicity of any kind under any circumstances. You understand?"

Hans was an achiever. In any legal organisation or business he would be in a position of high authority, with a large amount of responsibility. He was very conscientious and considered it an affront to his pride if he couldn't, for whatever reason, complete any task he was given. The success of this particular job was doubly important to him because of his previous failure. He confirmed his understanding of Max's instructions, waited until his employer had hung up and then dialled the hotel's reception desk. He asked them to arrange a hired car immediately, a Mercedes. He then turned to his large companion, Ernst, who was lounging on one of the twin beds, watching an adult movie on the TV while preparing a spliff.

"Come on," he said impatiently, "I've told you before about smoking that shit, it'll mess up your brain. You can do what you want when you're working alone, but don't use that stuff when you're with me. Do you understand?"

Ernst looked at Hans resentfully.

"And let's get one thing perfectly straight, shall we?" Hans said. "I don't care if Max is your uncle, I'm running this show and you'll do exactly what I tell you to do. Is that clear?"

Ernst nodded slowly.

"Good. Now, this almost certainly has got to be an inside job and the driver is probably the man responsible, so first we will speak to him," Hans said.

Hans knew he was in a very dangerous position. He'd have to be very careful about how he spoke to and treated Ernst because of the younger man's relationship to Max, but at the same time he had to make sure they found Max's missing property, otherwise he'd be for the chop.

21

George was already at the allotment when Joe arrived early the next morning. His mouth dropped open in amazement as he looked around the shed, and then he turned to his friend with a question on his lips.

George held up a pacifying hand to halt the onslaught before it began.

"I'll put the kettle on first, mate, and then explain everything."

George sat his friend down, made the tea and gently told him the story behind the boxes, bulbs and the cash. Joe listened with a look of utter disbelief on his face, especially when told that he was now in line for a full share of the money. When told how much actual cash was involved, his lower jaw dropped open again and remained like that for quite some time. It even remained open for a good thirty seconds after George had finished his account. Then, recovering somewhat, he started to ask questions. Most, George could answer, but not the one Joe most wanted an answer to, what were they going to do with so much money?

"You'll be able to buy Brenda whatever she wants. Pay off all the outstanding bills, even pay off the mortgage in full. Imagine what that would feel like, mate, waltzing into the building society and slapping all that money down on the counter. Then you could be off on a long holiday somewhere sunny, not Scarborough or Whitley Bay, but the Bahamas or some other sunny Caribbean island. Or anywhere else in the world where you fancy. And, not just for a week or a fortnight, but for a couple of months or longer. In fact you needn't come back at all, just imagine that."

Joe's eyes were slightly glazed as he imagined that, and then they cleared as he thought of new objections. "There'll definitely be enough for us all to live off for the rest of our lives," Joe confirmed. "But we're risking an awful lot."

"I know that. As near as we can tell there's about five million pounds in there. A lot less would be more than enough for all of us to live on for the rest of our lives, you can be sure of that, mate."

"It sounds alright," Joe was weakening. "But I'll have to talk it over with Brenda."

"Look, Joe," George said. "You can't go and talk it over with anyone. The fewer people that know about this, then the safer we're going to be."

"I talk everything over with Brenda. She knows everything I do. We don't hold anything back from each other. No secrets. I've got to get her opinion on this or I don't get involved at all."

George nodded. "I thought that you were made of better stuff than that, mate, but then, Brenda was always one for getting her own way, wasn't she?"

"I don't much care what you think. That's the sort of relationship we have with each other. We've had money problems in the past that nearly broke up our marriage. We managed then and swore that we'd always be totally honest and up front with each other about everything. That's the way things are and that's the way things are going to stay. If you don't like it, then tough, you can lump it. Alright?"

"Alright, Joe. Just calm down, mate," George said. "There's nothing wrong with you talking things over with the wife. Nothing at all. Brenda's got her head screwed on and she won't tell anybody about it. So don't worry, just take it easy."

"How many people are involved in this anyway?" Joe asked.

"Me, you, Alan and Nobby. That's it." George answered. "Four of us. And, everything will be split exactly four ways. But we'll have to know very soon whether you're in or not."

Joe nodded. "I'll let you know tomorrow. That alright?"

George nodded his consent.

"And anyway, even if I decide not to get involved, neither me nor Brenda will say anything to anybody, you know that, don't you?"

"I know that, mate. I know. Whatever you decide, we'll have to get together with Alan and Nobby and sort something out. We obviously can't leave the stuff here; it's too risky, and spending that much is going to be a problem."

"I never thought that having too much money would be a problem, but you can't just walk into a showroom and buy a new car for cash, can you? People will ask questions."

22

Ernst went to buy the drinks and Hans sat down at a window seat with the driver. They had brought him to the café in the service station where the theft of the lorry had taken place, hoping that the location might trigger the man's memory.

The driver was surprised by Hans's questions and more than a trifle intimidated by his interrogator's appearance. He sat opposite Hans looking like a rabbit cornered by a hungry wolf and watching Ernst's hulking figure make its way to the counter. Hans sat quietly and watched the driver closely. He'd received the man's details from Max and knew that he was English, thirty-eight years old, had worked for the haulage company for four years, was a fairly conscientious worker and as far as they knew, apart from adding the odd hour or two to his overtime sheet, honest. He was married with a young family and didn't have a criminal record. Ernst returned with the coffees and the men added various amounts of sugar according to their personal tastes.

"Look, I've already told the police all about this, not that they seemed very interested," the frightened driver said as he stirred his coffee with a slightly trembling hand.

"That may be so, but my employer is concerned at losing these bulbs. They are of special interest to him and he wants them back. He is also concerned that this might set a precedent and he doesn't wish anything like this to occur ever again. You understand, ja?" Hans said.

Ernst slowly sipped his coffee and stared silently at the driver.

The driver nodded. "But I've told you everything that happened."

"You've told me everything you told the police?"

"Yes, everything."

"Do you normally stop at this particular eating place?"

"No. I generally drive all the way to Birmingham without stopping at all."

"So why stop this time?"

"I was hungry and needed the toilet." He hesitated. "My stomach was upset. The crossing from Amsterdam was a bit rough and it upset my stomach. I didn't have any breakfast on the ferry." With noticeably trembling hands the man picked up his coffee, using both hands to steady the cup and sipped the hot liquid. "Then, as soon as I got inside the café I realised I'd left my cigarettes in the cab and came back out to get them. That's when I saw the lorry being driven off."

Hans studied the driver closely through narrowed eyes. He prided himself on being a very good judge of character and was almost certain that this man was telling the truth. His nervousness was something that Hans was used to. Most people he spoke to became nervous very quickly. "When you got out of the lorry, before you came into the café, was there anybody loitering around outside, apart from the two men in the van?"

"No, no ..." the driver said. He paused and distorted his facial features as if trying to remember the scene. "No. There was nobody hanging around. There was just the parked van with the two men in it. Just the van, a white, Escort-type van."

Hans looked at him. "An Escort van?" he prompted

"Yes. It must have driven into the car park behind me and it parked next to my lorry. It was the only space left. I walked past the van on the way to the café and its engine was still running. There were two men in the van and they both looked away as I walked past."

"So these are the ones that stole your lorry?"

"Yes."

"Tell me what these men looked like."

"One was about twenty-one or twenty-two, and was not very tall, well below average height. He had jet-black hair combed straight back with the front pulled forward."

"Pulled forward?"

"Yes," the driver confirmed, using two fingers to tease his own quiff down over his eyes. "Like Elvis. And he had his shirt collar turned up," he demonstrated with his own collar, "and wore a leather jacket with studs on the back that spelled 'Elvis The King' in big letters."

"What about the other one?"

"He was a bit older, I think. But I didn't really get a proper look at him."

"What makes you think he was a bit older if you didn't get a good look at him?"

"I don't really know. It was just an impression. He seemed older. Maybe he moved slower or something. He was the one that got in the lorry and drove away. The short one ran back to the van and followed the lorry."

"I don't suppose you noticed the registration of the van?"

"No, I never gave it a thought when I walked past it and was too far away when it drove off and followed the lorry."

"Was there anything at all that was unusual or out of the ordinary about the van or the men?"

"No, nothing." He hesitated and seemed to be thinking.

"What?" prompted Hans.

"Well, it's probably nothing but I did see that it had an Up North Combine sticker on the windscreen."

"Up North Combine?"

"It's a racing pigeon organisation. They transport birds to various locations in Britain and the continent and release them so they fly back home. I sometimes see their transporters on the road."

Both Germans looked puzzled.

"They drive the birds a long way away, then release them and the fastest bird gets back first and wins," he explained.

Hans nodded his understanding. "Ah, I understand. Homing pigeon racing? So perhaps these thieves have some connection to this Up North Combination, this is right, ja?"

"Combine," the driver corrected. "It's Up North Combine, not combination, and yes it's possible that they might have something to do with pigeon racing. Then again the sticker might have already been on the van when they bought it, or stole it."

"Did you tell the police about this Up North Combine sticker?"

"Er, yes I did. I remembered seeing the sticker on the van's windscreen."

"Pity."

The driver swallowed hard, intimidated by the big man's tone.

"Now where can we find this Up North Combine?"

23

Trev stopped the car and leaned across to open the passenger door. "You want a lift?"

Elsie smiled and climbed into the car gratefully. "Thanks, Trev, I've been standing there for ages. You can't rely on the buses nowadays."

Trev, seeing Elsie standing at a bus stop outside the railway station carrying a small holdall, guessed that she had just been released from prison, but tactfully didn't mention it.

But Elsie knew that he knew. "It's nice to be home, back in familiar surroundings and seeing friendly faces again," she said. She looked at Trev appraisingly. "You stopped your gallivanting about and got yourself a nice decent, young lass yet, Trev?"

"Er, not yet, Elsie. But I'm looking."

"I'll bet you are. And trying them all out for size as well, I'll bet," Elsie said and laughed. But then she suddenly became serious. "I always thought you and that musician lass would make a go of it. She seemed to be a nice girl."

"I thought so as well, Elsie, but it didn't work out. She fell for somebody who played in the same orchestra."

"Pity. I just wish our Alan would find himself a nice girl and have some kids. I'm at the age now when I should be a grandmother." She shook her head. "The girls he takes out aren't nice and he doesn't seem interested in settling down at all."

Trev remained silent until they reached Elsie's house. "Here we are then, Elsie," he said stopping the car. "Hang on and I'll give you a hand with that holdall."

"No, don't you bother yourself. I can manage it easily," Elsie said getting out of the vehicle. "Thanks for the lift, Trev, you're a diamond."

Elsie waved Trev off and then walked slowly down the path to the front door, savouring the familiarity of the street and her own garden. She opened the front door with her key and stepped inside, dropped her holdall on the floor and burst into tears.

"Is that you, Mam?" Alan shouted from upstairs.

Elsie walked into the kitchen dabbing at her eyes with a tissue. "Yes, it's me," she shouted up the stairs as she filled the kettle from the tap. "They let me out a day earlier than I expected. I don't think the bastards can count."

Alan came running down the stairs and hugged his mother. "I was expecting you tomorrow. I was going to come and pick you up at the station."

"Well, you needn't bother. I'm home now. Trev saw me at the bus stop and gave me a lift home."

"Was it alright?" he asked, looking into her eyes with concern.

"Oh, aye. No bother at all, son," Elsie said shortly, pouring boiling water into the tea pot. Her back to Alan now, she checked her eyes in a wall mirror and dabbed the last of the moisture from them. Despite her long and industrious career as a shoplifter, Elsie had never actually been imprisoned before. The last few months inside had been an experience for her and something of a shock. It wasn't that the prison regime was unduly harsh, or the officers or other inmates hostile, in fact just the opposite, she had made some good friends inside. No, it was simply the shock, the physical reality of being away from her family and familiar surroundings, the first time in her life she had ever been away from home.

"Margaret was asking when you were due out. She stopped me in the street yesterday," Alan said. "Her and Sharon are really grateful to you for taking the rap, you know."

"And so they bloody should be," Elsie said, sniffing, as she poured two cups of tea and passed one to her son. "Here, put your own milk and sugar in."

Elsie and two of her shoplifting associates had been caught red-handed with a number of stolen items concealed about the three of them. Her companions had multiple previous convictions and prison sentences for shoplifting and if convicted again would have received lengthy sentences, so Elsie had volunteered to say she'd stolen the goods and had asked the others to carry them for her. She swore that they were entirely innocent and didn't know she had stolen the items.

Neither the store detectives nor the police believed a word of her story, but they couldn't disprove it, Elsie was charged and the other two released. As she'd been charged and convicted previously, but never imprisoned, they all confidently expected her to be fined again, or maybe given a year's probation, but to their surprise and disgust, she'd got six months. Even the police were taken aback.

Elsie and her friend Margaret were almost certainly the best shoplifters in the country, but they never seemed to make much of a profit, preferring to give most of their plunder away to hard-up friends and neighbours for nothing or almost next to nothing. There were always strikes or lay-offs from the local yards and factories, and recently, with all the yards closing, their services were more in demand than ever. They didn't consider their activities were really theft at all, and genuinely thought that they were involved in some sort of Robin Hood operation, robbing the rich to help the poor, rather than in organised shoplifting. It was their opinion that if they could help friends to obtain some good quality clothes at a reasonable cost, and make a few pounds for themselves while doing it, then what was the harm in that? They reasoned that stores could claim the losses from their insurance companies, which charged them hugely excessive premiums anyway. And the stores made massive profits by charging hugely inflated prices for their goods, the women rationalised. The women charged their customers, who were their friends and acquaintances, at most only a quarter of the store prices, and there was no shortage of takers, they regularly got orders for specific types and sizes of clothes.

Their regular customers almost always made their own selections, browsing the shops for the particular goods they wanted, picking the exact style, colour and sizes. If the right size or colour wasn't in stock then they'd ask the store to order it in, then they'd notify Elsie or Margaret, who would then go and steal the item for them. Elsie wouldn't take any money at all from some of the worse-off families, and provided their clothes free of charge, considering herself to be a sort of cross between a female Santa Claus and a fairy godmother to the struggling families. Even in this modern society, which was supposedly awash with benefits of one kind or another, it was the worst-off families which always slipped below the safety net of social security payments. Elsie was actually the very embodied essence of the motherly figure, loving, warm and kind. She couldn't bear the thought of children doing without clothes or toys, especially at Christmas, and took it upon herself to provide them, if necessary for free. She didn't tell Margaret this, and so was totally unaware that her friend had also come to the same conclusion, and had made similar arrangements herself for certain of her customers.

"Come on then, son, get the chocolate biscuits out."

The pair sat opposite each other in armchairs in the living room, sipping tea and eating biscuits, Elsie now at ease, happy and content, wearing her favourite, extremely comfortable slippers, back in her own home at last.

"Come on then, Mam," Alan was bursting with questions

"Come on then, what?"

"What was it like? What did you do?"

"Well, you know after a month I was sent to Ashdown open prison?"

Alan nodded. Ashdown was at the other end of the country and he knew no one had travelled down to visit her. It was a long and difficult journey and most of her friends were ex-prisoners and disqualified from visiting her anyway. Alan was inside himself, of course.

"The second day in there I was interviewed by a social worker or somebody and she asked what courses I was interested in doing. Rehabilitation they called it. I had the choice of about six or seven." She counted them off on her fingers. "There was hairdressing, dress making, fabric cleaning, you know, furniture and carpets and stuff. What else? Oh yes there was massage with oils, aromatherapy or something they call it. Painting and decorating was another, beauty therapy and I can't remember the other one."

"Bloody hell, Mam, which one did you decide on, then?"

"Dress making."

"Why dress making, for God's sake?"

"I thought it might help me alter some of the knock-off stuff, you know, make it fit if I've nicked the wrong size," she laughed. "Anyway, knowing something like that will always be handy, won't it?"

Alan agreed and joined in her laughter.

"It was alright. The lasses doing the aromatherapy used to practise on me. I had a bloody good, full-body massage every day. I was so relaxed they had to wake me up when it was time to go to bed." She laughed again. "And those doing hairdressing did my hair every week and I got facials nearly every day from those doing beauty therapy."

"It certainly hasn't done you any harm; you look about ten years younger."

"It was like a holiday camp, son. I wouldn't mind all that much going back in, to be honest," her eyes became moist again. "It's just the being away from home for so long, son, you know?"

"I know, Mam," Alan said, going to her and putting his arm around her shoulder.

She patted his hand on her shoulder. "You're a diamond, son, a genuine diamond. I've really missed you."

Elsie had brought Alan up single-handed. Her husband had left them when her son was very young. She'd told Alan that his father was in the navy, he believed it and that's what he told his friends. But he realised as he grew older, and his father never came home, that it couldn't be true. Elsie eventually told him the truth, which was that his father was in prison. He'd actually been on the run for years before being arrested, convicted and sentenced to fourteen years. He served every day of the term, not earning a single day in remission. He'd returned home after being released some nine years ago, when Alan was twenty-two. Elsie had agreed, with grave reservations, to him staying for a limited period until he got on his feet again and found somewhere else to live.

Alan's early memories of his father were shrouded in a fog of sentimental nostalgia and a son's natural affection and hero worship of his father. Despite his mother's warnings of her now ex-husband – she'd divorced him while he was in prison – being a nasty, violent man, Alan had befriended and spent a great deal of time with him. Then, within weeks, to Alan's surprise, disbelief, and great fury, his father had disappeared with Alan's entire savings. This further betrayal had a profound effect upon Alan's already scarred emotions. It reinforced his early inbuilt instinct of natural distrust. He knew then that he'd been stupid and weak to trust his father, to trust anyone, and he would be very careful not to do it again.

Alan kissed the top of his mother's head. "I missed you, Mam. I missed you a lot and I'm really glad you're back."

24

The secretary of the local Up North Combine was very helpful and very talkative, especially as Hans kept buying him drinks. They met in the bar of a workingmen's club the following lunch time, after Hans's telephone call to the local office, and it soon became obvious to the Germans that the man liked a tipple. He started off drinking pints of brown ale, but quickly switched to whisky when it became obvious that Hans was happy to pay. Hans played the part of a long lost friend of the short Elvis fanatic who drove a white Escort van and who he thought probably kept pigeons. He expected the secretary to tell him that the police had been round asking the same questions, but he didn't. Hans assumed he was either playing his cards very close to his chest, or the police hadn't bothered to follow up the lead. While Hans talked to the man, Ernst took the opportunity to disappear and Hans was certain he was smoking pot in the toilet and made a mental note of this unacceptable behaviour.

The secretary's memory wasn't what it once was, he told Hans, but he was sure that it would return to its normal excellent capacity once he'd refreshed his intense thirst.

Hans played along, considering that getting the information this way would be easier, quicker, more accurate and more discreet than threatening and shaking the information out of the man. He was right. Finally, after about three hours and numerous whiskies, the man gave Hans the information he wanted, in fact more than he was expecting, in quite a slurred manner. He told him the name and address of Nobby and the location of his and Alan's pigeon loft. He also gave the German details of Nobby's longstanding partner in crime, Alan Spencer.

25

Joe told Brenda about the money stashed at the allotment. Her reaction surprised him. She listened quietly until he'd finished talking and then sat down without comment.

"Well, what do you think, love? Should I get involved or keep well away from it all?" he asked, taken aback by her reaction. He'd fully expected her to explode in anger, rubbish Alan and his thieving and insist that he have nothing to do with the money.

Brenda reached out and took Joe's hand, "Sit down, Joe, I've got something to tell you."

Puzzled, Joe sat next to her on the settee. "What is it, Bren. What's wrong?"

"I'm pregnant."

The implications of her stark statement didn't register in Joe's mind for a few seconds. "But what should I do about …?" he started to ask and then the full impact hit him. "You're what? How? Are you sure?"

"How do you think I got pregnant, you daft thing? And yes, I'm sure. I thought I was for the last month and I've been to the doc's this morning and he's confirmed it. I'm definitely pregnant."

Joe slumped back on the settee, his mind reeling. "But how? How has it happened now, I mean? We've been trying for years and suddenly you're pregnant, just like that."

"That's just the way it goes, love. They come when they want, not when we want them to."

The couple had wanted children since they married, but Brenda had her hands full looking after her handicapped younger sister, as well as trying to do a part-time job in a factory. Since her sister's death six years ago, the baby issue had come to the fore again. As the years passed they began to worry and each had tests done to confirm they could have children. All the tests were positive, they were both fertile and there was nothing stopping them from having the children they wanted. But still nothing had happened until now.

Joe shook his head as if to clear it. "This is going to take some getting used to. Me, a father. I thought it would never happen."

"Well, it's happening now alright, love, so you'd better get used to it. And this money has turned up at exactly the right time, hasn't it? It's a godsend, Joe. There'll be a lot of extra expense with the baby and we're never going to be able to make the mortgage repayments on dole money, are we?" She paused. "Even if you get another factory job, the money's poor and you hate being stuck inside and chained to a machine."

Joe nodded. "I though the money would be welcome myself and that's before I knew you were pregnant. We'll need to buy a pram and clothes and a cot and playpen and …"

"Take it easy, love. The baby won't be here for a while yet and you know what you're like. You'll worry yourself sick about everything. Just relax, try to take it easy and remember we don't have to worry about money now."

26

Back at the hotel the Germans considered their next move. Hans had totally discounted the driver, he was in the clear and they now had two avenues of investigation to follow and Hans decided they would take one each in order to multiply their chances of success. Hans would find the allotments and check out Alan Spencer and Nobby's pigeon loft, while Ernst visited Nobby's address.

George puffed contentedly on his foul-smelling pipe as he busied himself putting together material for the local history book. He'd written down memories of his schooldays in longhand and hoped they would be good enough to be included. The book was a local history project and all members of the group had been asked to submit suitable material. He'd included pieces about his school friends, his not so fond memories of school and of what he recollected about the area at the time, buildings, industry and social conditions. He had done a fair bit of research into his family history and this had in turn led to an interest in local history. Some of his recollections, although interesting to him, would not, he knew, be suitable and he was busy deciding which to remove, when the doorbell rang. He put down his pipe and opened the door and was surprised to see his estranged wife, Violet, standing on the doorstep.

"Hello, and to what do I owe this honour?" he asked sarcastically, looking up and down the street. "You come back for the family silver, have you?"

Violet followed him into the house, closing the door behind her.

"That your boyfriend out there in the car, is it?"

"Yes, George it is. Look, I don't want any arguments or shouting matches, okay. I just need you to sign these papers." She pulled an envelope from her handbag and removed some papers.

"He looks a bit young for you, Vi. He your toy boy is he? You'll get done for child snatching, you will, if you're not careful."

"Just sign the papers please, George. That's all I want from you."

He took the papers from her hand and quickly scanned the top one. "You want a divorce, that it?" he said, shocked.

She nodded.

"This is a bit sudden isn't it? Don't you want to wait a while and see how things work out?"

"It's been seven months, for Christ's sake. How long do you expect me to wait?"

George sat down, as if his legs had suddenly gone weak. "Do you want a cup of tea?"

"No, George, I just want you to sign the papers."

George stared down at the forms blankly, his eyes glazed but his mind racing. "Look, Vi, I know we had a blazing big argument and you walked out in a huff, but I wasn't expecting this."

She sat down opposite him. "Just what did you expect, then, George? You didn't come after me or try to find me in the seven months since I walked out, did you? And some of the things you said were absolutely terrible. How could you say that I never did any housework or cleaning, was always out at the club or at the bingo, didn't cook or wash for you etc, etc?"

"I know I shouldn't have said all that. I didn't mean it. I was annoyed, that's all, mad 'cos you'd gone and got a full time job, were out all day and my meal wasn't ready when I came in."

"Have you any idea what it was like for me being stuck in here all day without anyone to talk to? I was going mad in here on my own. Since the girls left home last year the place had been as quiet as the grave. I'd been going slowly barmy on my own in here."

"I miss the girls as well."

"But you were out at work all day, weren't you, and not stuck in here on your own?"

"There's letters on the mantlepiece from both of them. Heather has settled in at university and Denise loves working in London."

She remained silent, she'd written to both her daughters and they were writing to her at her new address.

"It wasn't really about my tea not being ready. I was upset, worried about a lot of things and … and …"

"And what, George?"

"And I just heard the rumour about the yard going to close and was upset. As it happens it turns out the rumour was right."

"So you took it out on me?"

George nodded. "I'm sorry, Vi. Look, I've found out just how much you do, did, in here since I've had to do it all myself. I didn't realise how much work was involved in running a home and doing a full-time job as well, that's a fact."

"Well, you've certainly learned the hard way, George, so maybe you'll appreciate and treat your new woman a bit better."

"I don't want any new woman, Vi. I just want you to come home, here where you belong."

"It's too late, George. Much too little, much too late. And it wasn't just what you said that night. We'd been going downhill for ages. You never talked to me, I'd sit here night after night and all you wanted to talk about was the yard, the allotment, football or your local history. Hardly riveting conversation was it? When we went out it was nearly always to the club where we'd sit with your mates and their wives and talk about what? The yard, the allotments, football, local history." She paused and shook her head in frustration. "Don't get me wrong, I like the other wives, but I didn't want to see them every bloody time we went out." She paused again and took a deep breath. "Look, I still want you to sign those papers so I can get things moving. Are you going to sign them or what?"

George signed the papers with a heavy heart.

27

Ernst, his senses still somewhat befuddled by the cannabis he had smoked earlier, finally found Nobby's house. It had proved hard to locate simply because there were no street names visible on the estate, their having been removed to confuse unwanted visitors and almost every visitor was unwelcome on this estate. Almost all the door numbers had also been removed by the residents. Everybody in the area distrusted men who came around asking questions about local people. Especially big, hard-looking, muscular men, with foreign accents. Nobby's immediate family was large and his extended family huge. He had eight brothers and four sisters and most of them were still at home, either because they were still young, were single mothers, or had married, separated and returned to the nest, bringing their own brood of children with them. The family lived in three adjoining council houses on the Westwood estate. They'd originally lived some distance apart, but gradually the neighbours in between them had moved out, or moved on, glad to get away from the street and the unruly family.

The German arrived in a taxi, which dropped him off at the entrance to the estate, the driver refusing to enter any further into the litter-strewn streets. Ernst walked to the house he'd been directed to by the taxi driver and stared in amazement at the display of discarded furniture and dismantled and burnt-out cars that occupied what were nominally supposed to be the front gardens of the houses. Half-naked children ran shouting and screaming toward him from the open front doors of the dwellings, demanding money and clinging onto his coat.

He reached Nobby's house and pushed past the garden gate that was leaning against the decrepit wooden fence. A large dog, shackled to the fence, snarled at him from the maximum extent of its chain, which was just short of the path. At the door to meet him was Nobby's mother, Nelly. Nelly was well known in the area for her raucous voice and fiery temperament. Nobody who knew, or had heard of her fearsome reputation would ever even consider crossing Nelly, as she was a real terror. Unfortunately Ernst didn't know this and even if he had, it is unlikely that he would have been impressed. His past history included some really nasty violent encounters and it is doubtful that he would have considered Nelly much of an opponent. This was a mistake.

"Aye? And just what do you want?" Nelly demanded as Ernst reached the front door.

"I'm looking for Mr Norbert Nordstrom," Ernst said in his thick German accent.

"And wae's asking?" Nelly asked, looking at the muscular visitor with suspicion.

Ernst ignored the question, mainly because he couldn't understand it, and persevered. "Norbert Nordstrom," he pronounced slowly, as if speaking to an idiot.

The woman looked at him silently as if trying to read his mind.

"Nobby?" he tried again.

"He doesn't live here, hinny," Nelly replied before the man had stopped speaking.

"Hinny?" Ernst repeated, looking puzzled. "No, not hinny, Nobby. Ja?"

"Yar? What're ye on aboot, man?"

"Norbert. I wish to speak to him, ja?"

"I've told you. There's nae Norbert here and nae yars, so get yersel away oot of it afor I set the dogs on ye, yar?"

Ernst looked at Nelly, more puzzled than ever. He was rapidly losing his patience, couldn't understand most of what the woman was saying and was getting nowhere. A dark thought was born in his mind. He decided to try his powers of communication and persuasion once again. "Look, Mrs …"

There was no response from the woman.

"Is it Nordstrom? Mrs Nordstrom?" Ernst persevered.

"It might be and then again it might not be," Nelly maintained. "Which Mrs Nordstrom do you want anyway?"

"Er, how many are there here?" Ernst asked shortly, becoming angrier and hopelessly lost in a tangle of unanswered questions.

"Here? Now? Let's see, there's Natalie and Nigella …" she continued to tick off the remainder of the names silently on her fingers until she'd filled one hand entirely. "At this minute there's five here and then there's me, that makes six," she announced triumphantly.

Ernst struggled to control his temper and tried yet again. "It is Norbert's mother that I am looking for, if Norbert isn't here, that is."

"That is, that is, what?" the sixth Mrs Nordstrom asked.

"If he's not here," Ernst said, almost totally exasperated.

"Wae's not here?"

"Norbert." The big German's temper exploded now. His suspicions confirmed. The woman was making a fool out of him and he didn't like it at all. He stepped to the door which was entirely blocked by Nelly, shoved her roughly out of the way; and walked inside and into the house. He entered the sitting room, which was so full of cigarette smoke that it caught in the back of his throat. A layer of thick smog hung across the airless room at about waist height, just about at the level of the heads of the seated occupants, who were watching television. The curtains were drawn, covering the windows, blocking any light, presumably to increase the television's visibility. The room smelled strongly of years of cigarette smoke, damp nappies and takeaway food. Evidence of the cigarettes and the food littered the floor and cigarette ash covered the carpet areas around the seated occupants of the room.

As Ernst entered the house, Nelly pulled herself up from the floor where she'd been pushed and launched herself at the intruder's back. She screamed like a banshee and grabbed him around the neck. The others occupants of the dimly lit room came to life at her scream and they also launched themselves at the intruder. The German, although much bigger and stronger than the women, was soon overwhelmed by their sheer numbers. The women used their nails and teeth, combs, ashtrays and vases, anything that they could get a hold of quickly to attack the man. After a few initial wild swings at his attackers, Ernst was overwhelmed by the onslaught, slipped on something wet and went down, face first on the not-too-clean floor. The women were merciless, punching, scratching and stabbing at their victim with anything at hand. He was hit on the back of the head by a heavy, blunt object. Two tormentors were now perched onto his back, weighing him down, their hands around his neck and interfering with his breathing. He shrugged his shoulders and pushed backwards, hitting one of his attackers on the door frame. She screamed and let go her grip, but was quickly replaced by another and equally determined Mrs Nordstrom. In addition to the women, a number of dogs had also appeared from somewhere and sank their teeth into any part of the man's anatomy that they could reach. He was badly bitten on his ankles, thighs and one enterprising dog, or it might have been one of the women, bit him in the groin. In complete agony, pain shooting through various parts of his body, he knew instinctively that if he didn't get up he'd be done for. In desperation he managed to force himself halfway to his feet, punching right and left. He pulled a large, eight-inch blade hunting knife from a sheath on his belt. He stabbed at Nelly's legs, which were wrapped around his waist as she was still clinging determinedly to his neck and hanging onto his back. She screamed in agony and fell to the floor, blood streaming from her wounds. Slashing at his tormentors indiscriminately, Ernst forced them back into the room as he made for the front door and away from the house. He was halfway up the street before he could shake off the following dogs. He hobbled his way out of the estate and back to civilisation. He'd have to report his failure to that prick, Hans, who wouldn't be happy at all. Ernst shook his head. This had started out as just another job, but now it was personal. He'd make sure that this Nobby paid for what had happened.

28

The pub was crowded and the ocularly challenged barmaid kept very busy, as was her wayward eye, which seemed to have a mind of its own. The growing band of criminal conspirators, now numbering four, met in the pub at lunchtime, where they were going to discuss their options in the lounge.

Joe, as proud as punch, gave the others the news about Brenda being pregnant and told them he was definitely in. He seemed to grow in stature as he accepted their congratulatory handshakes and backslaps.

The men stood at the highly polished pub counter. Alan paid for the pints and shook his head as he counted his change as they took their seats in the corner furthest from the bar where they wouldn't be overheard. "We'd better enjoy these pints, lads, because they're liquid gold."

"Paying for the new carpet, aren't we? The brewery has to get its money back, you know," George said. He took a long swallow of his beer. "Never mind, we can afford it now. Come on then, Alan, what's the plan?"

Talking quickly and quietly, Alan outlined his plan. "I don't need to tell you that we are in a unique position. We've got an absolute embarrassment of riches, so to speak."

The others nodded their heads in silent agreement.

"So, what I suggest is to get information from someone who knows all about finance and investment and stuff and let him do all the financial stuff for us."

The listeners were all ears and remained silent, waiting for him to finish.

"So think now, who do we know we can trust, and is in a position to get us expert financial advice?" He looked at the others expectantly.

They looked back at him blankly.

"Come on, think." Alan said. "Someone we know and trust and is in financial services?"

Still a row of blank, uncomprehending stares.

"Alright, I'll tell you – Trev."

"Trev?"

"Yes, Trev. He's in insurance isn't he? And they do all that investment stuff, don't they?"

"But he's only been doing it for a few weeks; he doesn't know anything about investments. He's still training."

"I know that, but he works with financial advisors, doesn't he, and can get us the info?"

This information was slowly absorbed by the others.

"Well I'll be. It should be a piece of piss for him, then." George said.

"Exactly," Alan replied. "It will be."

"It's going to be even easier than we thought. Trev will be able to sort all the cash out and we'll all be in clover," George said. "It sounds good to me."

Despite George's enthusiasm the others weren't so sure and asked a number of pertinent questions, which Alan answered glibly.

"It means another share if we bring Trev in, that's the only problem," Alan pointed out.

"Well, then we'll just have to manage on a million or so each, then," Joe said. "How will we ever manage on just that, eh?"

The men discussed the plan for the next fifteen minutes and none was particularly concerned by the possibility of another partner.

Alan said he had to go and see a man about a pigeon, drank his remaining lager and left.

They watched Alan leave and Nobby got up to buy more drinks.

"What do you think, Joe?" George asked, as he produced his pipe and baccy tin.

"I don't know. The way Alan talks it's as easy as falling off a log, but it can't be that easy, man, can it? And, he's not exactly a master criminal, is he? He's not long out of prison, for God's sake."

George nodded as if his friend had mirrored his own thoughts. "But there's not much else we can do, is there? What are you going to do with your money? You really going to book a cruise?"

"Yes, I am. I'm going to book a Mediterranean cruise on one of those big luxury liners, like I told you. First class all the way. I'll have all those waiters running around after me and Brenda all day and all night," Joe said.

"Cruises are very expensive, aren't they?" George asked, as he painstakingly filled the pipe.

"Yes. Those trips cost an arm and a leg, but what the hell, man." He paused. "You think about it for a while. When did you ever think that you'd have this much money? I'll tell you, never, mate. That's when. Why don't you just say that you'll come?"

George seemed to consider this point. "So, when are you booking it?"

"As soon as I can. I'll book a cabin with a balcony. Ocean views from our bed, that's what the brochure said. Fancy that. Sitting up in bed, eating your breakfast and watching dolphins and stuff swimming past outside in the sea. Marvellous, eh?" Joe stopped speaking and had a faraway look in his eyes, probably imagining what it would be like. "That'd be great wouldn't it?" he enthused, becoming more enamoured by the thought of the cruise, and infected by his own enthusiasm. He was already imagining himself on board, swanking about like King Dick, surrounded by waiters and attendants as he made his way regally from deck to deck as the ship sailed into the sunset.

George, seemingly, was also enchanted by the image that his friend had conjured up. "That'd be really something. Violet would really be impressed by something like that, she would," he said wistfully, putting a lighted match to the full pipe bowl.

"What are you going to do now that you don't have to work?" Joe asked, changing the subject.

"That's a good question, mate. I've not given it any thought at all. What about you?"

"I don't know. I haven't thought about it either."

"You know what you could do, now you've got plenty of time and money?" George said as he puffed on the pipe, drawing in and then expelling pungent smoke from his mouth.

"No. What?"

"Join the Samaritans." He dropped the extinguished match into an ash tray.

"The Samaritans, you're joking?"

"No I'm not joking. You're a natural. You've always got time to listen to people's problems and will go out of your way to help anybody, it's your nature. You'd be good at it. Really you should consider it; they always want volunteers to man the phones."

"Well, I don't know, but I might have a word with Brenda about it."

29

Hans walked slowly up to the brightly painted fence around the pigeon cree. This had to be the one; it was exactly as described by the Up North Combine secretary. It was the most garishly coloured, and stood out from its neighbours on account of having the words Elvis The King spelled out in foot-high, gold-coloured wooden letters on the roof. There was no one here now and they might have to come back later to find Nobby. Hans studied the position of the cree with professional interest. The place wouldn't be easy to stake out. It was accessible from a number of directions, too many for only two men to observe. There wasn't anywhere to park a car without it being immediately noticeable and nowhere else to watch from cover. The cree was near the allotments and easily visible to anyone in any of the gardens. Hans, having already spoken to a number of the allotment holders, had learned they were highly suspicious of strangers and totally uncommunicative when questioned about Nobby or Alan Spencer.

30

It was raining heavily. Joe and Alan were cosily ensconced in the allotment shed, finding space wherever they could amongst the boxes. The windows had steamed up and the lads were sipping piping hot, freshly brewed tea. After a lot of argument they had finally agreed to approach Trev and ask for his help in contacting a financial advisor and had invited him to the allotment.

Trev arrived over an hour late and refused a seat, saying he preferred to stand.

"Where you been, then, we've been waiting ages for you?" Alan asked impatiently.

"Is there a problem, Trev," Joe asked quietly, knowing instinctively there was something wrong.

Trev looked sheepish. "I know I'm late, sorry, lads, but I had to go to the doctor's."

"What's wrong? You ill?" Joe asked with concern.

Trev smiled wanly. "No, I'm alright. It's just ..." He looked even more sheepish.

"Come on then, out with it. What's up?" Alan demanded.

"Well, you know that lass I've been seeing on the debit?"

"Aye, Ginger something or other's her name isn't it? The whole estate knows you're shagging her," Alan said eagerly. "What about her?"

"Well, she's, how can I put it? She's very energetic and adventurous in bed, you know?"

"No. I don't know. Come on let's have all the sordid details," Alan demanded.

"Well, last night she was giving me a blow job–"

"That'll be stripping paint with a blow torch, Joe," Alan interrupted. They all laughed. "Come on then, Trev, let's have the rest," Alan said.

"–and when I got to the vinegar stroke, she sort of …" he hesitated again.

"Come on for God's sake. What did she do then?"

Trev was silent for a few seconds, looking more sheepish than ever. Finally he spoke. "Then, just as I was coming, she stuck her finger up my backside," he said quickly, as if to get it over with.

Joe and Alan exploded with delight. They laughed loudly and Trev's embarrassed expression only made them laugh all the more. Finally most the merriment subsided, much to Trev's satisfaction.

"Bit of a surprise for you, then, Trev," Alan said, still laughing quietly.

"You could say that," Trev said, not amused.

"You enjoy it, did you?" Alan asked slyly.

"Well, it certainly was an eye opener and that's a fact."

"So why have you been to the doc's, then?" Joe asked, wiping the tears from his eyes with a handkerchief.

"You've never caught something off her, have you?" Alan asked.

"No, I haven't caught anything off her. I've been to the doc's because she caught my hole with her fingernail and I'm bleeding."

The laughter exploded again. Trev looked on resignedly as the pair doubled up in mirth, tears streaming down their faces. It took a few minutes before they finally began to gain control again.

"And before you ask, no the doctor hasn't given me a bandage to stick up my arse, or a sling, or a big fucking sticking plaster to put on it," Trev said wearily, pre-empting what he assumed would be their next comments. This set them off laughing again.

Joe recovered his composure first. "I'm really sorry, Trev," he managed to say without laughing. "Seriously, was there anything he could give you for that, then?"

Trev shook his head. "No. The doc said it's an anal fissure, and it should heal up on its own. It was just seeing the blood this morning, in the toilet bowl. It gave me a right shock."

Joe was instantly sympathetic. "I suppose it would be a shock," he hesitated, "is that why you don't want to sit down?"

Trev nodded warily, half-expecting them to explode with laughter again. "It is a bit sore."

"Brenda's pregnant," Joe said, changing the subject so as to spare Trev any more embarrassment and because he was unable to hold his good news any longer.

"Congratulations, mate." Trev shook Joe's hand. "Well done. You must be cock-a-hoop?"

"Thanks, Trev. I am really pleased."

"Okay then, Trev, you just stand while I tell you why we wanted to talk to you," Alan said, now completely serious again, and went on to explain a version of the situation.

Trev listened intently and was, of course, very suspicious. "Let's get this right in my mind. You two and George have won a fair bit of money on the pools and want me to get some advice about investment for you?"

"That's right, Trev," Alan agreed. "You've got it in one."

"You've kept that very quiet, haven't you?"

"Well, you know how it is, Trev. It was only last week and we didn't want everybody to know."

Trev nodded his understanding, but was hurt that they hadn't considered him trustworthy enough to be entrusted with the information. "So how much have you lucky bastards won?"

"Over a hundred thousand pounds," Alan said quickly.

Trev gave a low whistle and then stared silently at the trio for a full minute. "Why didn't the pools company offer you expert financial investment advice? They do that with all big winners," he asked suspiciously.

"Er, they did, but I didn't want them knowing our business," Alan put in before George could speak. "We'll make it worth your while; see you alright, of course."

Trev nodded slowly, but obviously wasn't convinced. "Okay. I'll set up a meeting with the company's investment expert. When would be convenient for him to meet you lads?"

The pair exchanged panicky glances. "Er, the thing is, Trev, we were hoping that you could do it all for us. Sort everything out so that we wouldn't have to see the advisor or anybody."

"Well, first of all, I'm not yet fully trained, qualified or authorised to give advice on investments. There are all sorts of rules about investing money now. So I'll have to do it though a financial advisor. And you'll have to see him. Otherwise how can he invest the money for you? He'll need your details and have to either set up joint investments of some sort, or invest the money separately for each of you. He'll need to assess your individual risk levels." Trev thought for a moment. "And of course you'll have to sign either joint cheques, or three single ones for him. Where is this hundred grand at the moment, which bank?"

His query was met with stony silence.

Alan licked his lips anxiously. "Look, Trev, the thing is that it's in cash."

"What?"

"It's in cash," Alan confirmed.

"But why? Why isn't it in the bank? What are you doing with it all in cash?"

Silence.

"The thing is, Trev …"

Trev snapped his fingers. "Got it. The money isn't from a pools win, is it? You've been up to no good again, haven't you? And hit the big time for once and no mistake. A hundred grand. Phew!" Trev smiled. He was relieved that the secret pools win had been a ploy, he'd really been put out to think that they hadn't trusted him with that but he could live quite happily with being out of the loop on this criminality.

The pair looked at him in silence.

"I'm right, aren't I; you've got this money illegally?"

Alan nodded. "Look, Trev, if you help us out with this little problem, we'll look after you, see you all right for money."

Trev nodded. "Why don't you just put the money on the horses? Each of you can go to different betting shops and back the favourites, or the possible winners in every race. Chances are that you'll lose a bit, but the ones you win should compensate for that and with a little bit of luck you'll even make a profit. Then you've got legit money from a legit source."

"The thing is, Trev, when I said we had over a hundred grand, I meant a fair bit over a hundred grand."

"Exactly how much over?"

"Five million."

"Five million? Fucking pounds?"

The pair nodded in unison. "We'll give you an equal share."

A sudden thought struck Trev. "George, he's in, right?"

"Yes."

"Nobby?"

"Naturally."

"Anyone else?"

"That's it. With you, there are five of us. It means we'll all get around a million pounds each." He paused, guessing what the next question would be. "The only problem is likely to be George, you know how he is, he's always on the drink since his wife left him and we're frightened of him opening his mouth when he's drunk."

"Wait a minute. I can understand Alan and Nobby doing this, and George at a push, but how come you're in as well, Joe?" Trev asked incredulously.

"He found out afterwards that the cash was at the allotment and had to come in with me and Nobby. Same with George. No choice really," Alan explained.

"Does Brenda know about this?" Trev asked Joe.

"Yes she knows and is all for it. She's thinking of the bairn now and anyway, she's sick of living hand to mouth all the time," Joe said.

"I could do an awful lot with that much money," Trev said wistfully.

"Well, why don't you take the chance?"

"Well, I don't know." Trev rubbed his chin ruminatively. "Where'd the money come from? Who does it belong to? Where is it now?"

Alan quickly gave him all the details.

Trev listened quietly and then shook his head. "It's too much of a risk for me. I don't want to hear any more about it about it."

"Just listen to me for a minute, mate," Alan came back aggressively. "This is money for absolutely nothing. It's a once in a lifetime opportunity that you can't pass up. It'll solve all your money worries for the rest of your life. You'll be able to buy anything, everything you've always wanted. Clothes, a nice big house, flash car, holidays in the sun. Why, man, you could even buy a house abroad. Just imagine that, anything you or they want. Just think. What would that make you feel like, eh?"

"This is going to change all our lives. It's big. Very big and the best part about it is that it can't be reported to the police because it's funny money," Joe put in.

"What do you mean funny money? Is it counterfeited then, or what?"

"No nothing like that. It's just that it's money that shouldn't be here. It's illegal and can't be traced or reported stolen."

"I still don't think it's a good idea," Trev said, reinforcing his opinion by shaking his head negatively. "Even if it's as easy as you say it will be there's still got to be a chance of us ending up inside and I'm not prepared to risk that."

Alan gave Joe a 'told you so' look. "Bollocks, it'll not come to that, no way. We'll get away scot free and ride off into the sunset and live happily ever after."

"So you say." Trev obviously wasn't convinced by Alan's rhetoric.

"But I'm right. It's a doddle, man. It's a chance in a lifetime and we'd be idiots not to take it with both bloody hands. These opportunities don't come along every five minutes, you know. And, when they do, you've got to be ready to grab them, because the chances are you won't ever get another chance."

"Anyway, I can't see how we can possibly walk away from this with a fortune and there be no comebacks. Somebody somewhere is going to be very, very upset at losing all that money and is going to come after us, sure as night follows day. Either that, or word will get out, someone will find out and the police will become involved and track us down," Trev said.

Alan shook his head dismissively. "Won't happen, mate, believe me." He held up his right hand, index finger raised. "First off, the money shouldn't be here at all. It's illegal and smuggled into the country to be laundered and probably to buy contraband goods, got to be. So, there'll be no hue and cry about it being stolen." His middle finger went up to join the index. "Secondly, whoever the money belongs to, they'll not want any attention drawn to them because of this. Apart from the fact that they'll lose considerable street credibility, you know, lose face with their associates, they're bound to have numerous other dodgy business interests and certainly won't want any big searchlight shining on them." His ring finger joined the other two. "And thirdly, although this will be an awful lot of money to us, to them it'll be a mere drop in the ocean. They'll probably not even miss it too much and certainly won't go out of their way to cause trouble and spend more money, incur more expense trying to recover it. It just won't be worth their while."

"He's right," Joe said. "The chances of us getting caught are very low. We'll walk away with enough for each of us to live comfortably for the rest of our lives, without worrying about the gaffer being on our backs and being ordered to do this, or do that. We'll be able to please ourselves, man. Just think what that would be like, eh? No more shite from the boss and enough money so we don't have to worry about bills again."

"We'll be okay as long as that baldy, drunken, old git keeps his big mouth shut," Alan said.

There was a sudden noise outside and they all turned towards the door. The shed door opened and George put his head around the doorjamb. "Is it alright for me to come in?"

The men looked at each other, each thinking the same thought. How long had the newcomer been outside the door and how much had he overheard?

"Aye, come in, George," Joe said, getting up. "Get yourself a seat and I'll put the kettle on again. That's all we seem to do, make and drink tea."

"Oh, I wouldn't say that. It sounded like you were all pretty busy in here as I turned up," George said, sitting down and making himself as comfortable as the old sofa would allow.

"What do you mean?" Alan asked sharply.

"Oh, nothing really. It's just that I couldn't help but overhear a few snatches of your conversation as I approached the shed, purely accidentally, mind." He looked around at the faces watching him. "Some of it sounded very interesting, very interesting indeed."

"And what bits would they be, then?" Trev asked.

"So, you have agreed to come in as well, Trev? Well, why not? The more the merrier, that's what I say. All that easy money, there's more than enough to go round. Plenty for all. And we can all do with it, can't we? What bits did I overhear you ask? Oh, you know, the bits about me shouting my mouth off when I'm drunk, they're the bits I'm interested in."

Alan brought the steaming mugs of tea across on a metal tray. "You must have misheard, mate. We weren't talking about you, we were just talking about the money and what needs doing. The lads here were offering to give me a hand." He looked at Trev and Joe. "Isn't that right, lads?"

They both nodded.

"I think I must have misheard, then," George said.

Did you explain to Trev here how easy it was going to be and there being no chance of it being reported to the police, unless some drunken, big-mouthed idiot lets the cat out of the bag?"

None of them replied.

"Look, George–" Alan started, but was interrupted by George.

"You don't have to explain to me, mate. You think that I'm a liability. You think I'm a drunken old bastard who can't keep his mouth shut. Well, I do like a drink, there's no denying that, and I wouldn't try to deny it, but as far as keeping my mouth shut, I'm like the secret service, drunk or sober. You can rely on me absolutely and that's a fact."

His audience stared silently at George. What he had just said had thrown them in a number of ways. It had become obvious to them that he must have overheard a good part of their conversation whether they liked it or not. And what he'd said made sense and they knew that he could be trusted, as long as he stayed off the drink.

"You'll be fine as long as you stay sober. We've asked Trev here for some financial advice, him being in that type of work and he's going to sort it for us. So he's in for a full share, okay?" Alan said.

"Right, okay then, Trev, you're in." George said, putting out his hand to shake Trev's.

Trev hesitated for a second and then nodded, smiled, and shook George's hand.

They each agreed to take a thousand pounds for initial spending money, but promised to be careful and not splash it around and attract unwanted attention.

Trev accepted the windfall with a reluctance that surprised him. He'd have thought that a bonus of this magnitude would have made him deliriously happy, but there was a deep sense of unease lodged in the pit of his stomach. There was no doubting that the full share he'd been promised would come in very, very handy, but it could also prove to be very dangerous. His first instinct was to contact the financial advisor he worked with at Capital Growth, his employers, but on reflection he decided to contact someone working for another company. He didn't want unwelcome questions being asked at work. It never occurred to him that work should now be the last of his concerns. He finally decided on an independent financial advisor who wasn't tied to any one particular investment company, calculating that he would be offered the best possible range of products that way.

31

The financial advisor looked puzzled and lit a cigarette. "Let me get this straight in my mind. You've got a fair bit of cash to invest, is that right?"

"That's right," affirmed Trev, shifting in the chair, his behind still sore. He wanted to find out how it was done before revealing exactly how much he had to invest.

The advisor looked pleased. "Right then, I can certainly help you with your choice of investments, but first I just need to fill in a couple of forms." He began to rummage though a pile of official looking papers in his briefcase.

Trev started to get concerned. "Er, look, I don't want to have to fill in any forms or anything."

"Don't worry. You won't have to. I'll complete all the paperwork; all you'll have to do is to sign them."

"Well. I suppose that'll be alright," Trev said reluctantly.

The advisor produced a number of A4-sized forms and placed them on his briefcase, which was perched on his knee. Taking a ballpoint pen from an inside pocket, he clicked the top and poised it over the forms. "Right then. What's your full name?"

Trev was asked his full name, his address, date of birth, details of his health and was urged to reveal information that he'd no intention of revealing. When he realised what was happening, he made up a lot of the details.

"Do you have a bank account?" the advisor repeated.

"Look, what's with all these questions? All I want to do is to invest some money with you, that's all. Why do you need all this information? It's me giving you my money, not the other way about," Trev complained.

"That's very true, Trevor, but unfortunately, I've got to take all this information. It's a main requirement of the 1986 Financial Services Act. Just been implemented this year it has, made a big difference to my job, I can tell you. I've got two hundred percent more paperwork now than I used to have. It's a nightmare, believe me."

Trev knew that the new rules had recently come into force, but wasn't sure of the exact details. "But I don't want to give you all this information. I just want to invest my money," Trev maintained.

"I'm afraid it's the law now. You see the information helps me decide what is the best advice for me to give you."

"But I've already told you, I don't want any advice, I just want to invest the money."

"Well, I could do an execution only. That means that I don't give you any information or advice on your investment at all, you tell me exactly what you want to do with your money. But to do that, you'll have to know already exactly what type of investment you wish to make. For instance, do you want to put the money straight onto the stock market? If so what shares do you want to buy? Or do you want to put some of the money into a fixed-term, guaranteed bond? If so, which one? Or what about putting some into a cash deposit scheme, government bonds, bank bonds, or investing in works of art, precious stones …?"

"Wait a minute," Trev protested. "You're getting me all confused."

"It is a very complicated subject, Trevor. That's why I need all that information, so I can advise you correctly. If you're a very cautious person regarding investment, then I'd be wrong to suggest something like stocks and shares to you, because they can sometimes be a very risky investment."

"Is there no way that I can just invest the money somewhere safe, where it can't be got at, or lost and I can get a good return on it?"

"Of course there is. But you'll have to tell me where you want me to invest it for you and I'll do it, no problem. But if I need to offer you any information or advice at all, then I need that personal information first."

Trev nodded, beginning to understand that his suspicions weren't unfounded. "Right then. So if I say to you, I want to put the money into that, that and that, then that's okay? But if I say to you, what do you think of me putting money into that, then you need all that info before you can tell me, is that right?"

"Spot on. That's exactly right."

Trev thought for a monument. This was the exact opposite of what he wanted. He needed advice about where to invest the cash and to get that he was going to have to reveal a lot of personal details. "I'll need to rethink this. I'll have to select some investments myself and then come back and tell you, and give you the money, so you can invest it for me."

"Then there's the Money Laundering rules to take into account," the advisor said quietly.

"The what rules?" Trev asked.

"Money laundering rules. That's another new law that's just come into force. Any amount of money over a certain amount that's invested has to be accounted for. Where it came from, that sort of thing. You said earlier that you wanted to invest all your money in cash, didn't you? So I'll have to record where it came from. It's designed to stop criminals legitimising money made from illegal operations by passing it through insurance companies and the like." He paused. "Criminals will still find a way around it, of course."

"How will they be able to do that?" Trev asked.

"Simple. All they've got to do is to buy goods and then sell them again for cash. Bingo, the money from the sale is then as clean as a whistle. By the way, how much cash do you actually want to invest?"

"How much is the limit before all these rules kick in?"

"Ten thousand pounds."

"That's a coincidence, that's exactly how much I've got, but what about if I had a cheque instead of cash?"

"That'd be fine. A cheque hasn't got any limit," the advisor said starting to complete the forms. "That's because they can trace it back to you. They know that all your details are correct because the bank makes all the enquiries and checks on you when you open the account. That's why you need references and everything when you open an account."

Trev's suspicions were now fully confirmed. He realised there was no way they could invest any sizable amount of cash anywhere without unwanted questions about the money's origin being asked. He answered all the remaining questions evasively and vaguely, none of them truthfully. What he'd hoped would be a simple procedure had turned into a bureaucratic nightmare. It seemed that there was no way he could get the bulk of the money invested in any sort of legitimate way without answering all sorts of tricky questions and having to account for obtaining his money. Cash seemed to be a curse rather than a blessing. It was untraceable, but it certainly wasn't unaccountable.

The advisor filled in lots of forms and asked Trev to hand over the ten grand in cash. Trev knew the advisor thought he had just made a good-sized commission, no doubt had achieved his weekly target in one fell swoop and thought he could now have tomorrow off to go shopping with his wife. Trev was almost sorry to disappoint him, telling him he'd think it over and would phone him when he'd made his decision. The financial advisor was very unhappy and tried all ways to get Trev to sign the papers then and there, and cough up the cash, but was eventually forced to give up and leave.

Alan's mind, despite his outward appearance, was in turmoil. He'd dreamed all his life about pulling off the one really big job that would set him up for life and now he'd actually done it. Trouble was, he hadn't a clue as to what to do with the money. He hadn't even planned or thought about what he was going to do with the money he expected to get for the VCRs and now was totally flummoxed by the unbelievable amount they had actually stolen. He spent a lot of time wondering about the best place to put his money, but never actually did anything with it for weeks. He stuffed the bag containing his spending money in the bottom of a cupboard and left it there.

Nobby was in a dream state. He couldn't grasp the magnitude of what had happened and didn't seem to understand how much money he had, and hadn't a clue what to do with his share. He thought ten thousand pounds was a fortune and his mind just wouldn't expand to take in the actual amount. He took three hundred pounds from the bag that held his money and put it in his pocket in case he saw something that he might like to buy, but the money was still there a week later, unspent. He wandered through the shops looking at the electrical goods, clothes, jewellery and everything else for retail purchases, but couldn't make up his mind what he wanted to buy. He had a vague idea that he should be having a grand old time, living high on the hog and partying, whatever that was, but he couldn't, for the life of him, decide where to start, or even what he was supposed to do to enjoy himself. He'd only ever really had a good time and enjoyed himself while being with his mates. He'd just decided that he'd go and find Trev or Alan and ask them what he should be doing with the money, when he met Norma.

Norma wasn't the type of girl who would normally be seen dead with Nobby or anyone even remotely like him, or so Nobby thought. After all, she was a good five years older than him and almost certainly a lot more experienced with the opposite sex than he was, as his experience with females was absolutely non-existent. When he first saw her he was convinced that she'd target men who looked like up-and-coming executives, wore expensive aftershave, dressed stylishly and drove shiny big, new cars. But there was something about Nobby that she was she was immensely impressed by. It wasn't his charm, personality or eloquence; it was his dress sense. She, like him, was a fanatical Elvis fan, and she was absolutely taken with his hair, studded leather jacket, with 'Elvis' emblazoned on the back, his drainpipe jeans and beetle-crusher shoes.

They met in the electrical department of a big store in the city centre, where she worked. He was wandering around aimlessly looking for something that he might like to buy, when a brand new video recorder caught his eye. He knew that his mother had said she'd like one, and Norman, one of his brothers had tried to nick one for her from the local social club last week. Even Nobby thought that Norman was thick, and his brother had proved it yet again by making a right hash of the break-in and getting caught.

Now Nobby had finally found something he wanted to buy. Something useful that would please his mum and the rest of the family, and show them what a good son and a clever person he was. Norma happily explained the operational intricacies of the apparatus, which naturally went right over Nobby's head, but he simply nodded and smiled anyway, enchanted by Norma's presence, perfume, smile and voice. He bought the video with cash and, his heart palpitating, asked her out. She agreed and Nobby went home in an ecstatic frame of mind.

On their first date they got on famously, not surprisingly as they talked about what they both loved, Elvis's music and films.

They saw each other regularly after that first date and had a good time every time they met. She asked him how he had so much money, and seemed happy with his explanation that it was his redundancy payment. After they'd been out a few times, she invited Nobby back to her flat. From then on Nobby stayed there regularly and they were almost inseparable.

Norma was adamant that Nobby continue his Elvis impersonations and perform at the semi-final of the Supreme Leisure Ballroom competition. She couldn't believe he was considering pulling out. She boosted his confidence by telling him that he was the best Elvis impersonator she had ever seen, his height was immaterial and he shouldn't take any notice of the scoffers because they were only jealous.

Trev decided he wanted to give some of the money to his friend Mickey. He felt guilty having all that cash when he knew his friend was skint and needed money for his family. The problem was Mickey was a very proud and honest man and wouldn't entertain anything that was not legal. But eventually Trev figured out a story that his friend would probably accept, knowing full well that he wouldn't take any money if he suspected it was stolen. He decided he'd talk it over with the others

    The lads debated for a long time over how much to give to Mickey and how to explain it to him. They all knew that he would never accept anything he thought was illegal and so they had to come up with a story that he'd accept as genuine. The amount was also decided after a long and hard debate. Too much and it couldn't possibly come from a pools win, too little and it wouldn't be enough for him to live entirely independently. The figure of five thousand was considered by the majority of the lads to be about the right amount and so that was the figure Trev would offer him. The others had all agreed to contribute an equal part of their share to fund Mickey's, except Alan, who had disagreed with giving him anything at all. Trev had agreed to contribute Alan's share as well, so he was paying double what the others were, but that didn't bother him in the least, he would have gladly paid a lot more to see his friend financially secure.

32

Mickey stood in the warehouse and wiped the sweat from his brow. He'd worked there for three weeks now and hated every minute of it. He'd tried to convince himself of the advantages of working in such a dirty, dusty and dark place, but couldn't think of many. The only usefulness of the backbreaking mindless labour that the job entailed, apart from helping to provide for his wife and two children, was that it provided him with a good physical workout every single day. An ex amateur heavyweight boxer, he was still something of a keep-fit fanatic and coached youngsters in boxing and martial arts at the local parish boys' club. Some of the boys showed excellent potential and were winning competition bouts on a regular basis. He was proud of his contribution to the club and being able to help and advise the youngsters.

   Mickey, although he wouldn't admit it, even to himself, was afraid of finding a more mentally demanding job and being forced to develop new skills and work with new people. He had worked in the yards since leaving school, knew all the other yard workers, having been to school with a lot of them, and was uncomfortable about meeting new people. The warehouse job was dirty and heavy work, but at least he generally worked alone, there being only him and the foreman at the warehouse, and he wasn't asked to do anything intellectually demanding.

He plodded on with the countless, mind-numbing repetitive tasks he was given and never complained at all. All day, every day, he moved boxes. He unloaded them from lorries and stacked them in the warehouse and took from the warehouse onto other smaller lorries for delivery to local retail shops.

He was a giant of a man and well muscled, kept himself fit and in good physical condition, road, weight and ring training regularly. Even so he went home very tired every night, sometimes too tired even for his boxing, or martial arts training. He finally almost convinced himself that he was doing the best thing and the right thing. It was honest work, very taxing physically and the money was rubbish. He still saw Trev now and again, although he couldn't afford to go to the pub very often, but when he did, Trev was pleased to see him and always bought him drinks.

On one of these occasions Trev gave Mickey some good news. "You know that pools syndicate we had when we were at the yard?"

Mickey nodded.

"Well, it turns out that there was some money left over in the kitty. Not a lot, but enough to put the coupon on for a couple of months."

Mickey nodded, but his expression showed he obviously didn't understand what his friend was on about. "And?"

"And we only went and won, didn't we?"

"So?"

"Well, don't you see?"

"See what?"

"Part of that money was yours. You were in the yard syndicate weren't you?"

Mickey nodded again, still puzzled.

"Well, there you are then. You were in the yard syndicate and so you're also in this syndicate."

"Don't give me that old rubbish, Trev," Mickey said. "You started a new syndicate when the yard closed and I wasn't in the new one."

"No. You weren't. But you were definitely in the old one. The one we had at the yard, and that's the one that had money left over in the kitty."

"Okay. Give me my share of the syndicate kitty money. How much is it, fifty pence, a pound?"

"You don't get it yet, do you? We used that leftover money, which was part yours, to stake the first couple of months' coupons on the new syndicate."

"So?"

"So, that means that you are entitled to an equal share of the winnings."

"An equal share …"

"Yes. Dead right. An equal share of the winnings," Trev confirmed.

Mickey gave Trev a hard stare. "You're trying to give me some money from something I wouldn't want to get involved in, aren't you?"

"Mickey, the money has come from our pools win, nowhere else. Do you think that I would implicate you in something iffy? Would I?"

"No, I don't suppose you would, Trev," Mickey admitted.

"Too true, mate," Trev said, trying to keep the relief out of his voice. "Your share comes to five thousand pounds." He watched Mickey's face as the figure registered in his brain.

"Five thousand pounds," Mickey said slowly and quietly. "But that's a fortune, Trev."

"It sure is, mate. What are you going to do with all that, then, eh?"

Mickey sat open-mouthed, staring unseeingly straight ahead.

"You alright, mate?" Trev asked. "It is a lot, isn't it? But you'll get used to the idea, don't worry."

Mickey shook his head violently, as if to convince himself he wasn't dreaming. "You sure about this, Trev? You're not having me on are you?"

"No, mate. It's true enough."

Mickey accepted the money. He was a bit shocked when Trev passed him the whole amount in twenty-pound notes in a plastic carrier bag, explaining that they had already cashed the pools cheque and had divided the money up. Mickey was at a loss with where to place the money immediately. Trev advised him not to place it in a bank, because it would attract unwanted publicity and suggested that he hide the bag at home until he'd thought things through and decided exactly what he was going to do with the cash.

He actually walked home with Mickey and saw to it that he did hide the bag, and then took him back to the pub for a celebratory drink.

Mickey's mind wasn't exactly full of ideas. He could pay off all his debts; take Tracy and the kids on a holiday. After that he ran out of ideas and Trev suggested a lot more things the money would allow him and his family to do.

33

George's reaction to the unexpected windfall was entirely predictable. He went on a week-long binge. He took five hundred pounds with him, distributed evenly between his various coat and trouser pockets and started to drink as soon as the pubs opened that morning.

He explained his new-found wealth by telling his friends he'd had a pools win. His regular drinking companions were pleased about his supposed win, as he stood each of them a drink as they entered the pub. However, it soon became apparent to him that most of his real friends, after the initial drink, moved away and left the pub for other drinking venues. He was left with a crowd of motley hangers-on, the no-hopers, the ones who wouldn't work and spent all their time drinking in pubs and threw away any money they had left backing no-chance racehorses and giving the money to the bookies.

The week passed in a blur for George. Swallowing gallons of alcohol in various pubs all day then back to his house and bed. Up and out the next morning in time for the pubs opening again. Pubs to bed, bed to pubs, was his routine day after day. He went through the five hundred pounds surprisingly easily, but then buying bottles of spirits for the hangers-on didn't come cheap. He kept replenishing his spending money and made sure that he, and his newfound friends, ate as well as drank often and well. He didn't want to end up with an ulcer like Joe.

By the sixth day, most of his new found friends had been replaced by even newer found friends, and even George was beginning to tire of drinking alcohol. At times all he wanted to do was lie down and sleep.

It was then the reporter found him. The journalist was from the local daily, the Northern Tribune. It reported local news and events and had a circulation of around half a million. The reporter was an ambitious young man named Arthur Jackson and he was out to make a name for himself in the newspaper world. He'd worked for the Tribune for about a year and as yet hadn't come across the headline-grabbing scoop that would lift him out of the northeast and into the fast-moving and exciting flow of London's Fleet Street as a crime reporter. But he lived in hope that the next story would be the very one to do just that. He lived and dressed the part, having invested in what he considered was a sleuthish looking raincoat and trilby, which he wore whatever the season or weather. The other reporters on the Tribune, somewhat derisively, called him 'Scoop' Jackson.

Arthur, the aspiring crime reporter, heard the rumours about a local pools winner throwing his money around and then someone told him that the lucky winner was in a pub in the town centre, buying everybody drinks. After first ringing the office and requesting a photographer he jumped on a bus and headed across town in search of the lucky winner.

He found George almost immediately in the second pub he tried. Arthur arrived just as big-hearted George was buying yet another round of drinks for his cronies. Seeing the lad come into the bar, George took the large, expensive looking cigar out of his mouth and called out welcomingly, "Come on, mate, what you havin'?"

"Er, thanks. I'll just have a Coke please." Arthur didn't want to give alcohol the chance to blur his thinking process. He was after a big story, and could smell a real scoop.

George paid for the drinks, making sure that everyone in the bar had one, and then turned to Arthur. "You're drinking Coke? Coke? What's wrong with a proper drink, like beer?" he demanded, waving his full pint in his hand and spilling a lot of it down the front of his shirt.

"I don't really drink, er ... Sorry, but I don't know your name."

"George. That's me, George," George said tapping himself on his chest proprietorially with his thumb.

"Pleased to meet you, George," Arthur said politely. "It's very nice of you to get me a drink, even if it is only a soft one." He looked around the bar. "You buying everybody drinks today, eh? You must have won the pools or something?"

George placed a fatherly hand on Arthur's shoulder. "There's many a true word said in jest, young 'un. Many a true word."

"So you have won the pools?"

George placed an index finger along the side of his nose. "Could be, young 'un, could be," he said mysteriously.

"You are the one that's won a fortune aren't you?" Arthur asked doubtfully, taking in George's rather scruffy, unshaven appearance, the grubby shirt, missing the two top buttons, and stinking of tobacco.

"Yes, that's right. We got lots and lots of lovely money. Money, money, lovely money," George slurred, and took a long drink from his glass.

"We? There are more than you, then? A syndicate win was it?"

George nodded, a bit confused.

"How much exactly did you win between you?"

"How much? Lots and lots of lovely money. That's how much we won," he wiped the back of his hand across his froth-speckled lips.

"How many are in the syndicate then, George?" Arthur persisted.

"Well now. There's me, Trev, Alan," he put up two fingers. "Then there's Nobby," he put up another finger. "And ... and ...? Who else is there?" he asked Arthur.

"I don't know, George. You know, how many others are there?"

"Oh aye. There's Joe. Er ... That's it, Joe."

"So, there are five of you, is that right?"

George drank off the remainder of his beer, and nodded. "That's right. Five of us."

"Do the others live around here as well?"

"Yes, that's right. They all live around here, matey. All local lads they are."

Just then the photographer arrived and seeing Arthur and George at the bar, made straight for them. "What's happening then, Scoop? Is this the lucky winner?" he said slipping his camera from its case and checking the settings.

George looked at the newcomer through an alcoholic haze. "Lucky? Lucky? Yes. That's me, Lucky George." Drunk as he was, something, some flicker of suspicious intelligence sparked up in his brain. "Here, what you going to do with that?" he demanded, shielding his face with his hand as the flash on the camera went off. "I don't want any bloody pictures, get out of it," he shouted as the photographer readied the camera to shoot again.

"Come on, George. Just a couple of photos and you'll be in tomorrow's Tribune along with all the other celebrities. Can you see the headline? 'Lucky George and syndicate. Local man wins fortune on the football pools'. You'll be famous. Come on, just a couple of shots," Arthur pleaded.

"Get out of it," George shouted again, making for the door and pushing the photographer out of the way. Unfortunately, as he put up his hand to remove the unwanted personage who was preventing him leaving, the man took another photograph, either deliberately or accidentally, and the flash blinded George temporarily. Unable to see, George again flung out his arm and this time it connected with something. The photographer's chin. The man went down like a sack of spuds, and George, his sight not fully restored, stepped forward and promptly fell right over the recumbent figure on the floor.

Near pandemonium broke out in the bar. George's drinking cronies, all very much the worse for drink, seeing their friend and benefactor struggling with an assailant on the floor, took immediate action. Well, they stumbled and staggered towards the sprawling figures, each prepared to assist their generous companion to fight off whoever it was attacking him.

George struggled half to his feet, just as the first of the hoard of rescuers reached him. Ran into him would actually be a more accurate description. The rescuer collided with George and both men fell on top of the photographer. The three men went down in a writhing heap, and a number of other rescuers, having now arrived at the scene of conflict, fell on top of them. The men eventually disentangled themselves, with the help of the bar staff, and pulled themselves to their feet. None of them was any the worse for their fall except for a few bruises, sore shoulders and knees, except the photographer who was unconscious.

The photographer came around after having his face gently slapped for a few seconds by the cross-eyed barmaid who maintained that she had done a first aid course some years previously. The man was a bit groggy when he stood up and had to be helped to a chair. He kept shaking his head, probably to refocus his vision and to clear it of the image of the barmaid's eyes staring at him from varying acute angles. He was shaken but seemed alright and not badly hurt, which was more than could be said for his camera, which lay in two pieces on the floor.

Arthur was still determinedly chasing more details for his scoop, and persistently asked questions, which George studiously ignored. "Come on, George, give me the details, man. The news is sure to get out sooner or later, and it might as well be reported in the Tribune as in some outside rag."

"I'm saying nowt," George announced loudly. "Nowt at all."

"What about my camera, then," the photographer complained. "They cost a lot of money, they do." He stood unsteadily and walked to where the camera lay. "Look at it. It's knackered altogether."

"Look mate," George said to the photographer, "Don't get yourself in a tizzy. I'll pay for a new camera for you, alright?" He peeled off five twenties from the wad in his pocket and stuffed the notes into the complaining man's jacket pocket. "There you are. That should get you a brand new one."

The man pulled the notes out of the pocket. "A hundred quid? You're joking, aren't you? That'll not buy anything half decent."

"Here then," George said and pushed the rest of the wad into the man's hand. You keep that and sort yourself out a new one, okay?"

The man looked down at the cash in his hand. "Alright then. Thanks," he said quietly.

"George …" Arthur started.

"Sorry. Got to go now. Had enough to drink for today. See you later." George waved to his newfound friends from the press and disappeared through the door and out into the darkened street.

34

Arthur was certain that he was onto a scoop. The pools win was a big enough story in itself, for the Tribune it was anyway, but something, his crime reporter's nose, he liked to think, told him that there was more to this than met the eye. A lot more, something that would be the making of his journalistic career.

He spent a restless night and early the next day he decided to do some checking. He wanted to establish some facts and intended to flesh out the story. The bare bones were no good, not for an ambitious young crime reporter who was determined to get to the top of his profession. He contacted the large pools firms, Littlewoods and Zetters. They were very cagey about the information they gave out concerning winners, and were reluctant about details, but they did confirm that there hadn't been any big, no-publicity requesting winners in the past few weeks.

He then tried the smaller firms, but couldn't get any information at all from any of them. He decided that their jackpot amounts probably wouldn't be enough to explain the large amounts of money he was trying to account for anyway.

Not satisfied, he decided to check the newspaper records for recent robberies, convinced that there was something suspicious about this mysterious 'pools win'. The only robbery that could possibly fit the bill had taken place four weeks previously in Leeds. A payroll van had been hijacked and the money, wages destined for a local factory, stolen. The amount taken was a fortune of £400,000 and the reporter's lips fairly drooled at the thought of being responsible for solving the crime and being on the inside as the police arrested the criminals and the story broke. The national newspapers would fall over themselves to buy his story and he could achieve his burning ambition and demand a job in Fleet Street.

He read and reread the various newspaper accounts recorded in the newspaper's library and made copious notes in his notebook. The police stated that the robbery had involved at least five, probably six men, all of whom were very probably experienced criminals. The job was carried out to a high standard of professionalism and the robbers hadn't left any clue behind them at all for the police to work on. The Leeds CID suspected that the robbers had received some help form an insider either at the payroll firm or the factory the money was being delivered to. Enquiries were proceeding and the security firm had put up a reward of £20,000 for information leading to the arrest and conviction of the robbers. The large reward merely added icing to the cake as far as Arthur was concerned. He could achieve his ambition and be paid a fortune for his efforts into the bargain. He decided to start his in-depth investigations and surveillance operations on the 'pools winners', right away.

He started next morning. Returning to the bar where he'd previously met George. He was on the doorstep at eleven o'clock as the manager opened up and followed the man back into the bar.

"You're first this morning. What's the matter, you after a hair of the dog?"

"No. Nothing like that. I'll just have a bottle of tonic."

The manager poured the tonic into a glass and took payment. He looked at his only customer shrewdly. "Well, if it's not a hair of the dog, what exactly is it you're after?"

"I was in here ..."

"I remember," the manager interrupted. "You're a reporter aren't you?"

Arthur was pleased to be remembered as a reporter. "That's right. Crime correspondent actually," he promoted himself, "from the Tribune."

"So, what do you want then? There been another Great Train Robbery, has there?"

"No. Nothing like that at all," he said hastily, regretting now calling himself a crime correspondent. "I get a lot of other assignments as well, of course."

"Of course, when there's not a lot of Great Train Robberies happening," the manager said seriously. "And there's not a lot of them around here at the moment."

Arthur looked hard at the manager, unsure if he was being serious or not. He decided that he was, and continued. "I've been asked to do a bit of a story on these pools winners."

"What pools winners are those then?"

"The syndicate that won a lot of money recently."

"It's the first that I've heard about any pools winning syndicate," the manager maintained.

"You don't know who they are?"

The manager shook his head.

"There was one of them in here yesterday," Arthur said.

"Aye?"

"Yes. I was speaking to him."

"Were you?"

"Yes."

"What, in here?"

"Yes. In here."

"Well then, you must know who he is, if you were speaking to him."

"That's the problem. I don't know who he is. But I need to find out not just who he is, but who the others in the syndicate are."

Just then the door opened and a customer entered. The manager walked across to serve him. He didn't ask what he wanted to drink, but immediately started to pull a pint of bitter.

Obviously a regular, Arthur deduced, and walked over to where the man was standing. "Can I get you that?" he asked, indicating the drink that the manager had placed on the counter in front of the customer.

"This here's a crime reporter from the Tribune," the manager explained to the newcomer, with a significant look, as he took the money from Arthur.

"Oh aye?" the customer said. "You trying to get some important information out of me, are you then? That why you buying me drinks, eh?"

"One drink, mate," Arthur replied. "So don't get carried away, I'm not on exes for this story." Not yet anyway, he thought.

"What story's that, then?"

"It's about some syndicate winning the pools, Alec," the manager put in, giving Arthur his change.

"Winning the pools? Who's won the pools then? Somebody drinks in here, was it?"

"I was hoping you'd be able to tell me."

Alec drank deeply from his pint glass and wiped his mouth with the back of his hand when he put the glass back on the counter. He looked at Arthur and shook his head. "I've heard nothing about any pools win, Mr Reporter. How much did they win?"

Arthur could feel a stone sinking to the bottom of his stomach. I'm just wasting my time here, he thought. "You've never heard anything at all?"

"Not a word. But I'll tell you what, you leave me a phone number and if I do hear something, I'll contact you straight away."

Arthur realised that this was about the best he could hope for and wrote the office number on a piece of paper for the customer. He left the bar disappointed but not disheartened. "Right then," he said to himself, "It'll have to be plan B."

When Arthur left the bar, the manager and Alec put their heads together. "We don't want word about George's win getting out do we?"

Alec shook his head. "Not likely, not if it's going to stop George spending his money in here and buying us drinks. The place will be full of reporters and people trying to beg money off him."

"Right. So, you'd better nip round and tell George that the prick is looking for him," the manager said. "And I suppose you'd better mention it to his mate Joe as well."

Alec drank the last of his beer and left immediately. "And Alec," the manager called after him.

"What?" asked Alec from the door.

"Tell all your mates as well, will you? We don't want any of them shooting off their mouths about George to the prick either, do we?"

Arthur toured the town for the next couple of days looking for George, or news of him and his syndicate. He found nothing. It was as if the whole thing had been a dream, a figment of his imagination and he was chasing shadows, a whole syndicate of shadows. Other things became pressing and his boss was demanding to know what he was doing wasting his time on a wild rumour of a non-existent pools win. So he gave up for the time being, but decided to keep his eyes and ears open for any sign of the project that he was sure would make his name, and possibly twenty thousand pounds.

35

Hans spent a lot of time preparing his report for Max, who was getting very impatient at their lack of progress. Hans methodically listed everything they'd done since their arrival and the results. Unfortunately, after what seemed to be a flying start, the driver's information leading them to the secretary of the Up North Combine and him to Nobby, the pigeon cree and Alan Spencer, they'd become becalmed and no further progress had been made, but he couldn't tell Max that.

Taking a deep breath, Hans rang the international number and waited with a feeling of dread for Max to pick up the phone.

"Yes?" snapped Max into the receiver.

"It's Hans, Herr Westlik."

"Well, Hans. I hope you have some progress to report this time. What's happening?" he asked impatiently.

"Well, Herr Westlik, we're continuing our search for the two people who stole your property. We are getting closer and should catch up with them very soon."

"Very soon? How soon is very soon? Do you actually know what you are doing over there? I'd have been better off hiring some local people to do the work."

"We have leads, Herr Westlik, and know the places frequented by these people, but they are keeping a very low profile at the moment. Do not worry, we shall find them." As soon as he said do not worry, Hans could have bitten his tongue off. If there was anything likely to annoy his employer, it was someone telling him not to worry.

Max exploded. "Do not worry? Do not tell me do not worry. I'm not in the least worried. It's you who should worry, my friend."

Hans grimaced. Being called 'my friend', by Max was comparable to a death threat from anyone else. "I'm sorry, Herr Westlik, I did not–"

"Listen to me." Max's voice was low and threatening. "You find these bastards and find them quickly instead of wandering around there like tourists. For God's sake, do I have to come over there and do the thing myself?"

Before Hans could reply, he heard Max slam the phone down.

36

The neighbours could see that the man was obviously a policeman. He was tall, wore a suit and tie and walked with the unmistakable confidence, nay arrogance, of a respected member of the constabulary. Detective Constable George Henry was indeed a policeman, a policeman on a mission. D.C. Henry hated Alan Spencer and would do almost anything to put him behind bars again. The policeman knew Alan of old; they'd actually been in the same class at school and had hated each other then, as only schoolboys can. In fact it had been hate on first sight. The boys seemed to hate each other instinctively, as if they sensed they would take diametrically opposite paths in adulthood. When they were both nine years old, Alan had stolen Henry's football boots. Not because he needed a pair, as he owned much more expensive boots provided by his mother, who was a proficient shoplifter even then. No, he hadn't needed the boots, but had stolen them and had cheerfully thrown them in the river on his way home. Henry knew Alan had taken them, but had no proof. The boys had quite a few scraps during their school years right up until their paths diverged shortly after they sat the eleven-plus exam, which Henry passed and went to a grammar school, and Alan failed and was sent to a secondary modern.

Henry had arrested Alan on a number of occasions since joining the force. Some years ago Alan had been instrumental in preventing the officer's chance of promotion. It was entirely because of the detective's efforts that Spencer was imprisoned on the last occasion and Henry was determined to do it again.

Although there was no evidence of Spencer being involved in the theft of the bulbs, the description the hijacked lorry driver had given Henry of one of the thieves exactly fitted one Norbert Nordstrom, who Henry knew just happened to be Spencer's constant companion and partner in crime. D.C. Henry was absolutely certain it was him, because his logic wouldn't let him believe that there could be another pint-sized, Elvis look-alike in the area. That was more than enough reason for Henry to want to interview Spencer as a suspect, especially as Nordstrom seemed to have disappeared from his usual haunts.

Alan waited until the man had actually knocked on the front door before opening it. He looked at the caller with polite enquiring expression. "Yes?"

The detective said nothing, simply held out his warrant card for inspection.

Alan attempted to look at the card, but it was quickly pocketed by the policeman. Alan looked up at the man's face and feigned recognition. "Oh, it's you, Henry. What can I do for you?" Alan asked.

"Can I come in?" the detective asked. "Unless you want me to ask questions here on the doorstep, where all your neighbours can hear what's going on?" Detective Constable Henry said tetchily, looking at the women peering at him from the adjacent doorways.

"No. No, please do come in," Alan said, putting out am arm to indicate that the policeman should enter. "Just go through the door on the left. That's it," Alan followed the man inside after closing the front door. "Take a ... oh, you already have."

"Let's cut the crap shall we, Spencer?"

Alan nodded. "Anything you say."

"Right then. There was a lorry load of bulbs stolen recently. Where were you at the time?"

"What time?"

"Friday 12th, I've just told you."

"No you didn't. You didn't say what date or what time. Come on, Henry, that's an old trick. I say I was at the pictures at half-past-one and you say, who said anything about half-past-one? I thought that you'd be better than that, Henry."

"Stop calling me Henry. You know my name's Detective Constable George Henry."

"Well then, George. I don't know anything about lorries or bulbs. What voltage were they anyway?"

D.C. George Henry looked confused. "Voltage?"

"Aye, what voltage? Or is it wattage?"

"Wattage?"

"Listen, George, slow down a bit eh? You're getting me all confused here."

"Voltage, oh, I see." The penny had finally dropped. "No, no, they're not that sort of bulb."

"Well what sort of bulb are they then? Bigger than that are they?"

"Bigger than what?"

"Oh, so they are watts after all, then?"

"Will you shut up about watts and voltages. They're not that sort of bulbs. I've already told you."

"What sort are they then, for God's sake," Alan said beginning to tire of the game himself.

"They're the sort that you plant. Plant in the ground. Dutch tulip bulbs, various colours," he added unnecessarily, not quite knowing why.

"Oh, those sort of bulbs. Well, why didn't you say so, then?"

D.C. Henry ignored the remark. He was beginning to realise that he was on the losing end of this interview. "Do you know anything about the theft of the bulbs?" he asked.

"No. Should I?"

"If you were involved in the theft, you should, yes."

"I don't know anything about them, Henry, sorry, George. I don't go in for gardening. Never could stand all that digging. I've got a bad back, you know. Ever since I was a kid. Done it in–"

"Shut up and answer the question."

"I don't know anything, honest."

"Honest?" The policeman was fuming now and red in the face. "You think because you say honest that it makes me believe you? That's about the last thing I expected to hear from you, Spencer. You're the biggest thief in the area, you and that pint-sized mate of yours. It's only by pure luck that you're both not banged up right this minute."

Alan didn't reply. He sat and waited for the detective to recover his composure.

D.C. Henry gradually calmed down and resumed his questions. "So where were you at approximately one o'clock p.m. on Friday the 12th, then?"

Alan appeared to consider this for a few moments. "At one o'clock, I'd be at the pigeon cree, I reckon."

The policeman's ears pricked up. "Pigeon cree? What were you doing there?"

"I was cleaning the cree out."

"Where is this cree?"

"Up on the Sandhill."

"There are allotments up there as well, isn't that right?"

"Yes," Alan said cautiously, unsure and therefore unhappy with this line of questioning.

"When I heard about these bulbs being stolen, I thought who on earth would want to steal tulip bulbs? Who would have any use for that many bulbs? And do you know what I thought then?"

Alan shook his head. "What?"

"Gardeners. Allotment holders like your mates, that's who."

"Oh, I don't think so," Alan said.

"What did you do with the bulbs?"

"Oh, we're back to the lights, eh? I've told you that I know nothing about any theft of bulbs, whether sixty, eighty, or one hundred volts, or watts." He noticed the detective's eyes narrowing dangerously and thought he might have gone too far. "Or the other kind that's planted in the ground, either," he added hastily.

"Okay then, Spencer. If that's the way you want to play it. But I'm warning you, both you and me know that you were involved in this thing and I'm going to make sure that I prove it. This'll be your what, sixth, seventh conviction? It's not that long since you got out and I'm going to make sure that you go back inside and for a very long time."

Alan's attitude appeared to change. "You've got me all wrong, Mr Henry. I've done the odd bit of larceny in my time, but there's no way I would risk getting nicked for a load of bulbs, dear me no. I'd never live it down, Mr Henry," he said with a smile. "I'd look like a right daffodil, wouldn't I?" He began to whistle Tiptoe Through The Tulips.

The detective stood up, walked to the door, turned and looked Alan straight in the eye. "I don't like you. You're too fucking cheeky, Spencer, always were. You've no respect. I'm not particularly bothered if you did nick these stupid bulbs or you didn't. If you didn't do this one, then you could have done, and you would have done given half a chance. And I've got no doubt that you'll have done others that you've got away with, so, just to let you know, I'm going to make it my business to pin this one on you, Spencer, you wait and see if I don't." He opened the front door, stepped out of the house and walked away up the street.

Alan watched him go. As the policeman disappeared in the distance, Alan's smile gradually faded, his shoulders sagged, his bravado seeped away and he was left feeling drained and depressed. This was getting serious, he thought. He'd been told that there'd been a big foreigner up at the allotments asking for Nobby and him the other day, and now no less than the northeast's answer to Sherlock Holmes was poking his nose in as well.

37

It was a few days later when Arthur spotted George again. The reporter was making his way back to the office from the magistrate's court where he'd spent most of the day listening to what he considered to be the most boring cases ever brought before a court. He'd been bored to tears, and on two occasions had nearly fallen asleep listening to the mind numbing indictments. The most exciting of the cases had concerned someone knocking down an outhouse and building a conservatory without applying to the planning department of the council for permission. He saw George from the top deck of the number 16 bus, which wasn't scheduled to stop for another half mile or so, and he could only look on impotently as George and another man went into the very same pub where he'd first seen him.

Arthur raced downstairs and rang the bell, but the driver didn't stop or even slow down and Arthur had to wait a while until the bus slowed to turn a corner before daring to jump off the still-moving vehicle. The conductor shouted something very uncomplimentary after him as he stepped off. Arthur ran back to the pub he'd seen the pair entering. He arrived breathless in the doorway and stood for a minute getting his breath back before opening the door. His breathing more or less normal again, he entered the pub and looked around the half-empty room for George. He wasn't there. Feeling panic beginning to tug at his insides, Arthur looked around again, slowly and more carefully this time, but no, George wasn't in the room.

Puzzled, Arthur walked to the bar.

"Yes?" the barmaid asked impatiently.

Arthur, not realising that she was talking to him, ignored her and continued to look around the room in search of the elusive George.

"Yes?" the barmaid demanded, more loudly this time.

Arthur started. "Oh sorry, I thought you were …" He glanced in confusion at the man standing next to him at the bar. "Er, I'll have a tonic please."

The barmaid flounced away to get his order.

As she placed his drink before him on the counter, he saw from the corner of his eye a door open near the corner of the room and George walked out. Arthur cursed himself for his stupidity as he realised that his prey had been in the toilet.

George vaguely recognised Arthur, and seemed to associate him with something unpleasant, but he smiled at him anyway.

"Ah, George, I'm pleased I've found you again. I was beginning to think that you were deliberately avoiding me."

"And why would I do that?" George asked suspiciously, as he lit a large cigar. He was beginning to recall something about the last time Arthur had turned up.

"The last time we spoke you told me you'd won the pools."

"So?" He blew thin blue smoke towards the ceiling.

"I've checked. You haven't won the pools in the UK, or any lottery in Ireland or Europe. In fact there's no record of any significant winners in the last few months."

"Ah, but we requested no publicity."

"There haven't been any no publicity request winners either."

George was silent, his reservoir of excuses entirely redundant.

"So, as you didn't win the money, where did it come from then?"

"You tell me, you seem to know everything else."

"What about Leeds?"

George said nothing. He was completely confused by the vast amount of alcohol he'd consumed over the previous days. What was this prick on about? Leeds? Was that where the lorry was going? He couldn't remember what he'd told his questioner the last time they'd spoken and didn't want to make matters worse by saying something incriminating.

"Thought so," Arthur said excitedly. "You were involved with that, weren't you? You didn't win any pools jackpot at all."

George was now totally befuddled and beginning to panic. "Might have been," he muttered, puffing hard on the cigar, feeling pressurised into saying something, but not wanting to incriminate himself.

"Who else was involved? There were five of you, right?"

"Don't know what you're on about."

Arthur was about to try and wring more details out of George when he felt a tap on his shoulder. Turning around he found himself nose to nose with the manager.

"That'll do. You leave George be. Sup up and get out," the manager said in an intimidating manner.

"But ..."

"Drink up and leave," the manager indicated Arthur's untouched drink on the counter. "Now. Or I'll put you out."

Arthur had no option but to leave the premises. He felt frustrated at being so close to learning more details of the Leeds robbery, or so he thought, but would have to be content with the little information he had, which wasn't a lot, but enough to interest the police.

Arthur explained his theory to a detective constable at the police station a couple of hours later. He gave the detective a copy of George's photograph and demanded to be considered for the twenty-thousand-pound reward and exclusive rights to any story that resulted from his information being followed up.

D.C. Henry readily agreed and thanked him for supplying the

information. Henry was interested, very interested and promised to investigate. But what interested him wasn't the possibility of George being involved in the £400,000 robbery in Leeds. He knew that Leeds CID had five men already in custody and they would almost certainty be charged for the robbery in the Yorkshire city. But what really interested him was the fact that this George was spending money like water and pretending to have won the pools. The man in the photograph that Arthur had left with him was same George who had an allotment near Spencer and Nordstrom's pigeon loft. Henry didn't for one moment believe that George or the others were involved in the Leeds robbery, but thought that there was a very good possibility they might be involved in the theft of some bulbs a lot nearer home.

Later, back at the station, D.C. Henry was filling in his report sheet and discussing his lack of progress with his sergeant. "This Spencer has got something to do with it, I'm certain of that. The driver's description fitted that mate of his, Nobby, to the letter and he said there was an Up North Combine sticker on the van."

"He's certainly a likely candidate, but nicking a few quids' worth of tulips is hardly his type of job. There must be more to it if he is involved," the sergeant said.

"Maybe he was expecting something else to be in the lorry," suggested Henry.

"Something else, like what?"

"I don't know, but he's a slippery one, he is. And he's definitely the type."

"Look, I know you want to nail Spencer more than anything, but we've got much more pressing crimes to solve than chasing some idiot gardener who has done off with a batch of tulips. I told you to just go through the motions with that, and then get back to something important?"

"Well, this is important, sarge."

"It might be important to you and to whoever owned the blooming bulbs, but not to anybody else. In fact even the owner and the garden centre they were supposed to be delivered to have given up on the things and written them off. It wouldn't surprise me if it was an insurance job, anyway." He looked at Henry and smiled. "Look, I know that you've got a thing about Spencer. He's no good and his father was even worse. Come to think of it, his mother's in a league of her own as well, she's 'a diamond', as she would say herself, but you'll just have to accept that you can't win them all. You lose some and you win some. Just bide your time, give him enough rope and he'll drop himself right in it sooner or later, you mark my words."

"But, sarge …"

"Leave it, alright?"

"But I just know that there's more to this than just a few bulbs. There's got to be something else. Spencer was definitely involved in this with Nobby and he wouldn't bother for a few tulips, as you said."

"You keep saying there's something more, but what?"

"I don't know, not yet, but I'll find out."

"Alright. You follow your tulips in your own time if you want to, but leave the thing alone while you're working, alright? Don't mess about, that's an order."

"Alright sarge, fair enough. I'll do it in my own time."

And D.C. Henry did follow the leads up in his own time. And he made some very interesting discoveries.

38

Nobby was as proud as punch with his new purchase. He'd racked his brains wondering what he could buy for his brothers. It had to be something that they could all use and enjoy. Money wasn't a problem now, of course, but at the same time he didn't want to be seen to be throwing too much of it around. It would only arouse suspicion. He arranged for his purchase to be delivered at a time when he knew that all the family would be in the house. He wanted to see all their faces when it arrived. The delivery was late of course, and he had a hell of a job trying to keep two of his brothers from going out, as was their habit at eleven o'clock on a Saturday morning. The betting shop and the pub beckoned and he was having the devil's own job delaying them.

   He did his best and had just about lost the battle, as his brothers were walking down the garden path, when the van pulled up outside of the house. The sight of the large delivery van stopped his brothers in their tracks, both being curious as to what the driver could possibly want at their address.

"He must have the wrong house," the elder brother said, as the driver jumped from his cab and approached them, whistling an unidentifiable melody loudly and tunelessly.

"This number 10 Westwood Road, mate?" he asked, affably enough.

The elder brother looked around suspiciously. "Depends. Who's asking?" Norman, the elder brother said.

"Take no notice of him. Aye, that's right, this is number 10 alright. Why? What you got then?" Neil, the other brother enquired, curious.

"Had a right bloody job finding you and no mistake. There's not a bloody street name or house number," the driver grumbled, as he pulled a crumpled delivery note from a pocket.

"Delivery for," the driver peered at his delivery note, "a Mr Norbert Nordstrom. He about?"

"That's me," Nobby piped up and walked to the gate. "Can you bring it in? Neil and Norman here will help you with it."

His two brothers didn't particularly look as if they wanted to be helpful, but were obviously curious as to what Nobby could have ordered and so complied, and helped the driver lift the large box from the back of the van and into the passageway of the house. Nobby signed for the package and the driver went on his way, whistling tunelessly.

"What you gone and bought?" his mother demanded from the smokey living room where she sat in state, her injured leg supported on a stool.

"Nothing much, Mam. It's just something for the lads out of my redundancy money, that's all."

"For us?" both brothers said in unison, and began to rip the cardboard packaging from the thing. They tore at it with their hands without making much of an impression.

Their mother, seeing their impatience, limped into the kitchen with the aid of a walking stick. She returned almost immediately with a large knife and set about the packaging as if it had grievously offended her in some way. She hacked and slashed at the cardboard and cellophane and the lads made sure that they kept well out of her way until she'd stripped the last of the packaging from the thing.

They stared in wonder as the delivery lay before them, stripped of all the packaging and wrappings, which lay around their legs; it was exposed to their amazed eyes.

"It's beautiful," the elder bother said.

"It sure is," the other commented.

"When can we use it, Nobby?" Neil asked.

"As soon as you can put it up," Nobby replied.

"And where do you think that thing is going to go, then?" their mother demanded. "It's far too big for down here, we'll not be able to move for it." She rubbed her chin ruminatively for a few moments. "Only one thing for it, it'll have to go upstairs, that's all."

The lads wasted no time at all in carrying their new prized possession upstairs, but after much muted swearing and cursing, pushing and pulling, 'to me, to you', type of instructions, they'd had the thing in and then out again of two of the bedrooms because it was too large. They finally erected it in the one remaining bedroom and just managed to squeeze the thing in there after much struggle and argument. Of course, the bed had to be dismantled and the wardrobe moved to another room.

The two youngest girls, Natasha and Noreen, who slept in that bedroom, were not happy about the new arrangements at all, especially as they were now obliged to sleep downstairs. They complained loudly, but gamely and patiently put up with this inconvenience because they were allowed to play on the new snooker table when the lads weren't using it and because they secretly enjoyed sleeping downstairs, where they could switch the TV back on after everybody else was upstairs in bed. They continued like this until the novelty of playing with the thing had worn off somewhat, and it was left unused and things went back to normal. But while it was there and used frequently by the lads, their playing improved significantly and they never lost a game. They had to be careful, of course, especially with middle-table shots as they had to open the windows to accommodate the lining up of their cues, their elbows and the ends of their cues disappearing out of the windows, and had to open the door to the bedroom when lining up long shots for the same reason.

All Nobby's brothers were grateful to him for getting the snooker table, which although it wasn't full size, of course, was still the biggest and the best they'd ever played on for free. They invited all their friends around most days and it became a regular little snooker hall, albeit a miniature one.

Nobby's mother and sisters didn't complain much either; well not really. He sweetened his mother by promising to buy her a new cooker, fridge and washing machine and his sisters were happy because the snooker table upstairs attracted their brother's friends, some of whom they thought were very dishy, and there were several the sisters had their eyes on. Consequently, all of the girls immediately expressed an interest in the game and wanted to learn to play it.

39

The dark-coloured car had been parked outside Trev's flat for three hours. The two occupants sat patiently in the car watching the building until night fell. The street was almost deserted when the light faded apart from the occasional passing car. As Trev left the flat the vehicle's engine started and it cruised slowly after him.

Trev noticed the car immediately he stepped into the street. He'd been worried that the owners of the money would be looking for him. Trev immediately put two and two together and came up with a terrifying four. It had to be the criminals looking for their stolen money.

As he neared the corner Trev took to his heels and ran speedily to the end of the street. He turned the corner, and out of sight of the car and stepped into a shop doorway. He stayed far back in the shadow of the doorway and held his breath as the car cruised slowly past. It travelled about a hundred yards along the street and then stopped right outside a bingo hall. The two occupants alighted from the car and looked around, obviously searching for Trev. They stood on the pavement and looked up and down the street, their arrogance and self-assurance obvious. People leaving the bingo hall stepped off the pavement to get around them. These men were used to people getting out of their way and stood their ground. Trev remained in the shadows and watched until they finally got back into the car and drove off. He watched them go with a sense of fear and dread. He knew that they'd be back, and soon.

Trev was still wary when he made his way home later that night. But he wasn't wary enough, because he never saw or heard his attackers until they were almost upon him. He half turned as the footsteps behind him became audible, but was too late and didn't see what hit him. He was punched hard in the back of the head from behind and stumbled forward, grasping the wall in a desperate effort to stop himself falling. He was punched again, on the other side of the head this time by the other man, and fell onto the pavement. He was dazed and his vision blurred. He knew that he had to get up or he'd be kicked senseless; in fact his assailants were beginning to kick him now, as he struggled to rise. He folded under another onslaught of blows, trying to protect his head with his arms. After what seemed an absolute age, his assailants stopped their vicious kicking and one bent over Trev. He could smell the man's rancid breath.

"Keep away from Ginger or you'll get a lot more of the same," he hissed. Both the men then walked off, leaving Trev exhausted, breathless and in agony, but relieved that the assault had ceased. He eventually found the strength to stagger to his feet.

He made his unsteady way home where he cleaned himself up. He was badly shaken, his face was badly grazed and bleeding from his fall on the pavement, his head and ribs hurt badly from the punches and kicks he'd received, but apart from that, he wasn't too bad. It was a bit of a relief to find out he'd been followed and attacked by some irate husband and his mate rather than the alternative, the money's owners looking for revenge and the return of their cash.

40

Next morning Trev found Joe and Alan ensconced in the shed at the allotment and wasted no time in telling them about the attack on him. They were very concerned until they heard who his attackers were.

"Serves you right, you horny git, you should keep it in your trousers," Alan said. "You'll have to be very careful from now on."

"I'd already decided I wasn't going to see her anymore, anyway," Trev said.

"Things getting too hot for you there, eh?" Alan asked.

"No. I'm just sick of one night stands and messing about. What I really want is a deeper relationship with a decent woman who I can love and trust, settle down and have kids with, you know."

Joe nodded. "I know what you mean, Trev, but you had us worried for a minute there. I thought it was the Germans who'd attacked you."

"Germans, what Germans?" Trev asked.

Joe brought him up to date about the German turning up at Nobby's house and Nobby's mother getting beaten up, stabbed and ending up in hospital, a German asking questions around the allotments and D.C. Henry interviewing Alan, and about how George was attracting a lot of unwanted attention from the press, and most of the drinkers in the surrounding neighbourhood.

"Nobby's mother in hospital? Is she badly hurt?"

"No, she's out now and okay, but she's certainly had a right going over. The docs were really worried about her at first, they couldn't stop the bleeding."

"Bloody hell, this is getting out of hand. These bastards are dangerous. Those boxes of bulbs are still next door and it's too risky to move them now, with all these people sniffing around. And there's that financial advisor as well," Trev said. "He's pestering the bloody life out of me to invest that money with him. He just will not give up. He follows me around like a bleedin' dog. He's like a stalker. We really need to get a handle on this, otherwise it'll get right out of control and we'll not be able to stop the whole story getting out one way or another."

"You're dead right there, but what can we do?" Joe asked. "All these people poking their noses in, it's terrifying. I wish I'd never got involved in all this. My stomach hasn't stopped aching since I found out about it."

"Stop moaning, will you? It's probably kicked off because you've gone and volunteered for the Samaritans. What you've gone and done that for is beyond me. All those suicidal nutters ringing you up and wanting to talk to you about their problems. We've got enough bleedin' problems of our own, mate, never mine other people's. You must be mad," Alan said.

"That right you've volunteered?" Trev asked.

Joe nodded. "Yes, George suggested it and I talked it over with Brenda and she agreed I should do it. I've already done some training and it's only a couple of hours every other week on the phones. They've put me with an experienced volunteer until I get to know the ropes. It's very interesting and it's satisfying being able to help people."

"Well, you've certainly got the right nature for it. I admire you for having a go, mate. I really do."

Look, I've been giving our problem some thought," Alan said

with the emphasis on 'our'. He didn't understand how anyone could give up their free time to help other people, when they had real problems of their own. The whole concept was alien to him.

"Oh yes?" Trev said suspiciously.

"Yes. What we need to do is to get all of us together, the five of us, and do off somewhere quiet. Like the old western bandits did. We need somewhere to hide out in the country where we can't be found. Somewhere where we can take our time, have a good think and sort things out."

"Like the Hole in the Wall Gang did in Butch Cassidy and the Sundance Kid, eh? I'm all for that," Joe said eagerly.

"You do know what happened to Butch Cassidy and the Sundance Kid at the end of the film, don't you?" Trev asked Alan.

Joe looked worried, but remained silent.

"Yes I bleedin' do know what happened at the end of the film," Alan answered shortly. "Look, are you up for this or not?"

"I suppose so," Trev said.

"Me too. And the sooner the better," Joe said.

"Right then," Alan said. "I've already got a few ideas we can discuss." He pulled a piece of paper from his pocket. "I've made a list of possible places we can hole up. What do you think about these?"

Trev, humming Raindrops Keep Falling On My Head, took the proffered list from him and Joe looked over his shoulder eagerly. They quickly scanned down the page.

"This is a list of country cottages for rent," Trev said incongruously.

"That's right. We can rent a cottage for a month or even longer and get ourselves sorted out. It'll get us out of the way of that friggin' reporter, the financial advisor, the police, the Germans and your girlfriend's husband for a while, and give us the chance to think."

"Why don't we go abroad somewhere? Somewhere warm and sunny?" Joe asked.

"Because most of us don't have passports and we want to get away now, in the next few days. Waiting around for weeks while passport applications are processed is not on, Alan replied.

"A cottage in the country means we'd have to feed ourselves, wash our own clothes and stuff. Why not book into a hotel; you know, a big posh one with all the amenities, room service and all that?" Trev said. "We've got the money so why not live like kings in a place like that?"

"If we did that, we'd draw attention to ourselves, wouldn't we?" Alan replied. "Five of us together like that. We'd be sure to attract unwanted attention. I've told you. I've given this a fair bit of thought and the cottage is our best bet. We'd be isolated, but all together. As far away from people as possible and we could sort out some sort of plan to stop all this shit, because if we don't, we're going to get lifted by the police, or worse, by the Germans, sooner or later, and it'll probably be sooner if we carry on like we're going."

"I suppose you're right," Trev said.

"Yes, I think he is," Joe said a bit reluctantly. "It's just that Brenda isn't going to be happy about me disappearing for a month."

"She'd be even unhappier if you got put away for twenty-odd years or so, or worse, got killed by those Germans." Alan said.

"I suppose you're right there," agreed Joe reluctantly. "So what's the next step then?"

"Well, there's not much we can do about Nobby at the moment because we can't find him, but we need to have a word with George," Alan replied.

"What? You mean you haven't even mentioned this to him yet?" Trev said.

"No. I wanted to speak to you two lads first. Don't worry, he'll agree, we'll talk him into it."

"I can't see George being very keen to go into hiding," Joe said.

"Then we'll make him," Alan said aggressively. "I'm not risking prison for an idiot who can't see that he's putting us all at risk."

"But there's not much we can do if he refuses, is there?" Joe asked doubtfully.

"Isn't there? I think there is. We can make him come with us if necessary," Alan looked at the others. "I'm serious about this. I'm not going down because of his stupidity."

George was difficult, as they thought he'd be. They found him drinking in a pub, bleary-eyed, three-quarters cut and determined to drink himself even further into oblivion. They escorted him to a secluded corner, away from the prying eyes and flapping ears of his thirsty entourage, and explained their proposition to him.

"Country cottage. I'm not going to any country cottage. I'm not going anywhere, so you can both take a running jump at each other," George told them, quite forcibly, and loudly.

"Shush. Keep it down, will you? Look, it's only for a few weeks, and it'll give us a breather, you know, time to sort things out," Alan explained again.

"No way. I'm not going anywhere. I'm staying right here."

"But …"

"Look, I've told you once and I'll tell you again, I'm not going anywhere. If you want to have a holiday, great, but don't expect me to come with you and hold your hands."

Alan was beginning to get angry. "Look, you drunken old …"

"That's enough, Alan," Trev interrupted, and indicated to Alan that they should leave. "Okay then, George, you just be careful and look after yourself."

Outside, Alan was still furious. "Why didn't we keep at the bastard?"

"It's no good. He's made his mind up and there's no way we can change it."

"So what do we do now then? Just give up, leave him here and go ourselves? He's the biggest problem for God's sake. He's the loose cannon."

"Well. He won't come with us willingly and we can't leave him here, so we'll have to make him come with us."

"And how do we do that then, kidnap him? Jump him and tie him up so he can't move and shove him into the back of a car, do we?" Alan asked sarcastically.

"That's exactly right. Spot on. We kidnap the bastard."

"You serious?"

"Bloody right I'm serious. We'll come back tonight when he's even more pissed and lift him then."

The three men sat in the van until George came out of the pub. Nobby couldn't be found and so they had decided to go ahead and kidnap George without him. They waited until he'd said his drunken and incomprehensible goodnights to his drinking companions, all of whom were as drunk as he was, and then watched their potential victim stagger off towards his home.

"It's amazing that the old git can still walk after what he's drunk tonight," Trev said conversationally. "He was three-quarters gone when we looked in at about nine o'clock."

"He can certainly put some stuff away, can George," Alan agreed half admiringly.

"He can that," Trev agreed. "How much drink are we taking up to this cottage with us then?"

"I don't know. I didn't think about that."

"Well we'd better give it some thought because it'll take a big bleeding' tanker load to keep George happy for a month."

"I'll get ahead of him," Alan said, "and we'll grab him as he turns down the alley."

Alan accelerated past the intoxicated man and drove the van further down the road. He stopped at the entrance of a narrow alleyway that their prey usually used as a shortcut.

"Right, Trev. You and Joe get into the alley now. It's dark in there and he'll not be able to see you. When he turns into the alley, you grab him. I will follow him in and get him from behind and we'll throw him in the back of the van," Alan said. "I'll pull the van further along the road a bit, so he won't see us sitting out here, alright?"

They all nodded their understanding.

"You're the boss," Trev said shortly.

"And what does that mean?" Alan demanded.

"Nothing. Look, you've got it all worked out haven't you? You're calling the shots. Just tell us what to do and we'll do it."

Alan repositioned the van and Trev and Joe took up their positions in the alley and waited as George slowly approached. He stopped a couple of times and appeared to be having a conversation with himself. They began to wonder what was keeping him. They'd just about given up and assumed that he'd taken another route home, when a shadow appeared at the entrance to the alley. Trev and Joe, waiting in the darkness, tensed as the figure took a step towards them.

"Now!" yelled Trev, and the pair made a grab for the figure. The narrowness of the alley left very little room for manoeuvre on either side, but somehow both Joe and Trev managed to miss their target entirely. With arms outstretched they tried to ensnare the figure, but he sidestepped them. Trev lost his balance and fell to the ground in the confusion. Then George, with the agility and fluidness only the totally intoxicated can hope to achieve, somehow leapt past them both and was now shuffling away down the alley towards the far exit. He scraped the walls on either side as he ran, bouncing from one side to the other as he progressed down the narrow passageway.

Trev and Joe recovered themselves and ran after the escaping man, but got entangled with each other and Trev fell again, completely blocking the alley and preventing Joe from chasing the fugitive. Reinforcement in the shape of Alan appeared at the entrance of the passage. Unable to see in the darkness, he nevertheless ran straight into the alley, predictably colliding with the still entangled Joe and Trev, who were trying to get up from the ground. It took the men some time to disentangle themselves and follow the escapee to the end of the alley, but by then he'd disappeared completely and was probably locked safely inside his home.

Back in the van the failed kidnappers nursed their bruises and massaged their egos. "I'd have had got him easily if you hadn't got in my way," Trev accused Joe.

"I wasn't my fault. Anyway, I said it wasn't right, kidnapping him like that. We might have hurt him," Joe said.

"He'll hurt us all if he gobs off about that money," Alan reasoned. "We've got to try again. There's no way we can just let him go on like this."

"Well, he's pretty much a man of habit," Joe said. "He'll be out again tomorrow, but I'll be surprised if he uses that alleyway again for a while."

"Then we'll grab him somewhere else. He's always pissed, for God's sake; it shouldn't be that hard to pick him up."

"He'll be on his guard now, though," Joe put in. "He'll have got a right shock tonight and he'll be looking over his shoulder all the time now. Still you never know, he might just give up on the drink altogether and then our problem would be solved anyway."

"Dream on," Alan said. "Look, lads, this is a serious problem we've got here and we'll have to do something about it very soon or we're all in the shit, so come on, let's have some helpful suggestions."

"What about drugging him, spike his drink?" Joe suggested.

"What with?" Alan asked.

Joe was silent.

"We could trick him somehow. Tell him we were taking him somewhere where he'd like to go and then, once he's in the van, we do off to this cottage," Trev said.

"Now that's not a bad idea, mate," Alan said. "That might just work. Now where would George be most likely to agree to go to?"

"Dog races?" Trev offered.

"A new boozer opening somewhere," Joe put in.

"Naw. That wouldn't work, he likes to use the same pubs, does George."

"What about a strip club then?" Trev said.

"He might go for that, but there's no strip clubs around here and he knows that," Alan countered.

"We could tell him that there is a brand new one opening and we've got tickets for the opening night," Trev said.

"And they're giving away free drinks the first night. He'd be all for somewhere like that," Alan added.

"He'll not be worrying about free drink, not when he's got all that money," Trev pointed out.

"That's not the point, is it?" Joe explained patiently. "If it's free, then it always tastes better than if you've bought it. That's a well-known fact. It's the principle of the thing."

"That might work," Alan said. "In fact the more I think about it, the more I like it. That's what we'll do, we'll tell him that it's free drink and naked girls, he'll never refuse those two."

"Don't you think he might be a bit suspicious?" Joe asked.

"He might be at that," Alan said. "I know, we could actually get some tickets printed up with the details on. We can show him those and it might make the thing seem a bit more genuine."

"This is getting silly, far too complicated," Joe said.

"Where is this hideaway, anyway?" asked Trev.

They looked at Alan, who shrugged his shoulders. "I don't know. I haven't booked anywhere yet, have I?"

"This is all bollocks," Trev said. "If we're going to trick George, or kidnap him or whatever, then we're going to have to rent somewhere to take him first, aren't we? We can't keep him tied up at the allotment for a couple of weeks or so while we make all the arrangements."

After a bit of thought, the others reluctantly agreed that it was out of the question. They also agreed to put any further kidnap attempt on hold until they had at least found somewhere for them all to hide.

41

George was really shaken up when he called at the allotment the next morning. He looked pale and frightened. "I was nearly killed last night," he told Joe.

Joe feigned surprise. "What happened?"

"What happened? I was set upon by a gang of muggers, that's what happened. There must have been six or seven of them."

"Six or seven?"

"At least. They crept up behind me, the cowardly bastards, otherwise I'd have killed them all with my bare hands."

"Oh yes?" Joe said.

"Yes. They came at me in that alley and I had a hard job beating them off. It's lucky I didn't have much to drink last night and had my wits about me otherwise I'd have been in real trouble."

Joe shook his head sympathetically. "Maybe it was the people who are looking for the money? Perhaps we should lie low for a bit, mate?"

"No. I'm not hiding away," he said as he pulled his old pipe and tobacco tin from his pocket. "No way. If they want me then they can come and get me. I'll be ready for the bastards."

Idle Hands

George calmed down a bit after a bottle of brown ale and a smoke. He and Joe sat and talked.

Joe had seen Mickey that morning and passed a few words with him in the street. "He didn't mention taking that money from Trev. To tell you the truth, I'm really amazed he took it, but he was probably thinking of Tracy and the kids. Tracy is a bag of nerves, always fretting about something or other. At the moment she's worried sick about their son having to do Irish Dancing at school, because he doesn't like it and doesn't want to do it and keeps playing truant. She's been down the school trying to get him exempt, but they are adamant that the lad's got to do it, there're no exceptions."

"I remember doing Irish Dancing when I was at school," George said reminiscently. "I hated the bastard as well. All the lads did. We couldn't see the point. We lined up with the girls in our class every week like fairies. I think the girls hated the lesson as much as we did. We sweated and strained, and we must have looked lovely in our stretch-sided black plimsolls, long woollen socks and short trousers. We felt as soft as clarts. We were flat-footed, clumsy, and acutely embarrassed, as we tripped up and down the church hall, to the piano music provided by the teacher, who was apparently blissfully unaware of the torture she was inflicting on us. We thumped noisily up and down the hall on the polished wooden floor, sweating like horses, our mouths set in grim thin lines, chins up, our hands by our sides, and our feet going all over the place. We must have looked a picture. Luckily there weren't a lot of cameras about then, or we'd have been a ripe opportunity for blackmail."

They laughed.

"Don't get me started about school," George said. "The kids nowadays don't know they're born. They've got football pitches and swimming baths, all the amenities. We had to get a bus to the public playing fields once a week for a game of football. It took us a good half-hour to get from the school to the bus stop, catch a bus and get up there. By the time we got there, changed into our kit and kicked off, we were lucky to get fifteen minutes play in before it was time to go home."

"Aye, right, George," Joe said incredulously, with a smile.

"It's true. It was the same for P.T., woodwork and science. We had to troop across town to use the church hall or another school's facilities, and the public swimming baths for swimming. I remember one time we were in the baths with a woman teacher, what was her name again? I forget. She was a young lass really, straight out of teacher college and they made her take us to the baths. Well, one of the lads had a willy like a baby's arm. Brian something or other they called him. Anyway he comes out of the changing room with a pair of those woollen trunks on and she very nearly collapsed with shock. His willy was lying across to one side like a flag pole. She didn't know where to look, poor lass. And then when he'd been in the water and got out again, his trunks were all sodden, you know the way they used to soak up water like a sponge, well they clung to you, didn't they? Being wet they emphasized the size of his willy even more. And they were very nearly around his ankles with the weight of the water they'd soaked up. He had to keep pulling them up, but they'd slip down again. The teacher's face was all the colours of the rainbow. She told us to get dressed and had us out of there long before the session should have finished. Mind, she never took us for swimming again after that."

Joe laughed. "You've got a way with words, mate, you should put all that in your history book, but I'm sure it wasn't as bad as all that. Anyway, never mind about your school horror stories, what about this cruise, you changed your mind about not coming or have you got something else thing planned?"

"No, I'm not going on any bleedin' cruise. All that water everywhere, it isn't natural." He sipped his beer and changed the subject.

"You hear about Alan's new pigeon?"

"No. He been buying birds again, has he?"

"He has. Funny thing about Alan, he's the biggest rogue walking, and would steal your eyes if he thought he could get away with it, but he doesn't half love them birds. In fact I think those birds are all he really cares about," Joe said.

"That's a fact. I think he likes the freedom they've got, flying around in the clear blue sky like that. It must be an exhilarating feeling for them and that's what appeals to him. He probably imagines himself up there with them, soaring and swooping, literally free as a bird." George drank off the remaining alcohol in his glass and opened another bottle. "He's a hard man to understand is Alan. You know he once went to the dole office to sign on and nicked the date stamp off the desk when the clerk wasn't looking. I ask you, what bleedin' use would a date stamp be to him?"

"I heard he once nicked a toilet brush from the dole office toilet and threw it away when he got outside," Joe added. "Walked out with it stuffed in his sock."

"He must have some sort of problem with authority, you reckon?" George said and they both laughed.

Alan did love pigeons but he didn't know very much about them at all. Of course he wouldn't admit this to anyone and liked to pretend he was an expert. However, he was aware that he needed a good, fast bird to balance his existing flock, a better bird than any he currently owned, if he was to make any impression in competitions. Alan heard that Albie Trainer, a pigeon man of some renown, had a good flyer for sale and Alan went to have a look at the bird with a view to buying it. Alan watched the whole of Albie's flock in flight and they all looked good to him. Alan was impressed with them all, and Albie could tell he didn't want to ask which one was the best bird, because he was trying to look like he knew what he was doing.

Alan didn't have a clue of course, so Albie pointed it out. "That one there, the one out to one side, by himself, he's the fastest. Beat three hundred competitors last week, he did. Flew all the way from France and was home a good two hours and thirty-five minutes before any of the others'.

Alan readily agreed. "Yes, I could see right away that it was the best one," he said, as if he knew what he was talking about.

"You've got an eye for a good bird, Alan." Albie told him. "I could sell him for nearly double what I'm asking, if I waited a few weeks. But things being like they are, I can't wait. I need the money now." Albie could tell that Alan wanted to buy the bird, but was probably suspicious that the price was too high. Alan had recently bought a whole new flock of pigeons at an inflated price and later discovered that the best birds, the fastest flyers, had been sold off to the seller's friends long before he'd even heard they were for sale, and he'd been left with the duds.

Alan thought long and hard. That particular bird looked to be a good flier and even to Alan's unseasoned eye, he thought it had to be a good buy.

Alan finally made his mind up. "Look, I'll give you a fiver below what you're asking," he said. "I'll pay you cash, here and now and when the bird comes back in, it's mine. Okay?"

Albie appeared to consider the offer. Even with a fiver knocked off, the price was still way above what the bird was worth. "Alright then, Alan, you've got a deal," he said, putting out his hand to shake the proud new owner's.

Alan was pleased with his new purchase. It complemented his existing birds and gave them a leader, a pacemaker. The whole flock improved their performance within a very short period and he thought that the time was near when he'd try a few of the best ones in a race. But shortly after he'd bought the new bird that he noticed something odd about it. At first he wasn't sure, but his suspicions grew as he continued to observe it, and he was eventually forced to accept it as a fact. He just couldn't believe what he'd discovered. The bird was frightened of heights. It tended to keep below the others when flying, and as time went on he realised that the others were also flying very low, as if aware of the other's problem and accommodating it. He pointed this out to Nobby.

"A pigeon scared of heights?" Nobby said. "Get away. You've got to be pulling my leg."

"It's true," Alan assured him. "Just watch."

The pair watched the birds in the sky above them. The birds flew fast and soared and swooped, but when they soared it was not very high. They confidently climbed to not much higher than the height of a three-storeyed house but then quickly descended again. They preferred to skim the rooftops. This caused Alan a lot of stress, as it seemed to him that they were constantly dodging chimney pots and other low-lying obstacles. He'd paid a fair bit of money for the birds and didn't want any of them to kill themselves by flying into something.

Nobby and Alan tried to think of ways to get them to fly higher, but couldn't. They racked their brains but for the life of them couldn't think of any way to increase the height they flew at. Alan was sure that the others had flown at a normal height before the fast bird's arrival and that the newcomer had influenced them. Nobby was no help, of course, knowing less about the birds than Alan did. Alan considered taking advice from the other pigeon men, but decided against it. He suspected that they were already laughing at him behind his back, as it was, and didn't want to give them any more ammunition to use against him.

He tried changing the bird's feed and that seemed to have a positive effect for a short time, but all it really achieved in the long run, was to upset their stomachs and give them diarrhoea. The only real effects were, as the birds were flying lower, their aim had improved when they shit. Alan was soon convinced that they were all aiming for him. He got a little paranoid about it after a while, as well as a little messy, and swore that they were deliberately targeting him.

Alan began to lie awake at night worrying about the thing and finally got himself into such a state that he was prepared to do anything to rid himself of the problem, even kill the bird. His reasoning was that if he killed the fast bird, then the others would revert to their previous method of flying at a normal height. However, he decided to give the bird a little longer to improve its disappointing performance before resorting to such drastic activity.

42

Nobby got though the semi-final of the Elvis impersonators' competition and qualified for the final, but he wasn't happy at all and told Norma he wasn't going to take part.

"But why aren't you going to go to the final?" a surprised and concerned Norma asked.

"They were taking the piss again. They were laughing at me and I just wanted the stage to open up and swallow me."

"The only people laughing and jeering were that Sid the Shiv and his gang of thugs. You don't want to let them put you off, love. They'd like nothing better than you pulling out of the final, so Sid's brother, that Ricky Fontain, can win. That's exactly what they want to happen. You just ignore them and win the final. And we'll see who is laughing then."

"That's another reason I'm chucking it in. Sid and his Teds will make trouble and cause mayhem at the final. You saw what they were like at the semi. They're sure to kick off and I don't want to get involved in all that bother."

"There'll be a lot of bouncers at the final and I'm certain Alan and the other lads will turn up to stop any trouble, love. They think a lot about you, you know."

"Alan and the other lads sometimes take the piss as well. They say they're only joking, but it hurts just the same. But I honestly don't think it's just about that, Norma."

"What do you mean?"

"I think they're taking the piss because I'm an idiot. I'm far too short to be anything like Elvis and am only making myself a laughingstock by going on stage." He paused and Norma could see he was very upset. "Even the ones that cheer and clap me are only egging me on. They pretend they like me and that I'm really good, but I'm sure they're just taking the piss as well, all of them are constantly taking the piss out of me. The only way I'll ever be really like Elvis is if I get fat. Fat, like he was at the end."

Norma shook her head and tried to think of something she could say to reassure him. "Don't be silly. You're the best Elvis impersonator there is. Everybody shouts and cheers for you because you're good, very good. They're not just taking the mickey. Look, all the family will be there and I'll ask Alan to make sure all the lads come as well. They really like you. You know that they will do anything for you." She paused, biting her lower lip as if undecided and then made up her mind. "Alan told me not to say anything to you, and I don't know what it is, but he told me that he'd have a surprise for you if you made it through to the final. Something you'd really appreciate."

Nobby nodded and smiled but didn't look convinced.

43

D.C. Henry tracked George, the elusive big pools winner, down. He found him in a bar, where else? Luckily, George was almost totally sober and had his wits about him

"So just how do you explain the fact that you've been going round telling everybody that you have won lots of money on the pools?" Henry asked.

"I've told you. I did win the pools and it was a fair amount, okay."

"That is a downright lie. I've checked with all the pools companies in the country and the lotteries abroad and there have been no significant winners in the UK or anywhere else recently. None at all."

George paused. "You have been busy haven't you?" His mind was racing as he thought, how the hell am I going to talk my way out of this one? "Okay, you've got me dead to rights," he admitted.

The detective was all ears. "Go on, tell me about it."

George sighed heavily. "You're right of course. I didn't win the money at all. I admit it."

Henry waited a few moments, but when nothing else was

forthcoming, he got impatient. "So, why did you say that you won a lot of money, then?"

"I put that story around so that my wife would come back to me, that's why. She left me some time ago and I wanted her back."

"But where did you get all the money you've been throwing around?"

"It was my redundancy money and it wasn't that much, anyway."

Henry was struck dumb. He thought that he had George dead to rights and that he would confess to something or other regarding the stolen bulbs or something perhaps even more serious. But this was totally unexpected and he was now at a loss to know what to do or say next.

George, aware of the policeman's confusion, did nothing to help him at all; in fact he did the opposite. "And do you know something funny?"

"What?"

"I've realised that I don't really want her now. All that effort and scheming and all for nothing, eh? Life can be strange at times can't it?"

D.C. Henry left the bar a little bit wiser about George's supposed pools win, but totally confused as to whether the story about the ploy to win back his wife was real, or another red herring thrown out casually to put him off the scent.

Back at the station he received a telephone call from Arthur, who requested an update on the progress of the investigation and wanted to know how close he was to his £20,000 reward. The detective told the reporter some of his progress to date, but kept the details as vague as possible. The truth was, of course, that he'd made very little progress at all, but he did inform Arthur about his recent interview with George and where his money had come from. He also told him about the five men in custody in Leeds, who had now actually been charged with the robbery.

Arthur was disappointed, not just because his chance of receiving the reward had gone, but also because his story, the scoop of the year, had also disappeared. No locals involved in the big robbery in

Leeds and none with huge football pools wins. He resolved to cut his losses, give up on the pools story altogether and just write a public interest piece about a sad man trying to tempt his wife back with a cock-and-bull tale of a pools win.

D.C. Henry made his way to the next interview he'd planned. He didn't really believe that this visit would produce any information at all, but he wanted to stir things up and cause the suspects to be concerned. He knew that Mickey was an associate of Spencer, Nordstrom and this drunkard, George, the phoney pools winner, and thought he might as well give him a visit even though he had no proof he was in any way involved.

Again his reception was somewhat muted. He knocked three times before he heard any movement inside.

Mickey opened the door slowly, his eyes taking in the policeman's stance, arrogance and in-your-face attitude. He didn't recognise the visitor but knew instinctively that he was a policeman and was on his guard immediately.

"About time," D.C. Henry said abruptly to the face peering from behind the door and flashed his warrant card. "Well, are you going to let me in, or what?"

Mickey opened the door and stood back to allow the man inside. He followed him to the living room and stood while the officer sat down, crossed his legs, lit a cigarette and made himself comfortable. He looked around the room with distaste. "Nice place you've got here," he smirked, taking in the frayed carpet, old black and white television flickering in the corner and the kids' toys lying about the floor.

"Thanks," Mickey said, ignoring the man's sarcasm.

"You going to tell me about this robbery, then?"

"What robbery would that be?"

"Here we fucking go," the detective said. "Right, I'll spell it out for you. A lorry has been hijacked recently and I believe that it was you and your mates that did it."

"You're wasting your time talking to me. I know nothing at all about it."

"No? You know nothing about it, eh? Well then, if that's the case, how come a lorry matching the description of the one stolen was seen parked at the boys' club where you help out?"

Mickey shrugged. "If that's the case, it has got to be a coincidence. I honestly don't think that it could have been anything else but coincidence."

"Coincidence, my arse," the detective said. "I don't believe in coincidences, but what I do believe in is deliberate, pre-planned robbery. I believe that you are involved in this up to your neck, and I think that you are worse than any normal, run-of-the-mill thief, and you know why?"

Mickey remained silent.

"I'll tell you why. Because you, honest Michael, put yourself up as second man to the Pope. You, bloody holy Joe, became involved in something like this, while making out you're a saint. It's disgusting. Just because you're friendly with the parish priest and help out with those hooligans at the youth club, you think that you're untouchable. You're a hypocrite. You make me sick to my stomach. I want to vomit. You're disgusting and I'm going to do you for it. Believe me, I'll do you good and proper." Henry stood up and strode from the room.

Mickey heard the front door slam loudly as the policeman left the house. He was glad now that he hadn't touched the money Trev had given to him. He'd known instinctively that it wasn't from any sort of win and had hidden it in the loft. He'd not told Tracy about it, knowing she'd want to spend at least some of it. He put his head in his hands.

Tracy came through from the kitchen. "Is that true?" she asked.

Mickey didn't answer or even look up.

"What he said, is it true?" she asked louder this time.

"No, it's not true."

"But you did let somebody hide the lorry at the club, didn't you?"

"I let them park a lorry there, but I didn't know anything about the robbery."

"That Alan Spencer was round here the other week," she said accusingly. "This little lot wouldn't have anything to do with him, would it?"

"Look, I've told you, I know nothing about it. Alan did ask me to let him park a lorry at the club, just for a day or so. He told me he was doing a favour for a mate. He never said anything about hijacking the lorry. He said he'd make a donation to the club funds, to help out with the sports gear and stuff we need desperately."

"Well, he wouldn't mention hijacking the lorry, would he? Did you actually believe that Alan Spencer would do something for nothing? That he would give money to the club out of the goodness of his heart? You want your head looking at, you do. It's not me that should be in and out of mental hospitals, it's you."

"Tracy–"

"Don't Tracy me. I can't believe you let that toe rag do that to you." Tracy was shouting now, her voice shrill and piercing.

"Calm down, Tracy. You're working yourself up into a right state."

"And you've gone and got us in a right state. I can't believe that you've let this happen. Conned again by that bastard, don't you ever learn? And it's not as if we're any better off, are we?"

"Better off? What do you mean?"

"I mean that most probably that bastard Spencer and his mates will be rolling in the money they made from this robbery. They won't be worrying about how to pay the bills and where to get the school uniforms from for next term, will they? No. But we are. And you, you helped them with this robbery, and don't make a penny from it, but who do the police come straight to, eh? You, you great big, daft lump. If you had brains you'd be dangerous, you would."

"Come on, Tracy, calm down, you'll make yourself ill again. Anyway, that's not the way it was at all."

"Isn't it? I'll bet it is, though. You get yourself round and see your fine friends, your mates, and I'll bet you'll be surprised." Tracy was red in the face and highly irate now. Her hands shook and she had to support herself with her hand against the wall.

"Why don't you sit down, love? I'll put the kettle on and we'll have a nice cup of tea, eh? Here, you'd better take one of your pills, you're upset."

"Yes, I think I will," Tracy felt drained and spent now. She sat down, still shaking and closed her eyes.

44

Mickey threw open the shed door and strode angrily inside, his large muscular physique filling the doorway and blocking the daylight as he towered above them. "I don't want anything at all to do with anything that's illegal," he said adamantly, throwing the wad of notes onto the ground.

Alan looked at the money and, mindful of Mickey's intimidating presence, paused as if uncertain whether to speak, but finally he did. "Alright, but we all think that you're being daft and passing up the chance of a fortune. Chances like this don't happen very often, mate. Just once in a lifetime, that's all, once in a lifetime."

"Well, this once-in-a-lifetime chance has been passed by, I'm not getting involved in it, and as far as I'm concerned that's the end of it, okay?"

"Please yourself, stupid," Alan said.

"You deliberately used me," Mickey shouted, grabbing Alan by the lapels. Mickey was very angry now. His face was flushed with anger and his hands, holding Alan on his tiptoes, were shaking. He was surprised by the violence of his own reaction.

"Look, Mickey ..." Alan said, his voice strained as his throat was constricted by Mickey's tight grip on his jacket collar.

"Don't 'look, Mickey' me," Mickey spat, his face inches from Alan's. "You are definitely the worst scum of the earth, the very dregs of the filthiest dirt imaginable." He shook Alan backwards and forwards like a rat.

"Take it easy, mate," Trev said, trying to pacify Mickey. "It wasn't that bad. There was no danger whatsoever."

Mickey swung towards Trev, still holding the gasping Alan by the throat. "That's not the point." He shook Alan again. "He used me, actually got me involved in criminal activity, that's the point."

"But, Mickey, mate. It wasn't that bad," Trev tried again. "Okay, he used you, but you didn't know anything about it. You didn't know anything about what was going down and you still don't. The club also made a bit of money for the new sports kits, or whatever they're raising money for. Alan here has already made an anonymous donation that takes their fund right up to and beyond their target."

Mickey seemed to be slightly pacified; he looked at the now puce-faced, Alan. "That right?"

Alan did his best to convey the affirmative by nodding his head as much as Mickey's huge hands would allow.

Mickey started to relax his grip and Alan's feet touched the ground again, the first time in a while, and his face immediately began to resume its normal colour. Mickey had actually calmed down enough to let go his grip altogether and Alan staggered backwards, his legs unable to support the weight of his body. Trev stepped forward and supported him with his arm on his shoulder.

"Thanks, mate," Alan whispered.

"Don't thank me, just get yourself down to the club and make that donation fast, or you're a dead man," Trev muttered under his breath.

"It was still a nasty trick to pull," Mickey said.

"Well, you're probably right, mate. But what else could the lad do? He had to think of something and time was short, so that was all he could think of," Trev explained.

"I don't want to know the details. I don't want to know anything at all about what you lot are up to. Just leave me right out of it altogether. You've got your money back."

"Come on now, Mickey. That money will help you in all sorts of ways. It's only right that you get something for your help. The club now has enough money to pay for its sports kits, so I don't see why you shouldn't have a little as well."

Mickey looked at Trev with something like contempt on his face. "That's the whole point. Can't you see that? The whole point is that I don't want anything that was obtained dishonestly. I don't want any of your dirty money. I helped him, did him a favour because he was a friend and I though he was genuine. I didn't know that he was using me for his rotten stealing."

Trev was silent.

Alan slowly regained his proper colour and his composure, but was cautious of opening his mouth and risking further injury. Eventually, after a full minute, he did break the silence. "Everything you've just said is true, mate. Everything. But nobody got hurt, did they? Nobody even got frightened, except me, of course," he attempted a feeble joke. "But you are right. I admit that. You're dead right and we're definitely in the wrong. But, and it's a big but, we were desperate. Really desperate. We've had enough of the rat race, the daily grind, the struggling for survival that takes all our energy, time and effort. We want something better. Something that will give us a much better standard of living, a better life in every possible way and we saw the chance to get those things. This thing, this chance just fell into our laps, more or less. Can you really blame us for grabbing it with both hands? We've risked imprisonment and worse to have a chance at this. Now I know, we all know, that you think differently. You're a good, practising Catholic and have profound religious beliefs. You have moral principals, and we all respect and admire you for holding those beliefs and principles, but we're lesser men. We're not strong and upright like you are. We can't accept our lot and make do. We tried for something better. I know you'll say that treasure here on earth isn't worth anything and that treasure in heaven is what you should be aiming for. But again,

I'm not as strong as you are, we're not that strong, only ordinary working men, who saw the chance to better themselves and took it."

Mickey nodded his understanding. "Alright, fair enough. I'm not asking any of you to be like me. What you do is up to you. But I don't want anything to do with that money," he indicated the cash still lying on the ground. "The club can keep theirs. What they don't know won't hurt them and the sports kit desperately needed replacing, but I wouldn't feel comfortable taking anything."

"Taking the money wouldn't do you any harm, mate," Trev said quietly.

"I think it would, and it's what I think that counts, where it matters, up here," Mickey said, pointing to his head with his index finger.

Trev nodded. "Okay, mate. Have it your own way. But there'd be no harm in letting Tracy and the kids have something, now would there? They haven't a clue as to what went on and could do with some new clothes, furniture, carpets or something. I'm sure Tracy, young Paul and Terri would really appreciate a holiday. They've never had a proper holiday, have they?"

Mickey didn't look convinced.

"Tracy would benefit from a nice holiday. A good rest would do her the world of good, you know?"

Mickey didn't answer.

"Alright, you needn't say yes now, but just you think about it, okay?" Trev said, pushing the money back into Mickey's pocket.

45

Hans and Ernst split up and asked around the town centre pubs for Nobby and Alan. They might as well have saved their breath because they drew a complete blank. Meeting up later Ernst succinctly expressed his frustration in a few choice words. "None of these bastards know anything at all and if they did they wouldn't tell us. These people have got to be the most ignorant on earth."

Hans agreed. "I don't think they like anyone asking questions about any of the locals. They'll drink all the beer you're prepared to buy, but tell you nothing at all."

"Why don't we just grab one and beat the shit out of him until he tells us what we want to know," Ernst said viciously. He was determined not to let this jumped-up employee of his uncle call all the shots and he was tired of being considered stupid by Hans.

Hans wasn't impressed. Ernst was getting more and more excitable and it worried him. The rumours regarding Ernst's drug taking had been confirmed when he'd caught the big man snorting cocaine in the hotel. Hans knew that the side effects of the drug included paranoia, delusions and lack of judgement, especially when combined with the large quantities of steroids the bodybuilder was taking. "I've considered that option, but it would attract too much attention. No. We will continue to watch the pigeon loft, this Nobby must go there sometime or other and when he does, we shall grab him."

"Why don't we just watch his mother's house? He's more likely to call there than at the pigeon loft, especially now that his mother's been injured," Ernst said. "She will be home from the hospital now and he's sure to call to see her."

Hans thought this suggestion over carefully. What Ernst had said actually made sense and watching the house would be a lot easier than keeping tabs on the loft. It was far too open up there on the hill and only pigeon men and allotment holders went up there. A stranger stood out like a sore thumb. The nearest watching position they had been able to use was far too far away and didn't cover the other access routes to the loft. But they could easily keep the mother's house under observation by simply parking unobserved on the main road. There were only two ways into the street and they could park in such a position so as to watch them both. "For once Ernst, you have had a good idea," Hans conceded. "We will concentrate our efforts on the mother's house as you suggest."

46

Unwilling to show themselves openly since the Germans had been snooping around and Nobby's mother attacked, the lads decided to lie low at the allotment during the day and even sleep there at night, except George, who had perversely opted to sleep at home to prove a point. Trev, Alan and Joe had been holed up in the allotment shed for three days, only venturing out one at a time in the early morning to buy food, drink, cigarettes and newspapers.

It had been Joe's turn to get the provisions this morning and he returned to the shed with his face buried in the newspaper. Once inside he passed the paper to Trev.

ANONYMOUS DONOR GIVES FORTUNE TO CHARITY, the headlines screamed. Trev, sipping a cup of coffee, nearly choked when he saw the headline and coughing and spluttering quickly scanned the smaller print for all the details. The newspaper account went on to describe how a mysterious benefactor had pushed a package containing £5,000 in £20 notes through the letter box of a local office of a children's charity. Staff had found the money when they'd opened up the following day. There was an anonymous letter with the money simply stating that the money should be used for the benefit of the children.

"The stupid bastard," he muttered. "He's only gone and done it."

"You seen this?" Trev threw the newspaper onto the bench.

"Yes, I've read it," Joe said.

"Told you so, didn't I?" Alan said, reading through the story.

"Didn't expect anything else from Mickey. He's a very honest type of man, you know," Joe said.

Trev nodded. "All that religious instruction we had brayed into us at school certainly stuck in Mickey's mind. In fact I think he got my share as well,"

"Anybody would think that he was putting up for bloody canonisation or something," Alan said scornfully.

"Now don't you run down Mickey just because he's got a bit more moral fibre than we have," Joe put in. "The lad's right really and it's us who should be thinking more like him, not the other way around. The lad's got a conscience, that's all, and I'll bet you'd rather have him looking after something belonging to you, than any one of us, if you see what I mean," he finished lamely.

"Yes, you're right," Trev said. "Mickey's honest that's all, and we don't like it because it shows just how crooked the rest of us are."

"But there's honest and bloody honest, Trev. Come on, everybody can't be perfect like him, can they now?" Alan said.

"He's only trying to live his life according to his beliefs, isn't he? And there's nowt wrong with him doing that at all. Now leave the poor bugger alone and think of somebody else we can talk about," Joe said with finality.

"But to give the bloody money away. What's the stupid bastard gone and done that for?" Alan said. "He's dropped us right in it, he has."

"How's that? They'll never be able to link us to that, will they?" Joe said naively.

"You want to bet?" Alan almost spat. "They'll be on to us alright. Newspapers first, then the bleedin' police."

"They'll want to find out who the donor is, and where he got so much money from," agreed Trev.

"They'll never think that it was the likes of Mickey who gave the money," Joe maintained. "Who would think that someone like him would have that much cash? And not only have it, but give it away. No. They'll probably be looking for some generous millionaire businessman. I can't see anyone even vaguely connecting Mickey to it."

"Well, I'm not so sure," Trev put in. "That bleedin' reporter has been sniffing around for weeks now. He's like a dog with a bone, following George around. He was sure we've got something to hide and he's a persistent bastard. I think he was starting to slacken off and get a bit tired of it all, but now this will give him a renewed sense of purpose and he'll be off again."

"Then there's that financial advisor you brought in," Alan said accusingly. "He's got an idea there's something iffy as well. He's been sniffing about ever since you asked all those questions about investing the cash."

"This is all getting out of control," Joe said. "George's permanently pissed out of his mind and it's only a matter of time before he lets something slip, or someone twigs, anyway."

"And there's still D.C. Henry. He's still sniffing about and it's only a matter of time before he gets hold of something to hit us with. He's a right bastard that one and no mistake. He's really got it in for me, ever since we were at school and especially since that time I accidentally caught him with my foot." Alan said.

"You caught him with your foot?" Trev repeated.

"Yes. Well, what happened was that I was climbing over a wall and he just happened to be on the other side of the same wall. I put my leg over, as you do, and my foot caught him on the side of the head. He would never accept that it was a pure accident."

"When was this, then?"

"Oh, four, no five years ago it'll be now. You'd have though that he'd have forgotten about it by now, wouldn't you? But he's a vindictive bastard that Henry is."

Trev digested the information so recently imparted by his colleague. "So, what were you doing climbing over the wall then?"

"What wall?"

"The wall you were climbing over when you accidentally caught D.C. Henry with your foot."

"Oh, that wall," Alan said, as if he was in the habit of regularly climbing over walls, and had trouble remembering which was which, which he probably did. "Er, I was getting over it because, what was it again?" he asked himself. "Oh yes, it was the dog. I was getting away from the dog, that was it."

"Dog?"

"Yes, the dog. It was attacking me and I legged it, naturally, as you would do."

"So why was the dog attacking you, Alan? And where was all this happening? Bloody hell, man, getting info out of you is like drawing bloody teeth," Trev complained.

"Well, I forget, man. As a matter of fact, I've been attacked by dogs on quite a number of occasions. It's these bleedin' shopkeepers. They leave the bloody things in the shops at night and naturally they get a bit miffed with anybody breaking into the shop, don't they?"

"So, you were actually breaking into a shop and this dog chases you over a wall and D.C. Henry is on the other side waiting for you, right?"

"Well, I suppose that's one way of looking at it."

"And so he grabs you, your leg anyway, and you kick out at him and kick him on the head, right?"

"Could be."

"Well, it's no bloody wonder that he's got the hump with you, is it?"

"Look, when they got me down to the nick that night, Henry made sure he escorted me to the cells, didn't he? And he made very sure that I fell down the steps, didn't he? Not just once either, but twice. And that should have been the end of it. You know, tit for tat? But no, that's not enough for him, not for that bastard. He was after me from then on. He considered me to be public enemy number one."

He paused seemingly deep in thought. "He never let up chasing me. Then there was that time he arrested me for being in possession of stolen goods. I told him they weren't stolen, but he wouldn't listen, would he? He searched my flat and found these porcelain figurines. Now a few weeks earlier there had been a burglary at a local councillor's house, a big detached house on the seafront and figurines very similar to those he found at my flat had been stolen. Henry wouldn't listen to my explanation, ran his big mouth off and insisted on having me charged, made a right fool of himself. He made a statement to the papers, well to a reporter. Actually, he didn't know it was a reporter until later. Anyway, he rattles off all this crap about how good a detective he is and all that. He made a lot of noise and was considered the best thing since sliced bread for a while, but then it all went rotten, didn't it?"

"How did it go rotten?"

"Well, they eventually did listen to me, my brief actually, and realised the stuff did belong to me, not to this councillor. I found the receipt for the stuff and the seller remembered me buying it from him. Impeccable witness he was. Had an antiques stall in the market. The police had to release me with an apology didn't they? Nearly killed the bastards that public apology did. The local newspaper made a big thing about it. And all this was taking place at about the time our Henry was being considered for promotion. What with all the bad publicity making him look a right idiot, he was turned down. It was another two years before he actually did get his promotion to the detective branch. He blamed me for it, didn't he? Still does."

Joe digested this slowly. "This witness, who exactly was he?"

"The witness? Oh, he was called Nigel. Nigel Nordstrom."

"Nordstrom, any relation to Nobby by any chance?"

"His uncle."

"Very interesting," Trev said. "But what are we going to do with all this money?"

"I think we should get rid of the lot," Joe said. "Just ditch it somewhere and then we can get back to normal."

"Normal, like struggling to make a living and getting shit on by the boss all day?" Trev asked.

"Well, at least we wouldn't be frightened of our own bloody

shadows, would we?"

There was a loud noise from outside. A screeching as the allotment gate was opened. The three men froze and looked at each other in panic.

"Who the fuck's that?" Alan demanded.

"How do I know?" Trev answered.

"Oh God," Joe said, looking through the dirty window. "It's Brenda."

Brenda pushed open the shed door so hard that it bounced off the wall and shook the whole shed. She stood silhouetted in the doorway for a moment before walking in. She looked around and sniffed as if she could detect something that displeased her immensely.

"So you're all in here, I thought you would be. Call yourselves men? I've known braver mice. Look at yourselves, holed up, hiding in a garden shed for days. Scared to death to show yourselves outside just because there are a couple of ugly foreigners and a flat-footed policeman asking a few questions. What did you expect, eh? Just what did you think would happen? Whoever the money belonged to was never going to just forget about it, were they? Or is that what you thought? Just what do you think you are going to do? Give the money back? Give it to charity like Mickey did? Throw it all away? Burn it?" She shook her head as if disgusted. "What about all that positive mental attitude that you were so keen on, Trev? What's happened to that? The first sign of a problem, a little difficulty and you run in here and hide like a bairn."

Trev looked uncomfortable but said nothing.

She snorted with disgust. "Listen; if you keep this money you're hurting no one. It doesn't seem to belong to anybody. Not legally anyway, and certainly nobody's come forward to claim it. So you've got all this money, there are millions of pounds just going begging and you are too frightened to take it. This is the biggest chance that any one of you has had in your lives and you are terrified by it. You can't afford to just let it go. If you are too frightened to grasp this once in a lifetime chance, and are going to give the money away and crawl under a rock somewhere and hide for the rest of your lives, well that's fine, but you can count me and Joe out." She looked meaningfully at her husband. Joe looked sheepishly down at his feet, avoiding her eyes. "We'll take the bloody cash. All of it. Every last penny. I want my baby to have a good start." She placed her hands on her stomach. "A bloody good start, not wanting for anything. I want the best for my bairn and intend to get it. Joe here will have a few sleepless nights and his ulcer will play up for a while, and then after a few months he'll get used to having the money and get used to spending it, while the rest of you go back to your miserable existence scrimping and scraping enough money to live on. I know an awful lot of things I could do with that money. If you're too frightened to keep it. We'll have it. That'll solve your problem, and ours, once and for all." She paused for breath, her chest heaving and nostrils flared like a beautiful wild animal.

"But Brenda, look what they did. They very nearly killed Nobby's mother," Alan said quietly, having found his voice.

"But they didn't kill her, did they? And the chances are they'll give up now and bugger off back to Germany, or wherever it was they came from. They'll know the police are looking for them now. Look, the best thing that you three can do is to start acting normally. Hiding away up here is simply drawing attention to yourselves."

The men looked at each other.

"I was thinking the same thing, actually," Trev said. "It's pointless being holed up here. In fact if those Germans are looking around the allotments for the bulbs this is probably the last place we should be."

"And meanwhile, George, a real prize leak if there ever was one, is wandering from pub to pub drunk as a skunk and throwing his money around and attracting attention," Brenda said. "At least one of you should be looking after him."

The leak joke went straight over Alan's head. "He won't stand for that, Brenda," he pointed out. "He'll do what he wants and go where he wants, will George, and wouldn't take kindly to anybody trying to babysit him."

Brenda looked witheringly at Alan. "If anybody needs babysitting it's you, Alan Spencer. It's your fault that we're all in this position at all. You were the one who stole the bloody money and roped in Joe, Trev and the others. You. Mr Big, the bloody criminal mastermind. You, the one who is always talking about how you are going to pull off the big one, the big robbery that is going to set you up for life. And now that's exactly what you've got, millions of pounds lying there and you're too bloody scared to take it."

It was Alan's turn to look shamefacedly down at his feet.

"Your mother would know exactly what to do with the money, wouldn't she? She'd say thank you very much, God, you're a diamond, and she'd take the cash and be off spending it. Not hiding in here like rabbits in a hole." She looked at each one of them in turn. Joe nodded in agreement, Alan continued to look at his feet, but Trev stared back at her with an expression on his face as if she'd provided the answer to their problems.

"Do you know what your mother's doing now?" Brenda asked Alan sharply.

"No, what?"

"She's out there now, at this minute, stealing baby clothes for me because she thinks we're skint. That's what. She obviously doesn't know the baby's sex so she's nicking all white baby clothes. When the bairn's born, no doubt she'll be out again and get the right coloured ones. That's what your mother's doing, bless her. And you, you hide in here with millions of bloody pounds that you're too scared to keep." Brenda, breathing heavily, sat down, seemingly exhausted by her emotional outburst. Joe fussed around her and made her a cup of tea and she soon revived.

After more discussion and a lot more impassioned, but more controlled, input from Brenda, the men agreed to leave the allotment and start behaving as normal, but to keep their eyes peeled for foreigners. They did, however, decide to keep to their sleeping rota in the shed going, so as to be able to guard the cash at night. They all left the allotment soon after, but Joe and Trev returned that night as it was their turn to guard the cash.

47

Trev shook Joe's shoulder urgently.

"What …?"

"Shushhh!" Trev whispered. "There's somebody out there."

"Somebody out where?" Joe asked, still groggy with sleep.

"Out there in the allotment," Trev whispered. "Keep your voice down, will you?"

Joe staggered to his feet, throwing off the old blanket that he'd wrapped around himself. Trev, already on his feet, had hardly got a wink of sleep, what with Joe's snoring and the various unaccustomed noises outside; it had been an ordeal for him. Joe, on the other hand, whatever his other phobias and foibles certainly didn't have any problem at all with sleeping. He'd drifted off to sleep as soon as his head had hit the improvised pillow.

Joe was more or less awake now and they both armed themselves with spades. Trev opened the shed door a crack and peered out into the darkness. There wasn't much of a moon, but it provided just enough light for them to see most of the allotment. They both stared out into the gloom; Trev standing and Joe crouched behind him. They remained in that position for some time and Joe was beginning to get pins and needles in his legs. He shifted uncomfortably, moving his legs slightly to help the circulation.

Trev was cold and beginning to think he'd imagined hearing the noise. That was when they saw the movement. They both saw the man at the same time, as the intruder darted from the back of the greenhouse, across to the leek trench and crouched down low behind it.

"Somebody's after the money," Trev whispered, his voice hardly audible to Joe, whose ear was only a few inches away from him.

"What are we going to do?" Joe whispered back.

"We'll have to stop him, won't we? We can't have people helping themselves to our bleeding' money can we?"

A sudden thought struck Joe. "How'd they know the money was there?" he asked.

"How the fuck do I know?" Trev was getting tense. "Come on, let's nail the bastard."

Without waiting for his friend to reply, Trev flung open the door of the shed and ran out towards the still crouching figure. Joe followed close behind. They were halfway to the intruder's position before the man moved. Becoming aware of the two attackers bearing down on him, he scrambled to his feet and ran. He ran towards the back fence, which was the direction he'd come from originally. Trev and Joe gave chase; neither of them had uttered a word. The man jumped the various obstacles in his way, the type of thing normally present in an allotment, cold frames, a water barrel, some chicken wire fencing. Joe running behind, observed this, and his brain automatically recorded the fact that the intruder knew his way around the allotment very well, even in the dark. He's obviously been in here before, Joe deduced.

The man had almost reached the back fence and safety; once over that and he'd have been able to disappear into the maze of other gardens and allotments quite easily. However, his luck ran out about three paces from his target. He tripped and stumbled into a cold frame containing a large prize marrow. The intruder fell, breaking the glass and ruining the marrow completely, falling right on top of the huge thing and squashing it.

Trev caught up with the man as he was trying to extricate himself from the frame. He was a pitiful sight, covered in the soft substance of the marrow and bleeding from various cuts caused by the broken glass.

Joe arrived, the spade above his head ready to strike, as Trev grabbed the man's arm. "Now then, you bastard. How did you know it was in here?" Trev demanded of the prisoner.

The man was shocked and shaking from his recent exertions and fall. "I er ... I ..." He stopped, took a great lungful of air and tried again. "But everybody knows it's in here," he blurted out.

"Everybody?" asked Trev dismayed. "How does everybody know?"

"Because they do. It's the only place that it could be, isn't it?"

Joe, silent up to now, stepped forward, lowered the spade and spoke. "Hey, wait a minute. I know you, don't I?"

"Know me? Know me? You should bloody well know me. I've been runner-up in the annual leek show for the last ten years, I have," the man said dejectedly. "Runner-up every year to your bleedin' first prize leek."

"It's Frankie, Frankie Lane," Joe said to Trev. The intruder's real name wasn't actually Frankie Lane, it was Francis Cain, but he'd naturally been baptised Frankie Lane by his workmates when he started work, as the country and western singer of the same name was very popular at about that time.

"Pleased to meet you, I'm sure," Trev said sarcastically. "And would Frankie here like to tell us what he's doing in your allotment at half past two in the bleedin' morning? Because he certainly isn't here to sing Ghost Riders in the Fucking Sky, is he?"

"Oh, aye. I'm really sorry about this, lads. It's just that I come second every year, I'm always runner-up and this year I thought I'd do something about it."

"About what?"

"About your prize leeks. I've got to admit that I was going to sabotage them," he admitted. The admission had a huge effect on the man. His guilt seemed to multiply and his face crumpled into a tearful sponge. "I shouldn't have done it, Joe. But our lass has been on at me for years about me not being good at anything," he sniffed. "She kept complaining that I couldn't do anything to satisfy her need …" he sniffed again, "… her need to have a husband who was somebody, who won something." He paused. "And she has a wicked tongue she has, if she puts her mind to it, never lets up for a minute."

"That's right, she has got a wicked tongue," Joe confirmed to Trev. "You should hear her when she gets started …"

Trev stared at Joe in disbelief and then back to Frankie and shook his head. "Alright, alright. I think we can safely assume that this isn't the bleedin' world famous Pink Panther jewel thief that we've caught breaking in, so why don't we all go back and sit in the shed, where it's nice and warm and we can have a hot cuppa?"

The three men made their way back to the shed and boiled the kettle. Trev was more relieved than he let on that it was only a leek saboteur that had come sniffing around and not someone after the money. His heart had nearly stopped when Frankie had mentioned that everybody knew that it was in the allotment, but thankfully, it was only the leeks he was talking about.

"I wasn't expecting anybody to be here," Frankie explained despondently, dabbing the blood from a cut on his arm with a none-too-clean handkerchief. "I know that George sometimes sleeps up here to keep an eye on his leeks, but generally that's not until just before the shows, not this early in the season." He paused as if he'd remembered something. "What are you two doing up here, anyway? Did somebody tip you off that I was coming tonight, eh?"

Trev paused before answering, his mind racing. He didn't want to arouse any suspicions in Frankie's mind. "Well, we did hear a whisper that something was afoot."

"Thought so. You can't trust anybody these days. Grass you up as soon as look at you they will," he sniffed.

Joe seemed to be genuinely concerned about Frankie's emotional state and encouraged him to talk about his fears and worries. "Get them all out and you'll feel a lot better, mate," he advised Frankie.

Frankie did. He unburdened himself to Joe and Trev, confiding in them all his problems with his overbearing wife, her even more overbearing mother and sister and the misery they put him through at home in his own house. Apparently all three of them made a habit of ensconcing themselves in Frankie's front room every afternoon and evening and gossiped and moaned about just about everything he did and worst of all, monopolised the television remote control.

"But that's terrible," Trev said. "How can they do that to you? How can your wife allow them to do that to you? It's not right. In fact it's a bloody disgrace."

"Yes, it's not right at all," Joe agreed.

"And, maybe it's not my place to say this, Frankie, but maybe you should be a bit more assertive, manlier, like?" Trev advised.

"Oh, I tried that ages ago," Frankie confided.

"And?" Trev asked.

"And she stopped my ration."

"She stopped your …?" Trev started to query, but stopped when the penny dropped. "Oh, I see. But that's not fair; you shouldn't let her get away with that."

Frankie shrugged. "She's always doing it. What can I do? She says I'm a failure, that I can't even win a leek club prize, and so, no ration. I'm a driver, do trips to the continent regularly and sometimes I'm away from home for weeks at a time. I come home and she says, no ration. That's not right, is it?"

The men agreed with Frankie that it wasn't right, then fell quiet, ruminating on this predicament that Frankie had found himself in.

Revived by the hot tea and some of the sandwiches that the pair of sentinels had brought with them, the three men, now calm and relaxed again, talked and smoked until the sky grew light. Nothing was resolved regarding Frankie's matrimonial problems or frustrations, but Joe and Trev did promise to give the matter more thought and see what they could come up with. They waved a weary Frankie goodbye and set him to the gate, from where they watched him descend the hill towards his home.

"We should do something about that, you know?" Joe said.

"About him trying to sabotage your leeks?"

"No. About his wife and her mother and sister. They're a right bunch of nasty bastards, they are. I can remember a few years ago, Brenda had a run-in with Frankie's mother-in-law over the kids playing football in the street and kicking their ball into her garden. She would never give them the ball back. Anyway, Brenda goes round to see her about the balls and she wouldn't open the door. She just shouted out from the upstairs window. Called Brenda all sorts of names. Right foul-mouthed she has. Wouldn't be reasonable and you know what she actually did? She burst all the balls she'd kept. She used a kitchen knife and slashed them and then threw them out of the bedroom window. The bairns' were crying their little eyes out, they were. Nastiest bloody woman that I've ever come across, she is."

"But what can we do about it? Anyway, it's got nothing to do with us really, has it? We wouldn't have known anything about it if we hadn't caught him breaking in here, would we?"

"It might not have anything to do with us, but I still think you're right and that we should do something to help the poor bastard out. It's the principle of the thing, man. We can't let them ride roughshod over him like that. It's definitely not right," Trev said.

"Well, I can't see as how we can do anything about it, anyway."

"Maybe, but don't forget that we know have almost unlimited financial resources, don't we? That could make all the difference."

Joe nodded. "That's right. Believe it or not, I'd forgotten all about the money. That might make a difference all right. Things always look different if there's no need to spare the expense, don't they? Tell you what, why don't we discuss it with the others and see if we can come up with some sort of plan or something?"

"That's a good idea. Between the five of us we should be able to come up with something useful, shouldn't we?" Trev said, but thought, don't count on it, mate, don't count on it.

48

"I must be careful not to damage any of your prize leeks, mustn't I?" Detective Constable Henry said, a smirk on his face. "I must admit that I can be really clumsy at times. If my concentration goes and I get distracted." He looked at Joe and smiled, a nasty, vindictive sort of grimace. He poked around in the leek trench with a short stick that he'd picked up in the allotment. The bamboo stick was about two foot long and could easily reach the bottom of the leek trench.

Joe watched closely, his eyes narrowing involuntarily every time the stick strayed near to the edge of the trench. Joe realised that the detective was probably looking for some sort of indication from him and so he looked away and studiously watched Alan's flock of racing pigeons flying around in circles, high above then.

D.C. Henry followed his gaze upwards. "Your mate's pigeons, are they? I hear that he's got some real good racers there. I really must pop over and have a word with him while I'm in the area. I've never actually been inside a pigeon cree," he mused.

Joe looked across and could see Alan cleaning out the nesting boxes in the cree. He wracked his brains but couldn't think of any way that he could warm his friend that the policeman planned to go across. He became aware that the policeman was speaking. "Er I'm sorry, miles away, what was that again?"

"I said that it looks like I must have caught one of your leeks by accident," Henry said, the same smile on his face.

Joe walked nearer to the trench. The bamboo had almost uprooted one of his best leeks. One of those he'd planned to show. "Don't worry about it. Accidents will happen, won't they? Never mind it's not a very good one anyway."

The detective looked rather disappointed that Joe wasn't more upset and that he didn't seem to consider the damage to be too severe. But he was tiring of his game of baiting Joe and was now a bit more inclined to be straightforwardly obnoxious. "Right, then. Enough of this horseplay. Let's get down to business, shall we?"

"Whatever you say, officer, but I really don't know what sort of business it is that I can help you with."

"For starters, what about the bulbs?"

"The bulbs?" echoed Joe.

"Yes, the tulip bulbs."

"I'm afraid I don't know anything at all about tulips. Leeks or marrows perhaps, but I've never been inclined to grow flowers of any type. The lad next door," he indicated Ralph's garden with his head, "he used to grow flowers, but then again I don't think he was one for tulips either, more like geraniums and stuff," Joe said affably. "Anyway he's been dead for a couple of months now."

"Don't give me all that old shite. You know perfectly well what I'm talking about. I'm talking about the theft of a lorry load of bulbs. Why you wanted all those bulbs, I'll never know. Probably nobody will ever know. Maybe you plan to sell them on, but not this year you won't, because I'll be watching you." Henry nodded in Alan's direction. "You and your mate over there, the bird man of Alcatraz, he knows all about it as well. The bloody tulips will have gone rotten by the time you can shift them. If you ever do get to shift them, that is."

"I really don't know what you are talking about, I really don't," Joe maintained.

"Yes you do. Don't lie to me. And, don't think that this little episode will just blow over and go away after a while. I'm not giving up on this. I'm going to keep after you and Tweety Pie there, or is it Doctor Doolittle? Until one of you makes a slip. And one of you is sure to, sooner or later, then I'll have you, you pair of bastards." The detective was so annoyed that he practically spat at Joe. "By the way, what's happened to your other mate, Trev? I can't find him anywhere, seems to have disappeared off the face of the earth, he has. Him and that other loser, Nordstrom."

Joe shrugged his shoulders. "I haven't seen either of them for ages."

"I didn't think you would have," the detective said disgustedly and turned and made for the gate, throwing the bamboo stick sideways towards the leek trench as he strode away. The stick embedded itself in the soil near the edge of the trench, exactly above some of the buried money, like a miniature flagpole, marking its position.

Joe watched anxiously as the policeman left the allotment, but instead of going left along the narrow path towards Alan's pigeon cree, Henry stopped as if struck by a sudden thought. He turned right and strode towards the adjoining garden and peered thorough a gap in the fence. He remained there for a couple of minutes before walking back to the main road where his car was parked.

Relieved that Henry had decided against visiting Alan's cree, Joe made his way to the shed for his cure-all, a cup of hot, sweet, tea. He didn't think that his nerves could take much more of this tension. His stomach continued to give him grief and he was taking double the prescribed amounts of his medication, He'd knew that he'd have to make another appointment to see his doctor soon. He rummaged in his jacket, which was hanging from a nail in the wall, until he found his tablets, and swallowed two while waiting for the kettle to boil. His stomach ached as if he'd been punched hard in the solar plexus and he comforted himself by placing his hands over the spot.

Alan watched the detective drive away. He'd been aware of the man's presence in Joe's allotment, but had pretended he hadn't seen him. Watching closely from the corner of his eye, he'd been alarmed to see the detective prodding around in the leek trench, but it looked as if he hadn't found anything. Alan smiled; he thought that if Henry had found the cash, he'd have made a lot more noise about it and that's for sure. Then again, what was Henry doing looking into old Ralph's garden? Joe wouldn't have told him anything, would he? The pair of them looked decidedly pally over there together. Alan was puzzled as to why Joe hadn't come straight across and told him what had happened. He didn't trust Henry as far as he could throw him. Trev and Nobby had gone missing and probably taken a load of the cash with them, George was definitely suspect, the weak link, and now he was beginning to have serious doubts about Joe as well.

49

Violet walked straight up to George and stood beside him at the bar. "Buy a girl a drink, mister?" she asked quietly.

George, startled, turned towards her and his eyes opened wide when he realised who it was. "Violet, what are you doing here?"

"Trying to get you to buy me a drink," she replied, smiling.

"Of course. What would you like?"

"You've forgotten already, George? You know that I don't drink anything but lager or vodka and orange. And tonight is definitely a vodka and orange night."

"Yes, that's right. Vodka and orange, of course. How could I forget?" He put his cigar into an ashtray and signalled to the barman, ordered her drink and another pint for himself. There was complete silence between the couple as they watched the barman filling the drinks, each seemingly lost in their thoughts. George's mind was racing, wondering what Violet wanted. Despite himself his heart was racing as well, because of her nearness. He couldn't understand her turning up like this.

As the drinks were placed in front of them on the counter, George reached for his wallet and immediately suspected why she'd turned up just at this particular time. Of course, it was the money. She must have eventually heard that he had been spending money like a sailor with no pockets. He'd hoped that it would attract her, and sure enough it had worked.

"You keeping alright, then?" he asked as he lifted the full pint glass.

"I'm fine thanks. You're not looking so good yourself," she said, taking in his unkempt appearance.

"Never felt better," he said dismissively.

"Bachelor life mustn't be agreeing with you."

"You might be right." He drank a good part of his pint, wiping the froth from his lips with the back of his hand. Picking up his cigar, he looked towards her. "Look, Violet, I don't know what you want, but whatever it is, the answer is no."

"What makes you think that I want anything?"

"Because that's the only time you are ever nice to me. That's why."

"You know that's not true. We used to have a very good relationship at one time."

"Yes, that's right, we did. Until you walked out."

"You really do have a way with words, George. I want to come back to you, how about it, will you have me back?"

George was shocked. He looked at her to make sure she wasn't making fun of him and swallowed hard. "What about your boyfriend, the toy boy?"

"There was never any toy boy, George. I just told you that to make you jealous."

"What about the fella waiting for you in the car when you came over to get those divorce papers signed?"

"I tore the papers up and put them on the fire. And that was my friend Silvia's son. He's only twenty for God's sake. That's where I've been staying, at Silvia's; she works at the factory with me."

George nodded. "So you think you can just walk back into my life and take up where we left off, do you?"

"Would you like that?"

He paused before answering, as if weighing his words carefully. He took his time relighting the cigar which had gone out. He knew that he'd been the cause of her leaving. It was entirely his fault. He'd got into a rut as he got older, and was never very talkative about anything other than his very narrow interests. It wasn't that he didn't want to talk about other things, or do other things; it was just that he was comfortable with discussing and doing the things he knew about. He'd become set in his ways, and he'd been totally out of order calling her lazy like that. He drew on the cigar and blew a smoke ring. "No. Too much water has gone under the bridge for that. I'm not the same man as I was, and I don't think that you are the same woman either. Well, you're not the same in my eyes, and that's what counts," he lied.

"Why don't you think about it, George? You always were a thinker. That's what I liked about you. You never did anything on impulse. You always thought things through before you did anything. Think of the advantages of having a woman around. You've been on your own for long enough now to realise what you're missing." She paused and took her first sip of her vodka and orange. "And I don't just mean the home cooking."

"I eat out nowadays, thanks, but no thanks. You've got a real nerve. What makes you think that I'd even consider taking you back?"

"Well, that's another thing I always liked about you, you're a straight talker. No beating about the bush with you, George, when you do say something, oh no, it's always straight out with it, isn't it?" She drank more from her glass. "You'll consider taking me back because you still love me, George. That's why. You love me like you did when you married me. You don't want another woman, because if you did, you'd have had another woman by now."

"Quite the amateur psychoanalyst, aren't you?"

"I know people, George, and I know you well enough, believe me. You aren't the most communicative man in the world, or the most emotional, but there's worse things than that."

"Why did you come back now, at this time, why now?"

Idle Hands

"Because, I love you, George, that's why. I've been thinking things over. And I've come to the conclusion that you're the man for me and I want you. It's as simple as that."

"And what you want, you get, is that it?"

"If you like, but you know as well as I do that we should be together and we will be. There's no argument. Neither of us can fight it."

"It wouldn't be that fact that you've heard that I've come into some money that made your mind up, would it?"

She appeared to be shocked at the suggestion. "How can you say something like that after all we've meant to each other?" she asked him, what appeared to be real tears appearing in her eyes.

George drank the remained of his pint, seemingly unimpressed. "You want another?" he asked her.

She appeared to consider the offer very seriously before committing herself to accepting anything further from him. Then she made her mind up. "I don't mind if I do."

He indicated to the barman to refill the glasses and placed a five-pound note on the counter. "I won't be long," he said and walked towards the toilet.

The drinks were on the counter along with his change when he returned. "Well, at least you haven't done off with my change," he said, pocketing the money and raising his glass to his lips. He took a long drink before placing the glass on the counter again. He looked at her appraisingly and then pulled a wad of cash from his pocket and placed it on the bar counter. "There's nearly three hundred pounds there. That's all I've got left. Pick it up and you can have it. If it's only the money you're after, I'd appreciate it if you just take that and we'll go our separate ways."

She looked at the cash and picked up the bundle. She held the money to her nose and smelled the notes then, smiling, pushed them back into his pocket. "Don't you think that money stinks? No, George it's not the money that I want, it's you. I'll tell you what made my mind up, shall I?"

He didn't respond.

"It was when I read in the paper that you were telling people you'd won the pools and were splashing your redundancy money around, just to tempt me back. And the police thought you'd stolen it."

"I haven't won the pools, Violet."

"I know that. It's your bit of redundancy money you've been spending, going round buying everybody drinks and smoking big cigars as if you had loads of money. If you'd waste your money like that, just to get me back it means that you must really love me, George. And I really love you."

"Look, Vi, I love you as well, with all my heart, but there's something you've got to know." He paused for a few seconds before continuing, as if weighing the consequences of what he was about to say. "It wasn't my redundancy money that I was spending, either. I just used that as an excuse when the police questioned me about the money I was spending…"

Violet held up her hand to stop him speaking. "I don't care where the money came from, I don't care. All I care about is you. I made a big mistake leaving you and I regret it. I'll gladly come back to you whether you've won the pools, robbed a bank, or even if you're skint." She smiled. "Well down to your last three hundred, anyway. That is, if you'll have me back?"

"Alright then," he said relieved and happy. "Here's to us the second time around," he said, smiling and lifting his glass.

50

D.C. Henry was excited. While he'd been peering over the adjacent allotment fence into Ralph's allotment, using his highly tuned observation techniques, he'd noticed that a lot of the soil had been recently disturbed, turned over in fact. Joe had just told him that the allotment holder was deceased and had been for about two months, so why would anyone turn the garden over? he asked himself. He'd checked with the council and the garden hadn't been re-let yet. It was hardly likely that anyone would put that much effort into the garden before it was re-let. Because that's where the tulip bulbs had been planted, that's why, he reasoned triumphantly. He was one hundred percent certain that Spencer and his cronies were responsible for the theft, and it stood to reason the bulbs were hidden in that garden. What he would really like to do was to stake the garden out and arrest the thieves when they came back for the bulbs, but he couldn't spend that much time on a stake-out without permission. He decided to put in an official request, even though he knew that it was too time consuming and required officers that couldn't be spared, and that it was not very likely that he'd ever get the relevant authorisation. He drove straight back to the station and told his sergeant of his suspicions.

The detective sergeant wasn't exactly ecstatic about his theory. "Do you know what sort of pressure I'm under? I've got three hundred tasks to complete this week and all of them are high priority rated. I've two officers down with sickness and another two on holiday. The inspector is also on the sick and I've got half of his bleedin' work to do as well as my own and you want me to give you men to stake out a bleedin' allotment for bleedin' tulips? Are you stupid, man?"

"Okay, forget about the stake-out. But those bulbs are buried in that garden and we wouldn't have to search far for them, sarge. They're all there in the one spot. I can lead the lads straight to them. All they'll have to do is pick them up and bring them in. It'll take an hour at the most. I guarantee it."

The sergeant still looked undecided.

"It'll look good, us recovering stolen property and it'll be another stat off the crime figures and all it'll take is one hour," encouraged D.C. Henry.

"Alright then. You arrange for a search warrant and come back to me with the details."

51

The lads knew that Frankie would be in the doghouse if he didn't win a prize at this year's leek and flower show at the club. They discussed the matter and argued back and forth as to the best way to help the man. George was all for just giving him their leek and marrow entries and letting him claim them as his own, but Joe disagreed, not because he was concerned about them not winning this year, but because Frankie's wife would be sure to smell a rat. Frankie had told Joe in the past that his wife took a great interest in his vegetables and was always calling in at the allotment and inspecting them.

"Sounds to me more like nosiness than interest," George remarked. "But what can we do?"

"Well, I suppose that we could always swap them over in the trench," Joe suggested.

"What, do a ringer, you mean?"

"Yes, why not? That way his wife would actually see the things in the trench, his trench, with her own eyes and he could perhaps get her there to see them when he digs them up. She'd have no idea then that they weren't his, would she?"

George pondered this point for a while; sucking gently on his foul smelling pipe and polluting the atmosphere in the shed with plumes of acrid smoke with bits of ash intermingled in it, like a small, smouldering volcano. He indicated with the pipe, taking it out of his mouth and pointing the tooth-marked stem at Joe. "Alright. We'll do that and give Frankie the leeks. What about the onions then? Are we still going to show those?"

"We could do, I suppose, seeing as how Frankie's knackered the prize marrow good and proper. One prize will be enough for Frankie. He'll be happy with that and so will their lass, and he'll get his ration rights back. If he won the onion prize as well, it would be too dangerous. Their lass would be all over him and he'd probably shag himself to death."

George puffed contentedly on his pipe and smiled. "Do you really think that we're doing old Frankie any favours by letting him win? I wouldn't like to have to shag their lass, would you?"

"Ah, but old Frankie doesn't have any option, does he? It's her or nowt. But I still think that we should come up with something else. This is too complicated. How are we going to swap the bloody leeks over? We can't very well just waltz along with a barrow full of out leeks pull his up and stick ours in, now can we?"

"Why not?"

"Because there's too many people will see us. You know what they're like around here. They're like bloody old women. All that's missing from some of these sheds up here is a few net curtains up at the windows."

"I never thought about that," George admitted. "I suppose that we could do it at night, when there's no one about, couldn't we?"

"I don't fancy doing a Cadbury's Milk Tray advert type of thing," Joe said. "What about getting the expert in."

"Who's the expert?"

"Alan."

"Alan Spencer? We don't want him involved in this do we?"

"Why not? It's horses for courses, isn't it? He's just the man if we want to break in somewhere; nobody around here has had more experience than he has at that type of thing."

George nodded. "I must admit that he probably is the best for something like this." He paused and smoked. Joe was never sure when George was finished speaking or if he was just pausing before saying something else. He was just pausing. "He's a big thief, but there's nowt else up there for him to steal, is there?"

"No, just veg and a few old garden tools. That's it then. Problem solved, we'll ask Alan to do it sometime this week and get the thing over with."

"You'll have to let Frankie know as well. We don't want him sitting up there with a shovel or something and braining Alan when he climbs over the fence, now do we?"

"Like I nearly did to Frankie? No, we certainly don't want him doing anything like that. But don't worry; he's away on a driving trip abroad this week."

Alan agreed to the task but had some questions. "It's going a bit far, isn't it? Why not just meet Frankie on the way to the show and swap the things over then, no fuss no bother?"

Joe explained the complications with Frankie's wife.

"Okay then. I don't suppose there's anything else up there to nick, is there? So I'll do it just for the devilment. Mind, one of you will have to come with me."

"Why?" Joe asked.

"Because, if I get caught, I'm not going to be believed by anybody if I say that I just happened to be passing and thought I'd nip in and swap some leeks, which I just happened to have with me, for Frankie's, now am I?"

"So what difference does having someone with you make?"

"Because if I'm caught, it's likely to be by one of your allotment neighbours up here, and if one of you is with me, then they'll believe you. But they sure as hell wouldn't believe me, will they?"

"I suppose you've got a point," George admitted.

"Too true, I've got a point, mate," Alan said.

"You volunteering to go with him then, George, are you?"

"Are you daft or what, man? I'm far too old to be gallivanting about in the dark, climbing over fences and the like. No you'd better go."

Joe wasn't too keen and tried, unsuccessfully to suggest someone else. "What about Trev? He'd be much better than me. He's more agile, a lot younger and he'd be able to climb easier than I will."

"No. Trev seems to have gone missing; he's not been sighted for a while. It'll have to be you. All the gardeners up here know you and trust you, so it's got to be you," Alan, excited now by the prospect of the nocturnal expedition, started singing, "It's got to be you, wonderful you …" and grabbed Joe around the waist, leading him off on a dancing trip around the allotment.

They settled in the shed and waited. They watched an old black and white television, making sure that the windows were curtained so as not to display any light from the flickering screen. The picture was sometimes marred by interference and when that happened, Joe nipped outside and adjusted the aerial, which was attached to the roof. Both men were bored and listless. Alan found some of George's brown ale and they decided to have a drink to relive the boredom and pass the time. Time passed slowly but gradually the light began to fade. Despite the late hour there were still a good many people pottering about in the various gardens. At this time of year they fussed over their produce as if it were their children and not merely some vegetables. Alan couldn't understand why so many people got excited about the shows. "But it's all just luck anyway, isn't it? You just stick the things in the ground and they grow. If you're lucky, yours grows bigger than everybody else's and you win," he maintained.

"No. It's not luck; it's an art, a skill, man. A lot of thought, planning and preparation goes into growing prize vegetables. You start by preparing the ground. I always think that a trench is best; you can get the depth, drainage, and can treat the soil properly, and it protects the plants. You've got to develop a feel for the things. You find out by experimenting just what sort of fertilizer they like and thrive on. You nurture them and mollycoddle then and bring them on. The following year you carefully select the seed you are going to plant, and that way you gradually build up the best show veg. And it's not just the prizes," Joe told him. "It's the prestige of winning, of growing better and bigger veg than someone else. It takes years of experience to be able to grow prize-winning entries. Take Frankie Lane, for instance. He'll be absolutely over the moon if we can swing this so he can just win the best of the leek category this year."

"Yes. And their lass might give in and let him have his ration now and again."

They both laughed. The thought of helping mild-mannered Frankie and putting one over on his overbearing wife appealed to them both and in that moment of alcohol-fuelled macho bravado, they were both looking forward to doing it.

They settled down again, watched TV and drank more of George's brown ale.

"What do you think has happened to Trev?" Joe asked.

"I haven't a clue. He seems to have disappeared off the face of the earth. No one's seen him for days now."

"You think those Germans might have got him?"

"No," Alan answered with a conviction he didn't really feel. "He's probably shacked up with a lass somewhere."

It eventually got completely dark and the activity in and around the other gardens ceased. They watched the last allotment holder walking through the gate and heading towards home.

"We'll give it another twenty minutes or so and then we'll start," Alan said. He looked around the shed. "You think it'll be safe to put a light on? There's nobody left up here but us now, is there?"

"Yes, we should be alright now. Mind, there are some who sleep up here sometimes before a show, like George does. Although that's generally because he's too pissed to walk home."

"Why would he do that?"

"What, get pissed?"

"No. Why would he sleep up here?"

"To stop people breaking into the allotment and interfering with the leeks. You'd be surprised how seriously some of these gardeners take things. There have been cases of whole gardens being trashed and the veg spoiled, so it was no good for showing. Even old Frankie Lane has a dog up there in his garden, or so I've heard. But don't worry, it's his brother's, a little Yorkie."

"I know. George told me there was a dog. I'm not worried about a bleeding Yorkie. Anyway, I've got some of that Anti-mate that Trev was on about, so that'll sort it out if it has a go at us." Alan shook his head in disbelief. He could understand people doing all kinds of dodgy things to make a few bob, but to vandalise a garden just to win a vegetable show, was a concept difficult for him to grasp. A sudden thought struck him. "Anyway, what do they do with all the veg after the shows, do they eat it?"

"Some do. But the majority of growers wouldn't eat any of the show vegetables. The ordinary stuff, yes – you can't beat the taste of home grown vegetables."

"Why don't they eat the show veg then?"

"Because they know what's gone into them, don't they? People put some funny stuff on their veg to force feed it."

"Like what?"

"Like blood from the abattoir, any type of fertilizer you can get a hold of, even human excrement."

"Human excrement? You mean shite?"

Joe nodded. "Yes, and worse if they can get hold of it. In fact I've even heard of–"

"No. Don't tell me. I don't want to know. I'll never be able to look at a cucumber again," Alan said. He looked at his watch. "Come on, it's about time we were going."

Despite the alcohol he'd drunk, Joe was nervous now that the time had come. He had been getting increasingly anxious all day and now that it was time to actually do the thing, he was shaking. "This will be okay, won't it, Alan?"

"'Course it will. Just follow me and keep quiet. Try not to make any noise and we'll be in and out of the place, with the stuff switched, in a matter of minutes."

"Are you absolutely sure that you can sort the dog?"

"Stop moaning and worrying. You sound just like an old woman sometimes, nag, nag, nag."

Earlier, while it was still light, they'd carefully loosened the soil around the leeks so they could be easily picked up and placed in trays when it was time to go. Now they carefully lifted them and placed them in shallow seed trays.

"Now then," Alan said quietly, satisfied with his work. "There we are, one tray each. We'll take only one tray each, that should be enough and we don't want to damage any of the bloody leeks, do we?"

The men carried the trays silently through the darkened garden to the gate. Alan was in front and went to open the gate. Joe whispered harshly, "Don't touch that, it squeaks."

But it was too late. Alan opened the gate and the thing screeched an unearthly scream that could be heard quite easily for miles.

Alan got such a shock that he dropped the tray on the ground. The prize leeks scattered everywhere. "Good God, I nearly had a bleeding heart attack, then." He placed a hand on the approximate position of his heart and took deep breaths. "You could have warned me about the gate," he complained to Joe.

"I did bleedin' warn you. Anyway, you've been coming up here for long enough, haven't you?"

"You didn't warn me until I had my friggin' hand on the thing and opened it," Alan's voice was quavering. "And anyway, it's not the same being here at night, it's a lot quieter."

"Come on, pick these up off the ground. The bloody things will probably not be any good for showing now," Joe said. He stood up with one in his hand and shone the torch on it. "Look at the state of this one. That was one of the best, that was."

"Put that light out," Alan ordered. "You want everybody to know what we're doing?"

"But there's no one up here except us."

"Just put it out. Somebody might be passing," Alan maintained.

They collected the fallen leeks as best as they could with minimal help from the torch and at Joe's insistence, left the whole tray just inside the gate. "Most of them are no good, but I'll sort them all out tomorrow," he complained.

They carried on with the one remaining tray, which Joe insisted on carrying. The pair sneaked through the maze of paths that surrounded the various gardens in the dark. "I hope that you're not going to ask me questions about this route later," Alan joked, but his humour was lost on Joe, who was much too nervous to appreciate it. They made good time, walking in a half crouching position, until they arrived at Frankie's allotment.

"Are you absolutely sure that you can sort the dog?"

"Stop moaning and worrying about the dog. It's only a little Yorkie."

They stood in the shadow of Frankie's allotment fence, which was unusual in the fact that it was made from old wooden doors fastened together to make a wall. Joe had often heard Frankie fantasise that they were all bedroom doors, and the insides of each door must have seen some sights over the years and would have some interesting tales to tell, if they could only talk, of course. The two men climbed the fence fairly easily, if a bit unsteadily and made their way across the garden to Frankie's leek trench.

"This is where we've got to be careful," Alan whispered. "Pass me that Anti-mate will you?" Armed with the spray, Alan edged his way carefully further inside the garden. In his other hand he held a lump of raw meat that he had appropriated earlier from a local butcher. "If the dog turns up and the meat doesn't work then I'll have to use the spray," he whispered as he moved further inside. There wasn't any other sound. "He must have left the dog somewhere else," Alan reasoned quietly. "Good old Frankie."

They made fast work of changing over the leeks, removing Frankie's from his trench and placing Joe's replacements carefully in their place. Then they filled the tray with Frankie's efforts, which even in the dark, Joe could see and feel were nowhere as good as his. They had just about finished when the dog appeared.

It came suddenly, seemingly out of nowhere. It was the biggest, fiercest, most aggressive Rottweiler that either of them had ever seen in their lives. Without warning, the dog leapt at Alan, who, when giving an account later, swore that it went straight for his throat. "A fucking man-eater," was how he described it. As the dog approached, Alan, doing what came instinctively to him, turned and ran. In his haste to get away he ran into Joe who was standing right behind him. The two men struggled for a second and then both of them took off through the garden and ran for the fence, abandoning the tray near the trench. Alan, in his flight, dropped the meat onto the ground. The dog smelled it, came to an abrupt halt and turning, sniffed the ground appreciatively until it found the meat, which it proceeded to eat. The men hesitated at the base of the fence, and waited, ready to leave but reluctant to do so while there was still a chance to retrieve the tray. They didn't want to leave Frankie's leeks lying there where his wife might see them and so give the game away, if they could help it. They watched with great interest as the dog ate the entire lump of meat. When the beef was completely consumed, the dog licked its lips, then its paws, and looked as if it might just be going to settle down for a long snooze. But no. It shrugged off any creeping lethargy and resumed its pursuit of the intruders. It came charging full tilt straight at the men as they loitered, trying to make themselves invisible against the wall.

"Shit!" they cried in unison. After a moment's confusion they began to climb the fence, moving with the sure swiftness and strength that only terror can instil.

Alan, being nearest to the dog, only got about halfway up the fence before the animal was snapping at his ankles. He half-turned and with one hand gripping the top of the fence, sprayed the dog full in the face with the Anti-mate. The effect was immediate and spectacular. The beast went absolutely wild. It started to run around the yard howling and barking, and jumped up and down, salivating profusely. It jumped so high that it actually caught Alan's ankle with its teeth, and he was now lying along the top of the fence. The dog was absolutely crazy. It was insane. Neither of the men had ever seen any animal behave in anything like this manner. Aware of the noise that the dog was making, and the need to make a speedy getaway, both men were torn between the need to flee and the desire to watch the dog. They were rooted to the spot and reluctant to take their eyes off the demented canine, which was now rolling over and over on its back and managing to cover almost every part of the garden. The manic animal scattered the tray and sent the leeks spilling all over the ground. It was still howling like a banshee while performing these acrobatics. Suddenly the animal stopped rolling on its back and stood up. It looked up at the two men perched precariously on top of the flimsy fence and charged. It didn't try to leap up at them, but simply ran its head slap-bang into the wooden doors like a battering ram, all the while howling like a banshee. Again and again it attacked the tottering fence. The men swung their legs over the top of the fence and dropped to the ground on the other side and ran, determined to get as far away as possible before the mad dog broke through. But they were too late. One of the doors fell flat on the ground and the animal bounded out over it, free. Terrified, the men ran back the way they'd come, primeval instinct taking over and making decisions for them. They ran as fast as they could towards their allotment and safety. Caution was thrown to the wind as they jumped fences and knocked over rain barrels or anything else that was in their way. The dog was right behind them and gaining. Both men realised that they weren't going to make it. The rabid beast would have them before they reached their allotment.

Alan was just in front of Joe, but tiring fast, despite the adrenaline flooding his body. "Quick, in here," he gasped as the dog snarled at their ankles. He pushed open the gate to old Ralph's garden and both men ran in, the slobbering, mad animal right behind them. Both men instinctively ran right through the allotment, down the side of a shed, the dog still right behind them. Jumping on top of a cold frame, the pair stepped from it, onto an aluminium ladder leaning against the shed, which their momentum caused to slide sideways against the fence adjoining their own garden. The men skimmed up the tottering ladder and over the fence, pushing the ladder away and trapping the dog inside Ralph's garden.

The dog barked and snarled its displeasure at them and attempted to jump over the fence, but it was too high.

"I'll nip round and lock the gate and trap that bastard in there," Alan said and ran off.

Joe peered nervously over the top of the fence at the frenzied Rottweiler and swallowed hard. Alan returned after a few minutes.

"That's got the bastard sorted. It'll not be able to get out of there in a hurry. Come on, let's get out of here."

The noise that the dog was making was beginning to attract attention, and lights were going on in the windows of houses at the bottom of the hill, a couple of hundred yards away, as the pair made their way away from the allotments. Alan, having twisted an ankle jumping to the ground, tried to limp as nonchalantly as possible. Joe ambled alongside him also trying to act suitably unconcerned.

"You said that it would be a doddle. They were your exact words. 'Don't you worry, Joe,' you said, 'it'll be a doddle'."

"Well, it would have been if that dog hadn't took a wobbler like that. Have you ever seen anything like that? That dog should be put down. It's mad. Anyway, you said it was a fuckin' Yorkie."

"I think it was that Anti-mate spray that did it."

"It didn't turn a Yorkie into a Rottweiler, did it, and I'm not a magician, am I?"

They were nearing the bottom of the hill when a front door opened, throwing light out into the street. "What's going on here?" a large man said as he stepped out onto the pavement in front of them.

"Search me, mate," Alan said with a shrug. "Sounds like some bloody dog's having a fit or something."

52

On the night of the Elvis competition final, Nobby and Norma were in his mother's house on the Westwood estate. The rest of the family had already left for the theatre where the final was being held. Nobby had said he'd be right behind them, but hung back, having decided he was definitely withdrawing from the competition. Norma, concerned they'd be late, kept asking him to try on a new costume she'd brought. Nobby eventually told her he wasn't going. Norma had been half expecting this and did her level best to persuade him to change his mind, but to no avail. She argued that all his friends and family were there, waiting to see him and he owed it to them to appear. Then she brought out her secret and final weapon and opened the cardboard box containing the new costume.

Nobby stared at the costume open-mouthed. "Where did you get that?" he asked Norma, who stood holding the sequined jumpsuit against herself, admiring it in the full-length mirror.

"Alan's mam, Elsie, altered it so it will fit you. I gave her your measurements. She's made a really good job of it. It's absolutely great. You'll look smashing in it, love."

"I don't know …" Nobby said hesitantly. He'd decided to withdraw from the competition because he was convinced he was being made a laughing stock. He was tired of the jeers and taunts shouted from the audience at the competitions and his confidence was shattered. He was surprised that someone took him so seriously as to get him a costume. "Elsie made this up for me?" he asked her doubtfully.

"Yes, she altered it to fit you. Took her hours to do it. Now, she wouldn't go to all that trouble if she thought you weren't any good, would she? And Alan and his mates are going to be out front, so if Sid or his friends try anything they'll regret it. There'll be no trouble tonight, love."

Nobby was totally gobsmacked. "Where would Elsie nick something like that from?"

"She didn't steal it, love. Alan bought it for you at an auction. He actually paid for it and it cost him a small fortune. He went down to London one day last week especially and got it for you."

Nobby was silent, stunned that they had gone to all that trouble for him. He stared at the elaborate stage costume which glistened and sparkled. It was covered in rhinestones and metal studding with an ornately embroidered American eagle with spread wings on the back. Despite himself he licked his lips with anticipation.

"Please, Nobby you try this on now, here and have a look in the mirror. It's a copy of an authentic Elvis jumpsuit he wore at Las Vegas. It's got a coordinated belt that knots at the side and hangs down, looks really sexy, and there's a cape. Go on, try it on and then make up your mind about whether to withdraw. Go on, it'll only take a minute. Try it on and then see what you think."

Norma knew that once Nobby had tried on the magnificent costume, there was no way he was not going to perform in it.

Nobby put on the jumpsuit and admired himself in the mirror. It fitted him like a glove; Elsie had done a great job with the alterations. He turned so that he could see the sides and back. The cape and flared bottoms looked very stylish. He looked really good in it. The very living image of his hero. He looked at Norma and smiled ruefully. "Okay. I'll do it."

"And you'll win it, love," Norma said, relieved and excited. She embraced him gently, careful not to crease the costume, and kissed him. "You'll have to hurry, mind. The final starts in three quarters of an hour."

Nobby looked at his watch. "I'll never make it in time."

Norma thought hard. There wasn't a bus that would get them there in time, and it wasn't any good trying to get a taxi, none would come to the Westwood estate, and anyway there wasn't a public telephone in the area that worked. "Is there anybody you know around here who has a phone in the house?"

"You're joking aren't you? A phone around here? No way."

Norma snapped her fingers as inspiration struck. "The bike next door. Borrow the bike from next door. You'll get there in time on that."

There wasn't anyone in next door, they'd all left for the final ages ago, but Nobby took the bike from the alleyway anyway. He knew they wouldn't mind him borrowing the old bike.

Norma saw him off, promising to get the bus and be there as soon as possible, and watched him pedal shakily down the road, the bike's front wheel wobbling worryingly.

53

The Germans' patience finally paid off. They'd watched all the other members of his family, including the hobbling Nelly, together with what seemed like the entire population of the street, emerge from their houses and board buses. Now they watched Nobby emerge from the estate on an old boneshaker of a bicycle. They'd spent a lot of their time observing the area and now their hours of waiting and watching were finally paying dividends. They saw Nobby ride the bike to the main road and pedal away.

"Follow him," Hans ordered Ernst. "And don't lose him."

"I can hardly lose him when he's dressed like that, can I?" Ernst, who hated taking orders, spat back at him.

Hans laughed. Things seemed to be going their way at long last. Their prey, dressed in a replica of Elvis's stage costume, complete with cape, and pedalling furiously on a push bike, would be hard to miss. "Where on earth can he be going dressed like that?" he asked rhetorically.

They followed Nobby for a mile or so, driving some distance

behind to avoid detection. Then they lost sight of their prey when he rounded a corner. Ernst increased speed to reach the corner and then slowed as he turned the car around it. They stared in disbelief. Nobby was nowhere to be seen. They scanned the roads in all directions and Hans just caught sight of the back wheel of a bike disappearing down an alley, further along the road. An alley that was much too narrow for any car to follow.

"Quick, drop me here. I'll follow him on foot," Hans said, opening the car door and jumping out as Ernst braked. "You drive around the block, see if you can find him again." Hans ran to the entrance of the alley, took a quick look in, and could see the unmistakable figure of Nobby about three-quarters of the way along the narrow pathway. Hans walked nonchalantly into the alley and then hurried his pace in an attempt to make up some ground on Nobby.

Ernst, excited by the chase and determined not to lose Nobby, drove off at speed and screeched around the corner almost on two wheels, much too fast. The car drifted across onto the wrong side of the road and straight into the front of a large delivery truck parked at the curb. The sudden impact didn't do a lot of damage to either vehicle, but it threw Ernst's head and chest into the steering wheel, with considerable force.

By the time Hans had cleared the end of the alley, Nobby had disappeared again, this time without any trace. Hans ran to a corner and looked both ways but still couldn't see any trace of Nobby. He then went to the other corner, and seeing the crowd around the collision, ran to the accident scene. Ernst was obviously in a lot of pain, standing outside the car, leaning on the roof and holding his ribs. There was a large gash on his chin which was weeping blood. His eyes were bloodshot and the skin around them swollen and already starting to discolour.

"You okay?" Hans asked.

"I'll live," Ernst muttered gruffly. "Let's get out of here."

A large man came out of a nearby house and walked to the truck. "Your mate alright, is he?" he asked. "I saw it all. He came around the corner much too fast, on the wrong side of the road and went

Idle Hands

right into the front of my truck," the man complained.

"Is there much damage to your vehicle?" Hans asked.

"No, just a scratch or two," the truck driver said. Then, scenting possible financial compensation, changed tack. "Mind you, I don't know what my boss is going to say. He doesn't like his vehicles being damaged, he don't."

Hans examined the front of the truck. There were only a few scratches visible. There was quite a crowd around the vehicles and they were attracting far too much attention. Next thing the police would turn up and the last thing he wanted was to come to their notice. "Look," he said to the driver, taking his wallet from his pocket. "I don't want to lose my no claims bonus, so here is, what? let's say, two hundred pounds to get the truck's paintwork repaired, okay?"

The driver wet his lips with his tongue and stared at the money greedily. "Er, right then. Thank you," he said taking the cash from Hans, calculating how much change he'd have left after buying a can of touch-up paint.

Hans helped Ernst into the passenger seat of the Mercedes. Ernst groaned and held his ribs. He was obviously in a great amount of pain when he moved. Hans drove off carefully and cruised around the area looking for Nobby. He stopped the car a number of times and Ernst leaned out of the window and asked pedestrians if they'd seen someone dressed as Elvis on a bicycle. None had, and most repeated the question incredulously, suspecting a wind-up. Some laughed out loud in Ernst's face and told him to fuck off.

Ernst was really wound up and getting more and more angry every time he received a dismissive reply. Hans had to physically restrain him from getting out of the car and attacking the last person they asked.

"I'm pissed off with this fucking, Noddy," Ernst shouted. "I'm mocked when I ask if anyone has seen him. I was attacked by his female relatives, and then nearly killed in a fucking car crash ..."

"You weren't nearly killed, and from the truck was stationary, so the accident was your fault anyway. And his name is, Nobby, not, Noddy."

"Well, I've got a sore chin and bruised ribs," Ernst complained. "And when I do get hold of this fucking, Noddy, I'm going to make him wish he'd never been born."

After another fruitless half hour or so driving around trying to relocate Nobby, the Germans finally saw a man dressed as Elvis turn a corner a few hundred yards away and hurry down a narrow street.

"He must have got rid of the bicycle," Hans said as he accelerated after the man. They caught up with him halfway down the street and the car screeched to a stop.

Ernst quickly leapt out and grabbed the man in the Elvis costume. He punched him repeatedly on the back of the head, letting the frustrations of the past few days explode. Then he tried to bundle him into the open back door of the Mercedes. The Elvis impersonator fought back, struggled and kicked out at his attacker, and caught the German's shin with the high heel of his boot. Ernst, bent almost double with the pain in his leg, and still handicapped by his bruised ribs, tried to keep hold of his opponent. The pair fell to the ground, rolling into the gutter. Hans, sitting behind the steering wheel, groaned, shook his head in despair and got out of the car to assist his colleague. Quickly looking up and down the street to make sure they weren't being observed, he pulled an automatic pistol from his pocket and hit Elvis on the head with the butt. The man immediately ceased to resist and went limp.

54

All Nobby's family arrived at the theatre together in their stylish new clothes and squeaky new shoes, all bought for them by Nobby. After a noisy and totally unnecessary argument with the door staff, Nelly led the excited group determinedly down the aisle to the front seats, hobbling, still recovering from Ernst's assault, but mobile enough with the aid of a walking stick.

The other family members followed in order of seniority, with the children in tow, kept in order either by constant threats, the occasional actual cuff across the ear, or the bribery of sweets, crisps and ice cream. The adults, cigarettes dangling from lipsticked lips, ash falling unnoticed onto the kids' heads or onto their new clothes, dragged their offspring to their appointed seats. The children sat reasonably quietly at first as they considered the likelihood of the threatened consequences actually being implemented. They settled in their seats and looked around to identify possible targets to annoy amongst the other members of the audience.

On the other side of the theatre, Joe and Brenda and George and

Violet sat together, not far from the front, with Alan and Mickey nearby. Mickey, who had his own reasons for coming, had been given a ticket by Alan. Trev was still missing; no one knew where he'd gone. George bored everyone within earshot, but they were all too polite to say so, with the history of the theatre they were sitting in, telling them which world famous stars had appeared there, including famous music hall stars of the nineteenth century that no one present had ever heard of. Seated not very far in front of them was Sid the Shiv, those of his family not currently serving at Her Majesty's pleasure, and his gang of Teds.

If Detective Constable Henry had been present that evening, he could have had a productive time serving numerous outstanding arrest warrants on the various members of both the Shearer and Nordstrom families.

No expense had been spared on the event. A full twenty-piece orchestra was present in the pit, with an extra four saxophonists in the brass section. The theatre was the biggest and most lavishly decorated in the area and seated seven hundred in the audience. The compère was a very experienced TV presenter and comedian, with a background in live theatre going back decades. He was very popular and well known to everyone in the country with access to a television set.

The compère warmed up the audience with a few minutes of chat, topical comments and jokes. He flattered the chairman of the company organising the event, which, after all was paying his wages, and then briefly described the order of the evening's events.

"Tonight we have six excellent Elvis impersonators. Six of the very best, who have fought their way through all the heats to the final of this very prestigious competition." He paused while the audience applauded.

"They are each going to sing two numbers and the judges will award each competitor marks from one to ten. At the end, after the last one has sung his second number, the judges will reveal their marks and we will know who has won. Marks will be awarded for the singing, stage performance and, last but not least, stage costume." He walked across the stage and peered down into the orchestra pit. "Can you hear me down there? You still awake? Yes? Good," he walked away shaking his head and making drinking motions with one hand, implying the musicians were drunk. The audience tittered.

"Right, let's have the first one out before the orchestra is too far gone to play those instruments." He stepped back and indicated the side of the stage.

Ricky Fontain, Sid the Shiv's brother, swaggered onto the stage and basked in the raucous applause, almost all of which came from a rowdy group near the front, namely Sid, his family and his gang of drainpiped Teds. Lots of cat calls and boos came from further back in the stalls, and from the direction of Nelly's large family group. Sid and his Teds stood up and tried to identify the dissenters, hands held above their eyes to shield them from the glare of the spotlights. Unable to identify the booers, they only sat down again when the bouncers turned up and threatened to throw them out. Undeterred, on stage, Ricky ignored the boos and strutted around waving to his fans in the audience, which again were mostly in his brother's group at the front.

The compère walked to the centre of the stage to formally introduce Ricky. "Best of order now please, ladies and gentlemen." He paused and waited for the noise to subside. "Thank you. Now please put your hands together for a young lad with stacks of potential … Ricky Fontain." He walked backwards into the wings his open arm directing the audience's attention towards the gyrating Ricky.

Ricky made a passable attempt at Jailhouse Rock, his brother's favourite for obvious reasons. His voice wasn't at its best, he looked nothing like Elvis, his costume wasn't impressive and his stage presence was dismal. There was only muted applause when he finished, and more booing. Sid and company made a lot of noise, but there was no mistaking that the performance was, at best, only average. Sid, obviously very unhappy with his brother's performance and the audience's reaction, turned and began arguing loudly with someone sitting a couple of rows behind him. The row continued, and escalated, as the compère introduced the next contestant.

The fight started just as the second performer started singing. Sid climbed over the back of his seat and launched himself over the row of seats behind to get at the heckler, who happened to be Alan. He got a punch in the mouth for his trouble and fell to the floor. Struggling to his feet, he found that a couple of bouncers had arrived at about the same time as his gang of Teds.

Vastly outnumbered, the bouncers gave a very good account of themselves, but were getting the worst of it. The younger Nordstroms took this opportunity to launch a variety of well-aimed missiles, empty coke cans and even one or two full ones at the Teds' camp, and scored quite a few direct hits. Alan and a few of his more disreputable acquaintances were in the thick of the fight, on the bouncer's side and giving at least as much as they got. The older male members of the Nordstrom family ran around to take an even more active role in the proceedings.

Fists were flying indiscriminately and one inadvertently happened to hit Mickey a glancing blow on the side of the head. Mickey, very unhappy with the unprovoked assault, and even more annoyed about an attack on one of his young boxing prodigies a month or so previously by a group of Teds, which was the main reason he'd accepted tonight's invitation, pushed himself into the melee to get at his assailant, which happened to be Sid himself. Mickey grabbed Sid's shoulder, swung him around and hit him on the jaw. Sid went down like the proverbial sack of spuds. Out like a light. Satisfied, Mickey turned his keen attention to other members of the Teddy boy gang.

Joe, with a protective arm around Brenda's shoulder, led her up the aisle, away from the disturbance. George and Violet followed them.

Alan, in the middle of the near riot, was acquitting himself very well. He'd managed to get in a number of very good blows on various members of the opposition, when he was hit from behind. The blow wasn't serious, but was hard enough to knock him over. As he fell, the theatre lights went on and the two bouncers, who were now pretty well badly beaten, were reinforced by the other two on the door, and the combined force started to make inroads. The Teds were more or less all together, and their dress made them easily identifiable. The gang was definitely getting the worst of it and it looked as if it was all over, when Sid pulled the knife. The bouncers changed direction and walked quickly backwards, away from the gleaming blade.

"You'd better put that away and fuck off," one of the retreating bouncers said. "The police are on their way and will be here in a couple of minutes."

Sid, bloody and angry, thought for a few moments, then made his mind up. "Come on, lads. This is a load of bollocks anyway." He started to walk up the aisle towards the doors. "We'll see you outside, Spencer, you big-mouthed bastard. And that fucking little garden gnome of a mate of yours will be for it as well if he wins." He pointed the blade of the knife at Alan, who was struggling to his feet, and made slashing motions.

Followed to the door from a safe distance by the bouncers, the gang, still shouting threats and insults, left the theatre and the rest of the audience breathed a collective sigh of relief. Although all of the Teds had left, Sid's family was still in situ near the front and were still a noisy distraction. The threatened police presence never arrived, not surprisingly, as they'd never been called. The bouncer had been bluffing. Two of the bouncers had received injuries serious enough to require immediate medical attention and were driven to the casualty department of the local hospital by one of their colleagues, leaving only one doorman on duty. Gradually things calmed down enough for the lights to be turned down and the proceedings restarted.

The compère, his nerves affected by the evening's events, his voice harsh and his hands visibly shaking as he held the mike, introduced the second contestant again, nodded to the orchestra, and hurriedly left the stage, probably in search of a stiff drink. The soothing balm of music filled the theatre again and the contestant did his stuff.

55

One contestant hadn't turned up, bad case of nerves probably, was the general consensus. It wasn't until later that it was discovered he'd been attacked and was in hospital. The other contestants performed fairly well. Nobby got there just in time, thanks to the borrowed bike, to watch contestants four and five perform. He considered both these to have performed excellently and knew that they were his main rivals, the ones he had to beat.

It was Nobby turn on stage at last. Almost the whole audience, certainly all his family and friends cheered, whistled and clapped as he walked out wearing the magnificent costume, drowning out the catcalls and boos from Sid's family. Shouts of 'Little Diddy Elvis' and 'you should be a rocking horse jockey', could be heard from their direction, but most of the noise was from the members of Nobby's clan, who screamed their approval. Some of the younger ones even ran up and down the aisle in their excitement.

Nobby absolutely oozed confidence and his stage presence was fantastic. He moved around as if the place belonged to him. The orchestra was already playing his opening number, Viva Las Vegas, and he started singing the number at exactly the right moment and in tune. The spotlight picked him up as the house lights dimmed, picking up the rich colours of his costume and reflecting the twinkling sequins and rhinestones. With nothing else on stage to provide scale, Nobby looked a lot taller than he actually was in the well-fitting costume and he seemed to fill the whole stage as he strutted around, swinging the cloak back over his shoulder with a flourish. He sang his heart out and the audience was enthralled, hanging on his every word as he worked his way through the number. The audience went wild when he finished and he took time to take a bow in the centre of the stage before standing stock still for a full half-a-minute, soaking up the applause. The orchestra struck up again with his second choice, a slow love song. Nobby looked down to the people sitting near the front and held out his hand, pointing to a breathless, but smiling Norma, who had just arrived and stood in the side-isle near to the stage. "I dedicate my final song, Love Me Tender, to the best girl in the world, the love of my life, Norma."

Again the audience went wild and cheered, whistled and applauded long and loud.

Nobby sang the number magnificently and with a great deal of emotion and again held the audience in the palm of his hand. There was hardly a dry eye in the house by the time he finished, on one knee, singing directly to Norma. Most of the audience rose as one and gave him a standing ovation as the lights came up again.

The compère hurried on stage and relieved Nobby of the hand mike. "Thank you, ladies and gentlemen. Please put your hands together again for Mr Nordstrom." He indicated towards Nobby so the audience would know where to aim their applause. After an appropriate amount of time, the applause faded and the compère raised the mike to his mouth again. "Would all the contestants please come back on stage for the judges' verdict?"

The other four Elvises trooped back on stage and stood alongside Nobby.

"And now it's the time we've all been waiting for, the judges' decision." The compère indicated the three judges sitting high and majestically in their box. More applause and shouting from the audience. When the clapping abated the compère spoke again. "Mr Earl and the other judges, do you have a winner?"

He held the mike out to hear the result from the chief judge. "Yes, we have an outright winner."

"Will you please tell us who that lucky winner is, Mr Earl?"

"I certainly will." He held up a card and read a name off it. "The winner is …" he hesitated to increase the drama of the moment, "… the winner is … competitor number six, Mr Nordstrom."

The audience went wild again and further words from the compère were drowned out by the din. The compère waved Nobby onto the centre of the stage and grabbing his hand, held it up above his head like a winning boxer. Nobby took a couple of bows and blew kisses to the audience, and to the judges.

"And now Mr Earl himself will present the first prize to the winner, a trip for two to America." He waited for the applause to die down. "Yes, the winner and his partner will travel first class to Graceland, the home of Elvis himself." More thunderous applause filled the theatre.

They were joined on stage by Mr Earl himself, the chief judge and millionaire owner of the large leisure organisation, who shook Nobby's hand violently before presenting him with the prize details contained in a large gold-coloured envelope. The momentous event was captured for prosperity by photographers from the local and national press. Although no one complained officially, if the few disgruntled competitors who disagreed with the choice of Nobby as the winner had pointed out that Mr Earl could have been a teeny bit biased, as at five foot one inch, he was actually an inch shorter than Nobby, they might just have had a reasonable complaint.

56

The two Germans ignored the doorman's demand to see their tickets, pushed past him and rushed into the theatre. The lone doorman, protesting, followed the pair and after a brief struggle in the foyer, he was knocked to the ground and savagely kicked in the head by Ernst. The big German was now angrier than ever because he'd just attacked the wrong Elvis in the street outside. It had taken them only a few seconds to realise the unconscious man wasn't Nobby, as he was a good foot taller than their prey, but the error, on top of the other mishaps of the evening, had compounded Ernst's anger against the Nordstrom family as a whole and Nobby in particular. The big German was literally hopping mad, any semblance of logical thought long gone from his seething mind. Bursting into the stalls, Ernst spotted Nobby on the stage receiving his prize and walked quickly towards the front, intending to grab Nobby immediately he came off stage. Hans, always more circumspect, let his more volatile colleague go ahead, but stayed at the back of the theatre and watched.

At the proclamation of Nobby as the winner, Sid the Shiv's family, upset that their darling, Ricky Fontain, hadn't won, showed their disapproval by throwing things at the stage and across the seats at the Nordstrom supporters, some of whom responded by again running around the front of the stage and attacking them. Some of the other competitors' supporters, not to be outdone, joined in the melee.

Nelly, sitting in an aisle seat, ignoring the pandemonium on the other side of the theatre, her fingers in her mouth, loudly whistled her approval for the choice of winner, and applauding so much her hands hurt, saw the German stride past her down the aisle and reacted immediately. She jumped up, hobbled up behind him and hit Ernst on the back of his head with her walking stick. "He's the bastard that stabbed me!" she screamed. "That's the one who did it."

Ernst, surprised by the sudden attack, and smarting from the blow to his head, instinctively hit out at Nelly, catching her on the side of the head with his fist. She fell to the floor, still screaming. Now pandemonium broke out on this side of the theatre. Some of Nelly's relatives rushed to her side to tend to her injury, while the other members of the family, both male and female, not engaged in the current mayhem across the way, attacked the German. Ernst found himself again struggling desperately to defend himself against an onslaught of Nordstroms. He hit out right and left and floored two of his attackers, but was gradually being overwhelmed by the sheer force of numbers. His teeth bared in an animal-like snarl, he pulled the large hunting knife and waved it around in front of him. The hoard of angry attackers backed off slowly. Keeping his back to the wall, Ernst inched toward the front of the theatre, the aisle behind him now blocked by angry Nordstroms. Ernst turned and ran towards the steps to the stage, which were on the other side of the theatre, pushed through the thickening crowd of rival supporters' intent on murdering each other, and raced up the short flight of stairs onto the stage. He made straight for Nobby, who was still standing there with Mr Earl and the compère, watching the amazing events unfolding in the stalls. Nobby stood still, gazing at the long shiny blade as if hypnotized. Mr Earl and the compère, seeing the large knife, ran for the front of the stage and jumped unceremoniously into the orchestra pit, landing among the alarmed musicians. The other Elvises and the photographers scatted in all directions.

More of the fighting crowd spilled across in front of the stage and prevented the horde of Nordstroms following Ernst, as they struggled to force a way through the mass of bodies.

Grabbing Nobby from behind, Ernst stunned him by hitting him hard on the side of the head with his fist, and held him in a headlock, putting the knife to his throat.

"This way, my little friend," Ernst hissed, and dragged his captive sideways towards the curtained wings.

Nobby, half-stunned, made a half-hearted effort to grab the German's knife arm with both hands and struggled weakly, trying to wriggle his way free. Ernst, the knife's gleaming blade in his hand, tightened his grip around his struggling captive's throat to control him. Suddenly Ernst was aware of a figure coming towards him across the stage, a very large, muscular man, as big as himself, but older and with a determined set to his mouth.

Still holding Nobby around the neck with one arm, Ernst slashed at the giant's eyes with the blade, but missed. Mickey hit the German once with his right fist and took the man clean off his feet; Nobby fell away to the side of the stage. Ernst landed in a heap with the wind knocked out of him, but adrenaline, the cocaine in his system and sheer fright ensured that he was up and running right towards Mickey, waving the knife in front of him.

The men circled each other warily. The pair looked to be evenly matched in size and muscle, but while Ernst was a lot younger, Mickey was fitter, his regular road and gym training paying dividends, while the German's use of steroids and other drugs adversely affected his fitness. Mickey was determined that he wasn't going to let the man get anywhere near him with the knife and Ernst was equally determined he wasn't going to be hit again by that huge fist. But he was. The pair feinted and parried, Mickey surprisingly light on his feet, neither man gaining an advantage. Mickey tried to draw the knifeman way from Nobby, so the lad could escape, but the German wasn't letting that happen.

Then, Ernst made a mistake. Aware that others were running towards the stage and desperate to escape before they could reach him he lashed out recklessly with the blade, again aiming for Mickey's eyes. This strategy had always worked for him in the past. Anyone threatened with a knife in the eye would always back off, or lose the eye. Either way, Ernst would win.

But Mickey didn't retreat. He blocked Ernst's knife hand with his tensed forearm, using a martial arts technique, bringing his arm from across his body and into contact with Ernst's arm with such power that it forced the knife arm away, and Mickey punched the German squarely in the nose.

Ernst's nose exploded and blood splattered all over his face. He screamed in pain, and ran into the wings of the stage, still holding the knife and again grabbed Nobby, pulling him to his feet and held the knife to his throat.

"You come near and I'll cut his throat," the German hissed, hitting his captive on the top of the head with the heavy horn handle of the knife to show he was serious. The blow stunned Nobby again, his knees buckled and blood immediately started to pour from his head.

Mickey held up his hands, indicating he wasn't going to attack, and Ernst pulled Nobby backwards into the curtains. Looking behind him quickly, seeking an escape route, the German saw an illuminated emergency exit sign and pulled Nobby in that direction. Still holding the knife at his captive's throat, he and Nobby blundered through the props, hanging ropes and backdrops that cluttered the area. Ernst blindly pushed them out of his way, while wiping the blood from his shattered nose.

The pair were almost at the door when Alan, who had finally reached the stage after what seemed to him an age of fighting his way through the chaos in the stalls, stepped out from the curtains.

"Let him go, you piece of shite," he demanded, stepping in front of the men.

Ernst was surprised and shocked by the voice, but soon recovered. Incensed that he was again being thwarted, he shoved

Nobby away, and launched himself at Alan with the knife.

"Run, Nobby, run!" Alan shouted to his friend.

Nobby, having somewhat regained his senses and finding himself free of the German, took Alan's advice and, holding the gash on his head with his hand, ran from the wings on unsteady legs and towards the waiting Mickey and the relative safety of the stalls and his family.

Ernst missed Alan's eyes with his first attack. Alan tried unsuccessfully to hit him. Ernst sidestepped the blow and collided with Alan. Both men fell to the floor, Alan desperately grabbing Ernst's knife hand. They struggled with quiet determination and rolled down the steps and into the emergency door.

Alan managed to struggle upright and took a swing at Ernst's head with his fist. The blow connected and the German reeled backwards against the emergency door. Alan lunged after him and swung at his head again.

But Ernst was also fully on his feet now, and avoided Alan's punch. The men struggled against the opening bar of the door, their weight pushing it upwards, releasing the catch. Their combined weight pushed the door fully open and the men stumbled outside into the daylight.

As they stumbled outside, blinking, into the bright daylight, Ernst plunged his knife deep into Alan's chest, right to the hilt.

Alan stared down disbelievingly at the blood pouring rapidly from the wound and spreading across his shirt. Clutching his chest with both hands, he slumped against a wall and slid slowly to the ground.

57

Ernst cast around in the alley, wiping the blood from his face and eyes, eyes not yet accustomed to the light after the gloom of the theatre. He became aware that there were other people in the alley. A lot of very disgruntled people. People who were still smarting from the beating they'd received inside at the hands of Nobby's family, friends and the bouncers earlier, and who were now intent on revenge.

Sid and the Teds recognised Alan, their arch enemy, injured and sliding down the wall, but not this other bloodied figure with him, who had burst through the emergency exit and startled the already tense group. They were expecting another fight, although not from this direction, but when they saw the big hunting knife in Ernst's hand they didn't hesitate for a second. They attacked him.

Trapped against the wall of the narrow alley, Ernst used every ounce of his strength and street fighting expertise, which was considerable, but he couldn't win this battle. There were too many of them and Sid and a number of his other attackers also had knives, which they used skilfully and with great effect.

58

Hans, watching the events unfold in the theatre with dismay, realised that Ernst's only possible escape route was the emergency door into the alley. He raced out of the front of the theatre to the car and drove the Mercedes down the alley, making as much noise as he could, sounding the horn, shouting out of the open car window, his automatic pistol on the seat, at hand, cocked and ready to use if he needed it. The gang of Teddy boys ran in the opposite direction as he approached, shouting their defiance. He found the two bodies in the alley, left for dead.

Hans ignored Alan and dragged his semi-conscious colleague to the Mercedes, rolled him onto the back seat and drove away carefully, aware of the sirens of the approaching police cars.

The lads found Alan lying in the alley. There was not much anyone could do to help him. He'd a deep stab wound in the chest and had lost a great deal of blood. Mickey, Joe and Nobby looked down on their friend, not believing what had happened.

"He told me to run," Nobby sobbed. "He told me, or I'd have

stayed with him."

"It's alright, Nobby. You couldn't have stopped this even if you'd stayed with him," Joe said quietly, putting a comforting arm around his shoulder. The paramedics arrived and tended to Alan and then placed him carefully in an ambulance, which raced off with its siren wailing.

59

Elsie cried silently as she sat by the bed, dabbing her eyes with a handkerchief. The intensive care unit was a sterile, silent place. The nurses hurried about on rubber-soled shoes and talked in hushed tones scarcely above a whisper. Alan, wired up to various machines and drips, was sometimes semi-conscious, but generally he appeared dead to the world. The only sign of his continued existence was the quiet ping of the pulsating heart monitor and the moving wavy line on the screen.

Nobby received treatment for suspected concussion at the same hospital. Nelly and Norma, in the waiting room, took the opportunity to really get to know each other. Norma explained to Nelly that she was now officially Nobby's fiancée. If Nelly was surprised, she didn't show it. "I thought he'd met somebody special," she confided to Norma. "Him going missing for all that time and when he does turn up, he's walking around with his head in the clouds, like he's in love."

Norma smiled. "Really?"

"Oh aye. I knew there was something up straight away. You're just what he needs, Norma." She patted Norma's knee. "A nice young lass like you to keep him right. He's a good lad, you know. There isn't a bad bone in his body."

Norma nodded. "I know that, Mrs Nordstrom, he's a really nice lad and I love him," she said shyly.

Nobby eventually walked into the waiting room some time later and smiled at them both. Norma jumped up and held his bandaged head gently in her hands. "Oh, Nobby. Look at what they've done to you, love. You sit down here. Are you sure you should be walking about?"

"They wanted me to stay in overnight for observation, but I'm going home with you. I don't want to stay in here, it stinks of disinfectant. But what about Alan? Is he alright?"

"All they'll say is that he's comfortable. He's in intensive care and Elsie's up there with him. They'll only allow one close relative in there at any one time and Elsie says she's staying all night," Nelly said.

"You'd best come home, love, and get some sleep. There's nothing you can do for Alan here," Norma advised.

60

Hans drove to a secluded country lane on the outskirts of the city and examined Ernst as carefully as he could without getting covered in the man's blood.

He shook his head and muttered to himself. "They've carved you up good and proper and no mistake."

Hans returned to the driver's seat and thought hard about his next move. He couldn't think of any alternative. Ernst needed urgent medical treatment, but there was no way he could take him to a hospital or doctor. Even dumping him outside an emergency department of a hospital was too risky because it would start a police investigation and the injured man might reveal something while semi-conscious. No. There was only one course of action.

Hans stopped the Mercedes' engine and peered through the tinted windows at Alan's pigeon cree. It was pitch black and the allotment holders and pigeon men had long since gone home. He'd have to break into the cree tonight and see if the boxes were hidden there, it was the only lead he had. If he drew a blank there, then his only other course of action would be to search as many allotments as he could before daylight. Glancing into the back seat, he reminded himself he'd also have to dump and torch the car before going back to the hotel. He was taking a risk driving it around; there was too much blood on the seats and floor. He'd report the vehicle stolen tomorrow morning.

Just as he was about to get out of the car, a pair of police vans raced past the Merc and screamed to a halt at the entrance to the allotments. Hans quickly slumped right down in the seat, and watched the police activity with alarm.

Uniformed police officers poured out of the vans and made for the gates of the allotment. There was a man in civilian clothes with them and it was he who opened the padlocked gates allowing the officers to enter unhindered. The German could see the policemen's torches flashing around several of the gardens until they'd obviously found the one they wanted and then all the lights converged onto one location. The activity in and around this particular garden was intense for quite some minutes before the watching man saw anything else of interest.

Suddenly the torches all moved swiftly in different directions, there were shouts and screams and an unnerving, unearthly howling, as if some monstrous beast was loose in the gardens. The din went on for quite a while and Hans could see that there appeared to be total confusion in the various allotments. Gradually things seemed to quieten down again. The torches slowly and gingerly converged together again in one place. Order seemed to have been restored. A few minutes later a wailing siren could be heard approaching and an ambulance duly arrived. It parked next to the police vans, the medics ran into the allotments carrying various pieces of equipment, including a stretcher. Shortly afterwards, they reappeared carrying the stretcher between them, the man in plain clothes was lying on it, face down.

Soon after the ambulance left, a line of officers made their way from the garden back to the police vans. When they exited the gates it became apparent that they were each carrying something in their hands. As they reached the police vans Hans could make out that the objects were boxes and each one was clearly marked 'Dutch Tulip Bulbs'.

The German watched intently as the police officers removed box after box from the allotment and placed them inside the vans. Some carried one, but most carried two boxes at a time. Hans tried to keep count, but soon gave up as there were so many officers placing boxes in the back of the vans at the same time. Hans shook his head, started the car and drove away.

Hans listened to the next day's local radio news reports with horror. An undisclosed, but very large, amount of money had been discovered concealed in Dutch tulip bulb boxes found at a local allotment. The allotment was apparently not currently rented to any individual, the previous occupant having died recently. The report went on to say that police were investigating the find of the boxes, which were reported stolen from a lorry some weeks ago. The police had recovered what they thought were tulip bulbs and it wasn't until the boxes were opened and examined at the police station that they discovered a very sizable amount of cash concealed amongst the bulbs. A police spokesman said that they were surprised and puzzled by the find of the huge amount of cash, as there were only bulbs in the boxes when they were reported stolen and it was a mystery where the cash had come from. The haulage company's head office spokesman had no explanation at all for the find and said they were as mystified about the origin of the money as the police were.

The same news carried a brief report of a man's body being found in woodland on the outskirts of the city by a dog walker in the early hours of the morning. The body carried no means of identification and had numerous knife injuries, but the man had died as a result of being shot in the head.

Hans had been up all night and rehearsed his report countless times. He had to convince Max that the failure had been entirely Ernst's responsibility, not his. He couldn't afford to let Max think he was at fault. He listed the sequence of events chronologically on a piece of paper starting with the interview of the driver, then Ernst's disastrous encounter with Nobby's mother and family. This was followed by their fruitless enquiries at the allotments and around the town centre pubs. And then, with nothing else to go on, their staking out of the Westwood estate until they at last got a glimpse of their prey; their following Nobby on that stupid bike to the theatre, the collision on the way and attacking the wrong man. And then the farcical finale to the whole thing, Ernst getting involved in the fight and getting stabbed.

He was careful to put the blame for each disappointing result squarely at Ernst's feet. Hans read and reread the sequence of events, trying different ways of saying what had happened to make it sound more efficient and professional, and more damaging to Ernst. He dreaded making the call and put it off for as long as possible. Finally he couldn't delay any longer and rang Max in Berlin.

Hans tried to explain what had happened on the telephone without using incriminating language that might have been understood by anyone listening in. "I'm sorry, Herr Westlik, but the boxes have been found by the official opposition and are lost to us." The term 'official opposition' would be recognised by Max as referring to the police. He went down the prepared list, licking his dry lips. "Unfortunately there has been unavoidable collateral damage …" This meant deaths.

"Theirs or ours?" demanded Westlik.

"Both I think, but defiantly ours, Herr Westlik."

"Ernst?"

"It was unavoidable, Herr Westlik."

Hans could tell that Westlik was angry, very angry; as he had expected him to be. The line was quiet for a long time before his employer finally spoke again.

"So, you have lost my nephew as well as my property," Max said slowly and quietly, controlling his anger with superhuman effort. "Okay. I want you to abort the mission and return immediately," he hissed. "I want you to give me a full report of this farce, in person. Meet me at the warehouse tonight at ten o'clock."

"Of course, Herr Westlik," Hans said and heard the phone slam down at the other end before he'd even finished speaking. Hans sighed and licked his lips nervously. He was going to have to explain this chain of events to his employer very, very carefully, and prove to him logically and beyond any reasonable doubt that he wasn't in any way to blame. Hans was nervous, but placed complete trust in his ability to be able to convince Max of his blamelessness. Trust which was misplaced.

Max broke the international connection and immediately redialled. "I'll have another bundle of rubbish to be collected from the warehouse at eleven o'clock tonight, usual rates," he said tersely into the mouthpiece.

61

The police interviewed all the allotment holders at their gardens over the following few days and were informed of mysterious, but vague, goings-on at night, strange noises, barking dogs, etcetera. They paid particular attention to the written statements made by George and Joe, which were taken not at the garden, but down at the police station by D.C. Henry, the hero of the hour. He bravely conducted the interviews himself and was rigorous in the extreme, despite not being able to sit down owing to a number of quite severe dog bites to his posterior. The dog had managed to escape in the darkness and confusion and despite a concentrated search of the area couldn't be found.

D.C. Henry cross-examined them in the best traditions of all TV detectives and thought he really couldn't fail to get confessions from them. But he didn't get any confessions. Both men were annoyingly vague and selective in their recollections, but stuck to their stories and were eventually released without further action being taken. The police seemed to be so surprised and excited by their find that they didn't search any of the surrounding gardens or pigeon crees.

D.C. Henry would have liked to also interview Alan, Trev and Nobby, but Alan was too ill in intensive care to see, Trev was still inexplicably absent and Nobby, although now discharged from hospital and well on the way to recovery, insisted he couldn't remember anything and had a medical certificate to prove it.

62

"Where the bleedin' hell have you been? We thought you'd done off with some of the money," George said.

"You should have known that I wouldn't do that."

"Well, where have you been, then?"

"I've been abroad solving our problem with finance. That's where."

"You've finally sorted the problem with the cash?"

"I sure have."

"You what?" Joe asked.

"I've finally sorted out our problem with the cash," Trev confirmed. "I went with Frankie in his lorry to Belgium. He had a load to deliver near Antwerp, I took half a million pounds with me. Frankie doesn't know about the money, by the way. It was easy. Customs just waved us through, no bother at all. When we got to Antwerp, Frankie directs me to the right part of the city, and the rest was easy."

"So what have you done with the money in Antwerp, then?" Joe asked.

"I've spent it."

"You've spent it? Spent it?"

"I've invested it. Put it somewhere safe as houses where it'll never be stolen, will increase with inflation every year, in fact it'll probably grow a lot faster than inflation."

"What have you done with the bloody money?" Joe asked. "Spent it on what exactly?"

"Diamonds."

"Diamonds?" Joe asked incredulously.

"You all suddenly gone deaf or something? Yes, diamonds. Brenda gave me the idea when she was having a go at us up at the allotment and used that saying of Alan's mother's."

Joe looked puzzled. "What saying?" he asked.

"'You're a diamond'. When I heard that it triggered something in my mind, took on new meaning and I knew that's what I had to do, buy diamonds with the cash. Everything fell into place. Frankie was driving to Antwerp, which just happens to be the diamond centre of the world, so I went with him and bought some. I got half a million pounds worth of cut diamonds in various sizes, from a half-carat, to two carats. I bought a few at a time from different dealers over a period of a week or so. They're expensive, but small and easily transportable. They hold their value and actually increase as time goes by. They're as good as currency if they're certificated, and all those I've bought are certificated. They're all genuine and the best quality gems. And we can sell them as and when we need to raise some more cash, although it's always best to make sure that we sell when the market price is high."

"So where are these diamonds now?" George asked.

"Where they are safe and will stay safe."

"And where's that then exactly?" Joe asked.

"In a safe. In a safety deposit box in a bloody big safe in the strongroom of a bleedin' great private bank in London. We can sell some through the bank any time we need money. They'll take a small percentage of course, but our anonymity and confidentiality will be guaranteed. Or we can always sell the things ourselves."

"So we can get as much cash as we want, at any time, without worrying about being caught?"

"That's right. Got it in one. But the main thing is, we haven't got to hide millions of pounds in cash around the allotment and worry about it being found. We can transport the rest of the money in the same way and buy diamonds with it at any time we want. We needn't necessarily go to Antwerp every time, we can go anywhere in the world," Trev said.

"Oh, and we've got the chance to buy a small haulage firm as well. I think it's a great idea and we should go ahead, but I wanted to speak to you lads about it first. I thought that it might come in handy for transporting the stuff on the quiet. The owner wants to sell up and retire because he's not in the best of health. He'll take cash with no questions asked. It's the firm Frankie Lane works for actually, and Frankie says it's a going concern, makes a good profit." He smiled. "I thought that we could make Frankie managing director, chief executive, or something. You know, give him a title and an office with a nice little secretary to keep an eye on him. But then I thought we'd maybe be better off making him foreman first and see how he does. Now that we're capitalists we want to be sure he's not going to do anything to bugger up our business interests before we make him chief. Making him foreman will mean he's got a bit of status, and their lass will think he's really clever. Maybe that's what we should do with some of the money; buy up small businesses for cash, or start some up ourselves. The likes of taxi firms, launderettes, sandwich shops and such, in fact any small, cash business."

"Why?" George asked.

"So then we'll have a ready-made answer if anyone asks where our money is coming from."

"We could maybe give Mickey a job. Something that would give him a decent wage for a change," Joe said.

"I was thinking along those same lines myself, mate," Trev agreed.

The others thought these were all very good ideas, and brought Trev up to date on all that had happened since he'd been away. He was shocked to hear of the fight at the Elvis competition final, and Alan's injuries, but amused to hear of the leek swap, the police raid on old Ralph's garden and the loose dog.

"Is Alan okay, then?"

"Aye, he's coming along nicely. He'll be alright," George said.

"That bloody dog in the garden, it very nearly gave me a heart attack," Joe said with feeling. "Turns out it was Frankie's brother's dog and he'd stuck it in there thinking he was doing Frankie a favour, him being away. We were luck to get away from the mad bastard dog and lock it in old Ralph's allotment. When the police went into there it went berserk, bit as many policemen as it could, especially D.C. Henry, and then ran off home."

The mention of the dog brought the whole escapade back to the forefront of Joe's memory. "That Anti-mate spray that you were telling us about, Trev, remember?"

"What about it?"

"Well, Alan bought some and used it when that dog came for us, and the dog went absolutely bananas. It sort of took a fucking flying fit, and was howling and barking and running round and generally creating like a lunatic. It even started to batter at the fence with its head. It was still mad the next night, when it attacked the police."

"Yes, the one I used the spray on did exactly the same. Went barmy it did."

"But you never said that it had that effect on dogs?"

"Well, you never asked me, did you? Anyway, what sort of effect did you expect it to have?"

"Well, I don't know exactly. I just thought that it might quiet the animal down a bit, I suppose. Curb its amorous instincts a bit maybe."

"Well, it certainly had a profound effect the only time I used it. That dog I was telling you about, Mrs Wilson's, went absolutely wild. It ran around howling and barking. Started to jump up and down, trying to get above the scent on my trousers, I suppose. I don't know what they put in that stuff but it certainty works all right. It took one little sniff at my crotch and was off straight away. The animal was in such a hurry to get away from me that it knocked the old lady right off her feet and then ran off through the back door. I had to help the poor old dear up. She was full of apologies, said she couldn't understand what had happened to her dog. The next time I called, she told me that it didn't come back for four days. After that she always locked the dog in the sitting room when I called."

"Was she alright then?" Nobby asked.

"It wasn't a bitch, it was a dog, that's why I got the Anti-mate, to repel dogs," Trev said slowly, as if he was taking to someone who was more than a little bit slow.

"Not her, you stupid git, the old lady, was she alright? You said the dog knocked her over when it ran out," Nobby clarified.

"Oh, old Mrs Wilson? Oh yes, she was all right. She's a lively old bird and fit as a fiddle. Anyway I only used the Anti-mate the once, and then chucked the can away. It was a lot more bother than it was worth, and much too dangerous to use again."

63

The lads were celebrating quietly in the back room of the local pub. George and Violet were sitting snugly together, next to Joe and Brenda. Nobby, his head bandaged, sat with Norma a short distance away, near to Trev, who was void of female company.

Nobby made to get up to buy more drinks, but was stopped by Trev. "I'll get them. I've told you, best you keep well away from that barmaid for a while, at least until your dizzy spells stop. One look from her and you're liable to have a relapse and end up back in hospital." He turned to Norma, Violet and Brenda. "Would you ladies like another drink?"

They told him their preferred tipples and he set off towards the bar.

Violet and Norma had now been taken fully into the lads' confidence and were aware of the financial situation. Although there was never any statement made by the police regarding how much cash they had actually recovered, the lads, by careful stocktaking, calculated that it must have been just short of £700,000. The lads were thus left with a very respectable and mouth-watering grand total of around £4,300,000.

While George and Joe passionately discussed the local football team's chances for next season, Brenda and Violet were talking excitedly about their imminent Mediterranean cruise. George had readily agreed to go as soon as he found out that Violet wanted to take the cruise.

"Is Joe's stomach alright?" Violet asked. "He doesn't want any problems while we're at sea, that would be terrible."

"Oh, his stomach is fine. Funny enough, his ulcer has been no real trouble since he joined the Samaritans. He says listening to all those people with real problems makes him realise just how lucky he is and just how small our problems are in comparison. He's just the sort for that type of job, lots of patience and concern for other people. He goes up to visit Alan in hospital nearly every night."

"How is Alan?"

"He's progressing well and is out of intensive care now. He had a punctured lung and the knife had nicked a nerve in his vertebrae or something. He's really lucky to be alive. I can't get over him protecting Nobby like that. He's got a terrible name and is not the sort of man you could trust with your money. If you shake hands with him, you've got to count your fingers afterwards, but he can't be as bad as he's painted, can he, doing something like that? You know, all he's worried about are his daft pigeons; with Nobby going away there wasn't going to be anyone to look after them. But Nobby has arranged for the secretary from the Up North Combine to look after them. Nobby had agreed to give the man the fast, but what did he call it? That's it, the 'altitudinally challenged' bird, in payment. I haven't a clue what that means. 'Killing two birds with one stone,' is how he put it, when I asked him."

"How's George? Is he okay about you both going on the cruise?"

"Oh yes. He was all for it when I said I'd like to go," Violet said. "And he's proud as punch that his history project has gone so well. They're using everything he wrote and have asked him to do more of the same for another book to be published next year, but the one next year will be entirely George's own writing."

"He must be pleased."

"You can say that again, but he's careful not to bore everybody with it. Well, not too much anyway."

They both laughed.

"It's a pity that Mickey and Tracy aren't coming," Brenda said.

"It is. Joe offered to pay for both of them, and Tracy's mother would have looked after the kids for a few weeks, but he wouldn't have it."

"You still seeing Tracy alright for money?" Violet asked quietly.

Brenda nodded. "I give her the cash every month. She's getting enough to buy a few luxuries for the kids and herself. I can't give her too much in case she draws attention to herself. Mickey doesn't know, of course, or if he does, at least he doesn't say anything about it."

"What about Nobby and Norma, don't they fancy the cruise?" Violet asked.

"No, not those two, they just want to be together. They're off to America to visit Graceland, Elvis's house, where else? Nobby's not going to let those tickets he won go to waste. And I think he really is expecting to be mistaken for the real Elvis when they get there. No, nothing is going to stop them going."

"What about Trev, he going?"

"I'm not sure, but I think he might be," Brenda said.

"He'll be looking for some dolly bird to go with him, no doubt."

"Well, I don't know." She lowered her voice. "He was telling Joe that he's really had a change of heart recently. He was very impressed with what Norma and Elsie did for Nobby, getting that costume and building up his confidence again." She looked around to make sure the men weren't listening. "And apparently he was pleased to see you and George back together again and really admired the way I had a go at them all when they were hiding in the shed, terrified to show themselves outside. He's now beginning to consider women as people again, individual human beings and not just deluxe willy warmers." They both laughed. "So, all in all, there have been a number of real eye openers for him recently. His opinion of women has gone up a hundred percent." She looked around again to be sure they weren't being overheard. "I'll tell you what was a really an eye opener for him. Did you hear about him and that Ginger …?"

Violet nudged Brenda with her elbow. "Shush, Trev's coming back with the drinks."

"Okay, I'll tell you later."

At about nine o'clock Frankie and his wife came into the lounge. George walked across to the new arrivals. "Congratulations, Frankie. You did well winning the best of show this year," he said warmly.

Frankie looked as proud as punch as he smiled at his wife, who was hanging on to his arm. "Thanks. It wasn't easy, mind, a lot of hard work, but I did manage to grow the biggest leek and won this year's show. Perseverance, that's the secret. I knew I'd do it eventually."

"That's right, and there was a lot of stiff competition this year, as well," George confirmed, winking conspiratorially at Frankie. "I'll bet you're really proud of your husband, Mrs Cain? And him getting promoted foreman at work as well."

"Oh yes, I really am," simpered Frankie's wife, hugging his arm possessively.

"I've told the mother-in-law and her sister," Frankie indicated the in-laws sitting in a corner of the room, glasses of sweet stout on the table in front of them, "that they'll have to stay out of our house a lot of the time from now on, because I've got to have peace and quiet to do all the administration and paperwork now I'm foreman," he said importantly, drawing himself up to his full height. "And I've got to read up on my prize-winning leek growing techniques. Takes a lot of time and effort you know, does growing prize leeks."

George agreed wholeheartedly and watched them walk away to join their company. Frankie will be alright for his ration from now on, he thought with satisfaction.

Idle Hands

PRISONERS IN THE NORTH

The best selling book by John Ruttley,

The book details the forgotten deaths at Harperley PoW Camp, which was used to incarcerate German Prisoners during the First World War. There were also PoWs held at Harperley during the Second World War. The camp near Crook was recently featured on BBC 2's popular Restoration programme hosted by Griff Rees Jones.

What the press said-

'Wonderful, fascinating, educational and informative-this book is all of those and more, but best of all, it is one of those books that you only come across occasionally. It is a book that once started, you can't put down until you've finished.'-Weardale Gazette.

'Wonderfully written, an enthralling and interesting read, a friendly but at times chilling tale, well worth reading.'-Teesdale Mercury.

'A fascinating tale of a strangely neglected episode of war.'- Durham Town & Country magazine.

'A fascinating contribution to local history.'- Middlesbrough Evening Gazette.

'Harperley PoW camp is of national importance-it's a time capsule.'- Sunderland Echo.

'A truly tragic end to their war.'-Northern Echo.

The book is Perfect bound, has a laminated full colour cover.
A5 size, it contains 79 pages plus another 8 pages of colour photographs.
It also contains a detailed plan of the camp with an index.

ISBN No 0-9543366-1-5,

Excellent value at only £6.50 inc. p&p

Order Now:
John Ruttley
PO BOX 1180, Sunderland, SR5 9AP

The Devil Finds Work…

By John Ruttley.

'The Devil Finds Work…' is probably best described by the words of TV personality, agony aunt and best selling author, Denise Robertson in her foreword -

"If, like me, you've searched in vain for an authentic description of life in the shipyards of Britain, you need search no longer. This book gives you the smell, feel and taste of shipyard life. It portrays the camaraderie and the hardship endured by the men who made ships and gives an in-depth description of their family life. As the men and their women struggle to survive in a climate of industrial unrest and threats to their livelihood they are faced with a stark choice.... to fight organised crime or go under. Add an intriguing plot to authentic detail and you have that most enjoyable of things, a damn good read."

Against a background of national industrial unrest, a small group of ordinary shipyard labourers fight a David and Goliath battle against organised crime as they battle to save their workplace from being taken over. They struggle to find enough money to survive during a series of unofficial strikes, which are endangering the yard's very survival. When they discover that an American crime syndicate is behind the yard's industrial disputes, proposed takeover and the death of a workmate, things really start to move.

Excellent value at only £10.00 inc P&P
Order Now from- PO BOX 1180 Sunderland SR5 9AP.
Please make cheques payable to John Ruttley.

ISBN No 0-9543366-2-3